MW00776989

She Was Made for Me

JEN MORRIS

Forbidden on FRUIT ST

This is a work of fiction. Names, characters, places, and incidents either are the product of the author's imagination or are used fictitiously. Any resemblance to actual persons, living or dead, events, or locales is entirely coincidental.

First edition September 2023

Epub ISBN: 978-1-7386153-0-8

Paperback ISBN: 978-1-7386153-1-5

Cover illustration by Elle Maxwell www.ellemaxwelldesign.com

For all the workaholics. You are more than your career. Take a day off.

Never get so busy making a living that you forget to make a life.

— Dolly Parton

AUTHOR'S NOTE

Please note that this book contains references to anxiety and panic attacks. It also contains an age-gap romance between a 25 year old woman and a 43 year old man, with lots of consent. There is cursing, on-page sex, and some very light BDSM (spanking). If that's not for you, no hard feelings. Otherwise, enjoy!

1

VIOLET

If I have one piece of advice for anyone trying to impress their boss, it's not to fall asleep face-down on the floor of their office.

I don't even realize where I am until I hear the click of her office door closing, the sound of her setting a grande Americano on her desk. An Americano *I* was supposed to have ordered.

Shit.

"Oh, Violet," she says as I rouse myself from my slumber on her carpet. "Not again."

"Sorry, Deb." I groggily pull myself up, rubbing my eyes. This is not the first time I've spent the night at the office, and probably won't be the last. I glance at the posterboard and Post-Its strewn around me and wince. After Deb went home last night, I stayed on to create a Gantt chart in an attempt to increase productivity for our latest project. I find it easier to work on the floor, where I can spread out.

And, evidently, *pass* out.

Deb peeks into the trash can. "Did you order dinner, at least?"

"I..." Crap. *Dinner*. I knew I'd forgotten something. "Um, no."

She sets her purse on her desk with a sigh, her ebony curls perfect as always, her mahogany skin glowing from her early morning workout. I've never seen Deb look disheveled, which only serves to highlight my own state of chaos right now.

I push to my feet, hastily trying to gather the Post-Its into a pile. There's a pink one in the middle of the board with a big question mark on it, indicating exactly where I ran out of steam and dozed off.

"I was working on an idea for next quarter." I pull the question-mark Post-It from the board, frustrated. "I know we use an Agile approach, but I was thinking—"

"That's not your job," Deb says gently. "You're my assistant, Vi."

"I know." And I really do; four years of fetching coffee, booking conference rooms, and taking meeting notes has made that abundantly clear. *She's* the project manager for our team at DigiSwap, *I'm* the assistant.

Despite having spent several years at college training in project management.

But I know how this works. I'm paying my dues, working my way up, proving myself and biding my time until it's my turn. And Deb is an awesome boss—she's always respectful and kind, never barks orders at me, and yeah, tends to get a little concerned when she finds me asleep on her office floor after pulling an all-nighter.

I give her a sheepish smile as I smooth my hair, my natural blonde waves a little matted on one side. At this point, Deb usually gives me a good-natured lecture about working too much, and I nod along, half listening, half thinking about the project I'd labored over the night before.

But today, she slides into her chair and clasps her hands tightly on her glossy white desk, a line of worry along her forehead as she watches me gather my things from the floor.

"You're the most dedicated person on our team," she murmurs. "You work your ass off."

I can't help but beam as pride warms me from the inside out. See? This is what it's all about. Sure, I don't have much of a social life outside the office, and yeah, I only sleep about five hours a night—but this is what makes it worth it. Getting this recognition. Advancing my career.

I hold my breath, clutching the posterboard and Post-Its to my chest, waiting expectantly. I have a feeling Deb is about to make a big announcement, and I know what it is. It's something I've been waiting to hear for months now, and it's about time. My stomach swirls with anticipation as Deb opens her mouth to speak.

"Violet, sit down. I need to tell you something."

Her cautious tone sends a chill across my skin, making my confidence waver. "Just tell me," I say, tacking on a lighthearted laugh that doesn't quite ring true.

She gazes at me for a long moment before taking a deep breath. "I don't know how else to say this, but..." Her breath comes out in a long gust. "I have to let you go."

The posterboard slips from my hands, hitting the floor with a thud, followed by the Post-Its scattering in a colorful pile at my feet like giant pieces of confetti. I drop into the chair opposite Deb with lead in my stomach.

"*What*?"

"I'm so sorry. I promise you, this is the last thing I want to do, but it's out of my hands."

My jaw sags as I stare at my boss, speechless. I've never seen her look so solemn.

"But... why? What have I done wrong?"

"Nothing," Deb says quickly. "You're an amazing assistant, and I don't want to lose you at all, but last week the board announced huge budget cuts to all departments, which means no more unnecessary spending."

A disbelieving huff escapes me at her words. I've worked at this company for four years, giving them everything, only to be described as 'unnecessary.'

Ouch.

"I can't believe this," I retort. "So all the assistants are just... gone?"

Deb grimaces again, this time not meeting my eyes. "Not exactly. Departments have to share assistants, going forward."

I watch her awkwardly twist her coffee cup back and forth on her desk, shame washing over me as the meaning behind her words becomes clear.

"Right," I mutter. "And I didn't make the cut."

Deb forces her gaze to mine. "Please don't think of it like that. I fought hard for you, Vi. You deserve this job more than anyone. Hell, they should have promoted you to assistant project manager years ago, but..." She shakes her head. "You know what this industry is like. It's a boy's club, and Scott has more pull with the board than I do, so—"

"I get it," I say, rubbing my face. I really wish I wasn't having this conversation with the imprint of Deb's office carpet on my cheek. I must look so unprofessional.

"I'm sorry. If it were up to me, you wouldn't be going anywhere."

I nod stiffly, untouched by her words. I get that *she* doesn't want to let me go—she's always been good to me—but it just goes to show how fickle this industry is, that this company doesn't value me at all.

I swallow back the acidic taste in my mouth, woodenly

rising to collect my stuff from the floor again, then stalk to my tiny desk in the corner of Deb's office, trying to ignore the burning sensation behind my eyes as I gather my things with shaking hands.

Don't cry. Don't give them the satisfaction.

It's not only the humiliation of not being chosen to stay; it's the fear gnawing in the pit of my stomach at knowing I have to go home, in the middle of the day, to an empty apartment. My job is—well, *was*—my life. It was my sense of purpose, my guiding star, my reason for getting out of bed in the morning. Without that, I don't know who I am.

Despite being at the company for years, it only takes me five minutes to pack up my desk. Deb tries to give me a lengthy goodbye, telling me how much she's valued me, how much she'll miss me, but I make my excuses to leave. Each word from her mouth only twists the knife.

I don't say goodbye to anyone else as I flee the building, the sting of humiliation threatening to send tears spilling at the slightest nudge. The air is cool as the elevator lets me out into the parking garage, my arms cradling a box of items from my desk. It's not much; notebooks, pens, stapler, photo frame with a picture of me and my parents at my graduation, and a sad little succulent that has been on the brink of death for six months.

It'll most definitely die now. I'm sure of it.

I dump the box into the trunk of my car and slink around to the driver's side. As soon as the door is closed, I drop my forehead onto the steering wheel and let out a low "ughhhhhhh."

I'm twenty-five and unemployed. What the hell am I supposed to do now?

———

By the time I arrive home, I'm fuming. How dare this company just dispose of me as *unnecessary spending*, like I haven't given them some of the best years of my life?

I storm into my apartment, throwing the box of desk supplies onto the kitchen counter and slamming the door closed behind me. The sun is a bright glare streaking in through the open blinds, and as I reach for the cord to close them, I have to shield my eyes. I'm not used to being home at this time of day—I'm usually up to my elbows in emails or fetching coffee from the in-house barista in the lobby of our building. I lose track of time when I'm at work, buzzing from the energy of a busy office, high on the constant stream of incoming tasks that keep me on my toes all day. By the time I leave the building, most nights the sky is a bruised purple. On a really productive day, it's pitch black.

But this morning it was a brilliant blue, and I hated every minute of the drive home. I hated seeing my neighbors trimming their roses, the power-walkers returning from their daily route to do God knows what all day. Why aren't these people at *work*?

I live in this Silicon Valley neighborhood only because it's close to the office, not because I love it. I feel a familiar pang of longing for home, one I've gotten used to tuning out in the years I've been away from New York. *If I was at work*, I think bitterly, *I'd be too busy to think about this.*

I gaze around my apartment—a place I've seen so many times before, but never stopped to really *notice*. The walls are painted an unassuming beige, and the sofa is a charcoal three-seater that came with the place. All the furniture did. I've never given it a lot of thought, because I don't spend much time here. But now...

Unease snakes through me at the knowledge that I have nothing planned for the rest of... well, however long it takes me to find another job. I can't remember the last time I had an expanse of free time, stretching out before me like a vast horizon. Some people might be delighted at the prospect, but not me.

In fact, I feel vaguely ill.

I drop onto the sofa and reach for my laptop, desperate to do *something*. I'll start by getting my resume out there. As an assistant I made plenty of contacts, so I have no shortage of people to reach out to. The sooner I get started, the better. I should have done this months ago. No—Deb was right —*years* ago.

My role as Deb's assistant was only supposed to be for six months, maybe a year at a stretch. I'd taken the job on the assumption that they'd promote me as soon as I'd proven myself, and Deb told me at every available opportunity how valuable she thought I was, that she wanted to promote me as soon as she could. It's not her fault I've ended up here. It's mine. When the one-year mark rolled around, I should have actively started looking for new roles. I should have realized that, despite Deb's best intentions, a promotion wasn't going to fall into my lap, no matter how much initiative I showed, no matter how many late nights I worked.

My fingers hover over the keys as I consider my options. I don't want to apply for another assistant job. I'm a qualified project manager, and it's time I get the job I deserve. It won't be as easy as getting into another assistant role, but I need to fight for this. I'm sick of not utilizing my talents.

In fact, being let go might actually be a *good* thing. A blessing in disguise and all that.

I've almost managed to convince myself when my phone rings. Dad's name flashes on my screen and despair rushes up inside me.

Shit. Who am I kidding? This isn't a fucking blessing.

I set my laptop aside and reach for my phone, swallowing against the sudden lump in my throat. "Hi, Dad."

"Hi, Sweetpea."

I sniffle at the sound of his comforting voice. It's almost as if he knows, somehow.

"I tried your office line, but someone else answered and said you don't work there anymore."

Okay, so he *does* know.

"What's going on?"

I clear my throat. "I, um… yeah." Of all the people I have to tell about this, my father would be absolutely *last* on my list. I was kind of hoping I might be able to get another job quickly enough that I wouldn't even have to tell him. Then I could casually mention it after the fact, like yeah, I'd been given an exciting opportunity at a new company, and how cool is that?

Instead, I have to tell him that his only child, his pride and joy, is now *unemployed*. I hate letting him down like this.

My face heats with shame as I mutter, "I was let go this morning. They had budget cuts, and…"

"What?" Dad's voice rises in disbelief. "How could they lose one of their most promising project managers?"

I press my eyes shut, my stomach knotting into a tight ball. God, I am the worst daughter on the planet, because not only was I *not* in a project management position, my parents were under the impression that I *was*.

It's not my fault. I mean, it *is* my fault, but really it's a misunderstanding I haven't been able to bring myself to rectify. I'd told my folks I'd gotten a job as an assistant *to* a project manager, but Dad misheard me and thought I'd said I *was* an assistant project manager. I took a breath to correct him, almost amused at how it was as if I was reading a script from an episode of *The Office,* but when he went on to say how proud he was of me, and how the money he'd spent on college had been worth it—gulp—I couldn't bear to tell him that no, I wasn't managing exciting projects, I was fetching coffee for the people who were. Besides, I'd reasoned, they'd promote me soon enough, so it didn't make sense to disappoint him.

And then, you know, four years somehow passed and here we are.

Anyway, it was all for nothing. I don't have a job or any prospects lined up. I have a handful of contacts, which will probably amount to nothing, and I've wasted years of my life. I might not quite be there yet, but I've got a pretty good view of rock bottom from here.

"Um, about that," I begin, taking a deep breath. Ugh, this isn't easy. My father's a successful attorney who raised me to work hard and make things happen for myself. To tell him that the wonderful things he's been thinking about me since I graduated were based on a lie... I'd rather perform naked gymnastics to a packed crowd at Madison Square Garden.

"Hang on a second." I hear the door to his office close, the familiar creak of his leather chair as he settles in front of his expansive oak desk. I only visited Dad's office once, years ago, but the feeling of it sticks vividly in my mind. The law firm had an air of *importance* about it—like the work they did mattered. It made me realize how much I wanted to do work that mattered, too.

I sigh, needing to get this out. If I don't tell him now, I never will. And I've lived with this untruth long enough.

"Dad—"

"You know what I think, Violet? Screw them. If they can't see what they're missing out on, that's their loss."

"Thanks, Dad. But—"

"What are your plans moving forward?"

I falter. Sometimes conversing with my father makes me feel more like I'm a witness being cross-examined on the stand than his daughter.

"I'm already sending my resume out and getting in touch with contacts I have."

"Excellent. Do you have anything lined up?"

Lined up? I only left the office an hour ago!

"Not yet, but it won't be long until I do." I pick at a nail, hoping my voice conveys more confidence than I feel.

Dad is quiet for a beat, and a slow churn begins in my gut. He's not buying this. Why would he? And I still haven't told him the worst part yet.

But he surprises me when he breaks the silence. "Why don't you come stay with us for a while?"

"Stay with you?"

"Sure," Dad says easily. "You can keep up the job search from New York. Who knows, you might even find something closer to home."

Home.

I sigh, thinking about New York. The truth is, I've missed it ever since I left. The bustle of the city streets, the convenience of having everything on your doorstep, and the beautiful row houses that remind you of the city's history. There's nothing like that here.

The problem is, most of the good project management jobs in tech are on the West Coast.

"Maybe," I murmur.

"I might have something to keep you busy in the meantime," Dad adds.

This piques my interest. I hadn't thought past my plan of sending out resumes all day, but who knows how I'll fill my time after that. I need something to do. I need a plan.

"What is it?"

"Ah." He chuckles. "Wouldn't you rather it was a surprise?"

I twist my lips to the side, frowning. As someone who likes to stay on top of every aspect of my life, surprises are not something I enjoy.

Take this morning, for example.

"Come on, Sweetpea." Dad's voice softens. "Your mom and I miss you. This is a great opportunity for you to come home for a few months."

I lean back on the sofa, turning the idea over. It wouldn't hurt to get a change of scenery, and besides, I'll have a little money from my severance to live off for a while.

One look around my stale shell of an apartment confirms it. The thought of spinning my wheels here indefinitely while I wait for something to happen on the job front makes me positively nauseated.

"Okay," I agree, but there's no way I'm moving back in with my folks. That definitely *would* be hitting rock bottom. "I'll stay at Sadie's, though. I haven't seen her in ages."

Sadie, my best friend from high school, has always been okay in the past with me crashing on her sofa. Usually we spend the time painting our nails and binge-watching reruns of *The Office* while talking about guys.

Okay, we did that once, six years ago, but I'm sure it will be fine.

"Great!" Dad says. I hear him tapping at his keyboard in the background. "I'll book your flight now."

In spite of everything that's happened this morning, I find myself smiling. Maybe going back to the city is just what I need.

2

KYLE

"I don't want to go back to the city." I answer the phone without a greeting, because when I see Richard's name on my screen, I know exactly what he's calling to ask. It's always the same thing.

"Well, hello to you too," Rich says wryly.

I chuckle in response as I step from my truck, tucking my notebook under my arm and turning to survey the dilapidated cabin in front of me. I grimace at the state of the deteriorated cedar shakes and the way the entire place looks as if it's leaning slightly to the right. It needs a lot more work than I realized. That's what happens when a cabin is in the family for generations—over time it falls into total disrepair, often past the point of being reasonably salvaged. This evening I'm meeting the owner to discuss the work that needs to be done, before deciding whether to take on this project. I glance at my watch, noticing I'm a little early, and figure I'll get a head start on checking out the exterior.

"You don't know what I'm calling to ask." Rich's protest brings my attention back to my phone.

"So it's not to come back to New York, then?" I begin

down the muddy path toward the cabin, careful not to lose a work boot in the mush. Mud season in Maine is no joke.

"Well, yes," Rich admits, "but it's not to come back to the firm. It's—" he cuts himself off mid-sentence, and I hear him cover the phone to talk to someone in the background. Shelley, no doubt, his assistant of twenty years. I know Rich is at the office, because he's always at the office. He spends more time there than in his own home.

Just like I did, once.

I wait patiently, giving the cabin a quick once over, before my attention is stolen by the view out over Lake Cobbosseecontee—known as Lake Cobbossee to the locals —just beyond the slanting front porch. Rich calls me regularly to ask if I'll consider coming back to work at Hudson, Oppenheimer & Stant, the law firm on Manhattan's Upper West Side where we worked together for years, and I always give him the same answer.

I turn back and take in the area surrounding the cabin. It's on a sheltered portion of land set back from the main road, quiet and undisturbed. The cabin itself is surrounded by pine trees, their scent as familiar as home. I hear a loon call out on the lake and smile. Why on earth would I want the madness of the city when I have the beauty of Maine every day?

"Sorry." Rich returns to the phone. "What was I saying? Oh—right. I have a project, and you're just the man for the job."

"A project?"

"You remember that townhouse I bought a few years back?"

I do remember the townhouse: a four-story redbrick building in Brooklyn Heights, just minutes from the Promenade. I grew up around there and know the area well. Rich bought the townhouse as an investment years ago, but it's sat empty and gathering dust ever since.

"Sure," I say, beginning to suspect where this might be going.

"I've decided now is the time to remodel it. I want you as the lead contractor on the build."

I scrub a hand across my beard, coarse and bushy under my palm. One of the benefits of no longer working in an office—I don't have to shave every damn day.

"Why me?" I ask. "I've never worked on a project like that. I restore old cabins, not townhouses."

"I know, but the previous owner did half the work before they sold it. Besides, it can't be that different, can it?"

"Actually—"

"Regardless," Rich says brusquely, and I stifle a laugh. He's a shark in court—always was a far better attorney than me—and I already know there's no way I'll win this battle. "You're the guy I want on this."

I hear the crunch of car tires on gravel, and turn to see a red Honda Civic pull up beside my truck. "I'll call you back," I mutter to Rich, watching an elderly lady with old money elegance climb from the car. "My client is here."

"This conversation isn't over," he says as I hang up the call. I stuff the phone into my pocket with a chuckle.

"Mr Armstrong?" The cabin owner—a woman named Muriel Murdoch who looks to be in her eighties, and assured me over the phone that the cabin was "in reasonable shape"—begins making her way down the path. I hurry over to help her. With the ground in this condition, she could seriously hurt herself.

"Please call me Kyle, Mrs. Murdoch."

"Muriel." She takes my arm. "And thank you. I always hate this time of year."

We make it to the cabin in one piece, which is a small miracle in itself because that mud-slicked path is a death trap, but as she fights to open the twisted front door, I begin to wonder if it's safer out here.

Once the door is finally open, Muriel gestures for me to enter first. I take a tentative step across the threshold, careful not to fall through rotten floorboards. It wouldn't be the first time. The planks creak under my boots, but nothing more, and I say a silent thanks. The smell of damp, musty cabin air swamps my lungs, and I wait for my eyes to adjust to the dim room. So many of these old cabins are dark, with few windows. I love finding a way to honor the charm and history of the cabin while also making them feel more open and bright, usually with an entire wall of glass facing the water.

I glance at Muriel as she steps in behind me, surveying the place wistfully. "I haven't been in here for at least a decade."

Sure smells like it, I think, but thankfully manage not to say. She draws back some filthy drapes to let more light in, and I set about inspecting the place in earnest. It's reasonably spacious, but the good points stop there. The walls are lined with a hideous fake-wood paneling that was probably installed in the seventies, and the ceiling tiles are water-damaged, sagging so low in one place I can see the insulation peeking out. When I give one tile a gentle nudge it crashes to the floor, exposing some kind of nest and animal droppings.

"Oh!" Muriel cries, startled.

"Very common in a cabin this age," I tell her. "You might not have been here for years, but plenty of critters have been living in the ceiling." I give her a smile to soften the blow, but she looks disgusted. Because it *is* disgusting.

Why did I choose this line of work again?

I wander over to one corner, prying back a piece of the wood paneling to inspect the wall cavity. "Squirrels have been living in the walls, too."

Muriel appears behind me. "How can you tell?"

I gesture to the piles of acorns inside the wall cavity and she blanches. Pulling back the paneling further, I notice a line of carpenter ants.

Excellent.

"How long have you been restoring cabins?" Muriel asks, hovering behind me as I yank up a corner of the linoleum to examine the floor.

"A few years." I scribble some notes in my notebook with a frown. I'm pretty sure we can't salvage the floors, and they'll be expensive to replace. I look back up at the ceiling. That will need to be ripped out, and the insulation will all need replacing too.

"And you do the work alone?"

"Uh-huh." Well, that's not entirely true—I have the occasional contractor who does jobs that aren't in my area of expertise, like plumbing and electricity, but for the most part it's just me.

"Must be lonely," she murmurs.

I glance at her over my notebook. Is it lonely? I guess I try not to think about it. I keep myself busy enough to get through my days, and the physical labor means I always sleep solidly at night. I have my own beautiful cabin on the waterfront, and a cold beer at the end of a long day. It's a different life from what I had in the city, and that's intentional. If I occasionally miss having someone to wake up next to as the yellow rays of the sun warm my bedroom ceiling each morning, that's a small price to pay.

I shrug, stepping back outside to check the foundations.

There's definitely a lean to the place—I could feel it as we walked around inside—and as I crouch at the back of the cabin, I can see why. The entire back sill is rotted through, so soft I can scoop the wood out with my fingers. It's too close to the ground, and snow piles up during winter, damaging the wood. None of these old cabins have pressure-treated timber, so they simply rot.

I rise to my feet with a sigh. This place has pretty much everything you could imagine wrong with it. Most of my jobs have at least one or two of these issues, but not all of them at once. She'd be better off tearing the cabin down and starting from scratch.

I thank Muriel for her time and tell her I'll be in touch with a quote for the work, but I'm not sure I want to take on the job. It's a lot of work for one person, and would take me forever to complete.

I take the scenic route home along the lake, stopping in at the market to grab some fresh produce for dinner. When I finally roll down my gravel driveway, I'm tired. It's been a long day finishing up a job on one site before meeting with Muriel at the house of horrors. I'm ready for a beer and a long sleep.

I take the steps two at a time up to the screened-in porch at the side of the house, and smile looking out over Lake Cobbossee as I kick off my work boots. I bought this cabin when I first came up here, four years ago. It wasn't in great shape—though nowhere near as bad as the place I just saw—and it took me months to painstakingly restore, learning everything as I went. Now, I can't imagine living anywhere else.

I grab myself a beer from the fridge, casting my gaze around. The kitchen and living room are open-concept, with a cathedral ceiling, supported by huge, rough-cut hemlock beams spanning the space overhead. There's a bathroom and bedroom downstairs, and a lofted bedroom above them, looking out over the living space below. The entire front wall of the cabin is made up of windows, framing an expansive view across the lake. In winter, I warm up by the wood-burning stove after an afternoon of ice fishing, and in summer, I have the windows open to let the breeze blow through—when I'm not in the water.

It is, in a word, paradise.

My phone vibrates in my pocket and I retrieve it with a chuckle, knowing it's Rich following up from our earlier call.

"You're not going to let this go, are you?"

My friend's voice is confident in my ear. "What do you think?"

I lean back in my chair and prop my feet up on the coffee table in front of me. It's made from local pine and took me hours to sand and polish to bring out the natural grain of the wood. It was one of the first projects I finished when I first moved, and reminds me of why I left the city. Up here, in the beauty of Maine, I don't have the stresses of corporate life that nearly killed me. I spend my days working with my hands, restoring neglected cabins in Kennebec County to their former glory. When I became an attorney years ago, I did it because I wanted to make a difference in people's lives. I still do that now, but in a way that doesn't cost me my health—or my sanity.

"I think you're a pain in my ass," I say good-naturedly, and Rich laughs.

"I try." His voice turns serious. "I want you on this project, Kyle. I'll pay you twice your normal rate."

I sigh. At forty-nine, Rich is six years older than me, and has always done this big brother thing—more so over the past four years, since my life fell apart and he scraped me up out of the gutter.

"You know I get plenty of work up here," I say gently. Though when I think back to the cabin I checked out this evening, I grimace. "I appreciate the offer, but I don't need—"

"It's not that. I know you're busy, and sure, it's not your usual job, but... you're the only guy I trust to do this."

I look down, brushing sawdust off my work shorts. The thought of going back to New York churns my stomach, but Rich has always been there for me, no questions asked. If he needs me, I'll have to make this work.

"You know this is too much for me to take on by myself," I tell him.

"Of course. I'll get a team together, and I'm in the process of getting a project manager as we speak."

I frown. I don't need a project manager to keep me organized, but that's the least of my problems right now.

"So you want me to start right away?"

"If you can," Rich replies. "I'm hoping we can get the whole thing done in a couple of months."

"Let me get this straight. Instead of spending summer at the lake, you want me to spend it in the city, sweating my balls off?" Richard barks a laugh and I continue. "Where will I even find a place to stay at this late notice?"

"You'll stay in the guest room at our place. We're out of town for a couple weeks over summer anyway, so you'll have the place to yourself for a while."

I contemplate this. A few months in the city, working on something different to help a friend.

Or removing dead animals and rot from a cabin I'd rather not step foot in ever again.

"Fine," I relent warily. "But you're not paying me."

Rich gives a scoff of disagreement. “I most certainly—”

“You can cover the cost of the materials, and obviously you’ll need to pay the crew, but I’m not taking a cent from you.” I have more than enough money to live off for the next couple of months, especially considering I’ll be staying with Rich and his wife, Diana. I can’t take their money after all they’ve done for me.

“Kyle,” Rich protests, but I know I’m going to have to stand firm on this. “Come on—”

“I mean it. If you want me on this renovation, those are my terms.”

He lets out a long sigh. “Alright. Whatever gets you back here.”

3

KYLE

New York is worse than I remember. Four years away from the city dulled my memory of how bad things were when I was last here, but being back instantly makes me edgy. I left Maine at 4 a.m. and spent six hours on the road, but that's not the worst part; it took me over an hour to crawl through Manhattan to get to the job site in Brooklyn Heights. By the time I park my truck, I'm crabby and irritable, my ears starting to ring in that way they do when I get tense.

I'm meeting Rich to look over the building and talk through his plans, and meet the project manager he's got lined up. I don't even know why we need a project manager—I never have them on my renos back home.

Still, this is a much bigger project than anything I've done in Maine. If I'm being entirely honest, I'm a little concerned there are aspects beyond my expertise, but when I mentioned that to Rich he wouldn't hear a word of it.

"You're the best carpenter I know," he'd said. I tried to point out that I was the *only* carpenter he knew, but he laughed me off. "You're who I want as the foreman, Kyle. I won't take no for an answer." And when I thought of the way he'd shown up for me when I was at my lowest point, I had no choice but to swallow my hesitations and agree to the project.

Now, as I step out of my truck, my doubts are back.

I wander around to the sidewalk with a sigh. I never used to be like this. When I was at the height of my law career, I had the confidence of a man who could hold the attention of the courtroom, who knew exactly what he was doing. I felt invincible.

I guess that was the problem. I wasn't invincible. Not even close.

Leaning back against my truck, I let my gaze wander up and down the street. At least Brooklyn Heights isn't Manhattan. It's quiet here. No billboards, no taxis crawling by, no tourists shoving past you. Instead, it's rows of brownstones and townhouses, quiet streets lined with oak and ginkgo trees, their leaves a fresh, vibrant green with the start of summer. A mom pushes a stroller past me, and a block away I can see a tiny coffee shop, but otherwise the neighborhood is still and calm. A gentle breeze carrying the sound of a siren somewhere in the distance is the only reminder that I'm actually in New York.

I relax as I scan the street. For a moment, I can pretend this isn't the city that filled me with stress and made me question everything about myself. No—this is the neighborhood I grew up in, filled with history. Mine, and the people who came before me.

My gaze lands on the building in front of me: number 14 Fruit Street. It's a four-story Greek revival-style townhouse, one in a row of three, joined with a continuous redbrick façade and matching details, like the brownstone steps with iron railings.

Each entryway is surrounded by tall brownstone pilasters, each with a triangular pediment on top, the doorways set back under a transom window, with sidelights and column details around a wooden door. From the street number 14 looks to be in decent condition; maybe one of the windows needs replacing, and the brick might need some work, but otherwise it doesn't stand out from any of its neighbors.

Rich assures me it's a different story inside, though. The previous owners abandoned it mid-restoration when their marriage broke up—or so he says—and it's a mess.

I glance again at the coffee place down the street. I'm a little early, and a decaf cappuccino would be nice.

The shop—Joe's Coffee—is busy when I enter, and I order a coffee before scanning the room for a place to sit. The walls are old brick, painted white, and the ceiling appears to be the original pressed tin tiles. I love that they've kept these features and not replaced them with something more modern.

I spot an empty table to one side and wander over, ready to claim my seat, when I notice a woman, standing with a to-go coffee cup in her hand, her back to me as she reads something framed on the wall. I don't make a habit of openly checking women out in public, but my gaze is riveted to her. Long, curvy legs stretch up from wedge sandals, disappearing into denim cutoffs that emphasize her wide hips. She's wearing a floaty pink blouse tucked loosely into her shorts, her blonde hair falling in delicate waves just past her shoulders.

She steps to her right to examine what else is framed on the wall, but her sandal catches on the uneven floorboard—one of the hazards of these old buildings—and she loses her balance, catching herself just as her coffee slips to the ground, exploding on impact. She leaps back, narrowly missing being scalded.

"Ughhh," she groans, surveying the dark liquid pooling at her feet. "Fuck, fuck, fuck my life," she mutters under her breath, which seems like an extreme reaction, even under the circumstances.

"Are you okay?" I ask tentatively, stepping closer.

She turns my way and I get my first real look at her. Big, hazelnut-brown eyes, bangs that frame her heart-shaped face, full, pink lips pressed together as she frowns. She's younger than I'd usually let myself look at—I'm guessing early thirties—but I can't help myself. She's beautiful. If I hadn't heard her just utter a mouthful of curses, her looks would have me believe she's soft and sweet, especially with the way her cheeks now blush a delicate pink. I find myself intrigued by the contrast.

"Bad morning?" I try again, attempting to lighten the mood.

"More like a bad week." She rubs her forehead in agitation. Sympathy tugs at me as she steps over the mess at her feet and glances past me to the counter. There's something almost familiar about her. I can't put my finger on what it is, but it draws me closer to her.

"Let me get you another. What were you drinking?"

"Oh," she says, flustered. "You don't have to do that."

"Hey, we've all had bad weeks. Let me make yours a little better."

She hesitates, gaze resting on my face. I rub a hand self-consciously across my unruly beard. For the first time in years, I find myself wishing I'd shaved this morning, maybe done a little more than pull on a dirty work shirt and shoved a cap on my head.

"That's really sweet." Her mouth lifts into a smile that

sends warmth rippling through my chest. It's a sensation I haven't felt in a long time, and it makes me want to flirt with this beautiful young creature in front of me. It makes me momentarily forget I'm not the young man I used to be.

"Well, I'm a *very* sweet guy." This time I earn a laugh, and fuck, that feels good. Before I can get too carried away, I ask again, "What were you drinking?"

"Triple shot Americano. Thank you."

"Whoa. That's an intense coffee order." I say it without thinking, and am relieved when she laughs again.

"Yeah, I need that much caffeine to function."

I remember a time when I needed that much caffeine too—I was working around the clock and ignoring all the signals my body was giving me to STOP.

"Case in point," she adds, motioning to the mess beside us, which is currently being mopped up by a brunette barista with a nametag reading 'Daisy.'

I grin. "Fair enough." I head back to the counter and order her another coffee, hoping I'll get the chance to talk to her again, even for a few minutes.

When I turn back she's still standing by the wall, reading the framed information. It's a history of the neighborhood, surrounded by modern, artistic photographs that focus on the architectural details of the old buildings.

"This is so interesting," she says when I reach her side again, and I take this as an invitation to continue the conversation.

"Yeah. There's a lot of history in this area."

"I didn't know Brooklyn Heights was America's first suburb," she utters in astonishment.

I nod. "The ferry meant that people could live here and work in Manhattan. Hard to believe it was all farms and orchards around here before that."

She lifts her eyebrows. Impressed? I can't tell. God, she's pretty.

"I grew up a block away," I mumble, pulling my cap off and raking a hand through my hair in a futile attempt to tidy myself up. "You're not from around here?"

"I'm a New Yorker, but..." She gives a shamefaced little laugh. "I don't know this area well." She turns back to look at the images on the wall and continues. "I was reading about how many buildings they tore down before this became a protected historic district. That's devastating. I love the old buildings. Such a shame to see that history lost."

There's a funny flip in my ribcage. Historical building preservation is something I've always been passionate about, especially growing up in this area. I've never met a woman who cares about that too.

"It is," I agree, wondering how insane it would be if I asked for her number. She must be a good decade younger than me.

My order is called from the counter. She lifts a single brow when I claim my decaf cappuccino, then turns back to the wall. Someone who consumes three shots of caffeine in one drink probably won't understand that a single shot of the stuff makes me agitated and jittery.

I hover near the sugar stand, wondering if I could get away with hanging around to talk to her some more. I might be a little late meeting Rich, but I'm sure he'd understand. He's been urging me to get back out there for ages.

The barista saves me from my nervous dithering by calling out her order, and I swoop in to pick it up and hand it to her. I cringe at myself as I reach her side again.

Play it cool, man.

"Your coffee, madam."

Nice one.

I tug the brim of my cap down to hide my embarrassment. Fuck, it's painful watching myself attempt to flirt.

But she laughs again, taking me by surprise. "Why thank you, kind sir."

I glance at her, my mouth pulling into a wide grin.

"Seriously, thanks." She raises her cup and taps it against mine as if to say 'cheers.' Her gaze flicks to the door, then back to me. Disappointment trickles through me at the thought of her leaving, until she says, "Which way are you heading?"

She's asking me to walk with her. I have to glance down to hide my smile.

"Uh, down the block that way."

"Me too. Shall we?" She motions for me to follow and I nod, pressing my lips together to hide my nerves as we leave the coffee shop. I don't know why she's giving me the time of day, but I'm not going to say no to a few more minutes in her company.

"So you grew up here?" she asks as we walk.

"Yeah. A block that way, on Cranberry Street, in an old brownstone. At the time the building was split into several apartments, but I think it's been restored to a proper five-story home."

We pause at a street crossing, and she glances up at me. She's a lot shorter than I am, probably even more with those heels off. My gaze strays to the creamy skin of her neck, then to the opening of her blouse, where I steal a peek of soft cleavage. I catch myself, whipping my gaze back to hers. There's a shimmer of amusement in her eyes that tells me she noticed my lack of self-control, and I'm about to apologize when she turns to step out onto the road.

"What's your favorite thing about the neighborhood?" she asks as I scramble to catch up with her.

"Uh... the Promenade." I gesture to our right. "A couple blocks that way. Beautiful views of downtown Manhattan."

"I'll have to check it out." Her walk slows, right in front of my truck. "I'm Vi, by the way." She extends her hand and I take it in mine, swallowing as her soft fingers brush against my calloused palm.

"Kyle."

Her hand lingers in mine, her gaze sparkling as we stand there, looking at each other. My pulse spikes, and I begin to think that coming back to the city was a very good idea indeed. I don't know how she knows to stop right here, or what her plans are for the rest of the day, but I think I'm about to ask this young woman out.

What the fuck is happening? I don't date, and I especially don't ask out beautiful women ten years younger than me, but there's something in the way she looks at me, the electricity between us. She could have left the coffee shop without me, after all, but she asked me to join her, and is gazing up at me as if she's waiting for something.

Of course, this could all be in my head. But when I think about letting her walk away... fuck it. I'll kick myself if I don't at least try. It's been years since I've even considered asking a woman out. I don't care if the odds are against me on this one. I'm going for it.

"Listen, uh..." Jesus, it's been way too long since I've done this. What do I say again? "This is probably a long shot, but is there any chance you might like to—"

"Oh, good. I see you two have met." I turn to see Rich approaching, hands in his suit pockets, smiling as his gaze moves between the two of us.

I glance at Vi, then at Rich, confused. But my confusion

evaporates when she steps up onto her toes to hug Richard, and says,

"Hi, Dad."

Dad.

Wait. What? This is Richard's daughter?

No, that can't be right. She's like... twenty, or something, isn't she?

I open my mouth to ask what's going on, but stop when her eyes swing back to mine, a little confused, a lot embarrassed.

Oh, fuck. She's his daughter. *She's his daughter.*

How the hell did I not realize that *Vi* is short for *Violet*? As in, *Violet Hudson*. And what is she doing here? I thought she seemed vaguely familiar, but... have I met her before?

Actually, yes, I think I have. Once, years ago, when she came to the office, but her hair was brown then, and she was a lot younger...

Because she is *a lot younger, jackass.*

I do some mental math. She was eighteen or so when she visited the firm. I remember because she was going off to college, and that was about... six years ago? So that would make her twenty-four, give or take. Not even *close* to early thirties.

And a hell of a long way from forty-three.

Nausea churns through my stomach and I avert my gaze from hers, my face hot.

I think I'm going to be sick.

I've spent the past twenty minutes hitting on my best friend's very lovely, *very young* daughter.

4

VIOLET

"Kyle!" Dad steps over and pulls Kyle into a hug, clapping him on the back. "I knew I could get you back here. It's been too long."

Kyle nods, half-heartedly clapping him back. This is *Dad's* friend, Kyle? Last time Dad mentioned him, he said Kyle was a contractor up in Maine. Come to think of it, I might have met him briefly once or twice, but he certainly didn't look like *this*. He'd been wearing a pristine suit, clean-shaven, and very frowny.

I stare at the two of them, trying to put the pieces together. Last night I had dinner with Mom and Dad, and halfway through our entrees Dad casually asked me to meet him at some random address in Brooklyn Heights this morning, but wouldn't tell me why. I deliberately arrived early so I could get my coffee fix after being kept up all night by Sadie and her boyfriend having unnecessarily loud sex (ugh), only to drop said coffee after one sip.

And when a guy asked if I was okay and if he could buy me another coffee, I found myself saying yes. He wasn't my usual type; I tend to go for the clean, tidy, and styled look.

This guy's beard was a mess and his hair stuck out at all angles from under his cap, but he was tall and well-built, with deep green eyes, the kind that crinkled at the corners when he smiled. I could tell he was handsome underneath all that scruff, that if he tidied himself up, he'd be unbelievably attractive. And I certainly didn't think he was *Dad's* age. Sure, he had some gray in his beard, but I know guys in their twenties who are going gray. It wasn't until he'd pulled off his cap to run his hand through that mop of hair that I noticed the gray on his temples, too.

Still, I felt myself drawn to him. He wasn't just ruggedly good-looking, he was sweet and interesting, and he made me laugh after what's been a pretty average week.

And, admittedly, it's been a while since a guy has paid any attention to me. I mostly worked with men at DigiSwap, but I learned early on that the only way to be treated with any kind of respect was to act like one of the boys. If that helped me get a promotion, then so be it. (Spoiler alert: it did not.) But it meant that after a while, they treated me like one of the boys, too. And given that I hardly went anywhere outside the office... Well, let's just say it's been a *very* long time since someone flirted with me. Add to that the fact that I've gained a few pounds from working around the clock and never making time to exercise or eat properly, and I haven't felt great about myself lately.

So it was nice to have Kyle's attention. The way he tried not to check me out—and failed—was adorable, and I could be mistaken, but I think he was about to ask me out right before Dad arrived. He looked nervous as he started to speak, and I felt a thrill, wondering if I'd get lucky enough to see what was beneath the flannel shirt that strained across his broad, muscular shoulders. Is it wrong that I wish Dad hadn't shown up just then?

Yes. He's your father's friend. That's weird.

Kyle's gaze clashes with mine before darting away, and my face heats.

"You remember my daughter, Violet?" Dad asks Kyle, completely unaware of the uncomfortable cloud that's descended upon us as he retrieves a set of keys from his pocket.

Kyle presses his eyes shut, looking ill. "Uh-huh."

I scrunch my nose, trying to suppress my disappointment at the misunderstanding, realizing it must be ten times worse for Kyle. I'm the daughter of his friend. Even I know that's a no-go.

"And you remember Kyle?" Dad asks me.

"Um, I think so."

"Great! Let's go in."

Dad starts up the front steps of a redbrick building. I follow, momentarily distracted from Kyle, who trudges warily up behind me. I still don't know why Dad has brought me here, of all places, but when I reach the doorway, my thoughts skid to a halt and my steps falter.

"Wow," I murmur, gazing around the entry hall. Much of it is in disrepair, but I can see the original beauty of the curved banister sweeping up the stairs to my left, the skylight several floors up bathing the landing in natural light.

"Yeah," Kyle says in agreement, pausing next to me. We stand side by side in the doorway, close enough that I can feel the heat from his large frame, and we glance at each other. Our eyes lock for a brief second, then he tears his gaze away, clearing his throat as he continues into the foyer.

I sigh and take a sip of my almost-cold coffee as Dad turns to us, beaming.

"What do you think?"

“Not bad,” Kyle mumbles, inspecting a crack in the wall. “Definitely needs work.”

Dad nods. “That’s why you’re here.”

Right, so that explains Kyle’s presence, but I still don’t know why *I’m* here.

I open my mouth to ask, but before I can get the words out, Kyle says, “What time is the project manager meeting us?”

A chill runs down my spine as Dad’s gaze swings to me.

Surely not.

“She’s already here,” Dad says, grinning.

He can’t be serious.

Kyle glances past me down the hall, as if he’s expecting someone might be lurking in the next room or hiding under the stairs. The expression on his face when he looks back at me is priceless. “You’re the project manager,” he says flatly.

Before I can respond, Dad says, “What do you think, Vi? Up for something a bit different?”

I glance between him and Kyle, at a loss for words.

“This entire place needs to be gutted and remodeled. I’ve got Kyle here as the foreman, and we need a project manager. I figured since you’re between jobs right now, it would be the perfect opportunity.”

I squeeze my eyes shut, willing the world around me to vanish. I should have told Dad the truth when I had the chance. I should never have agreed to visit him in New York. I should have known better when he said he had something to keep me busy for a while. I don’t know what I was expecting, but it wasn’t this.

“I’ll pay you,” Dad adds, chuckling. “Whatever the going rate is for a project manager on a renovation project like this.”

I wince, staring at the floor. How the hell should I know what that is?

The weight of Dad and Kyle's gaze presses against me, and I force my eyes up. What can I say? I can either tell Dad the truth now, in front of Kyle, which will be twice as humiliating, or I can agree to something I have no clue how to do.

Okay, yes, I know how to manage a project, even if I've had no direct experience doing so. But remodeling a historic building in Brooklyn? I wouldn't know where to start.

I make the mistake of meeting Kyle's eye. He's gazing at me curiously, and on instinct I straighten up, lifting my chin.

"Uh, why me, Dad?" I ask, stalling for time.

"The timing is perfect," he says again. "You don't have anything to do for a while, and I think you'll do a fantastic job."

His unwarranted belief in me makes me cringe. I don't doubt my ability to manage a project, but I don't relish the idea of jumping in at the deep end in a completely new industry and under the watchful eye of my father.

And that's before we even get to the fact that I'd be working with Kyle, the thought of which is equal measures awkward and appealing.

Dad looks between me and Kyle, smiling. "I wanted the two people I trust most on this project."

Oh, God.

Guilt gnaws through me and I twist my hands together, miserable. I can't tell him the truth now. It would crush him. I'm going to have to do this.

Dad's right, anyway—I don't have anything else to do. I've sent out resumes, I've emailed contacts, and I've heard nothing back. I can't sit around twiddling my thumbs, waiting. I'll go crazy. I'm already feeling antsy at having nothing to do.

Besides, part of me reasons, if I do this then I'll have *actual* project management experience to put on my resume, which is huge. And it's not like I'm not trained in this. I know what to do. Sure, the building stuff will be a steep learning curve, but I'm a fast learner and I love a challenge. This will definitely keep me busy while I wait for a real job opportunity, and it will help me *progress* in my career, rather than tread water.

I swallow, giving Dad a weak smile. "Okay, count me in."

"Excellent!" The way his face lights up makes me want to shrivel up and die, but he doesn't notice, turning to lead us further into the house. "Right, let's have a look at what we can do with this place."

I trail behind Dad and Kyle, barely able to focus as Kyle asks all kinds of questions, jotting things in his notebook. We step into a large room, which Kyle refers to as 'the front parlor.' I'm momentarily distracted from the situation by the beauty of the room—the intricately detailed crown moldings, the rich dark wooden floors, the rosette around the light fixture on the ceiling that Kyle points out. He explains the history of these types of townhouses—I hear him use the term 'Greek revival'—and despite myself, I'm riveted. His eyes are bright as they move around the room, his deep voice ringing with passion as he speaks, and I almost forget Dad entirely as I watch Kyle. When he moves near me to show us the pocket doors, my body tingles with awareness.

"That's great," Dad says, bringing my attention back to him, "but I'm thinking of a more modern feel. I want the place split into several apartments."

Kyle frowns, scrubbing a hand over his messy beard. He opens his mouth to say something, but appears to bite his tongue.

I don't say anything either, but have to admit that seems

like a shame. After spending so long in the commercial area of Silicon Valley, a place with so little character, the charm of this neighborhood—this building—is hard to deny. The thought of deliberately stripping away that history to create a bunch of apartments feels like sacrilege.

Still, it's Dad's place, not mine. He's the client in this situation. He's the one we need to please. I'm sure Kyle is used to working with people who have a different vision for a project from his own.

We head from the front parlor to the back parlor—because apparently one parlor wasn't enough in the nineteenth century—and out to what looks like a balcony. Kyle says it's a later addition, and that these spaces were often used as tea rooms. I don't drink tea, but I imagine the balcony would be a nice place to bring my laptop and work outside.

There are two floors above this one, each with two bedrooms and a bathroom, but they're a mess, with brick and wiring exposed in places as half the walls have been torn out. It gets worse when we go down to the basement. Kyle explains it's a 'garden-level basement,' which means it's half below street level on one side, but you can walk out into the yard at the back. Whatever it is, this is apparently where they stored all their junk. There's no sign of the kitchen that Kyle tells us would have once been here, and as for the yard, it's little more than an overgrown tangle of weeds and building materials.

By the time we're back in the entry hall, my head is spinning, wondering what I've gotten myself into. Not just with the house, but with the foreman, who I can't seem to take my eyes off.

"I trust you'll know what's best for the place," Dad says with a grin. I'm not sure if that's directed at me or Kyle, but either way it's the vaguest request I've ever heard from a client on a project. I can't decide if that's a good thing or not.

Dad gets Kyle and I to swap numbers so we can set up a time to get together and begin our plan for the work. "My two favorite people working together," he says, squeezing me on the shoulder with a chuckle. "She's a handful, Kyle. I hope you're up for the challenge."

Kyle pulls his cap off, sighing as he runs a hand through his hair.

My face warms and I shoot Dad a sarcastic smile. "Thanks."

"Seriously, Sweetpea." Dad pulls me into his side, the heat in my face intensifying as he uses his childish nickname for me in front of Kyle. "I think you'll do a wonderful job."

I can only hope he's right.

5

KYLE

"You okay, honey?" Diana, Richard's wife, hovers above me where I'm seated on the sofa, lost in thought as I stare into my beer bottle.

Rich wanders into the living room, loosening his tie with a chuckle. "He's fine; just realizing what he's got himself into with the place on Fruit Street."

I give them a grim smile. It might have been the job I was worried about to begin with, but not anymore.

"It's a beautiful building, isn't it?" Diana says, handing Rich a bottle of beer.

He shakes his head. "It's completely outdated. We're going to modernize the whole place."

I twist in my seat, focusing on the conversation properly. "About that, Rich. I've been thinking. I know it's old, but there's a lot of history in that neighborhood. It was the first suburb of New York when the ferry service started in the early nineteenth century."

Rich waves a hand. "But it's not anymore. It needs to be brought into the *twenty-first* century."

"Well, it's a historic district," I remind him. "There are restrictions on what we can do."

"Sure, on the exterior. But inside we can gut the place and start from scratch. Carve it up into multiple apartments, which is far more useful."

I grimace at the thought of gutting that beautiful row house, turning it into apartments instead of the stately family home it was designed to be. I know it needs a lot of work, but there's so much charm in the original layout and features. It just needs to be restored to its previous glory.

"What did Violet think of the building?" Diana asks, joining us with a glass of wine in her hand. I haven't seen Diana in years, but we spent a reasonable amount of time together when I was at the firm, attending company dinners and client events. Looking at her now, it's so obvious she's Violet's mother—same blonde hair, brown eyes, warm smile. How I didn't connect those dots earlier today, I have no idea. I guess it never occurred to me their daughter would be there. Last I heard she was living on the West Coast.

Rich rubs his chin. "She seemed distracted, which is unlike her. I thought she'd be going around with her notebook, asking questions and grilling me for details, but she was strangely quiet."

I shift my weight, taking a swig of beer. "She's not normally like that?"

Diana and Rich laugh.

"Not our Vi," Diana says fondly. "She's very outspoken. You have to be when you work in a male-dominated industry."

I nod, absorbing this. "Last time I saw her she was going off to college. How old is she now?"

Rich smiles. "Twenty-five. My little girl is all grown up."

His use of the term 'little girl' makes my stomach turn over. I think of the way he called her 'Sweetpea' today, like she was eight years old, and shake my head to myself. I have never felt more like a dirty old man than I do right now.

Diana sips her wine, thinking. "She loved her job. Such a shame she was let go."

I frown. "She was let go?" That's rough. Her words from the coffee shop—about how she'd had a bad week—come back to me. Suddenly the overreaction to the spilled coffee makes a lot more sense.

Di nods. "Maybe that's why she was quiet today," she murmurs to Richard. "Her confidence is shaken."

"Maybe." Rich sips his beer and glances at me. "Well, you can keep an eye on her for us, can't you?"

As much as I want to shake my head, I nod. "Sure."

"You know what guys are like on these kinds of job sites. I don't want any creeps trying to take advantage of her."

Guilt claws up my throat and I try to swallow it down with my beer. Thank God Rich doesn't know I'm the creep who hit on her today.

"I'm sure she can handle herself," Diana says with a laugh. "She's not a little girl anymore."

No, she most certainly is not.

"Still." Rich looks at me pleadingly. "You'll look out for her. We're going out of town next month and it makes me feel better knowing you're going to be there."

I can't help but laugh. "Rich, she's *twenty-five.* She doesn't need me looking out for her."

"It's not only that." Rich sighs, setting his bottle down. "This is her first project like this and she has a lot to learn."

"What do you mean, this is her first project? I thought she'd done this before?"

"She has a background in project management," Rich

hastens to assure me. "But not in renovation. She comes from the tech world."

Irritation flickers in my ribcage. "So she doesn't know a thing about remodeling a house?"

"She's a very fast learner," Di says. "But this is new to her, so she might need some guidance."

I take a long chug from my bottle to hide my frown. I already felt uneasy about being back in the city and taking on this project, and this doesn't help. I'm about to ask why he's hired her if she's so inexperienced, but I already know the answer. She was out of a job and her father, being the good guy he is, wanted to help her out. It makes sense, but it doesn't make the job any easier for me. It's bad enough that I have to work with a woman who is both attractive and completely off-limits, but now I have to babysit her? Micromanage her so she doesn't fuck things up?

This is too much.

I open my mouth to protest, but Diana rises from her chair with a smile. "Is Mexican still your favorite, Kyle? I was thinking of making fajitas for dinner."

Any annoyance I feel quickly dissolves. "I'd love that, Di. Thanks." I swallow, gratitude warming me through. "You always take good care of me."

She pauses to squeeze my shoulder on the way past. "Of course, honey." She wanders into the kitchen and Rich smiles in the way that says he's glad I'm here—that I'm always welcome here.

These two took me in when my life fell to pieces four years ago, and have worried about me ever since. The least I can do is keep an eye on their daughter while we work together.

But how am I going to do this? This morning I was

seconds away from asking her out and now I have to pretend I'm not interested in her.

I mean, I'm *not* interested in her. She's twenty-five and Richard's daughter, for God's sake.

I'll have to put some proper, professional distance between us. No more laughing and flirting, obviously. No mention of what happened this morning; that would be inappropriate. All I can do now is pretend it was an innocent coffee, nothing more. Instead, I'll focus on needing to keep an eye on her, and how annoying that is. Rich never told me, when he strong-armed me into this job, that it was also a babysitting gig.

I repeat this fact to myself like a mantra, stirring the irritation inside me again, letting it fester.

It's the only way I'll survive this.

6

VIOLET

I used to wake by 5.30 a.m. most days, sometimes earlier, but since leaving DigiSwap I struggle to drag myself out of bed in the mornings. It's as if my body somehow knows I no longer have a job and is taking the chance to catch up on all those years of missed sleep.

Well, I *didn't* have a job, but now Dad's roped me into doing this project. I'm still in two minds about it, to be honest. When I got home yesterday I did some research about how to manage a renovation like this, and while some of it was familiar—I'd get to use my beloved Gantt charts, yay—a lot of it wasn't.

Then there's the rugged foreman I met yesterday, and the unusual predicament we seem to find ourselves in. My belly flips with nervous excitement when I think about working with him, but I get the sense he wasn't thrilled when he learned I was Richard's daughter. More like mildly horrified. Still, I can't seem to bring myself to message Dad and tell him no, so that means Kyle and I are officially working together. We need to forget about what happened yesterday and focus on the job, which suits me just fine. If there's one thing I'm good at, it's prioritizing work.

I roll over and check the time on my phone, surprised to find a text waiting for me.

From Kyle, of all people.

Kyle: Meet me at the house in an hour to discuss planning.

No 'hello' or 'good morning' or 'hey I was going to ask you out yesterday but then you turned out to be my friend's daughter and now I don't know what to do'—straight to business.

I had planned to use this morning for more research, to learn about the type of building we're working on, and some common pitfalls in townhouses of that era. I'd begun this late last night but barely made it to 11 p.m. before my eyes started drooping. Only a few days out from leaving my job and I'm already losing my edge.

I check the timestamp on the message from Kyle, frowning when I notice it was sent forty minutes ago.

Shit. Research will have to wait.

I throw the covers off and lurch upright on Sadie's sofa, scrambling for my toiletries bag and a change of clothes. I fire off a quick 'sure thing' in response, have a three-minute shower, throw on my clothes, then pause in front of the coffee maker. I could grab a coffee now, or I could stop in at Joe's again and grab one for both me *and* Kyle—an apology for being late and a peace offering after the awkwardness of yesterday. A sort of *I know that was weird, but let's start over and kick butt on this project together* gesture.

"Morning," Sadie sing-songs as she breezes into the kitchen, her saffron-yellow silk robe billowing out behind her. "How'd you sleep?"

I turn to my friend with a smile. "Good, thanks." It's true.

Her boyfriend didn't stay over, so my ears were blissfully free from the sounds of them going to town on each other.

"Sorry I can only offer you the sofa." She tucks a strand of her unruly red hair behind her ear and reaches for a coffee mug. "I know it's not that comfortable."

"No problem. I appreciate you letting me crash." Although that raises a good point. If I'm sticking around for a while to manage this project, I'll need somewhere to stay besides my friend's couch. Especially if I want more uninterrupted nights of sleep.

I push the thought away, telling myself that's something to worry about later.

"Where are you headed?" Sadie asks as I reach for my bag.

"Meeting with Kyle on the job site today." I told Sadie all about yesterday's events: the handsome-underneath-his-scruff stranger who bought me a coffee and flirted with me, how I was sure he was going to ask me out, and then how he turned out to be Dad's friend. She thought it was hot that Kyle is older, and I agree. Last time I hooked up with a guy my own age I had to pay for dinner *and* drive him home. And don't get me started on how mediocre the sex was.

Sadie's lips twitch with a barely restrained smile. "Seeing your dad's hot friend again? Nice."

I wince. "Can we not call him 'my dad's hot friend'? That's weird. True, but weird."

She laughs into a sip of coffee. "Sure. But you're going ahead with the project?"

I chew my lip, nodding. "I think so." Sadie knows all about the misunderstanding between me and Dad, and when I said I wasn't sure about this project, she told me there's no reason I shouldn't take it on.

"Good. You're qualified and I think you'll be great." She grins at me, full of confidence. "You've got this, babe."

"Thanks." It's nice to have someone believe in me *without* their conviction being based on a lie.

She turns her attention to the refrigerator and I remember I'm running late.

"Have a fab day." I wave over my shoulder as I dart from the kitchen.

"You too!" she calls. "Sneak a picture of that scruffy hottie for me!"

I'M a little late meeting Kyle. I would have been earlier if I hadn't stopped for coffee, but that's a necessity. And I really want to smooth things over with him, so we can start off on the right foot.

In hindsight, arriving on time would have helped that, but it's too late now.

It took two trains to get here from Sadie's apartment in Bushwick, and when I finally climb the front steps to the building, I realize I'm nervous. Which is silly, of course. Kyle might be Dad's friend but he's also a nice enough guy—that much was clear yesterday. I just need to hand him the coffee, address the elephant in the room, then we can put it behind us.

"You're late," Kyle grumbles when I push open the front door.

Jeez, I'm not even in the building yet.

"Sorry, yes." My hands are full with the coffee, so I push the door closed with my butt and turn to smile at him.

He's standing in the entry hall in shorts and work boots, a red flannel shirt open over a plain white tee, sleeves rolled to the elbows. The same cap from yesterday contains the mass of dark hair on his head, and he holds a clipboard in one hand as he frowns at me.

He's cuter than I remember, even though I now know he's nearly fifty.

Which is double my age. Yikes.

"I, uh, stopped to get us coffee." I hold his decaf cappuccino out with a sheepish smile. He seems tense, and I guess that's not surprising. If I can only get him to laugh like yesterday, to relax, this job might actually be fun.

He stares at the coffee cup in my hand, brow pulled low, apparently deciding whether to accept it. "Is it decaf?" he asks at last, and I nod. "Thanks." I notice he's careful to make sure his fingers don't touch mine as he takes the cup from me. Have I become poisonous overnight?

I tap my cup against his like I did yesterday, and he flinches. "I owed you anyway," I say, trying to segue into addressing the delicate issue at hand, but before I can continue, he lifts his gaze to meet mine.

"You didn't have to do that. I was trying to do something nice to make your day better."

"You did." I smile, letting my gaze rest on his face. Smooth, light-olive complexion, strong nose, beard that would have once been a rich brown but is now threaded with gray. His eyes are a darker shade of green today, a lush forest after rain, and small creases fan out beside them as he studies me. God, I could get lost in those eyes.

Snap out of it.

I swallow. "You definitely did," I murmur, my voice huskier than I intend.

A flicker of something passes across his features, then he seems to catch himself, clearing his throat and glancing away. "Well, thanks for the coffee." He taps his clipboard. "Now, we need to—"

"Actually, um, before we do that, can we talk about..." Kyle looks back at me impatiently, but I square my shoulders, trying to do the right thing and clear the air. "I know this is all kinds of awkward, having to work together after... you know."

He stares at me, unmoving. "No, I don't know."

I huff an uncomfortable laugh. *Way to make this even more awkward, Kyle.*

"Well, it seemed like you were going to ask me out yesterday, I think?" Why is my voice so squeaky? "And then you realized... Anyway, I don't want things to be weird, so—"

"I wasn't," he says sharply.

"What?"

"I wasn't going to ask you out." He clears his throat again, his cheeks turning pink under his beard as he pretends to study something on his clipboard.

Okay, so he's embarrassed. Fair enough.

"Look, you didn't know I was Richard's daughter, I get it. I didn't know you were Dad's age, either—"

"I'm not," he cuts in. "I'm only forty-three." Then he frowns at the clipboard, as if it has personally offended him.

Right, so he's *not* nearly fifty. That makes sense. He certainly doesn't look it.

"It's okay," I say gently. "We were hitting it off. But obviously now—"

"It's not okay. I bought you a coffee, nothing more."

Irritation fizzles in my stomach. Is he freaking serious right now? I'm almost *certain* he was about to ask me out—it was basically out of his mouth just as Dad arrived. Why won't he admit it?

I put a hand on my hip. "Are you kidding?"

He takes a long sip of his coffee, buying time. Eventually, he swallows and says, "Nope. Not kidding. And I don't want to waste time talking about something that doesn't matter when we've got shitloads of work to do."

I give a scoff of disbelief. He wants to be like that? Well, he can be like that. I've worked with plenty of difficult men and I can give as good as I get.

"Fine." I motion along the hall. "Lead the way."

He tightens his grip on the clipboard and nods. "Great." He turns and stalks into the front parlor—a ridiculous name in this day and age, but I digress—and reads from the notes on his clipboard. "First thing we need to do is meet with a structural engineer to check the integrity of the building. Once we get the all-clear there, we can meet with an architect."

I wander across to the fireplace and set my coffee down on the mantel, rifling in my bag for my notebook and a pen.

"Hey, whoa." He strides over and snatches my cup off the mantel. "That's antique black walnut. Don't throw your coffee down on it."

I narrow my eyes. Is he referring to me dropping my coffee yesterday? That was an *accident*. I'm not some klutz—I tripped in my sandals. Today I'm wearing much more sensible Converse sneakers.

"No, that's not—" He shakes his head, clearly frustrated with himself. "Just—that mantel is over a hundred and fifty years old. We need to be careful."

"Oh." I take my coffee from him and step back to assess the mantel. It's a large wooden structure with small decorative columns running up each side. A layer of dust covers a thick slab, once painted in what I think may have been white, but now appears to be a dirty taupe color, soot-blackened in places. I can imagine what it looked like back in the day, though, a roaring fire inside the black cast-iron grate, maybe some oil lamps or pictures or whatever it was people put on their mantel a hundred and fifty years ago.

"Got it. Don't touch the priceless mantel." I glance from the fireplace to Kyle, who's standing right beside me. He's much taller than I remember—almost a foot more than me, which would make him around six-four.

Which is not relevant, I remind myself.

I shake the thought from my head, gesturing to the elaborate mantel. "Will this be staying, though? It's not very modern, and Dad said—"

"I'm not removing an original mantel in good condition like that," he says gruffly. "We'll make it work."

"Okay then." I glance around for somewhere safe to set my coffee down. There's a spot on the dirty floor in the corner, and I gingerly tiptoe across and place my cup out of harm's way. On closer inspection, I notice the floor is quite damaged in places. "Have you seen this floor?" I ask, turning to find Kyle watching me.

He heaves an exasperated sigh. "Yes, Violet, I've seen the floor."

I resist the urge to roll my eyes. I didn't mean it *quite* so literally.

"No, I mean the damage to the wood. Will we replace this? Maybe put down some vinyl, or..." The horror on Kyle's face makes me stop short.

That's a no, then.

Admittedly, it wouldn't be my first choice, because the wood is beautiful and worn in that way that only old wooden floors can be. But some of these boards are really damaged—how would we even find replacements that match? And old wooden floors don't exactly feel modern...

"We'll restore the floors," he says, as if it's obvious. "We can take spare boards from a closet or something upstairs to replace the damaged ones. That way they'll match."

Huh. That's clever.

I grab my pen and note this down, along with what he said earlier about the structural engineer and architect. I'm assuming we'll need a plumber and electrician at some point, probably a landscaper and decorator as well, so I note that down too without saying anything.

Kyle and I talk for a little longer, him pointing out things that are apparently obvious but I completely miss, me taking notes as he talks. Ultimately, we both agree that we can do nothing until a structural engineer assesses the place, so I leave with a promise to organize one as soon as possible. Kyle tries to insist on contacting one himself, but I remind him that, as the project manager, liaising with contractors is one of my main tasks. He reluctantly relents.

It's a relief to get out of there. If I thought yesterday was uncomfortable, today is worse. What happened to the sweet man I met in Joe's? I get that things didn't start off great, but I don't know why he's so touchy. And the fact that he wouldn't admit to flirting with me yesterday...

I shake my head as I walk back to the subway, dropping my empty coffee cup in a trash can on the way. I'm not full of myself—it's not like I think all men want me, or whatever, but I feel kind of... ripped off. We definitely had a connection at the coffee shop. I haven't felt a spark like that in a long time, and I know I didn't make it up.

Anyway, that's the least of my problems right now. I felt like an idiot in there, not knowing about the mantel or the flooring—or anything else, for that matter. I need to contact a structural engineer as soon as I'm back at Sadie's, then I've got some serious research ahead of me.

7

KYLE

To clear my head, I've started running early in the mornings. Though I'm generally fit from my work, I haven't gone running in years. It's taken me a few days to get back into it, but it was like muscle memory—throwing on my shoes at 6 a.m. and heading up Central Park West, cutting into the park through Strawberry Fields and Cherry Hill. In a way, it's almost like I never left my life on the Upper West Side, four years ago.

Almost.

At least my anxiety is nothing like it was then, although it's definitely increased since being back in the city. I can tell by the way my ears ring like they used to, the way my thoughts race more than usual. The Violet debacle certainly hasn't helped.

Things with Violet have been as difficult as expected. It started when she confronted me about the fact that I was flirting with her before Rich showed up. I didn't want to lie, but what was I supposed to say? *I thought you were beautiful and interesting and yes, I was about to ask you out*? What if she told Rich? No way could I risk that.

And she knows nothing about the house. It's not like I expect her to recognize black walnut on sight, but to at least have *some* knowledge of a renovation like this would be useful. I'll have to hold her hand throughout this whole damn project, all because Rich wanted his daughter to have something to do while she was out of a job.

I sigh, turning to head back to Rich's place, reminding myself that it doesn't matter. I owe Rich big time, and I want to be there for him like he was for me. Even if being there for him really means being there for Violet.

Still, if I wasn't here doing this for Rich, I'd be pulling animal feces out of Murial's cabin back in Maine, and this is much better.

I think.

Back at Rich and Diana's, I shower and eat, thinking about the day ahead. We got the report from the structural engineer yesterday, and besides some rotten oak planks on the staircase—which I already knew about—and some mortar that needs replacing in the brick façade, the house is in reasonable shape, structurally. Pretty surprising, given the building dates back to 1847.

And Rich wants to modernize the whole thing and carve it up into apartments? I shudder at the thought. It was designed to be a beautiful family home, and I don't know if I can bring myself to destroy it like that—even if four floors is a little excessive for the average family. Usually I trust Rich's judgment without question, but I think he might be wrong on this one. Besides, he said he trusted me, didn't he? Even if technically he is my client, and even if technically he is *allowed* to alter the interior to that extent, I feel the need to protect the history of the neighborhood I grew up in.

Which reminds me, I'll need to contact the Landmarks Preservation Commission before we can begin work. No doubt I'll have to jump through a stack of hoops for this project, unlike back home. I'm not used to working like this, but if it means the history of Brooklyn Heights is preserved, I'm all for it. People have already erased too much of this city's past.

I head out the door to my truck, making a mental note of what I want to do today. I'm planning to go to the site and make a more detailed list of what needs to be done, and which contractors I'll need for more specialized tasks. I haven't asked Violet to meet me, because really, what's the point? I don't need to babysit her again, and I definitely don't need the distraction of her wandering around in those denim cutoffs.

It takes me forty minutes to reach the job site, which wouldn't bother me if I was driving through the beautiful Kennebec County, but irritates the shit out of me when I'm stopping at traffic lights in Manhattan every fifty feet. If a job was far enough away in Maine, I'd take an air mattress and stay out there for the week. It allowed me more time to relax in the evenings; instead of driving for hours only to be exhausted when I got home, I could use my time after work to swim or hike nearby, cook on an open fire and listen to music under the stars. I've made a promise to myself that my job will never take over my life again, and balancing rest with work is essential. While there's no swimming or hiking here, it might be good to stay on site to avoid the traffic and enjoy being in the Heights more. Plus it would give Rich and Di their guest room back. They've done enough for me.

I grab a coffee from Joe's then head to 14 Fruit Street. The front door is already unlocked when I arrive, and I pause in the doorway, wondering if I forgot to lock up—I'm sure I didn't—or if someone has broken in. A few tentative steps into the house reveal it's neither. Violet is here, sitting cross-legged on the floor of the front parlor, leaning over the glowing screen of her laptop. Scattered around her are books, notebooks, and pens; behind her stands a large dry-erase board on wheels, dotted with Post-Its. She's set a drop-cloth down underneath her, a careful island containing her chaos, and something tugs in my chest. She's trying to protect the floor.

"Hey," I say, my voice strangely rusty.

She doesn't notice, though, because she's too busy leaping out of her skin.

"Jesus!" she shrieks, one hand flying to her chest. "I didn't hear you come in. Were you tip-toeing?"

Despite myself, a laugh slips out. "No. I think you were just very focused."

She glances at her laptop, rubs her eyes, then looks back at me and closes the lid. "Sorry. I'm trying to get a handle on things after we got the engineer's report yesterday."

I nod, looking down at the single coffee cup in my hand and feeling like an asshole. If I'd known she was here, I would have bought her one.

Then I remember I'm not supposed to be chummy with her—I'm supposed to be putting distance between us.

So, here I am. The jerk who accepts her free coffee and doesn't reciprocate.

I don't like being this guy.

She pushes to her feet, stretching her arms overhead and yawning. Today she's in a periwinkle-blue floral cotton dress that rises above the knee as she stretches, revealing the soft, creamy skin of her thighs. My fingers itch with the urge to reach out and touch her.

Christ.

I stumble back, hitting the doorframe.

Ouch.

She gives me a strange look. "Are you okay?"

"Fine," I grunt, lifting my coffee and taking a scalding sip. I hiss out a breath, both in pain and irritation. I was looking forward to a distraction-free day so I could make some progress. "What are you doing here, Violet?"

Her brows draw together under her bangs. "I'm working on this project too, remember?"

How could I forget?

"I didn't ask you to come in," I retort, more sharply than I intend.

She snorts, placing a hand on her hip. "First of all, you're not my boss, so I don't need your permission. Secondly, this is *my* father's house, so I can come whenever I like. And thirdly, I have work to do, so I'm here working."

I blink. She has no trouble talking back to me, that's for sure. It's both frustrating and, weirdly, kind of arousing.

Fuck. I'm in hell.

Work. Focus on work.

"Alright," I mutter, humoring her. "What have you been doing, then?" It can't be anything useful, that's for sure. She might be gorgeous but she doesn't know the first thing about what needs to be done here.

She glares at me, one eye twitching with barely restrained anger. I'm being a dick and I hate myself for it.

"Well, *Kyle*, I've put through applications for two different permits with the Landmarks Preservation Commission for a start."

I rub a hand across my beard, attempting to hide my surprise. "Two?"

"Yes. We need one for the interior and one for the exterior, as well as a permit from the Department of Buildings, which I've just sent off. I had a lovely chat with Ruth at the

DOB who's going to try to push our permit through within the next few days."

Okay, *that's* impressive. Permits can take weeks to come through, if not longer.

"And I've got an architect coming to meet with us on Monday. His name is Ben, and his firm specializes in townhouses like these."

Huh. I may have underestimated her.

I sip my coffee, trying to appear underwhelmed. "When were you going to tell me this?"

She lifts her brows. "When were *you* going to tell me you were coming here to work today?"

"Uh..." Shit, she's got me there.

"Exactly." She smirks. "Anyway, you're welcome." She pivots on her heel, as if to head out of the room.

"Where are you going now?"

"To the bathroom." She throws an indignant look over her shoulder. "Or do I need your permission for that, too?"

Normally on a site like this I'd say yes, but given the engineer assured us the plumbing is all in working order—apparently the people who owned the place before Rich had it redone—I shake my head.

I force myself to stare at the crumbling ceiling as she leaves the room.

VIOLET and I manage to avoid each other for most of the morning, and when I pop out to grab a late lunch, I consider asking her if she wants anything, then decide against it.

She's a big girl and can clearly handle herself.

But when I come back to the house after three, she's still

hunched over her laptop, showing no signs of having taken a break at all.

"Hey," I say, and she jumps.

"Shit." Her hand goes to her chest but her eyes don't leave her screen. "You sure love to sneak up on me."

"I wasn't..." I shake my head. *She sure gets lost in her work,* I think, but I don't say it. "Did you eat?" I know I should leave it but I can't help myself. I used to skip lunch all the time and my body paid the price. Rich asked me to look out for her, after all. Though I'm not entirely sure this is what he meant.

She waves a hand, eyes glued to her laptop. "I'll eat later."

"It *is* later."

She finally looks up at me. "What? It's only—" She glances down to check the time on her screen and her eyes widen. "Crap, I didn't realize." She snaps her laptop closed and rises to her feet, and this time I make sure to turn away when she stretches.

"Sitting on the floor like that can't be good for your back," I mumble, then I feel about a million years old. Twenty-five-year olds don't tend to worry about shit like that.

She shrugs, but I make a mental note to look for the fold-out camping chair I always take to job sites. It's somewhere in the back of my truck. She needs a desk, really. Maybe there are some stray building materials in the basement or yard I can cobble together into something—

Or maybe you should focus on the job and stop thinking about what she needs.

"I want to start putting together a plan for how the project is going to unfold," Violet says, apparently forgetting about lunch again.

Something comes back to me from my days in law, something I haven't thought about in ages: Gantt charts. They're essentially a bar chart that shows how a project schedule will unfold. Rich used to go on about how they were a useful tool for planning legal projects and communicating procedure with clients, and insisted we all use them. I'd never considered their application in a reno project, but I can see how they might be useful in a large-scale one like this.

"What about a Gantt chart? It's a tool that shows how to structure..." I trail off as Violet looks irritated. Or is it amused?

"You don't need to mansplain. I know what a Gantt chart is."

Of course she does. This is her job, you fuckwit.

"What do you think this is for?" She gestures to the dry-erase board behind her. "Pictionary?"

I stifle a chuckle because even though she's clearly still irritated with me from this morning, that was kind of funny.

Goddammit. The last thing I need is for her to make me laugh.

"Yeah, alright," I mutter, frowning down at the floor. "Then let's figure this out. First of all, we need to decide what we want to tell the architect on Monday."

Violet lifts a shoulder. "We know what to tell him. Split the place into apartments. Make it modern."

"Yeah... We're not going to do that."

There's a beat of silence, and then, "Excuse me?"

"I told you, we're not removing those original features."

She rolls her eyes. "I know, you want to keep the mantel and the floor, but—"

"We *will* be keeping those things," I say firmly.

Her hands go to her hips as she glares at me. "What makes you think *you* get to decide that?"

"I'm the foreman. Rich asked me to head up this project."

"Yeah, and he asked *me*, too."

"But you don't know anything about remodeling a house," I say, my voice rising in exasperation.

Her eyes narrow, and guilt darts through me. Her father told me that in confidence, and she's trying her best. Even I can see that.

"Maybe not," she forces out through gritted teeth, "but I understand the importance of meeting client expectations on a project."

"That's not..." I shake my head, looking away as I realize there's more to this than only her lack of experience. I think back to the woman I met in Joe's, the one who admired the history of this neighborhood and felt sad to see it erased. "You know what's pissing me off the most, Violet?"

She throws her hands up. "I have *no* idea."

"When we met, you talked about how much you love these old buildings. Now you're doing your best to strip the history out of this one."

"Oh, *now* you want to talk about what happened the day we met?"

"That's not what I mean," I say, caught off-guard. The last thing I need is her pressing me again to confess that I was about to ask her out. "In Joe's you said—"

"I know what I said. Unlike *some* people"—she looks at me pointedly—"*I* can actually remember what happened that day."

Don't bite.

"Then why, if you mean what you said about the importance of preserving old buildings, are you so insistent on destroying this one?"

"That's a little dramatic. We're hardly *destroying* it. But Dad said—"

"So it's because he's your dad?"

"No, it's..." She shifts her weight, suddenly looking uncomfortable. "It's because he's our client," she says after a pause. "It's important to make the client happy."

"It is," I concede. "But he was vague, and said he trusted us to do what was right. I've known Rich a long time—"

Violet looks at me like I'm completely dense. "I *think* I've known him longer."

I lift my gaze to the ceiling, trying to stay calm. "Technically, yes, but not as an adult. Not as a friend. And I think we can make this project better than even he could envision. He chose me to head this project, and he knows the way I operate. It's a risk, but I truly believe he'll be grateful in the end."

She opens and closes her mouth, all the fight draining out of her. "You don't get it," she mumbles, turning away. And before I can say anything more, she shoves her headphones in and returns to her laptop.

8

VIOLET

On Saturday morning, Sadie tells me I need to take a break from work. Ever since Kyle accused me of knowing nothing about the work we're doing—quite rightfully, too—I've been glued to my laptop, learning as much as I can. I try to tell Sadie that I *can't* take a break—I still have so much research to do—but she insists that a few hours away from my laptop and Post-Its will do me good.

We take the train into Manhattan, because she wants to visit the huge Barnes & Noble store at Union Square. "They have the best range of romance," she told me when I asked why we had to trek all the way over there. Sadie loves her romance novels.

I'm happy to oblige. She's letting me sleep on her sofa—even if most of my nights aren't as restful as I'd like—and besides, I haven't hung out with her properly since I arrived. I dove head-first into work, like usual.

I stare out the window as we head across the Williamsburg Bridge, flashes of the Empire State Building and East

River appearing between the steel bridge beams like the flickering of an old film reel. Something stirs in my chest at the sight of the city I grew up in, the city I left for work and returned to in a moment of desperation. I haven't stopped to appreciate that I'm here—that I'm *home*—and it's really nice. I missed this place so much.

When we climb out of the subway at Union Square into the warm sunshine and the hum of the city, the feeling intensifies. We walk through the leafy shade of the small park, the sounds of traffic and people milling about the farmers' market reminding me how alive this place is.

Sadie was right—taking a break from work was a good idea.

"You're quiet," she says, nudging me as we cross the park. "You okay?"

I smile. "Yeah. Just thinking about how much I missed New York."

"Really?" She turns to me excitedly, her wild red curls spilling over her shoulders. "Does that mean you're moving back for good?"

I can't help but laugh. Sadie and I were inseparable in high school, then I went out of state for college and straight into work at DigiSwap, and our friendship faded from long-distance calls to the occasional text. My career became the center of my universe and left little room for anything else. Sure, I missed Sadie, but most of the time I was too busy to think about it.

Being back here with my friend, I begin to wonder how I could let that happen—how I could just let our friendship go like that.

I put an arm around her shoulders and squeeze. "I'd definitely consider it," I say, surprising myself. "But..." I sigh.

"I need to get a job here, and most of the good jobs are on the West Coast."

"Most," she agrees, grinning at me hopefully. "But not all."

I laugh as we head into Barnes & Noble, buoyed by Sadie's optimism. The store is huge—four floors of books that rise before us like a temple of literature right in the middle of the city. Sadie sighs in satisfaction as we step onto the escalator. This is her happy place.

"Come check out the romance section with me, will you?"

I glance away from Sadie, dragging my bottom lip between my teeth. The last thing I want to think about right now is romance. My life has been woefully devoid of it for a long time. It wasn't something I gave much thought to until a week ago, when, for a brief moment, I thought I'd met a really nice guy; a serendipitous encounter in a random coffee shop while waiting to meet my dad. For a few minutes, I'd let myself bask in the attention of this kind and handsome stranger, imagined what it might be like to go out with him. And my heart leapt in a way that was both unfamiliar and pleasant when he opened his mouth to ask me out.

Well, that part is apparently debatable, isn't it? I know I didn't imagine it, and I'm still frustrated that he can't even bring himself to be friendly to me, let alone admit the truth about that moment we shared.

So, no. I'm not really in the mood for romance.

"I might, uh, look at magazines for a while. But I'll meet you there?"

"Sure," Sadie says, and I wander off to the magazine section while she heads up to romance.

Ugh, I don't want to look at magazines. My mind has

strayed back to work, and the argument Kyle and I had yesterday. We've got the architect coming to meet with us on Monday, and we can't agree on what to do with the place. I need some inspiration, something to prove to Kyle that we need to go modern, like Dad asked.

After several wrong turns, I find the architecture section, and hunt for books on remodeling old houses. I come across several, all massive tomes, so I pull them out and sit cross-legged in the aisle, flipping through them.

One in particular—titled *Restoring a House in the City*—shows a lot of townhouses similar to ours, renovated in various ways. Some are restored to their former glory, and look like they're straight out of the mid-nineteenth century, with elaborate plaster details on the ceiling, original wood flooring, and—yup—mantels similar to ours. Others have a much more modern twist, with bright pops of color, lots of steel and glass, and no sign of the original details.

I sigh as I pore over the book, comparing the different styles, and my heart sinks.

As much as I hate to admit it, I think Kyle might be right. The modern houses, while beautiful in their own way, *do* completely eliminate the history of the building. Sure, from the outside they look like the original—they have to, thanks to the Landmarks Preservation Commission—but inside they could have been built yesterday. They lack the charm and character that the house's façade promises.

I think back to the buildings I'm used to from the commercial hub in Silicon Valley—almost all of them modern, with little character or history. There are plenty of places like that in the world, and we have a rare chance to preserve something that has meaning, that holds stories from years gone by.

But when I think of Dad insisting on the place being

modernized, my stomach wobbles. Plus he wanted it to be split into multiple apartments, not kept as one big home. How can we please him and also preserve the building's history? Can we reach a compromise that somehow does both?

"There you are."

I glance up to find Sadie, her arms piled with romance novels. I blink. "Oh, hey."

"I was calling you. It's been over an hour."

"What?" I pull my phone from my bag, surprised. I shouldn't be, though—I often lose track of time when I'm working.

Which I'm not supposed to be doing today. Whoops.

I give Sadie a shamefaced smile as I push to my feet, stretching out my back. Kyle's right, sitting on the floor all the time isn't good for my posture. I think it's giving me headaches.

Dammit. I hate that he keeps being right.

"Sorry." I grab a handful of books from the floor and hold them to my chest. "I got distracted."

"Working," Sadie says, but her tone is affectionate, not judgmental. "You really love this project, huh?"

I consider this as we make our way to the register. Admittedly, I wasn't sure about it when Dad first proposed it —awkward Kyle issue aside—but the more I learn about buildings, especially these old ones, the more interesting it becomes. In tech, so much of what we did was intangible, but with a project like this, I can look at the house and envision how it can be different. Be better. We haven't started work yet—we're still waiting for the go ahead from the Landmarks Commission—but I'm excited to begin. I'm excited to watch something physically take shape in front of me.

"Yeah," I say, placing my books on the counter. "I didn't expect to, but it's interesting."

Sadie smiles. I wait for her to make a joke about Kyle, 'my dad's hot friend' but she doesn't, and I'm relieved.

I'm going to have to do some serious groveling on Monday.

9

KYLE

Violet looks nervous when she arrives Monday morning.

I don't blame her. I've felt shitty all weekend after the way we left things on Friday. I still stand by not modernizing the building, but I hate that we yelled at each other and that she looked so upset. I had to distract myself with a project to make sure I didn't text her.

"Hey," she says warily, closing the front door.

I grunt in response, doing my best to appear aloof. Like I haven't been waiting for this moment for forty-eight hours. But then I ruin it: her arms are piled with books, and on instinct I step forward to grab them.

I am so bad at this.

"Oh." Her eyebrows pop up in surprise. "Thanks."

We stand in the entry hall, staring at each other awkwardly. She's wearing skinny jeans that cling to every inch of her generous curves, a loose Nirvana T-shirt tied at the waist. I wonder if she's actually ever listened to Nirvana or if it's just one of those trendy shirts young people wear because it's 'vintage.' It occurs to me that Kurt Cobain died before she was even born, and I feel ancient.

"So, um." She shifts her weight from one foot to the other. "I owe you an apology."

Guilt trickles through me. I sigh. "No, you don't, Violet. You want to do a good job on this project, and your dad—"

"No, hear me out. You were right."

Okay, I can't have heard that correctly.

"Come again?"

A reluctant smile plays at the corner of her mouth, but I can see she's trying to fight it. "*You were right*. We can't modernize this place."

My eyebrows hit my hairline. "You're serious?"

She nods, gesturing to the books in my arms, and I look down. *Restoring a House in the City*—that one I haven't read. But the other two—*Bricks & Brownstone*, and *Old Brooklyn Heights*—are books I know well.

Wow. I was not expecting this.

"I did some reading over the weekend, and I think the history of these townhouses is important. We can't strip that away."

I glance up at her, warmth suffusing my chest. She actually paid attention to the things I said. She cared enough to purchase these books and spend time reading them.

"And what about your dad?"

"Well... yeah." She pulls her bottom lip between her teeth, nibbling at it in thought. God, it's cute when she does that. I force my gaze back to the books.

After a moment, she says, "It's important to me that he's happy with the project."

"Yeah, it is to me too."

"So, maybe there's some sort of compromise we can

come up with. Like, we split it into multiple apartments, but we keep the original features."

I shift the books to my other arm, thinking. "Maybe. But we'd still have to lose a lot of the history to do that, because we'd have to change so much to accommodate a kitchen and bathroom on every floor."

Her shoulders slump. "Yeah, I guess you're right."

"But… what if we did two apartments, each split over a couple levels? Then we could keep a lot of the original features, but still provide two separate places." I scratch at my unkempt beard, considering how this could work. "Basement and first floor could be one apartment, and they get the yard, then the top two are another."

Violet gazes at me, her head cocked to one side in thought. "I could see that." Her eyes sparkle as she turns the idea over in her mind. "We'd keep the historical features throughout the building, like the original floors and the plaster moldings and the fireplaces, but we could also add some modern touches in unexpected ways, like a bold color palette, and brass fixtures in the kitchen and bathroom."

I nod, the image forming in my head. I can absolutely see how that could work. It's like what I do with cabins back in Maine—I preserve what history I can, but I also add in more modern elements like bigger windows. And, you know, running water.

"I like it," I say. "And I think your dad will too. He wants the apartments to appeal to buyers, which is far more likely to happen if they're unique. And that's exactly what we'll create."

"Okay," Violet says slowly, nodding. "Yeah, okay. I trust you."

"Really?" I shouldn't pull at this thread, but the word is out of my mouth before I can think twice.

Her eyes narrow slightly as she studies my face. I don't know why she would trust me. I've lied to her about what happened the day we met, and I've been nothing but an asshole around her since. I hate myself for it.

"Yes," she says at last.

It feels so good to finally agree about the project that I can't help but grin. She grins right back. We gaze at each other a moment longer, the light in Violet's eyes shifting from excited to something else, something more heated. The silence between us becomes heavy and loaded, and Violet swallows, running her tongue across her bottom lip as she looks at me.

I tear my gaze away, frustrated. *This* is why I need to keep her at arm's length, because the minute we get along, the feeling between us shifts back to what it was the day we met at Joe's. That feeling where we connected and flirted and both saw something more there.

Something we can't have.

"Great, well, we agree then," I mutter, turning to head back into the parlor room.

Violet hesitates, then follows me in. She stops short when her eyes land on the desk in the corner, with the fold-out chair tucked behind it.

Oh, shit. I'd forgotten about that.

"Is that... for me?" she asks uncertainly.

"Yep." I set her books down on top, admiring the finish. It's nothing fancy; an old door I found lying in the basement that was far too gone to be used as a door again, but once I varnished it and added legs, it made a great desk. It's big enough to spread her shit out, and hopefully stop her from hunching over her laptop so much.

She wanders across and sets her bag down, looking at the desk. "Did you make this?"

I nod, turning to head back out of the room before she can ask too many questions. Yes, I spent the weekend making her a desk, carefully planing and sanding and varnishing the old wood of the door to make a smooth surface for her. Yes, it was a lot of work. No, I probably shouldn't have done it.

"This is… wow. Thank you. It's perfect." Her voice is reverent, and despite myself I glance at her. She's leaning forward over the desk, admiring it, and I foolishly let myself admire the way her jeans hug her perfect ass.

Before I can stop myself, I imagine walking up behind her, pressing myself to her soft curves, and burying my face in her hair.

Disgust washes through me as soon as I have the thought. I should not be thinking about my friend's daughter in this way.

"You're welcome, Vi," I say, my voice gravelly. It's the first time I've called her Vi, and I wonder if she'll notice.

She does.

She turns back to me, her eyes wide, her mouth curving into a tentative smile.

It hits me hard in the chest, and I glance away, shoving my hands into my pockets. "I don't want your stuff all over the floor," I mumble. "It's getting in the way."

I leave the room before I can register the expression on her face.

I PUT the notes from my clipboard on Violet's new desk and head out to lunch without saying a word. I've spent the entire morning avoiding her—again—which is hardly helpful given we need to be working together. At this rate we won't even *start* the project, let alone finish it.

I take a long lunch, sipping coffee and writing notes at Joe's, trying to get my head on straight. We've had our permit from the Department of Buildings come through, and are only waiting on the Landmarks Commission. This afternoon we're meeting with the architect, and then we can get in the guys Rich organized to begin the demo phase.

These are all things Violet and I should map out together, but I find myself wanting to be around her as little as possible.

That's not true—I *want* to be around her, a lot—but I know I shouldn't want that. I know wanting that makes me a bad guy, the exact kind of guy Rich was worried about on the job site.

The thought makes my stomach sour, and I set my cold coffee aside, sighing. Guess I can't avoid the place forever.

When I get back, Violet is busily working at her dry-erase board, sticking Post-Its and humming to herself. The tune is familiar but I can't put my finger on what it is. She turns to me, grinning as I enter the room.

"Guess what?"

"What?" I mumble, wishing she wasn't so... effervescent. So damn pretty.

"We got our permits from the Landmarks Commission! We're good to go."

"Oh." A smile creeps onto my face too. "That's awesome."

"I know!" She motions to the board behind her. "I've been working on a Gantt chart"—she shoots me a smirk—"for how it's going to proceed, using your notes. The architect will be here soon, and after we finalize our plans we can begin demolition, and..." she trails off with a frown. "What?"

It's not until she stops that I realize I'm staring at her intensely, because she's done exactly what I wanted her to do, without me having to ask, and she's happy and excited about it. A week ago she didn't know the first thing about this project and now she's up and running as if she's been doing it for years.

God, she's so smart, so hard working—and so fucking sexy.

I close my eyes and drop my head into my hands, groaning to myself. This is my own personal hell.

"That's great, Violet," I mutter, refusing to look at her. "That's... yeah. Good." I turn to leave the room, because I honestly don't know what else to do, when her voice stops me in my tracks.

"What's going on? I thought you'd be happy?"

I sigh, not glancing back. "I am. That's great news."

"Then why—"

She's interrupted by a knock on the door as the architect arrives, and I breathe out in relief.

Will this get any easier?

10

VIOLET

For the first time in years, I leave work early.

Well, there was that time I was let go and had to walk shamefully to my car with a box full of my stuff at nine in the morning, but I think we can agree that doesn't count.

The meeting with the architect went well—at least, I thought it did—but Kyle was tense the whole time. I assumed since we were finally seeing eye to eye on this project he'd be in a better mood, but if anything he seemed worse. He shuffled around behind Ben and I, barely saying two words, refusing to look at me.

I step off the train at Halsey Street, shaking my head. I don't know what's going on with him, but it's getting annoying. He's made it clear from the moment Dad announced I was working on this project that he doesn't want me there. Admittedly I didn't make a fantastic first impression, but I've been working my ass off to learn everything I can and prove I'm an asset rather than a liability to this project. But it doesn't matter what I do—the minute I feel I've done something well, he finds a way to make it clear I'm not welcome. I'm starting to wonder if he's actually trying to drive me off this project altogether.

But then I think of the desk he made me, and confusion clouds my head. Why go to the trouble of making such a lovely desk if it was just to get me out of his way? A tiny part of me wants to believe he made it because he likes me, but I don't have much to support that hypothesis, not when every word coming out of his mouth tells me otherwise.

I turn into Sadie's street with a sigh. At least I'll have a couple of hours alone before she gets in from work. I love her, but I miss having my own place, coming home after a long day at work, putting on my softest PJs and curling up in bed with Netflix and a pizza. I feel rude doing that here, and if I'm home when she's eating I'll join her. And it's rarely just Sadie—her boyfriend Tim is there more often than he's not, and I can't exactly complain because he's not the intruder here, I am. No matter how much Sadie assures me I'm welcome.

I let myself into Sadie's, looking forward to the quiet. I'm just going to use it to work anyway. I've still got to research—

"Ahh!" I lurch back, hitting my shoulder on the door frame as my hands fly to my eyes.

"Shit, sorry!" Sadie's voice is high-pitched as she and Tim scramble for their clothes.

That's right—I walk in on them having sex. On the living room floor. At three-thirty in the afternoon.

"I'll go," I say, turning blindly for the door. I dropped my keys in shock and start fumbling for them on the floor, one hand still firmly over my eyes, but it's too late now—the image of Tim's bare butt is seared into my retinas.

Ugh, I want to bleach my brain.

"No! Don't be silly," Sadie says, more calmly. "We're dressed. Come in."

My hands close around my keys and I straighten up, reluctantly uncovering my eyes. Sadie is sitting on the sofa, her cheeks flushed as Tim slinks from the room.

"Sorry." I cringe. "I should have knocked, or—"

"No, *I'm* sorry. We don't usually..." She shakes her head, giving an awkward giggle. "But I got the afternoon off work, and Tim was free, and"—she shrugs, grinning—"you know how it is."

No, I don't know.

"Mm," I say noncommittally, hanging my keys on the hook by the door. I haven't had sex in months—or is it years?—and the last time wasn't anything to write home about. I might not love seeing my friend and her boyfriend all over each other, but I have to admit I'm a little jealous of their chemistry. I've never been with someone who couldn't keep their hands off me, who wanted me so badly we ended up going at it on the living room rug on a weekday afternoon.

Against my better judgment, Kyle appears in my head. We mostly argue and it's exasperating, but I've noticed that I enjoy pushing his buttons, that I get a little turned on when he's stern and gruff with me. I wonder if he's bossy in bed, if he'd take charge and tell me what to do. If I'd let him.

Heat blossoms between my thighs at the thought, and I shake if off with a frown. I'm nothing more than an inconvenience on the job site to him, regardless of what my poor, neglected libido might like to imagine.

"You're home early," Sadie observes, smoothing her mussed hair. "But actually, that's good. There's something I wanted to run by you."

I step over their sex spot on the floor to perch on the sofa beside her. "What's up?"

"Tim and I have decided to move in together."

My eyebrows leap in surprise. "Oh! That's cool." Makes sense—they spend almost every night together.

"Yeah." She smiles giddily to herself. "He's going to move in here, but I wanted to check that you're okay with it."

I tilt my head to the side. "It's *your* apartment, Sade."

"I know, but you're staying here for a while, so this affects you as well."

That's sweet. Sadie's always been a bighearted person who worries about others. But I'm hardly going to tell her—when she's glowing with happiness—that listening to her boyfriend make her orgasm night after night is actually a little awkward so no, thanks, he can't move in.

"I've been thinking of finding my own place," I hear myself say.

"You don't have to. I don't want you to feel unwelcome." She looks concerned and I pat her on the arm.

"You've been wonderful, but yeah, I need my own space. I don't know how long this project is going to last and I can't stay on your sofa forever. I think it's really great Tim's going to move in. You guys are a good couple."

I just don't want to, you know, witness it quite so much.

"Okay, if you're sure."

I smile. "I'm sure."

Now I have to figure out where to go.

SADIE INSISTS we all have one last meal together, which she cooks from scratch, while Tim studiously avoids eye contact with me. I pack my stuff into my duffel bag and do a quick search on AirBnB for any last-minute places, but they cost a small fortune. I have my severance, and Dad said he'd pay me for this job, but I feel uncomfortable taking a paycheck from my father. I'm still paying rent on my apartment back in Silicon Valley and I don't know when I'll get my next real job—still nothing in my inbox from the feelers I've sent out —so I need to be careful with the money I have. I absolutely do not want to end up having to move back in with my parents, unemployed *and* broke.

Halfway through dinner, it hits me. I'll stay at the house on Fruit Street. It's a huge pain having to take the subway forty minutes each way to get to work there anyway—time I could use either working or sleeping. There's electricity and running water, and best of all, it's free.

I stop in at Target to pick up a few essentials, like an air mattress, a lamp, some towels, a sleeping bag, and a couple of folding chairs—maybe Kyle is annoyed I'm using his?—before taking an Uber to Fruit Street. It's almost dark by the time I arrive, the June sun bathing the street in a copper glow as it sinks below the horizon.

This neighborhood really is beautiful. Rows and rows of brownstones and brick townhouses, carefully preserved. They look almost ethereal in the evening light, as if I've stepped back in time to the nineteenth century, when this neighborhood was born. The only thing reminding me it's the twenty-first century are the cars parked along the street and the distant sounds of traffic.

I smile as I climb the front steps to the building, my arms laden with my supplies. I can see why Kyle fought so hard to preserve the history of this project. The entire neighborhood has a magical feel to it in a way that modern areas just don't have.

I leave one folding chair in the parlor room—I've gotten

used to calling it that now—and go down to the basement to set up the rest of my things, because I'm trying to be stealthy and I'm less likely to be spotted from the street with my little lamp down here. There's a lot of junk from the previous renovation attempts, and mountains of dust, but I spend a few minutes making space and sweeping a clear area for myself. I decided to splurge on a fancy air mattress that's the same height as a normal bed so I could get a decent sleep after Sadie's sofa. It also has a built-in electric pump, because I'll need to take it down every day and store it out of the way of the crew. No way do I want to spend an hour each evening inflating it. Knowing the late hour I usually crawl into bed, I'd probably just give up and sleep on a pile of my clothes.

I'm ecstatic to learn it only takes five minutes for the bed to self-inflate, during which time I venture into the small bathroom to brush my teeth and change into my pink PJ shorts and tank top. Then I stand in the dim basement, lit only by the tiny lamp I bought, listening to the silence.

Ahh, finally. Peace and quiet. No foreman growling under his breath about what a terrible job I'm doing, no friend having mind-blowing sex with her boyfriend. Just the sound of my own breathing, my footsteps on the dusty tiled floor.

It's almost *too* quiet. The kind of quiet where my mind can start to whir with boredom, where I get fidgety from not working or doing something. I pull my Bluetooth speaker from my bag, needing something to fill the silence, and select one of my favorite bands on Spotify: Rogue Valley. Then I put on their song *False Floors*, turning it up. The music moves through me and I sway my hips, dancing around beside my bed, singing along. I can't remember the last time I danced, and it feels both weird and good. I glance down at my phone in my hand, cuing up the next song with a smile.

But when I look up, the silhouette of a large man appears in the doorway, and I scream.

11

KYLE

Violet flings her phone in shock and it hits me squarely on the cheekbone.

"Ow!" I say, raising a hand to my face.

"Oh, shit!" She scurries across to me, her brow dipped with concern in the half light. "I'm sorry! I didn't know it was you."

I press my fingers to my throbbing cheek. She has good aim, I'll give her that. What the hell is she doing here at this time of night?

"Here." She guides me to a chair, nudging my shoulder to sit down. It's only then that I notice a large air mattress and huge duffel bag.

Wait, is she *living* here?

She turns the music down on her speaker, then pops into the bathroom, returning with a wet washcloth. "I don't have any ice, so this will have to do." She presses the cool washcloth to my cheek and I wince. Her lips twist into a wry smile. "You should have learned not to sneak up on me by now."

"I didn't mean to. I heard music and wondered who it was."

She folds the washcloth and repositions the cool side on my skin, saying nothing.

"What are you doing here, Violet?"

Her eyes won't meet mine. "I could ask you the same thing."

I sigh, looking down at my hands. The truth is, I didn't feel like going back to Rich and Diana's place tonight. I didn't feel like smiling and making polite conversation with my friends, knowing the things I've been thinking about their daughter. Every time Rich asks me how Violet's doing, I choose my words carefully, in case they give me away, and then I feel like a complete dirtbag. What kind of asshole gets a crush on his best friend's daughter?

"It was a pain having to drive all the way back to Manhattan in traffic every night," I mumble. "I'm crashing here, upstairs. I used to do it on job sites back home all the time." At least it's not a lie.

Violet is quiet for a beat, then says, "My friend's boyfriend moved into her tiny apartment and I wanted to give them space."

I glance up to see her nose scrunched in disgust, and curiosity gets the better of me. "You don't like him?"

"It's not that. He's alright. It's just..." Her cheeks color slightly and she focuses intently on pressing the washcloth to the spot on my cheekbone, which is now nothing more than a dull ache. "I walked in on them having sex this afternoon on the living room floor. It was awkward."

I huff a laugh, dropping my head to hide my gaze under the brim of my cap. "Yeah. That would be awkward." Before I can stop myself, I'm wondering when she last had sex—must have been more recently than me, that's for sure—and if she's the kind of woman who likes casual sex or prefers relationships. Rich has never mentioned anything about her having a boyfriend, and that makes sense when I think of how dedicated she is to her work. She probably doesn't have time.

Which is a shame. She's young and beautiful and full of life. Any man would be lucky to have her.

Violet places a hand under my chin, gently guiding my head up so she can examine the damage. My breathing is a little off as she studies me, and I hope to God she can't read my thoughts on my face.

"It's not too bad." She brushes the pad of her thumb softly across my cheek. It sends a shiver through me, which I pray she doesn't notice. "But you'll probably have a bruise. Sorry."

I swallow. There's something about the tender way she's caring for me that cracks my chest open, just a little. It's been a long time since a woman has shown me this kind of care—and it's the last thing I deserve after the way I've acted around her.

Her gaze lingers on my face, as though she's searching for answers to a question she hasn't asked. She's close enough for me to smell her; a sweet vanilla scent that makes my mouth water. Her hand still rests on my cheek, and my pulse accelerates as she strokes her thumb across my skin again. I try to keep my expression neutral, but I must not do a very good job because her breath catches and heat flares in her eyes.

Shit. I have to stop this.

I lean back in the chair, away from her touch, trying to be nonchalant. "You have good taste in music."

She tugs her gaze to the washcloth in her hand, breathing out hard. "You know Rogue Valley?" she asks in a tight voice. When I give a casual nod, she relaxes. "My friend Sadie introduced me to them ages ago. They're my favorite."

"Mine too." I've liked them for years, but I don't know anyone else who's familiar with them. I'm guessing it's the same for her, because her face lights with a surprised smile. It's the kind that makes me want to pull her close and press my mouth to hers.

Instead, I rise from the chair and grab her phone from the floor, desperate for a moment to collect myself. I inspect it for damage before handing it back to her.

"Why did you throw your phone at me, anyway? If I was an intruder, you would have wanted to call the cops."

She laughs quietly. "Yeah. You're probably right. It was a reflex."

I stand with my hands on my hips, letting my gaze drift around the makeshift bedroom she's created down here. I hate the thought of her sleeping somewhere like this.

"You could stay in the guest room at your folks' place, since I'm staying here. You'd be more comfortable there."

"No." She shifts her weight. "Thanks, but I don't want to move back in with my parents. It's bad enough that I've taken a job from my father. Besides"—she glances around with a shrug— "it's fine here. I don't have to take two trains back and forth each day, and I can keep an eye on the project."

I have to admire her determination to be independent. I'm sure plenty of kids her age would eagerly accept help from their parents without a second thought.

I remove my cap to run a hand through my hair, thinking. It would make sense for me to leave, because I'm not sure I'll be able to sleep knowing she's in bed only a few floors away from me. I don't need that kind of temptation.

But when I think about her sleeping here alone, at an empty job site... I frown at the thought. I can't leave. I need to make sure she's safe.

Violet's eyes narrow, misreading my expression. "I'm not leaving," she says firmly. "And I'm not only talking about living here."

I pull my cap back on. "What?"

"I know you don't want me working on this project. You think I don't know what I'm doing and I'm getting in the way, but—"

"That's not true at all," I say, surprised.

"You told me as much, Kyle. I'm not stupid."

I let my breath out slowly. She has a point there.

"Well, yeah," I begin, "at first I was a little annoyed that you didn't seem to know much about the remodel. But I can tell you've been working hard to catch up." I meet her steely gaze. There's something about being here at night with her that feels so different to the time we spend together during the day. Something that nudges me to say, "I definitely don't want you to leave."

Her eyebrows tug together under her bangs. "Then why have you been so difficult? When we met in Joe's you were nice and we really clicked, but working with you... you're like a totally different person."

"I know," I mumble. I *have* been a different person—a person I don't even recognize. Gone is the carefree guy up in Maine who never takes on more than he can handle, who lives a carefully constructed life to ensure he stays mentally and emotionally healthy. Now I'm the guy who's worried he's taken on a job that's too big for him, the guy who's developed inappropriate feelings for his best friend's daughter. I've become the guy who has trouble falling asleep at night, whose ears are ringing from the creeping sense of anxiety about it all.

I wipe a hand down my face, frustrated. My cheek still tingles from her gentle touch, and I'm desperate to tell her the truth—that I haven't been able to stop thinking about her since we met, and working with her is only making it worse. But I know that once I tell her, I can't take that back, and I'm not sure what it will do to our working relationship.

Worse, I'm not sure what it would do to my relationship with Rich.

"I'm sorry, Vi. The truth is, I have found it difficult working with you." I'm trying to walk the fine line between not revealing too much while still being honest with her. She looks hurt and I shake my head, quick to add, "It's not your work ethic, or your knowledge of the project. You've impressed me with how much you've learned in such a short time."

She crosses her arms, her brows still low. "Then what is it?"

I rub the back of my neck, avoiding her gaze. I hate this. It's not fair for her to be in this position.

"I... I can't really explain." I want to leave it there, but in the dim light of the basement I hear myself continue. "I'm just... having a hard time, is all. Every time you laugh, or smile at me..." I trail off with a grimace as she tilts her head, examining me.

Ah, fuck, I've said too much. I should have kept my mouth shut.

She stares at me for a long moment, her face giving nothing away. I shift my weight uncomfortably. She opens her mouth to say something, and I silently pray she won't ask me to elaborate. When she closes her mouth again, I'm equal parts relieved and disappointed.

We gaze at each other in silence, the words I'm not saying filling the space between us. The air becomes so thick I'm almost afraid to take a breath.

"Well, the house is what matters most here," she mutters at last. "This is all temporary anyway—we're only here until we finish this project, then we both go back to our real lives. Right?"

I nod, not letting myself think about what my life will be like once she's no longer in it. It's an absurd thought to have after only knowing her for a week, but it's there nonetheless.

"So let's focus on the job," she adds, "and try to stay out of each other's way."

Even though it's exactly what I need, it still feels like a punch to the gut, because I don't want to stay away from her. I want the opposite.

And I'll never be able to have that.

I force myself to nod. "Good idea," I say, not meaning a word of it. I turn for the door before I say anything else I can't take back. "Goodnight, Violet."

"Goodnight, Kyle." She gives a quiet sigh as I leave the room, and I pretend not to hear.

12

VIOLET

The air mattress is ten times more comfortable than Sadie's sofa—*and* I don't have to listen to anyone having sex just a few feet away from me.

And yet, I hardly sleep.

Instead, I spend all night wondering where in the house Kyle is sleeping, and trying to make sense of our conversation. He'd looked so agonized when I asked him why things had been tense between us, and he couldn't explain exactly why. I'd just assumed he'd been annoyed about my inexperience with this project, but he was pretty clear last night that it's not about that.

Every time you laugh, or smile at me...

I lie awake in bed, the early dawn light seeping in through the half windows of the basement, replaying his words from the night before. I held my breath as he said those words. Words he didn't finish.

What? I wanted to ask him. *What happens when I do those things?*

I'd been so busy trying to learn everything I could about this project, worried he thought I was useless, that I couldn't see what was staring me in the face: he's struggling because he's attracted to me. That's what he was saying, right? I know he didn't use those words, exactly, but the electricity between us last night, the look in his eye as I moved closer and touched his cheek...

A thrill pulses through my body at the memory, and I roll over and punch the pillow in frustration. It doesn't matter, does it? Nothing will come of it, because we've agreed to keep our distance.

Look, it's not like I thought something would happen between us, but after our conversation last night—the most honest conversation we've had since the one at Joe's—I keep replaying his words, wishing he'd finished the sentence. Wishing he'd actually *said* that he wants me. God, I want to hear those words from him.

He'd never say that, though. He's a good guy and Dad is his best friend. He knows it's not okay to come onto your friend's daughter, even if you're both consenting adults. That's probably why he never admitted to asking me out the day we met; he was trying to do the right thing. Trying to be a good friend to Dad and not complicate the situation.

I haul myself from the bed, pushing thoughts of last night from my mind. I'm here to work and prove I can manage a project on my own. Besides, with his unruly beard and shaggy hair, it's not like Kyle is my type. In fact, I tell myself, I'm not even that attracted to him.

I almost believe it.

With an exasperated shake of my head, I pad into the bathroom and splash some water on my face. This room seriously needs to be re-tiled, I note as I brush my teeth. The house wouldn't have had bathrooms when it was built because only the very wealthy had indoor toilets at that time, and bathrooms were added later on the landing of the stairways or in closets upstairs. I don't know when this one was added, but it's definitely more practical than pretty. We'll need to change that.

I dress quickly and find a protein bar in my bag for breakfast, then head out to Joe's for my daily caffeine hit. Given I hardly slept at all, I can't skip that. In fact, would it be too much to ask for a quadruple shot?

My phone buzzes in my pocket as I walk. It's a text from Dad, saying he and Mom want to meet with me and Kyle for lunch, to catch up and talk about progress on the house. Nerves flutter in my stomach as I read his words. We've got a crew arriving today to begin demo, but other than that there's not much to update him on.

Well, there's the decision Kyle and I made to stick to a historical restoration and not do what Dad actually asked for. Thinking about that makes me uneasy. How's he going to take it?

I swing into Joe's, absently staring at my phone as I line up to place my coffee order. At the counter I slide my phone away and ask for my regular Americano, then hesitate.

"Is that all?" the barista asks.

"Uh..." My instinct is to get one for Kyle, whether by kindness or out of habit because I always got coffee for Deb, I'm not sure. But I sense that's not the right thing to do anymore. "Yes, that's it."

She nods, grabbing a pen and a paper cup. "What's the name?"

"Violet."

The barista smiles as she scribbles my name on my order. "My name is a flower too," she says, motioning to her nametag. For the first time, I notice the word 'Daisy' pinned to her shirt. I've seen her working here but haven't ordered from her before. "I'm named after my favorite flower," she tells me, and I pause, wondering how that works—how her parents could have known her favorite flower before she was born. But before I can ask, she adds, "What about you?"

"My dad got my mom violets on their first date," I say with a laugh. "Apparently it stuck."

"What a sweet story." A grin brightens her pretty, freckled face. "Well, your coffee won't be long."

"Thanks." I turn and step away from the counter to wait, smiling to myself.

My smile quickly drops away when I notice a certain tall, broad-shouldered contractor with a messy beard and cap standing on the other side of the coffee shop, his eyes on me.

I stumble in surprise, quickly catching myself and glancing away as if I didn't see him.

Well. This is awkward.

Kyle appears at my side with a sigh. "You don't have to act like we're strangers," he mutters.

"Sorry. I wasn't sure if I should say hello."

He doesn't respond, but I can feel his gaze on me. Eventually I can't take it, and glance at his face. His green eyes look tired, and I wonder if he spent the night like I did, tossing and turning, thinking about our conversation.

When he finally tears his gaze away, I notice the purple bruise on the side of his cheek. I want to reach out and touch him, to apologize again, but I stop myself. Instead, I say, "Mom and Dad want to meet us for lunch to discuss progress on the house."

"I know." He won't look at me, and seems relieved when his coffee order is called. "We're going to be pretty busy with demo today," he says on his way past me to the door. "So you should probably stay out of the way." Then he steps outside, saying nothing more.

KYLE and I walk two blocks in uneasy silence to meet my parents at a cafe on Pineapple Street for lunch. True to his word, he's been busy with the demo crew, so I made myself scarce and spent the morning in Joe's with my laptop, occasionally chatting to Daisy. I hadn't planned to walk to lunch with Kyle, but I came out of Joe's right as he passed and there was nothing to do except fall into step beside him. Besides, we're going to have to be around each other at lunch anyway, and we'll need to do a better job of acting like things are okay in front of Dad for him not to wonder what the hell is going on.

"Wait." I grab Kyle's arm, stopping him outside the cafe, and he turns to me with a frown. "I want to tell Dad."

His eyes widen and I realize I need to clarify.

"I mean, I want to tell him what we're doing with the house. That we're doing something different to what he asked."

Kyle regards me carefully, stroking his beard. "You don't want to surprise him at the end?"

I wring my hands, feeling queasy at the thought. "No. I want to make sure he understands our reasoning and is on board. It's important to me that this goes perfectly."

Kyle studies me for a moment longer, and something in his face softens. "Okay. We'll walk him through it today."

"Thank you."

He nods, turning up the steps to the cafe, and I follow him inside. We thread between the tables and outside to a paved area bordered with raised gardens, tucked between the back walls of the neighboring buildings. One wall is painted in fruits of bright colors, honoring the street names of the area, which makes me smile. My parents are sitting under a large umbrella, shielding the table from the midday sun.

"Hi, honey," Mom says, rising from her chair to hug me. I haven't seen her since we had dinner on my first night back, and she squeezes me tight.

"Hi, Mom." I turn to Dad and hug him too. He's in his work suit, as usual, probably planning to make up for lost time later.

Dad shakes Kyle's hand and Mom pecks him on the cheek. I try not to feel jealous because honestly, what the fuck is wrong with me?

"How are things with you?" Mom asks me once we've ordered. I've always had a good relationship with my mom, and I suddenly wish I could talk to her about everything—what Kyle said last night, the feelings I'm developing for him despite trying to convince myself otherwise, how nervous I am about this project and letting Dad down. But even if we were alone, I couldn't. Not when all my problems lately seem to be about hiding things from Dad.

"Good," I murmur in response.

Mom nods and glances at Kyle, who's studying the label on his beer bottle. "Everything okay, Kyle?" She smiles at him, sipping from her wineglass. "I didn't hear you come in last night."

"What?" He glances up. "Oh, yeah." His gaze finds mine, and I silently plead with him not to say anything about me sleeping in the basement on an air mattress. I don't know why, but it's something I'd rather Dad didn't know.

He clears his throat, turning back to Mom. "I decided to sleep at Fruit Street. It's easier than hauling my truck back and forth, trying to find a parking spot each day."

Mom's brow clouds and she reaches to place a hand over

Kyle's. "You know you're welcome at our place, as long as you need."

"I know." He smiles, but it doesn't quite reach his eyes. "This is much more convenient for now, but I'll keep that in mind. Thanks, Di."

She gives his hand a squeeze and lets go, and Dad cuts in with a grin as Kyle raises his bottle for a sip.

"We thought maybe you'd met some pretty young thing and spent the night with her," Dad says, chuckling.

Kyle chokes on his beer, lowering the bottle as he coughs.

"Rich," Mom scolds, glancing at me, and I laugh.

"It's okay, Mom. I'm familiar with the concept of casual sex."

All three of them look at me and my face heats.

"I mean, not *me*, I just... ugh, never mind." I reach for my glass of wine and take a huge gulp, wanting to die.

"I do wish you'd meet someone though," Mom tells Kyle. "It's been so long since Lisa."

Lisa?

My ears perk up at the mention of another woman's name. I sneak a glance at Kyle, but his face is unreadable.

"I agree," Dad chimes in. "Why not have a little fun while you're in town? You might even meet someone worth sticking around for."

Kyle rolls his eyes with a good-natured smile. "And then end up back at the firm, Rich?"

"I miss the old days," Dad admits. His expression shifts. "But I know things are different now, and you won't be back at the firm. There could be something to this townhouse remodeling business, though."

Kyle doesn't say anything, but I don't miss the twinkle in his eye at Dad's suggestion. It doesn't surprise me in the slightest—he's so passionate about these buildings, it would make sense for him to work on them full time.

"Speaking of," Dad continues, "how's the house coming along?"

Kyle glances at me, then back at Dad. "Good. We've got all our permits and plans, and we've begun demo today." He pauses, and I wonder if he's actually going to discuss the changes—and if I'll have the courage to bring it up if he doesn't.

There's a knot in my stomach as the waiter delivers our lunch, interrupting the conversation. For a brief second, I consider blurting out that I've never been a project manager and that Dad was wrong to trust me on this project, but Kyle catches my eye and, somehow, seems to sense my nerves. Despite the lingering tension from our conversation last night, he sends me a reassuring smile.

"Violet and I have spent a lot of time learning the quirks of the building," he begins, taking a fry casually from his plate. "We think your idea to split it into apartments is sound, especially for resale value."

Dad nods, throwing his tie over his shoulder before picking up his BLT.

"But we thought that what really makes these buildings unique—what would make them stand out in a crowded market—is their historical charm."

I have to admit, Kyle is good at this. Instead of just telling Dad we don't want to modernize it, he's building a case to support what will work best for Dad. But then he used to be an attorney, didn't he? It's easy to forget that when he's stomping around the job site in work boots and flannel, his hair sticking out at all angles from under that hat.

Dad chews thoughtfully on his sandwich and Mom nods.

"I think you're right," she says. "The building is beautiful, and that's what people love about this neighborhood. The history."

Dad isn't saying anything, and I feel that same swell of unease.

"We'll definitely add modern elements," I say in a rush. "Things that make it feel contemporary, while respecting the character of the building."

Under the table, Kyle's knee nudges mine—whether to reassure me or shut me up, I don't know.

"We think we can create two spacious apartments that capture the charm of the building," Kyle says smoothly, "with modern elements that appeal to the style-conscious home buyer."

A smile slides onto Dad's lips. "You sure you don't want to come back to the firm?"

Kyle chuckles, reaching for his beer, and Dad gives a thoughtful nod.

"Alright. I trust you both. You know your stuff, Kyle, and I know you will have done your research, Vi"—he winks at me—"so whatever you think is best, let's do it."

Relief settles cool in my chest, and Kyle's knee brushes mine under the table again. When I meet his gaze, there's warmth there, and my heart skitters. For a split second I forget all about our conversation last night, because it feels like we're on the same team, and it's so good to have achieved something together. But when I return his smile he tugs his gaze back to his plate, stuffing fries in his mouth.

"You know what?" Dad says after a pause. "If you think the history of the building is its most important feature, then let's do this right. Instead of apartments, we'll keep the original layout as a single home, and sell it as a historical restoration with modern touches."

I blink in surprise. Kyle was right, of course—Dad trusts him implicitly. I can't help but smile, knowing we don't have to lose the charm of the house.

"I think that's a great idea." Kyle is grinning too, clearly thrilled that Dad's on board. "Then instead of being like every other New York duplex, or apartment conversion, it will stand out as a beautiful family home."

"Exactly." Dad nods. "I'll get a realtor to come out and meet with you. See if he has any advice."

"Couldn't hurt," Kyle agrees. "He can give us an appraisal before we start the build, so we can see how much value we add."

"I'll organize that, Dad," I offer, still feeling the need to prove myself. "Let me know which company you want to go with and I'll call them."

Mom spears a salad leaf with a smile. "Who knows? You may want to buy the house yourself, Vi."

I laugh, finally contemplating my lunch now that the conversation is over and my stomach is more settled. As if I could afford a house around here. And what about work? I'll be heading back to the West Coast as soon as I've got another job lined up.

A funny sensation washes through me at the thought of leaving New York for California again. I'd always reasoned it was a small price to pay for my career, but since being back in the city I haven't thought about Silicon Valley at all. I definitely don't miss it, even if I miss having a real job.

I shake the thought from my head and concentrate on lunch. No point thinking about any of that while I'm on this project. I need to focus and make sure Dad's faith in me isn't completely misguided.

13

KYLE

Living with Violet has taught me several things about her. Not that we're really living together; in the evenings I make a point of staying upstairs, so we don't spend any more time together than we did previously, but I've noticed things that I hadn't before.

Like how she doesn't ever seem to eat a proper meal, or how she hardly sleeps—I know because I see her light on when I go out running early in the mornings, and sometimes late at night if I can't sleep—or the fact that she works around the clock. The other night I came down to get my phone charger from the parlor room at 11 p.m. and she was still there, fiddling about with her Gantt chart, books spilling off her desk, the blue light of her laptop giving the room an eerie glow. She never switches off.

Three days have passed since lunch with Rich and Di, and Violet and I have kept our distance from one another. I don't know if she figured out what I was trying to say the other night—what I *didn't* say—and I'm trying not to think about it. She's right; we need to focus on the project then return to our normal lives.

I've kept myself busy with the crew doing demo, which we've just finished. They're a nice enough bunch—two guys in their sixties called Bob and Dale who have a lot of experience on restoration projects like this, a young guy around Violet's age called Phil who's pretty green but a quick learner, and a guy in his forties called Ryan who's a bit of a joker. They're hardworking and listen to what I say, and I haven't yet seen one of them leer at Violet, so I'm happy.

Today we're beginning to frame up the bedroom walls upstairs, now that we've demolished all the damaged plaster. After an hour of work, I remove my tool belt and leave the guys to meet with Owen, the realtor Violet contacted at Rich's suggestion.

Violet's already at the door when he arrives, leading him inside as I appear in the foyer. Owen looks to be in his mid twenties, in a crisp navy-colored suit with shoes so shiny I can see my face in them. His hair is blond and swept to one side with an inordinate amount of hair product, his jaw clean. I'm not too manly to admit he's a good-looking guy, and as Violet's eyes follow him through the doorway, I can see she's noticed it too.

He shakes Violet's hand enthusiastically as they make introductions. His gaze sweeps across her figure when she glances away, following the curve of her hips to her cleavage. I can't help but clench my jaw in irritation as his eyes swing to me.

"And you must be Violet's father?" He extends his hand and I shake it stiffly.

I already hate this kid.

"No." I may grip his hand a little harder than necessary.

"Forgive me," he says, not looking even slightly remorseful. "She mentioned in her email that her dad owned the place, so I assumed..."

Beside me, Violet snorts a laugh into her hand.

I frown at her, then at Owen. "I'm the foreman. Her father is a friend of mine."

"Right. Of course." He flashes a dazzling smile at Violet and she practically swoons. I trail behind as she leads him into the parlor.

"This is quite the place you've got here," Owen remarks, glancing around.

The house is a mess at the moment, as we've ripped several of the plaster walls out to re-frame and re-insulate, exposing the rough brick underneath. It pained me to see some of the beautiful molding torn down, but it was too damaged to salvage. We'll replicate any of the molding that was lost, and I must have taken hundreds of photos to ensure it gets redone properly. I open my mouth to tell him as much, but Violet speaks first.

"We're in the middle of working on it, obviously," she begins, "but what we hope to achieve is a contemporary feel without losing any of the historical features of the building."

Owen smiles, apparently impressed. "These old places are cool. It's nice to see you keep the original features rather than remove them." He glances at me and I nod begrudgingly. At least he can appreciate that.

"I agree," Violet says, and I swear to God she's fluttering her eyelashes. "Shall we start the tour?"

"Absolutely." Owen grins—two rows of perfect white teeth that make me think of a cartoon shark.

They turn for the stairs and I hesitate. I'm tempted to leave them to it so I don't have to witness whatever the hell is going on here, but the thought of leaving her alone with him makes my stomach roil. I tell myself it's because I'm supposed to be looking out for her, nothing else.

Heaving a sigh, I plod up behind them as they ascend

the wobbly staircase, feeling like a chaperone on prom night.

"As you can see, it's a blank canvas at this point," Violet says. "But we'll have two large bedrooms here, with walk-in closets." She motions to the ceiling. "We've lost some of the plaster moldings in the demo, but they'll be replaced with ones that perfectly match the originals."

"Nice," Owen murmurs, but his gaze isn't on the ceiling at all, and I want to kick him.

Violet's oblivious. "It's a very specialized art, replicating plaster moldings. We'll have a professional do them." She turns to Owen with an amused expression. "I was reading the other day that the original plaster contained crushed limestone or shell, and was often mixed with cattle hair." She giggles—she fucking *giggles*. "Isn't that gross?"

Owen laughs too. "Yeah, it kinda is."

"Of course," Violet continues, with an air of expertise, "after around 1830 a lot of the ceiling plasterwork was mass-produced by steam-powered machinery, and made from papier-mâché or stucco, so I'm not sure if these are true plaster."

"They are," I mutter, but neither she nor Owen notice.

He gestures to the floors. "What's the plan here?"

"Oh, we'll restore the original oak flooring. It's too precious to lose. Any damaged boards can easily be replaced by taking them from spaces where they won't be missed, like the upstairs closets."

Owen looks impressed. "That's a good idea."

Yes. It is.

Violet's too busy fawning all over him to notice how I'm glowering at her. She didn't know the first thing about any of this two weeks ago. While I've enjoyed teaching her things about the house, and the extent of her own research is admirable, I can't say I love that she's using it to impress another man.

In fact, I downright hate it.

She leads Owen to the fireplace, explaining the details of the mantel, and I remain rooted to the spot, arms folded across my chest, grinding my molars. If he asks her out in front of me, I'll kick his ass.

I catch myself, turning away.

Jesus fucking Christ, what is wrong with me? I'm supposed to be focused on the house, not Violet, but I've never felt this protective before. As much as I tell myself it's because I'm looking out for her for Rich, I know damn well that's not true.

I just... I think back to the day we met, when we talked about the buildings in this neighborhood and I felt the first buds of hope begin to unfurl; that I'd met a pretty woman who shared an interest of mine, that maybe I was ready to ask someone out again for the first time in years. That maybe I had been lonely up in Maine, as Muriel had pointed out, and I only realized that when I met a woman whose company I wanted more of.

Then I find out she's Rich's daughter and just like that, it's over. I lost her before I even had her, which I know is an irrational thought, but also... that's what it feels like. It feels like I lost something that should have been mine. Something that *is* mine.

But she's not, is she? She never will be, and I have no choice but to accept that.

I follow Owen and Violet to the top floor where the guys are working, and Violet introduces him to the team. Dale talks him through the bedroom layout up there, and how the bathroom will be remodeled, but Owen's eyes barely leave Violet. He watches her like the proverbial cat that got the canary, apparently forgetting I'm even here, and I swear any minute he's going to ask if she's free tonight.

Which would be completely unprofessional, I might add.

Eventually they head back downstairs, and it couldn't come a minute too soon.

Owen pauses at the bottom of the staircase in the foyer. "This balustrade is nice. Will you restore this too?"

"Definitely." Violet hovers beside him, gesturing to the decorative swirl at the top of the last baluster. "Isn't this newel post lovely? Did you know that there's a chamber inside where they originally stored the deed of the house?"

I lift my eyebrows, impressed that she knows this little historical tidbit, though she doesn't notice of course.

"I didn't." Owen flashes her his trademark grin. "You have such an extensive knowledge of these buildings," he adds, and she beams back.

The scowl on my face deepens as they gaze at each other. They may as well begin fornicating on the stairs right now.

I cough loudly, reminding them I'm here.

Violet glances back at me, a blush staining her cheeks, then she pulls her gaze back to Owen. "Would you like to see the basement and the yard?"

"I'm sure he's got other things to do today," I interject sullenly.

"Actually—" Owen begins, but I've had enough.

"It's your standard Brooklyn backyard," I say flatly. "You've seen one, you've seen them all."

Violet narrows her eyes at me. I ignore her.

I climb down a step, my closeness forcing Owen to step back onto the floor of the foyer. "We won't take up any more of your time." I step down again, noticing I'm still half a foot taller than Owen when we're on the same level. I extend my hand, which forces him to back up further, until he's almost at the front door.

"Uh—" He glances at Violet and she folds her arms, giving me a look.

"Thanks for stopping by." I pump his hand firmly, not budging.

He squares his shoulders and reaches for the door handle. "I'll be in touch," he says, looking past me to Violet, and I resist the urge to clock him in the jaw.

"Great. Bye." I close the door behind him, breathing hard.

Pull yourself together.

I wait a beat before turning around, directing a tight smile at Violet. "He was nice," I say, but it doesn't sound convincing, even to my own ears.

She stares at me, mouth hanging open. "What the hell was that?"

I shrug. "We have work to do."

"Really?" She smirks at me. "Or are you pissed because he thought you were my dad?"

Yeah, that sucked.

I grunt, ignoring her comment. "Come on. He was supposed to be assessing the place and instead he was all over you."

She arches an eyebrow. "Jealous much?"

I roll my eyes. "Grow up, Violet." I regret the words as soon as they leave my mouth, because she's spot on—I'm jealous as hell. The way she looked at him, with that stylish hair and pristine suit, the way he eagerly looked back...

The very fact that he's *allowed* to look at her at all.

So yeah, I behaved like an ass. Apparently that's just who I am now.

Violet's staring at me, arms crossed, shaking her head. "I may be eighteen years younger than you, but I'm not the one who needs to grow up."

My heart sinks as I watch her storm back into the parlor room. I try to tell myself that at least I've done an excellent job of pushing her away today, but I still feel shitty. I pull my cap off and rake a hand through my straggly hair, suddenly feeling in desperate need of a haircut.

14

VIOLET

I probably shouldn't have flirted *quite* so hard with Owen in front of Kyle, but it wasn't exactly a hardship. He was attractive, if not a little too smooth, a little too... something.

Young? Shiny? Nice, maybe?

But after the past couple of weeks with Kyle stomping around the place, maybe that's what I need; a nice, uncomplicated man who openly likes me and doesn't hesitate to show it. Physically, Owen is much more my type than Kyle, plus he's already emailed to ask if I'm free for dinner sometime, which is refreshing.

So why am I not excited about it? Why did I feel more of a thrill from arguing with Kyle after Owen left?

"We're going to start on the upstairs bathroom today," Ryan, one of the crew members, says to me.

I glance up from my morning coffee, pushing away thoughts of grumpy, shaggy-haired foremen. "Did you finish framing up the bedrooms yesterday?"

Ryan sips his own coffee. "Mostly. Bob and Phil will

finish that up and begin the insulation while Dale and I start tiling the bathroom."

I nod, glancing at my Gantt chart. So far, everything seems to be going to plan, and the crew is good at checking in each morning to make sure they're on track. I'm used to working with groups of men, but these guys are far nicer than the team I worked with back in Silicon Valley.

The other guys arrive and mill around the parlor room, drinking coffee and talking. I bought a tray of donuts which they help themselves to, thanking me.

It doesn't hurt to bribe them with sugar, too.

"How are you this morning, love?" Dale asks, his chin dusted with cinnamon sugar. He's a sweet, old-fashioned kind of guy who always checks in with me. He once told me he's got three daughters and can't imagine any of them holding their own with a crew of contractors like I do, even though they're all older than me. I get the sense he likes to make sure I'm safe. He reminds me a little of my grandfather, who died when I was younger, and it's given me a bit of a soft spot for him.

I smile. "I'm good, Dale, thanks."

"That realtor kid seemed like a nice guy," he says, his eyes taking on a twinkle I pretend not to notice.

Phil snorts over his coffee. "Kyle didn't like him."

"Speaking of," Ryan interjects, "where is our fearless leader?"

I drain my coffee with a shrug. I haven't seen Kyle since late yesterday afternoon, when Sadie showed up and dragged me out for a drink. I told her about Owen, leaving out the way Kyle behaved. I don't know why, but I didn't want her to judge him. I mean, *I'm* judging him—the way he acted wasn't cool—but I feel protective of how she might see him.

Which is ridiculous, because it's not as though I *like* him. He was kind and sweet when we first met, but I've seen very little of that since. And as for his appearance... Look, I'm not shallow, but between the dirty work clothes, the worn old cap, and the hair that sticks out in every direction—from both his head and his chin—he's a mess. Sure, his shirt strains over his biceps in a way that makes my thighs clench, and his eyes are like pine trees in summer, and when we're alone there's a spark between us that sometimes short-circuits the logic center in my brain...

But that doesn't mean I'm into him. Right?

"Ah, here he is," Bob calls, and I make sure not to glance Kyle's way. I don't want to give him the satisfaction of even a simple "good morning."

Beside me, Phil wolf-whistles. "Looking sharp, boss."

"Whoa, who the hell is this guy?" Ryan asks behind a grin.

I force myself not to look, focusing on straightening a few of the Post-Its on my chart.

"Ha, ha," Kyle drawls behind me. "It was time for a trim, that's all."

"Did you go to that place over on Montague?" Dale inquires.

"Uh-huh."

"They're good," Bob agrees.

Okay, now I'm curious.

I twist around, meaning to casually glance at Kyle and then down at my laptop, but my eyes find him across the room and refuse to leave.

Oh, *holy fuck*.

It's the first time I've seen him without that cap on his head, and he looks... different, to say the least. His messy hair has been neatly trimmed, close on the sides, longer on top, the hints of gray at his temples more subtle now that it's shorter. And his beard—honestly, if you'd asked me yesterday, I would have said he needed to shave the whole thing off, but he hasn't, and I'm glad. Instead, it's been trimmed and groomed, so it's much neater but still a full beard, dark with flecks of gray. And, well, let's just say I think I'm a beard girl now.

Kyle is strapping on his tool belt, above which I notice a clean white tee under a forest-green plaid flannel shirt, sleeves rolled back to the elbows. It's the same sort of thing I've seen him in many times before, but it looks different. Cleaner. Tidier. Sexier. Have his forearms always been that muscular?

His gaze lifts to find me staring, and something flashes in those piercing green eyes. Satisfaction, maybe, but I can't be sure. Whatever it is, I feel a bolt of awareness spread through me, a tingle of heat low in my abdomen.

Christ.

I whip my gaze away, my cheeks warm. Overnight he's gone from being my dad's rugged, kind-of-handsome friend to a freaking *smokeshow*.

Goddammit. How am I supposed to focus now? I can't even remember what we're supposed to be doing today. Instead, all I can think about is walking across the room and running my hand over his beard. I wonder if it would be coarse or soft. I wonder what it would feel like against my neck. Between my thighs.

So much for not being into him.

Argh. Fuckity-fuck.

This is a problem. This is a real problem. In all my time working with men, not one of them looked like a sexy carpenter from some kind of HGTV wet dream. Who knew that was my type?

It doesn't matter. You have a job to do.

I blink, forcing my attention back to the task at hand. I'm here to work, not ogle the foreman. I need to get my head on straight.

So I do the only thing I can think of.

"Yes, Kyle, you look very pretty," I say dryly. "Now, if you ladies are finished exchanging beauty tips, maybe we can get to work?"

This earns a few chuckles from the guys, and Kyle's eyebrows slam down. I'm relieved when he plods up the stairs, followed by the crew. It gives me a chance to catch my breath.

Right. Work. I need to work.

I glance at my laptop, feeling antsy. I don't want to sit still right now. I need to move. There's a weird itchy energy running through me, something I'm not used to. Something I need to work out of my body.

I take the steps two at a time down to the basement, then stride to the doors leading out to the garden. Well, 'garden' is a little generous; it's more like an overgrown tangle of weeds, old building materials, and what I think was once patio furniture. We haven't had a landscaper out here yet because we've been focused on getting the interior work done, but I'll need to organize one soon. Until then, I can make myself useful by clearing away some of this mess.

I find an old wooden ladder leaning haphazardly against the exterior wall of the house, probably left over from the previous attempt at renovation. Tugging free some vines tangled around it, I drag it to the back wall and prop it against the brick. This yard faces onto the back of another building; four solid stories of white brick, with some kind of ivy-like plant spilling down over it. In the middle of the yard stands a tall magnolia tree, the last of its pink and white blooms falling to the ground as the heat of summer starts in earnest. The yard would be pretty if the brick was cleaned up and the other weeds weren't threatening to engulf the back property.

I climb the ladder carefully, determined to strip away some of the weeds along the back wall. The ladder wobbles a little and I pause, making sure it's steady. Some of the rungs have seen better days, but it feels fine, so I continue.

Once I'm high enough, I grab a handful of the weeds and yank. They tear away from the brick with a satisfying snapping sound, and I toss them to the ground below, grabbing more. It feels good to work with my hands. I spend so much time sitting at my laptop inside that I sometimes forget how much better I feel for moving my body in the fresh air. The sun hits the yard at this time of the morning, the warmth soaking into the exposed skin on my arms and legs.

"What are you doing?"

I sigh when I hear the gruff voice of our foreman down below.

Here we go.

"I'm getting started on this yard," I say, without glancing back. "Felt like working outside today."

There's silence for a beat, and I think he's gone back inside, but then he says, "Don't talk to me like that in front of the crew again."

I stop what I'm doing and turn to glance back at him. "Excuse me?"

"Earlier. Don't talk to me like that in front of the crew."

I give a huff of annoyance. "Are you serious?"

"I mean it, Violet."

"I said you looked pretty." I snicker, and his brows slash together.

"I'm the foreman. You can't talk to me like that."

Anger ignites hot in my belly. "But it's okay for you to be a dick to me whenever you feel like it?"

That makes him pause. I give him a look that says *exactly*, and turn back to tear another weed from the wall, yanking harder than necessary and almost losing my balance.

"Be careful." His voice moves closer. "You should be wearing gloves."

"Don't tell me what to do," I retort, pulling out another weed and dropping it on my pile below. I'm so annoyed that he'd dare to complain about my joke when he's been an ass for weeks, that it's easy to forget how hot he looked coming down the stairs this morning. How my body responded to that look in his eye.

This is better, though. If I'm angry with him, I can't be attracted to him. I can focus on work.

"Seriously, Violet, be careful—"

I grab another weed and wrench on it with two hands, taking my anger out on the unsuspecting plant. Something slices into my palm, and I jerk back in surprise, losing my balance. My arms windmill at my side, the ladder falling out from beneath me, and I watch in what feels like slow motion as I tilt away from the brick wall.

"Shit!" Kyle's voice is a distant echo as I brace myself to hit the ground, knowing this is going to hurt.

But I don't hit the ground. Instead, I'm stopped midway through the air by Kyle's arms swooping underneath me. My head hits his chest and he stumbles back a step, but he's got me.

I clutch at his shirt, my heart thundering, my breath coming in short, sharp bursts. Tears press unexpectedly at my eyes, and I bury my face in his shoulder, steadying myself. His arms tighten around me, and for a brief moment I hope he never lets go.

When I finally glance up, Kyle's eyes are wide, his chest heaving underneath me. "Are you okay?"

I give a quick nod, my heart still racing. "Yes," I manage. "I'm fine."

"Good." His concern is quickly replaced with a frown as he sets me down on wobbly legs. "I told you to be careful. You need three points of contact on the ladder at all times. You could have broken your neck."

Despite the adrenaline still coursing through my veins, I grit my teeth. "I would have been fine if you hadn't come out here to yell at me."

"I didn't yell." Infuriatingly, he keeps his voice even. "I simply asked—"

"More like demanded," I snap, cutting him off. I tear my gaze from his stony face to examine the stinging on my hand. There's blood trailing across my palm and I close my hand, grimacing, hoping Kyle hasn't noticed.

But he has.

"Hey." His voice softens, all traces of irritation gone from his face as he reaches for my hand. "You've cut yourself."

"It's fine," I say, yanking my hand away, turning toward the house.

"Violet." Kyle steps in my path, hands on his hips. "It's not fine."

I glance up to find his face lined with worry, his eyes on my left hand. What happened to the grumpy fuck who came out here to lecture me?

"You're hurt," he murmurs, reaching for my hand again. I uncurl my palm and let him examine the damage. His fingers are rough and calloused but they're gentle when they brush against my skin, sending tingles up my arm. I'm shaking, but I can't tell if it's from his closeness or from nearly falling to my death. Somehow, they almost feel the same.

Kyle's gaze moves from my hand to my face, assessing. His green eyes swim with concern, and there's a wrench in my heart.

Don't be nice to me, I silently plead. *If you start being nice to me while looking like that, it will be game over.*

"Come on." He motions over his shoulder to the house. "I've got a first aid kit inside. Let's get that cleaned up."

"I don't need your help." I give him a defiant look, well aware I'm being a brat, but too afraid to give in to his kindness. "I can manage it."

"Of course you can," he says, speaking with the indulgent tone one uses with a child. "But I'm going to help anyway."

I follow him inside the house, back through the basement. He gestures for me to sit on my air mattress, which I didn't deflate today because I knew they were working upstairs. He hands me a washcloth to press to the wound while he goes to fetch the first aid kit. It's the same washcloth I used on his forehead after I hurled my phone at him the first night here, and I think back to that moment, to his words.

Every time you laugh, or smile at me...

God, I wish he'd finished that sentence.

Kyle reappears with the first aid kit, lowering himself onto the bed beside me. The mattress shifts under his weight, making me lean closer. I should move back but I don't want to. I can smell his scent, a combination of an earthy, musky cologne, and something woodsy—probably sawdust. It's *his* smell, I realize. So perfectly him.

With a gentle touch, he takes my hand in his, turning it over so my palm is facing up. I watch as he carefully cleans the cut, which isn't too deep, thankfully. It must have been a thorn or something on one of the weeds I was tackling.

He doesn't say anything as he works, but there's no need for words right now. Not with the way he's touching me so tenderly, with the attention he's giving the task, with the way I can feel his warmth beside me, on my bed.

I press my eyes shut, imagining for a moment what it would be like to close the distance between us, to brush my mouth over his and pull him down on top of me.

As he dresses my wound with such care, I can't remember what I was so mad about outside. All I can remember is the nice version of Kyle—the one who made me a desk, who helped me convince Dad about the restoration, the one who laughed and flirted with me in Joe's and nearly asked me out.

He did. I'm sure of it. I've always been sure of it, regardless of his denial, and I've always wished he had, that Dad hadn't shown up at that moment.

I stare down at Kyle's gentle hands, my heart thrumming in a steady rhythm. I've been kidding myself that I haven't been into him this whole time, messy hair or not. It was easier to deny when he acted like a jerk, and it was definitely easier to pretend before he tidied himself up.

But now that he's sitting here, being so kind and caring, looking so fucking good and smelling like some kind of sexy forest...

Crap. I'm in big trouble.

15

KYLE

"Good work today, guys." I close the door as Ryan and Phil leave, glad it's quitting time. It's been a long, hot day restoring the oak staircase on the upper level, and I'm ready for a drink.

I think back to my house on Lake Cobbossee, wishing I could dive into the cool water right now. I haven't minded being back in New York as much as I thought I would—especially not here in the Heights—but I miss the beauty of Maine and the convenience of living by the lake in the summer. I can't exactly go for a dip in the East River.

Oh well. A cold beer and a good meal will have to do.

I enter the living room to find Violet peering down at the cold scraps of pizza left over from the lunch she ordered for the team today. I wrinkle my nose. That was shitty pizza six hours ago; there's no way it's gotten better since then.

"Are you sure you should eat that?"

She looks up at me with a frown. "Don't body shame me."

I recoil in shock. "*What*?"

"What I eat is none of your damn business. Okay, yes, I

should probably eat better, given that this"—she smacks her ass—"isn't getting any smaller. But right now I don't have time to—"

"Whoa, whoa, whoa," I say, raising my hands and taking a step back. Holy crap, have I wandered into a minefield here. "I didn't mean..." I begin, but I don't know how to tell her that I asked because I'm worried about her, not because I think there's something wrong with her body. I never see her eat—even at lunch with her parents she basically just pushed her food around her plate—and now she's considering eating something this nasty? She deserves to have someone take her somewhere elegant, or better yet, cook for her. She deserves more than disgusting cold pizza for dinner.

And as for the suggestion her ass is too big... just, no. I haven't been able to keep my eyes off her perfect proportions since we met. I'd give anything to have my hands on that gorgeous backside of hers, even if thinking that makes me a creep. I can't fucking help myself.

She's still glowering at me, the pizza looking less appetizing by the second. She's been in a mood all week, ever since we argued in the yard, but goddammit, she's lucky I was there—she could have been seriously injured.

My mind flashes back to the way it felt to hold her in my arms in the garden, the softness of her hair tucked against my shoulder, and the way she clung to me for a moment, as if I was her safe space. And when I saw that she was hurt, there was no mistaking the way my heart clanged violently. I didn't stop to think, I just knew I had to care for her. It wasn't until we sat on her bed, so close I could breathe in her sweet vanilla scent, her hand in mine as I cleaned the cut, that I realized what a mistake I'd made. All it would have taken was a few inches and her mouth could have been on mine. God, I wanted that.

I was relieved that she avoided me for the rest of the day, and seemed to return to being annoyed for the remainder of the week. It's better when we're arguing, even if I sometimes imagine what it would be like to pull her onto my lap and give her a good spanking when she uses that smart mouth on me. I wonder if she'd enjoy that.

Or maybe she'd think I'm a complete pervert.

I shake my head, disgusted with myself. What the fuck would Rich say if he knew I was thinking these things about his daughter? What is wrong with me?

I force my attention back to Violet, hovering over the pizza box. It might be better for us to be at each other's throats, but that doesn't mean I'm going to let her eat this trash for dinner. I'm genuinely concerned about her health at this point. I think of Rich asking me to look out for her, and wonder if he knows how hard she works and how little she takes care of herself. If she's not going to do it, someone else will have to.

And even though it's against my better judgment, part of me wants that someone to be me.

I sigh. "No, Violet. I just think you deserve to eat something better, that's all." I swipe the pizza box into the trash before she can protest, then gesture to the stairs. "Get changed. I know a place."

She lifts her hands to her hips. "I can't go out right now. I have work to do."

"Work can wait." She opens her mouth to protest, and I add, "Violet, it's summer. You're young, and"—I almost say beautiful, but catch myself just in time—"single... and you're choosing to spend this stunning evening with your laptop and cold pizza."

She twists her lips to one side, considering this. "You make it sound so sad."

I cut her a look that says *it is sad*.

"Ugh, fine." She sulks off downstairs to change, and I grin to myself. At least she'll have a decent meal tonight.

VIOLET APPEARS in the parlor room thirty minutes later wearing a pretty white dress with loose sleeves, a low-cut neckline, and a hem that stops mid-thigh. She's got the same wedge sandals on from the day we met, her legs long and shapely. Not going to lie, my cock twitches at the sight of her, at the way she looks both innocent and sexy at the same time. I don't realize I'm staring until she shifts her weight from one foot to the other and laughs uncomfortably.

"Is this okay? I don't know where we're going, so..."

I tear my gaze from her, reaching for my wallet. Taking her out is a terrible idea. What the hell am I thinking?

You need to calm the fuck down.

"Yep," I mumble. "It's fine." It's better than fine—it's gorgeous and I want to rip it off her.

It will be okay, I try to tell myself. *As long as you're out, as long as you're not alone, it will be okay. You can control yourself. You're not an animal.*

We head out into the bright summer evening, the air still hot and sticky from the long day. The place I'm taking her is only a few blocks away on Montague Street, so we walk. As we cross the streets of Brooklyn Heights, I'm reminded of the day we met, the day I almost asked her out to dinner. It occurs to me that, technically, I *am* taking her to dinner, but under very different circumstances. Even if I wish the evening would end much the same way as a date.

We reach a Mediterranean restaurant and I pause, making sure Violet is okay with the choice. Her gaze swings from the tables and chairs spilling out onto the sidewalk to me, and a smile curves along her mouth in response.

I swear, that smile is going to kill me.

We find a table outside where we can enjoy the warm evening air, both of us feeling a little awkward and uncertain. I want her to stop worrying about work and relax. She deserves a night off.

"You're being so nice to me," Violet murmurs as I pull out her chair.

Huh. Maybe I should stop acting like I'm on a date.

I wonder if the same thing is running through her head —that this is like the date we never got to have. Probably not, since I've denied the fact that I was going to ask her out from day one.

Still. She's not stupid.

I settle myself into the chair opposite, ignoring her comment as I reach for the menu. "What do you feel like?"

She studies the menu in silence, and for a second I wonder if this place was a bad choice. But then she looks up at me with wide, excited eyes.

"It all looks so good."

My mouth pulls into a grin before I can stop it. "It is good. Let's get a bunch of dishes."

"Okay," she agrees, grinning back. As much as I tell myself I need to push her away, that it's better for us to bicker our way through the project, I can't deny how good it feels when we get along like this. While I shouldn't let myself have even this with her, tonight I can't stop myself.

I flag down the waitress and order way more food than we need, plus a beer for me and Riesling for her—the same drink she had at lunch with her parents last week. She seems surprised that I remember, and I pretend not to notice.

She's quiet for a moment, then says, "Sorry I snapped at you earlier. When you were telling me not to eat the pizza, I thought..." Her cheeks color and she looks relieved when the waitress brings the drinks.

"I'd never tell you what to eat."

Her lips quirk. "But you're happy to tell me what to do around the house."

"That's for your safety, Vi." And a little, I realize, because I love the way she gets fired up at me. "I don't want you to get hurt," I add.

"I guess that makes sense." She shifts in her seat, dropping her gaze to the table. "Well, anyway. I just haven't felt that great about... myself lately, so I assumed you were, you know, commenting on my body."

I consider how to answer. Somehow I don't think saying *your body is so divine I want to put my hands all over it* is an appropriate response.

"Why are you feeling bad about the way you look?" I ask carefully.

"I've, um, put on a little weight. I should make time to exercise, or maybe cook healthier food, but it just feels like there aren't enough hours in the day."

God, I understand how she feels. I lived for decades like that—working all hours, convinced there was never enough time in the day, but that always comes at a price. I want to tell her this, but I don't know how to do it without sounding like I'm lecturing her. If there's one thing I've learned about Vi, it's that she hates being lectured.

The food arrives and she looks down at it with a crease in her brow. I get the sense she's uncomfortable eating in front of me after that conversation, and I desperately want to make her feel better.

"You have nothing to worry about." I busy myself with my napkin so I don't have to meet her gaze. "Seriously. You're..." Fuck, I think I'm going to say it. "You're beautiful." That's not inappropriate, right? It's an observation. I'm merely stating a fact.

There's a long silence while I reach for an olive, chewing slowly as I cast my gaze out across Montague Street. It's a bustling little shopping and dining area between the more residential streets of Brooklyn Heights, and tonight the restaurants are packed with people high on that summer night feeling, enjoying the fading light.

Eventually I can't stand the silence, and let my gaze wander back to Violet. She's studying me over her glass of Riesling, her hazelnut-brown eyes warm in the golden glow of the evening.

"Thank you." Her voice has taken on a husky purr that makes my pants a little tighter. "You're not too bad yourself, you know."

My chest expands and heat swirls down my limbs. I made an effort tonight, putting on a fresh maroon-colored T-shirt over clean jeans and boots, and even styled my hair with a product my barber recommended, since Violet seemed to like the way Owen wore his. I'm not sure it was a conscious decision, but as her eyes drink in my efforts with obvious approval, I feel like a fucking king. She's looking at me the way she looked at Owen, and God, it's the best damn feeling in the world.

Shit, we are getting into dangerous territory.

I clear my throat, looking down at my plate.

Don't smile. Do not *smile.*

"I mean, uh…" She shifts in her seat, trying to backpedal. "You look a lot less wild since you had a haircut."

I want to tell her that I can be very wild under the right circumstances, but instead I say, "I think you mean I look pretty. Isn't that what you said?"

A laugh tinkles in her throat. "Yeah. *Very* pretty." She gives her words a sarcastic edge which breaks the tension, and I breathe out in relief.

Right. Time to change the subject.

"Well, I'm glad I managed to tear you away from your laptop for one evening," I say, nudging her plate toward her. I'm aiming for lighthearted teasing, but it sounds like I'm being critical.

She frowns. "I enjoy working, being busy. I get bored when I have too much free time."

"I didn't mean it like that, but yeah, I know what you mean. My life used to revolve around work too."

"Used to?"

I nod, wondering how much to share. "Until a health scare forced me to realize there was more to life."

She glances up in concern, looking as though she wants to ask me for details, but she doesn't, and I'm glad. I'm not sure I'm ready to share that part of my life with her. God knows how she'd see me after that.

I reach for my beer. "I'm more careful now to choose jobs I know I can handle, and set my own work hours, taking it a lot easier than I used to."

She looks thoughtful. "But don't you miss challenging yourself?"

I turn this question over as I twist my beer bottle. Since arriving back in the city to tackle this huge house project, my stress levels have been higher than I'd like, but now the work has actually started, I feel better. With the support of the crew, and Violet overseeing the details, it hasn't been as overwhelming as I'd worried it would be. In fact, I'm enjoying the challenge of a more complex project.

And then there's seeing Violet everyday. That has been an unexpected, sometimes frustrating, but very enjoyable, distraction.

"I think it's good to get a sense of purpose and satisfaction from work," she adds. "That's important to me."

"Sure, I get that." I dip some bread in olive oil. "But you deserve a life outside of work too. Who are you when you're not working?"

She glances up from her plate, looking mildly shocked. Her mouth opens, then closes, and her frown deepens. It doesn't surprise me that she has no answer to that question. For most of my working life, I didn't either.

"Well, who are *you* when you're not working? What do you like to do?"

"All kinds of things."

"Like what?" she presses.

Warmth spreads through me at the curious expression on her face—as if she really wants to know more about me—but I quickly tamp it down. "Hiking, reading, cooking..." I think for a moment. "Ice fishing, in winter. I kayak on the lake in summer. Things like that."

She nods, her expression clouded in thought. "I honestly don't even know what I like to do outside of work. My life revolves around my job. That's why I took it so hard when I was let go from DigiSwap. I'm sure you remember I wasn't at my best the day we met."

She's broken our unspoken rule—not to talk about the day we met—but I nod anyway. "I remember," I murmur.

"I wouldn't have taken this job with Dad if I wasn't desperate. As you made clear at the start, I didn't know anything about the industry. And then there's the fact that —" She snaps her mouth shut, fixing her gaze intently on her wineglass.

"The fact that?"

She shakes her head. "Nothing."

I study her curiously. There's something she's not sharing with me, but I know better than to push her right now. I decide to take a different tack.

"Why did you get into project management?" I ask, spreading hummus onto a piece of pita bread.

She pulls her bottom lip between her teeth, nibbling on the plump flesh, and I smear hummus across my palm.

Dammit. Why is it so sexy when she does that?

I reach for my napkin, wiping my hand clean, and she sighs.

"I wanted to get into law, like Dad, but..." She shrugs as she dips some bread in the olive oil. "It didn't work out."

"What do you mean?"

She chews her bread slowly, avoiding my gaze. "It's hard to explain. I did a week of pre-law, but... I had to switch my major."

There's something about the change in her tone, the shift in her posture, that makes me set my drink down. "What happened?"

"I freaked out in one of my political science classes. We had to do an impromptu debate—I can't even remember what the topic was now—but I just... couldn't do it. I froze. And something weird happened to me. I got all shaky, I couldn't breathe, I couldn't think, I just had to get out of there. Then I couldn't make myself go back. Every time I tried, I was terrified it would happen again."

"Oh, Violet," I murmur. My heart aches for her. "You had a panic attack."

She glances up at me, surprised. "You think that's what it was?"

"I... yes, I do." I wish I could tell her I have a lot of experience with panic attacks, but I can't get the words out.

She lifts a shoulder, glancing away. "Well, whatever it was, I knew I needed to change my major. I remembered the career adviser at high school had said project management was a growing field, so I changed to that. But then Dad..."

I raise my eyebrows as she trails off again. "He wasn't happy?"

She shakes her head. "I couldn't tell him for months. I was so worried he'd be mad."

I can't imagine Rich being angry with Violet for having a panic attack. Not after he was so understanding with me.

"When I eventually told him," Violet continues, "he didn't say much, but I could tell he was so disappointed in me."

I frown. There's a difference between him being disappointed because she changed her major, and him being disappointed because she felt she couldn't talk to him about something so important. I open my mouth to say as much when she speaks again.

"And now, with this project..." She stares down at her Greek salad, letting the words hang in the air. There's definitely something she's holding back, and I get the sense she wants to share. That there's a weight she's carrying, and I could help to lighten that load if she'd let me.

"What about this project?" I prompt gently.

She lifts her gaze to mine, letting it rest on my face for a moment. "Okay," she says at last, blowing out an unsteady breath. "I'll tell you, since you're being so nice to me, but you have to promise not to tell Dad."

My brows tug together. I take a swig of my beer,

conflicted. On the one hand, I really want to know whatever it is she's going to say. On the other hand, I don't know how comfortable I am keeping a secret from Rich.

Still, I reason, nothing can be as bad as the feelings I've developed for his daughter. That's one secret I won't be sharing with him, well, ever.

"Okay," I reluctantly agree.

"And..." Worry flits over her brow. "You have to promise to be kind to me when I tell you."

That one is much easier to manage.

"Of course."

"Right. Okay." She gulps down a mouthful of wine, swallows, then takes a deep breath.

Man, whatever she's going to tell me is a big deal. Maybe I shouldn't have agreed to keep this from Rich.

"I've never worked as a project manager before," Violet mumbles in a rush, staring at her plate as her cheeks redden.

"You mean, on a reno project?"

"No." Her blush deepens, and it's the most endearing thing. "Like, ever. Back in Silicon Valley..." She presses her hands to her cheeks, as if to hide her embarrassment. "I was an assistant *to* a project manager, but Dad thought I was an assistant project manager."

Despite her discomfort, I smile wryly. "Do you watch *The Office*?"

A laugh slides from her lips. "Yes. I love that show." It seems to help her relax a little, and I'm glad.

I take a second to digest her revelation while she reaches for the iced water on the table and takes a long sip. I think about what she's just shared with me—the panic attack she had in class, how she felt she couldn't tell Rich about changing her major. And now she's too afraid to tell him she doesn't have experience for this job. No wonder she was so adamant we do everything by the book, why she's so concerned about his approval of her work. That explains a lot, but I would never have known she was inexperienced if she hadn't told me. I might have doubted her knowledge when it comes to the house itself, but not with the other stuff.

"I worked closely with Deb," she adds, avoiding my gaze. "She was my boss at my last job. I learned a lot from her. But, yeah... this is my first project."

I drain my beer. "So what? I think you're doing a great job. I know I was hard on you to begin with, and"—I cringe—"I'm sorry for that, but, truly, you're killing it. It's running like clockwork. That almost never happens on a project like this, and I think it's because you're good at what you do. Even the guys have said so."

A smile touches her mouth at this. "Really?" I nod, and she sighs, her smile sliding away. "Well, that doesn't change the fact that Dad gave me this job under false pretenses. That he's spent the past four years thinking something about me that isn't true."

I twirl my empty beer bottle. "Why didn't you tell him the truth?" I ask, even though I know the answer.

"At first it was a misunderstanding, but then he was so proud, and..." She grimaces. "I couldn't stand to let him down. Not again."

I nod, understanding. I know what it's like to let down the people you love.

She straightens up. "Anyway. That's why it's important that this project is a success. I just want to do *one* thing that makes Dad proud—that makes *me* proud of myself."

Everything in me softens at that comment. We've spent weeks arguing, disagreeing, generally just not getting along, and that's because of me. I've made this project much harder than it needs to be for her, and for what? Because I don't trust myself not to act on my feelings toward her? I've made my attraction *her* problem, rather than handling it myself. I can't do that anymore—not when I know what this means to her. Not when she's trusted me enough to share this with me, when I can see how hard she's trying.

Not when I can see what's on the line.

16

VIOLET

Kyle gazes at me across the table, compassion warm in his expression. I've never told anyone about what happened in class that day, and I have to wonder how he knew it was a panic attack.

What he doesn't know is what caused it.

The thing is, he's Dad's friend. I don't want to say anything that would make him think badly of Dad, because I know it wasn't Dad's fault. Sure, he worked long hours and never seemed to have much time for me as a kid, and yes, he broke a few promises to me growing up, but it's not like he did it on purpose. His job was important—I learned that years later.

But that didn't help me at the time.

The memories flood back uninvited, and I press my eyes shut. It was senior year of high school and I'd been instrumental in getting our debate team to the regional championships. Dad was thrilled when I told him. He was a very successful attorney, with high standards for his only daughter, even making the time to help me prep for the debate. We spent an entire week of late nights researching possible topics, brainstorming arguments, and rehearsing rebuttals. It was the most time we'd ever spent together, and I'd never felt so close to my father as I did that week. When he promised he'd be there to support me on the big day, I knew he wouldn't let me down.

I was understandably nervous the day of the debate. It was so hot on that stage, and my teammate Naivasha had been undermining me all morning. We never got along, but I knew that dealing with difficult people was an important aspect of law, the career I planned to pursue, so I tried to view it as good practice.

Randy opened the debate, his confident tone doing nothing to soothe my nerves as I scanned the crowd for Dad. Mom was there, a few rows back, her face stretched wide in a proud grin, but she was alone. I assured myself that Dad was probably running late and there was still a lot of time before I gave my closing remarks.

I don't know what it was about that day that felt so important. It was as if everything in my life led to that one moment, and Dad had to be there. He *had* to.

I struggled to focus as the debate wore on, keeping one eye on the door to the auditorium. My hands were sweaty, my shirt sticking to me under the hot stage lights. It all happened so fast—too fast—and then it was my turn to wrap up our argument and bring it home. I was good at this —I'd done it dozens of times before—but tonight my pulse was erratic, my chest tight, and I felt like I couldn't draw a deep enough breath.

He promised, I thought, staring blankly at my notecards before sweeping my gaze around the auditorium again. *He said he'd be here.*

There was no more time to wait. Everyone was looking

at me expectantly, and my father was going to miss it. My proudest moment.

Except it wasn't my proudest moment—far from it. I struggled to get the words out, and when the door to the auditorium swung open I actually stopped, mid-sentence, desperately praying for it to be Dad.

It wasn't. The disappointment I felt was so overwhelming that when I looked at my note cards, they blurred through my tears.

I don't know how I got the rest of the words out, but I did. I muddled through my closing comments, but did it so poorly we lost the debate.

To this day, I can still remember the scathing look Naivasha sent me as they announced that the other team were the winners. I'm surprised it didn't reduce me to ash on the spot.

When Mom found me after the debate she pulled me into a hug, beaming. "You did great, honey!"

I couldn't tell if she genuinely meant it or if she was only being kind, but it didn't matter. We'd lost the championship because of me.

"Where's Dad?" I finally managed.

Mum wrinkled her nose. "I'm sorry, honey. He's been stuck in court all day. You know how it is."

I did know how it was. How it always was. That no matter what I did, it was never enough to make him put me before his work. It was never enough to make him truly proud.

I swallowed back my tears and told myself I was fine, tried to bury the humiliation of that moment on stage deep inside. I thought I had, until that Poli Sci class. Until it all came back to me in such a vivid way that it felt like it was happening all over again.

The decision to change my major wasn't easy, but even worse was the knowledge that Dad would be disappointed. That's why I couldn't tell him for so long. Why I could barely look him in the eye when I finally did.

And why I can't seem to bring myself to tell him the truth now.

"I won't tell Rich," Kyle murmurs, bringing me back to our conversation.

Relief washes over me at his words. "Thank you." I do my best to shake off the memories and focus on Kyle. "I swear, I'll keep working hard, I'll—"

"I don't doubt that at all." His mouth curves into a smile as he pushes his plate away. "I think you need to work *less*, Vi. You can still do an excellent job while having a life outside of work."

I look away, unconvinced. It doesn't matter anyway—the mere fact that I've shared my secret with him and he hasn't judged me, hasn't spluttered in outrage and disbelief... I can't describe the relief. I don't know what inspired me to be so honest with him. He's been like a different guy this evening, insisting I take a break, asking me about my life—and that's before I even consider the fact that he told me I'm beautiful. Sheesh, that nearly did me in. The nicer he was to me, the more I felt that untruth sitting between us, gnawing in my gut, and in a moment of trust, I decided I wanted him to know. I didn't want to hide anymore.

I should have known he'd be kind. He might make a show of being grumpy, bossing me around at the house and keeping me at arm's length, but I'm coming to see that's not who he really is. He's the guy I met in Joe's. The guy who bought me a new coffee to make me smile.

I know I shouldn't be fanning the flames of this crush. As disappointed as Dad would be if he knew the truth about my career, I can't imagine how appalled he'd be if he knew the things I've thought about his friend.

But I can't seem to help myself. I'm beginning to think I'm past the point of no return. It doesn't matter that I know I *shouldn't* get close to Kyle. I desperately want to. It's almost as if I'm drawn to him by a force I can't control. A force that started the day we met in Joe's. It's only gotten stronger since.

He pays for dinner—despite my insistence that I can pay —and we head out into the hum of Montague Street, walking slowly past groups of diners crowding the pavement. I don't dare think about what comes next, or that this whole evening has felt like a date and I don't want it to end. I don't know if he's thinking the same thing, but he also seems to be lost in his thoughts as we walk.

"Did you ever go see the Promenade?" he asks, breaking the silence. I wonder if he's been remembering the day we met, walking through the Heights, talking about the neighborhood.

"No." I give him a self-deprecating smile, pointing a thumb to my chest. "Workaholic, remember?"

He chuffs a laugh. "Of course. Well, I guess I'll have to take you there now." He hesitates, glancing at me. "You didn't have other plans, did you?"

"You mean, besides work?"

"Right." He rolls his eyes, smiling in that good-natured way he has. "Then I definitely have to take you, if only to make sure you have a full night off."

I smile down at my shoes, trying to match my steps to his. He's a lot taller than me, so his stride is longer, plus I'm in heels. He notices and slows beside me. I think about how he remembered my wine order from last week, how concerned he is about my work habits, about what I was planning to eat for dinner tonight—if I ate at all. I can't remember the last time someone looked out for me like this, and it's the nicest feeling.

We cross Pierrepont Place, and as we approach a path between two buildings—a huge brick apartment block on our left, a massive brownstone mansion on our right—I pause.

"Wow, this house is beautiful," I say, gazing up at the brownstone in awe. "Look at the Renaissance revival details, like the frieze and cornice hoods on the windows, and the Corinthian pilasters on the doorway."

I step back to get a better look at the house—it's actually two brownstones with a continuous façade—and realize what's missing. "Wait, I know this place. The Pierrepont mansion was right there"—I motion to the far right, where a playground now sits—"but it was demolished in the mid-twentieth century, leaving only these two." I frown, thinking about how impressive the three buildings would have looked all together. "That's such a shame."

I glance back to find Kyle gazing at me, head tilted to one side, eyes dancing as they move over my face. "How do you know all that?"

"I read something about it in one of my books."

"You learned about the Pierrepont mansion to help with our restoration?"

"Well, no." My cheeks warm. "I started because of the restoration, but I found myself doing extra-curricular reading because it was so interesting." Kyle gives me a look I can't interpret, and I huff an awkward laugh, adding, "Nerdy, I know."

"Not nerdy," he says, his voice pitching lower. His gaze moves to my mouth, his eyes darker than before. It sends a delicious shiver through me, and I want to step closer.

Before I can, he looks away, motioning to the pathway running to the left of the brownstone. "The Promenade is through here."

I follow him, gazing up at the house through the branches of the huge honeylocust tree beside it. The path opens out to a long, paved walkway on the bluff along the edge of the Heights, looking directly over the East River to lower Manhattan. The sun is finally slipping below the skyscrapers of downtown, giving the sky a pink and orange glow. My breath catches at the sight.

"I can't believe I've never been here." I wander across to lean on the iron railing that runs the length of the Promenade.

"See what you miss when all you think about is work?" Kyle murmurs beside me, and I glance at him with a smile. I've missed a lot over the years, and I'm only just realizing. This beautiful city, meaningful friendships, having fun—but also passion, falling in love. I've never been in love and I wonder what it feels like. What it would feel like to be loved by a man like Kyle.

I force my gaze back to the view. "Do you miss living in New York?"

"Not New York, so much, but I miss Brooklyn Heights."

"I can see why," I say, thinking of the beautiful neighborhood. "I think I'll miss it when I go." I'm struggling to picture myself back in Silicon Valley right now, but I shake the feeling off.

"You're still going to go back?" Kyle asks.

"Of course. My whole life is there." Well, my career, which I guess is the same thing. "I just need to do a good job on this project so I can prove I have project management experience, which will help me move into a better role when I go back. That's why this needs to be perfect."

I stare across at Manhattan, listening to the sound of the Brooklyn-Queens Expressway that runs beneath the Promenade. The city glitters in the dusky pink light and I try to ignore the way my heart aches at the thought of leaving this place again.

"I'm so sorry, Violet," Kyle says. When I glance at him in surprise, he's looking down at his hands.

"Why?"

"I know I haven't been easy to work with. I've made the situation harder than it needs to be, and I didn't even consider how that could affect you."

I study him in silence, the ache in my chest growing stronger. His broad shoulders slump, and he runs a hand wearily over his face. I love the dark cut of his beard against his cheek, the way his green eyes cloud when he's lost in thought. I think back to last week, when I finally let myself acknowledge how much I liked him, and how hard it was to focus on work after that—how it was easier to act like a child, or avoid him altogether.

"It's okay," I mumble. "I understand why you did."

Clouds gather above us and a breeze lifts off the East River, ruffling my hair. Kyle reaches out to brush a strand back from my face, his eyes searching mine. "You were right, you know."

I have no idea what he's talking about, but my breath falters at the intensity in his gaze. "About what?"

"That day in Joe's, when we met. You were right."

He's standing so close to me that I can barely think straight, so it takes me a few seconds to understand. "You mean… you were going to ask me out?"

His Adam's apple bobs as he swallows hard, and nods.

My stomach flutters in response, sending a thrill through me. I knew it. God, I knew it.

"I wish you had," I whisper.

He looks pained, drawing his hand away, the spell apparently broken. "It's probably a good thing I didn't."

I feel cold at the loss of his touch. "Why?" I ask, even though I know the answer.

He gives a hollow laugh. "Do you know how inappropriate it is that I hit on the daughter of my best friend? I thought you were in your thirties, or something. And as for being related to Rich—"

"You didn't know," I say gently. "I didn't know who you were either."

He gives a slow nod, looking at Manhattan across the river. "But I do now, Violet."

"Yeah," I murmur, because I understand exactly what he's saying. Now that he knows my real age, that I'm Rich's daughter, he can't unknow that. He probably thinks it would be a betrayal to Dad, even if I'm a grown woman who can make my own decisions.

Even if I want him more than I've wanted any man I've ever met.

There's a loud crack in the sky above and we both startle, glancing up. I hadn't realized how gray the sky had become because I'd been too focused on Kyle, but now a fat raindrop lands on my cheek, followed by another.

"We should go." Kyle steps back from the railing. From me. "This way."

I follow him north along the Promenade, watching people scatter, dodging raindrops as they fall, that familiar smell of fresh rain on pavement clinging to the air. Kyle breaks into a light jog as the rain picks up, but I can't keep up in my sandals. I stop to take them off, and he notices, turning back for me. He takes my shoes, then slides his other hand into mine, and we begin to jog as the rain pelts down in sheets. It's only a few blocks, but I'm out of breath by the time we arrive at the house. Kyle, on the other hand, hasn't even broken a sweat.

We tumble into the entry hall, rain lashing against the door as it closes behind us, and I step away from Kyle, taking a moment to catch my breath. We're soaked through, my hair trailing rivulets of water down my chest and shoulders, Kyle's beard dripping on the foyer floor. And my dress is stuck to me, no doubt revealing some things that probably shouldn't be revealed.

I glance up to see if Kyle has noticed, but he's too busy peeling his sopping wet shirt from his body and tossing it into a soggy pile on the floor.

I stop breathing altogether at that point.

Holy hell, he is pure eye candy. He's in such good shape—hardly surprising given his job and his level of fitness—and while he's not sculpted in the way a man who spends his life at the gym might be, he's muscular and solid from long days of hard work. The salt and pepper hair on his chest tapers to his navel, and my eyes stray to the top of his jeans, desperate for him to keep undressing. I almost beg him not to stop but catch myself just in time, letting out a tiny squeak instead.

Fuck. Me.

He lifts a hand to rake it through his damp hair, unaware of my roving eyes, and I catch a glimpse of a tattoo on his upper bicep and shoulder that I didn't know was there. It's a moose in front of a forest and mountains.

Jesus, Mary, and Joseph. He has a tattoo. *God, that's hot.* Everything about him is so freaking hot and I think I might be losing my mind a little bit over here.

He doesn't notice, though, because his gaze has found me—slowly working its way up my legs, over the soaking wet dress stuck to my thighs, and when I glance down I notice you can see my underwear through the fabric—lacy red panties and a matching bra.

I should feel sorry about that, but given the expression on Kyle's face, I'm not sorry one little bit.

His gaze finally meets mine and his breath comes out as a hard rasp. His eyes are dark pools of desire, his face intense with want, and I could be wrong, but I swear there's a bulge in his jeans that wasn't there before.

I've never felt so damn good about myself as I do in this moment.

I know he doesn't want to hurt Dad. I don't either. But we're adults, we both want this. Do we have to fight it so hard?

"Violet," he says, his voice rough in a way I've never heard. It sends heat shooting through me and I press my legs together, itching for his touch.

Come here, I silently plead. *Come here and kiss me, take me to bed. Please.*

But he stays where he is, curling his fist into a tight ball at his side. He swallows, his jaw clenched. Now I can't tell if he's angry or turned on. Maybe both.

"I'm going up to my room," he grits out, turning from me and stalking upstairs before I can protest. My heart falls as he plods up the steps.

"Thanks for a great evening." My voice is hoarse as I call after him, and I'm not sure he hears me.

I sigh, traipsing downstairs, and peeling off my clothes. I take a long hot shower, hoping it will soothe me, but when I climb into bed I'm too agitated to sleep.

I can't stop thinking about Kyle, how vulnerable he looked when he apologized, the gentle way he brushed my hair from my face, the way his body looked in the entry hall, all hard lines and firm muscle under glistening raindrops.

Fuck, I'll never sleep now. Not like this.

I snake a hand under the covers, into my panties. I'm not surprised to find I'm already wet, thinking about the way his voice sounded when he said my name. I wonder what sounds he makes in bed. I wonder how he likes to fuck. Does he take control or let the woman take the lead? I wonder what his face looks like when he comes.

Oh, God. *Yes*.

Thinking about Kyle, I orgasm in three seconds flat.

17

KYLE

I pace the top floor of the house, feeling like a live wire, restless and dangerous. I heard the shower turn on in the basement as I climbed the stairs, and knowing Violet is down there, naked under a stream of hot water, is driving me fucking crazy.

Why the hell did I let my guard down with her tonight? Laughing and talking over dinner, apologizing for the past few weeks, and then admitting that I was going to ask her out... What was I thinking? All that has done is turn the heat up on this pressure cooker.

I replay what she told me tonight—about having a panic attack in class, how worried she is about letting her father down. I wanted to pull her into my arms and tell her I understand, that we're more similar than I realized. I wanted to press my mouth to hers and erase any pain she's ever felt.

I think of the way the wind blew across her face as she looked at me on the Promenade, the husky catch to her voice when she told me she wished I had asked her out, the sad look of resignation when I made it clear nothing could happen.

I hadn't meant to grab her hand as we rushed home through the pelting rain, but I needed to make sure she was safe beside me. And I certainly hadn't meant to undress her with my eyes in the entry hall, but that wet, see-through dress left very little to the imagination. From the flare of her wide hips to her narrow waist, and her perfect, round breasts heaving with her rapid breathing... I've never wanted someone so badly in my life. And then there was the red underwear I could see under it all...

Fu-u-uck.

My cock hardens remembering the way she looked at me with pure, unrestrained lust. She wants this as badly as I do, and the thought makes me dizzy. Harder.

"No," I mutter, stripping off my wet jeans and trying to ignore the way my cock throbs as I brush past it. It knows what it wants. The only thing separating us is four floors and my own dwindling self-restraint, but that is going to have to do. I will not fuck my friend's daughter in the basement of his house, no matter how much her eyes were begging me to do just that.

I let out an agonized groan as I stalk across the floor to the bathroom, locking the door. This room was re-tiled in an emerald-colored subway tile last week, perfectly matching with the brass fixtures Violet suggested. After meeting with an interior decorator, she finalized the color scheme for the house—a mix of dark green, navy blue, and apricot, offset with neutral creams. The bathroom looks really good, but I barely notice as I peel my wet underwear off.

I glance at my erection, an angry red-purple, aching for release. I lift my fist, then hesitate. Jerking off while thinking of Violet isn't much better, is it? I've resisted since we met, knowing that once I fantasized about her sucking me off, about being inside her, about the sounds she might make as she comes, it would be almost impossible to look her in the eye.

Still, I reason, doing this might be the only way I can keep my hands to myself. As much as I want my hands on *her* instead of on my dick, they can't be.

I turn on the shower and step into the tub, drawing the shower curtain. As steam curls up from the spray, I wrap my fist around my length, feeling equal parts horny as fuck and ashamed.

She'll never know, I tell myself, but more importantly, Rich will never know.

I push the thought of my best friend from my head, letting the image of his daughter appear instead, needing to make this count as I'm only going to let myself jerk off to her once. Has she ever touched herself while thinking of me? What would she do if I walked in on her? She'd be on her bed, legs spread, fingers in her underwear, eyes closed...

I let myself slip into the fantasy as I grip my cock and stroke. In my mind, I stand in the doorway to the basement, watching her pleasure herself until I can't handle it anymore.

"Need some help?" I rasp, and her eyes fly open in surprise, a gasp escaping her lips.

"What are you doing here?"

I ignore her question as I stalk across the room, coming to stand at the foot of her bed. "Were you thinking of me?"

Her cheeks turn that beautiful pink they get when she's embarrassed, and she nods.

"Take your panties off," I command, and she hesitates for a moment, then obeys. "Your bra, too." She does as I say, then leans back on the bed, naked and spread out for me. "Good girl." I strip my shirt off, then reach for my belt, but she sits up.

"Let me." Her hands fumble on the buckle, as if she's nervous, then she slides my zipper down, releasing my erection. My jeans fall to my ankles and before I can do anything more, her fist wraps around my length and my eyes roll back.

"Oh *fuck*," I say thickly. "It feels so good to have your hands on me." I kick my pants off and lower myself to the bed beside her. Her dark brown eyes are round, excited, and hungry for me.

"Are you finally going to give me what I need?" she whispers, and I nod.

"I am, sweetheart. You've been so patient with me."

I brush my mouth over hers, heat pouring through me as her tongue laps against mine. My hands roam her beautiful body, cradling her pert breasts, stroking her nipples. Her back arches and she moans...

"Jesus," I mutter out loud as the water streams over me. I brace myself against the shower wall and fuck my hand, imagining how soft her skin would feel, how sweet her little moans would be, how she might like to be touched. I let the fantasy take over again.

"I need you here." She takes my hand and lowers it between her legs. My fingers touch her wet heat and I groan. "Yes," she breathes as I circle her clit, stroking, pushing inside her tight wetness, then circling back.

"I can't wait anymore," I growl, nudging her back onto the pillow and climbing over her. "I need to feel you." I spread her thighs and sink into her perfect tightness with a low groan. Her pussy grips my cock like it's been waiting for me, like I've finally come home.

"Oh God, Kyle." Her mouth finds mine and our tongues collide as our bodies rock together. Her lips are so sweet and

I drink down her kiss, thrusting hard. She moans as I change the angle, going deeper.

"You like that, sweetheart?"

"Yes. Fuck, yes."

I pin her hands above her head and she watches as I take control, holding her down and pounding her hard.

"Yes, yes, yes," she pants, her hips bucking beneath me. "I'm going to come."

That's all it takes. I come so fucking hard, imagining the pleasure on her face, her legs wrapping around me as I bury myself deep.

The sound of water hitting the tub brings me back to my senses. My chest is heaving as I rinse off, feeling only a fraction of the satisfaction I was hoping for. More than anything I feel dirty, uneasy, as if I've crossed a line I shouldn't have.

I shut off the shower and dry myself, pulling on fresh boxer-briefs and sinking onto my air mattress with a sigh. I reach for my phone to check the time, and there's a text waiting for me.

From Rich.

Like he knew what I was doing and wanted to remind me I'm a complete dirtbag.

Rich: Up for an early game of racquetball tomorrow?

Guilt lashes through me as I stare at his words. The last thing I feel like doing is seeing my friend in the morning, knowing what I just imagined doing to his daughter.

Kyle: We've got a lot of work to do at the house.

I send off my lame excuse, hoping he'll let it go. If there's one thing Richard understands, it's work.

Rich: Come on. It's our last chance before Di and I go out of town tomorrow night.

Shit. I forgot they were heading out of town for two weeks.

Rich has some clients to meet up with in Boston, and Di talked him into making it a summer holiday on the East Coast. How she got Rich to agree to that much time off work is beyond me.

I sigh, giving in to my friend.

Kyle: Okay. Usual time and place?

We used to play weekly, back when I lived in the city, so he'll know what I mean.

Rich: See you then.

I throw my phone onto the bed and lie back to look at the ceiling, at the plaster that still needs to be repaired, but I can't even muster the energy to care. All I can think about is how I'm going to look Rich in the eye tomorrow.

18

KYLE

I slam the ball into the wall and instantly feel better.

"There he is," Rich says as my serve ricochets off the front wall and sails past him. "Just as sharp as ever, I see."

I laugh, catching the ball and preparing to serve again. It's been a long time since I've held a racket, let alone played, but being back here with Rich feels good. When I left the city I was trying to escape the hectic life I'd built for myself. I didn't realize what else I'd lose in the process.

Rich doesn't miss this time, and we rally for a few minutes, dodging each other, eyes glued to the ball as it flies around the court. At the end of the first game, we stop to catch our breath.

Rich reaches for his water bottle with a smile. "How are things at the house?"

"Good." I inspect my racket, refusing to meet his gaze. As if something in my eyes might give away what I did last night and Rich will realize what a bad friend I truly am.

"Are you looking out for my girl?"

Despite myself, I feel a prickle of jealousy at the way Rich refers to Violet as 'his girl.'

Because she is *his girl—she's his daughter, for fuck's sake.*

"She's fine," I mutter, prepared to leave it at that, but there's a pinch in my chest as I think again of what she told me at dinner—how scared she is that Rich will be disappointed in her. That he won't be proud. "Very good at her job," I add.

"Yes, she's hardworking." Rich sets his bottle down. "Though sometimes I worry she works too hard."

"I wonder where she gets that from," I respond dryly.

He chuckles. "Yeah, but I'm an old man. She's young, with her whole life ahead of her. She needs a life outside of work, too."

I nod, picking up the ball and bouncing it on my racket. "That's what I told her last night."

Rich gives me a curious look. "You saw her last night?"

Shit.

I feel the color drain from my face and concentrate on bouncing the ball. I can't lie to my friend. "Yeah, we ended up grabbing dinner together after work."

I try to console myself with the knowledge that we didn't do anything wrong—merely ate dinner and talked. I had every chance to do more than that, and I didn't.

Rich is quiet for a while and my stomach churns with unease. I glance over to see if he's figured it out—that I want his daughter more than anything and I've let myself imagine what it would be like to have her—but he's just busy tying his laces.

"I'm glad she has you there," Rich says when he straightens up. I should be relieved, but his words make me feel worse. "You two seem to work well together."

"Uh-huh." I toss the ball to Rich, hoping that's the end of

this conversation, but instead of serving, he holds the ball and studies me.

"Everything okay? You seem preoccupied. You were like this at lunch the other week, too."

I twirl my racket, considering how to answer. I really don't want to lie to him, but it's not like I can tell him what's on my mind.

"Would it help to talk?" he asks gently, and guilt swamps me. I'm instantly transported back to four years ago, to the way Rich was there as my life crumbled around me.

It started with what I thought was a heart attack: chest pains, shortness of breath, palpitations, dizziness—all the usual signs. I was admitted to the hospital and run through every test they could think of, only to turn up nothing. I went home feeling stupid, and quite frankly, terrified. They said it was nothing, but it wasn't nothing. I'd felt something. Something I didn't understand.

It happened again a week later, in the middle of court, and Rich took over for me without a word. I saw a different doctor this time, a woman who suggested I was having panic attacks.

I thought she was joking. "I don't panic," I'd said.

But once she'd explained what a panic attack was, how it felt, and how it could seemingly come out of nowhere, I knew she was right. I was at the top of my career, about to be made partner, and I was having panic attacks.

It was humiliating, to say the least.

So I did what I'd always done and put my nose down, ignored the problem, and vowed to work harder. It didn't hurt that Lisa, my girlfriend of five years, supported this approach, and it wasn't long until I was back to being on top of the world, handling the stresses of my job like a pro.

But here's the thing about the body, it has an intelligence

the mind does not. It knows when it can't handle any more, even when the mind wants to push it past all reasonable limits.

And it tells you when it's had enough.

While I could hold it together at work, the panic attacks started happening in the middle of the night. I'd wake up in a cold sweat, my heart racing, struggling for breath. At first Lisa was concerned, holding my hand and helping me through them, but she grew tired of it and started sleeping in the spare room. I figured it was a phase, and reasoned that as long as they didn't happen at the office or in court, it was fine. But soon they happened all the time, any time, and I could never be prepared.

It was Rich who talked me into going to a therapist. He found someone and took me to my first session, waiting outside while I told a stranger what was happening to me, and how I couldn't understand why.

It was Rich who suggested I lighten my workload at the firm. When that didn't help, it was his suggestion for me to take some time away from work, from the city. And when Lisa kicked me out...

Anyway. If it hadn't been for Rich and Diana's kindness, their care and concern, I don't know what I would have done.

And now here I am, fantasizing about their daughter like some kind of depraved creep. Rich has been the best possible friend I could ask for, and how am I repaying him? By betraying his trust. It doesn't matter that I haven't *acted* on my feelings for Violet, having them in the first place is enough of a betrayal.

I need to remember what matters most here, and it's not getting my dick wet.

I shake my head. "No, I don't need to talk about it, but

thanks. It's just... something at the house. But I'll sort it out." It's not the full truth, but it's not a lie, either.

Rich nods, accepting this. "That reminds me. How did it go with the realtor? I never heard."

It occurs to me then that neither did I.

I scrub a hand across my beard, trying not to scowl at the thought of Owen coming onto Violet in front of me. My grip tightens on my racket when I remember that he thought I was her father. *As if.*

"I'm not sure. I'll have to check with Vi," I say carefully. "Maybe he contacted her."

He'd better fucking not have, I think, against all better judgment.

Rich nods again and returns to the game, serving the ball. For the next hour, I whack the shit out of that ball, pretending it's not Owen's face I'd rather be hitting.

19

VIOLET

"Morning, gorgeous." I glance up from my laptop to find Sadie grinning at me from the doorway.

"Oh! Hey." I push my laptop away and stand from my desk, stretching. "I didn't hear you come in."

"I knocked, but there was no answer." She sweeps her red curls over one shoulder as she enters the room. "The door was unlocked so I let myself in. I hope that's okay."

"Of course." I wouldn't have heard her over the music from the Bluetooth speaker on my desk and the banging on the floor above me. The guys are framing up the bedroom walls on the second floor, but I haven't seen Kyle this morning. Probably for the best, after the things I pictured him doing to me last night...

I clear my throat, feeling warmth touch my cheeks. Sadie's eyebrows rise, but before she can say anything, I ask, "What are you doing in this neighborhood?"

"I've got a meeting with a potential client on Clark Street. Thought I'd see if you're free for a coffee first." Sadie works at a respected marketing firm in Manhattan and I've always admired her for it.

I glance down at my laptop, then over at my Gantt chart. We've got a countertop being delivered today, ready for the kitchen install starting next week, and I'm not sure when it's arriving. "I don't know if I can get away," I say. "I might need—"

"You should go." Kyle's voice enters the parlor and Sadie spins on her heel to see who it is. By the looks of things, Kyle has just arrived from the gym. He's a little sweaty, his moist tee clinging to the hard swell of his biceps and the broad expanse of his chest.

Oof.

"Hi." Sadie steps forward, hand extended. "I'm Sadie."

Kyle drops his gym bag on a chair and takes her hand. "Kyle."

"Oh, *you're* Kyle." Her gaze sweeps over him, assessing, then swings to me. Her widened eyes and barely contained grin tell me she approves.

Kyle glances at me, mirth shimmering in his eyes before they quickly swing back to my friend. "You've heard about me, have you?"

Sadie, realizing her mistake—and that I'm going to kill her—hastily backtracks. "Well, Violet mentioned you're the foreman. That's all." She beams up at him innocently and I roll my eyes.

"Right," Kyle says, clearly unconvinced. A Rogue Valley song comes onto my Bluetooth speaker and his eyes flash to mine, then away.

I sigh. Last night was magical, but today he can barely even look at me. This sucks.

"Ooh, I love this song." Sadie leans over to turn up my speaker. "They're playing a show next week."

"Really?" This seems to pique Kyle's interest. "Where?"

"Dumbo, I think." She glances at him. "You like this band?"

His gaze meets mine again and he nods. When he doesn't immediately look away, a little zing of adrenaline zaps through me. I feel it in the way my heart skips and goosebumps spread across my arms. It's summer, for God's sake.

"Anyway," Kyle mutters, wrenching his gaze away and reaching for his clipboard. "You should go for coffee, Vi. We can handle things here for an hour."

"Are you sure—"

"Yes. Go."

I reach for my purse with a frown and follow Sadie outside. The minute we're down the front steps, she wheels on me with a wicked grin.

"Oh my God, Vi. He is capital H *hot*."

"Shhh," I hiss, grabbing her arm and dragging her away from the house. But as soon as I'm sure we're out of earshot, I can't help but join her. "He is, right? *So* fucking hot."

She nods vigorously as we head to Joe's. "He's got that sexy daddy thing going on."

I glance at her. "Daddy thing?"

"Yeah, you know. An older man who knows how to take control."

I snort a laugh. "Well, I won't be calling him *Daddy*," I say, thinking of my own father and how horrified Kyle would probably be.

Sadie waves a hand. "You don't have to call him that. It's like... an energy. A vibe. Anyway, the technical term is 'Stern Brunch Daddy.'"

I laugh as we step into Joe's and wait to order, even more confused. "What does brunch have to do with it?"

She cocks her head. "You know, I'm not sure. It's from my

romance novels. It basically means he's both sweet and caring, but also fierce and protective."

"Huh." I mull this over while Sadie orders for us both, then finds a table.

Kyle is all those things and more. I think of when he cared for me after I cut my hand, how much he worries about my work habits. Then I think of the way he practically pushed Owen out of the house that day, and stifle a smile. I've never had a man do that before.

Which reminds me, I never did respond to Owen. Truthfully, I hadn't known what to say. He was nice enough, but I didn't really want to go out with him, and I hadn't figured out how to say that without coming across as a bitch. I'm not used to having to turn men away.

Daisy, Joe's regular barista, brings our coffees to the table. I smile my thanks and take a sip of my Americano, waiting for the caffeine to hit my veins. Nothing tastes as good as the first sip in the morning.

"What's it like living with Tim?" I ask.

Sadie smiles, stirring her latte. "Good. Really good." Concern creases her brow. "Are you okay sleeping at the house, though? I worry about you staying in that big empty place alone."

I shift in my seat. She's going to love this. "I'm not alone. Kyle's there."

She sets her spoon down. "He's staying at the house too?"

"Yup."

She rocks back in her chair with a smug smile. "Right. Okay. It's all making sense."

"Shut up." I swat her across the table. "Nothing has happened between us."

"But you want it to?"

God yes.

"It probably shouldn't," I say, dodging her question. "He seems to think it would be inappropriate, and he's not wrong."

"Why? You're both adults."

I gaze into the dark liquid of my coffee with a sigh. "Yeah, that's what I thought too, but Dad wouldn't be okay with it, and it's important to me that this project goes well."

"I guess," Sadie says. "But—"

My phone buzzes on the table between us and I glance down, expecting to see Kyle or Dad's name there. Surprise jolts through me when I see Deb's name. My old boss.

"I'm sorry." I pick up my phone, curious. It must be early on the West Coast. "Do you mind if I take this quickly?"

"Go for it."

I rise from the table as I answer the call, wandering across to the wall where I first met Kyle.

"Violet! How are you?" Deb's voice is as familiar in my ear as if I'd just heard it yesterday, and there's a little tug in my chest.

"Hi, Deb. I'm good. How are things?"

"Good, good. I'm calling because I wanted to let you know about a possible opportunity here at DigiSwap."

My ears perk up. "Oh?"

"Nothing is official yet, but there might be a project manager position opening up in Scott's team. You were the first person I thought of."

My heart does an excited little jump. "Me?"

"Of course."

"Is it an assistant project manager job?" I ask, because that would be the next natural progression for me.

"Nope. You'd be a fully-fledged project manager. It's what you deserve, after all the work you've put in here."

I inhale, a little shocked. That would be a *huge* step for my career.

"Is it something you'd be interested in?"

"Yes!" I say, turning away from the crowd in Joe's to hide my grin. My eyes land on the framed images of old Brooklyn Heights along the wall, and my heart sinks. "But I'm working on a project in Brooklyn right now, so I won't be free for at least another month."

"That's okay," Deb assures me. "This is still in the works. Are you managing the current project?"

"Yes." I leave out the part where my father hired me because he didn't know what a little liar I am, and how guilty I've felt ever since.

"Excellent! What is it?"

"Historical building restoration. Probably not relevant to the work at DigiSwap."

"I disagree; it shows you're able to adapt to a range of projects and environments. Can you get a letter of recommendation to me sometime in the next few days? That will really help things here."

A letter of recommendation. I twist my lips to the side, knowing that Dad would probably give me a glowing recommendation, but that it won't count if it comes from someone with the same last name as me.

On a sigh I realize exactly who I'll have to ask.

"I can probably get one from the foreman. I'm working closely with him. Would that work?"

"Definitely. Get him to send something through and I'll keep it on file for when things start moving here. I'm going to do everything I can to make sure you get the job." She's quiet for a beat, then adds, "It will be so good to have you back."

I study the frames on the wall—the pictures of brownstones and old streets, the history of the neighborhood around me—trying to imagine myself back in soulless Silicon Valley.

But what alternative do I have? This project will end soon, and if I don't take this opportunity, I'll be back where I started: unemployed and lost. This is what I wanted all along—a real project management position—and a month back in New York hasn't changed that. My career matters to me just as much as before, if not more now.

"Thank you so much, Deb. I can't wait to come back." I end the call, ignoring the hollow feeling in my chest as I return to the table.

"Who was that?" Sadie asks. "You seemed to be grinning pretty hard there for a moment."

"That was my old boss, Deb. She said there might be a job opening back at DigiSwap and she's going to suggest me for it."

"Awesome!" Sadie high-fives me across the table. "Although, I do wish you'd stay in the city. It's been so nice hanging out again."

"It has." I take a long sip of my lukewarm coffee. "Anyway, I might not get it. I have to ask Kyle for a recommendation, and God knows how that will go down."

"You don't think he'll do it?"

I lift a shoulder. "He's so hot and cold with me, I have no idea. I like to think he's professional enough to do it, but..."

Sadie nods, setting her coffee cup down with a twinkle in her eye. "What if we could give him a little nudge in the right direction?"

"If you're about to suggest I use sex to bribe him, I really don't think that will help."

She laughs. "Not sex, but there might be something else."

I lift my eyebrows with interest, but she catches sight of the time and jumps up from the table. "Shit, I'm going to be late. I'll call you, okay?"

"Wha—"

"Bye!" She pecks me on the cheek then whips out of Joe's before I can ask anything more.

IT'S two hours later when she calls me—two hours I spend agonizing over the best way to ask Kyle for a letter of recommendation and coming up with nothing.

"Did you get my email?" Sadie asks breathlessly on the other end of the line. I slink down the stairs to the basement so I can take the call in private, then switch my phone to speaker.

"No. Hold on." I open my mail app and see something from Sadie—an email with the subject line PROBLEM SOLVED, and an attachment. It's two tickets to Rogue Valley. "What is this?"

"He likes them, right?"

"He does," I say, thinking back to that night we both discovered we loved this obscure band, and how it almost seemed as though we'd found a kindred spirit in each other.

"So, take him to the show. Use that to grease the wheel."

I frown. "How much did these cost you?"

"I got them through a contact from work, so they were free. Oh, but I was wrong—it's not next week, it's tonight."

I look at the attachment again, checking the date, and see that she's right. Shit.

"I'd go myself," she adds, "but Tim has a work thing he wants me to go to tonight."

"I can't take these." I think of Sadie's generosity since I

returned to the city, not sure I've earned it. "It's too much, Sade."

"Vi, they were *free*. If I can't go, you should at least go, and take that man of yours."

I glance at the doorway, quickly taking my phone off speaker. "He's not my man," I say in a low voice.

"I know, and I've been thinking about what you said earlier. You're leaving town again soon, right? If you two like each other, I see no reason why you couldn't have a little fling. Why does your dad even have to know?"

I open and close my mouth, unsure how to answer. It's not like *I* would tell Dad, but I'm sure Kyle wouldn't be comfortable with keeping something like that from him.

Would he?

"I don't know," I mutter, sinking down onto my bed.

"Either way, take him to the show. At the very least you'll have fun, and hopefully he'll be happy to write the recommendation for you after."

"Okay," I agree. "And thanks, Sade." Now I just need to figure out how to ask him.

20

KYLE

It's nice to have some time in the house without Violet after last night; a chance to get my head on straight and focus on the work. I spend the morning helping the guys frame up the bedroom on the second floor, and don't realize Violet is back until I head out for lunch a few hours later.

I find her on the sidewalk, assessing the front façade of the building. We've got scaffolding scheduled for set up in the next day or so to get the mortar and brickwork restored, and I assume she's making sure the space is ready for it.

"Hey," I say, descending the front steps into the midday sun. The heat envelops me on the sidewalk. New York doesn't do summer by halves, and the days are scorching. I miss my lake house on days like today.

Violet glances at me. She's in her denim cutoffs again, a loose tee hanging off one shoulder and tied at the waist. It's the most simple of outfits but it makes her look like a goddess. What I wouldn't give to make her *feel* like one, too.

Stop.

"Hey." She offers me a tentative smile. "I'm just making sure we're ready for the scaffolding."

Of course she is. Always on top of everything.

"Good." My stomach rumbles and I turn to head off for lunch, then remember. "Did you ever hear back from Owen? Rich asked this morning about the appraisal."

She lifts a brow. "This morning?"

"We played racquetball."

"Ah." She nods, then does that bottom lip thing I find so adorable. She doesn't answer my question, and a feeling of suspicion creeps over me.

"You didn't hear from him?"

"Uh..." She shifts her weight. "Yeah, I did."

"And? Did we get the appraisal?"

"Not yet."

I narrow my eyes, not liking where this is going at all. "Then what did he contact you for?"

She looks down at her shoes, folding her arms. "Um... he asked me out."

I knew this was coming, but it still feels like a kick in the stomach. I clench and unclench my fists, trying not to flip out. Because why should I? I have no claim to her.

"Right," I say through gritted teeth. My jaw aches, and I realize I'm clenching it hard. I take a deep breath, my appetite gone.

I don't want her to go out with him. It's completely unreasonable, given I have no intention of doing anything with her, but I still don't want her with him.

I don't want her with anyone.

"I'm not going to say yes," she says gently, eying me.

Good. Okay. Leave it there.

But for some reason I feel the need to say, "You can if

you want." Then I desperately hope, against all reason, that she'll say she doesn't.

She lifts a shoulder. "I'm not sure I want to."

Oh, thank fuck.

"Why not?" I hear myself ask. Determined to press my luck, apparently.

She tilts her head to the side, giving me a look. "You know why."

It takes every muscle in my face to hold in my triumphant smile. She doesn't want to go out with that greasy little shit. She wants me.

And you can't fucking have her.

"I should get to lunch," I mumble, looking away.

"Before you go, there's something I wanted to ask you." She sounds uncertain and I force my gaze back to hers.

"What's up?"

"Um..." She rubs her face. "Do you have plans tonight? Because Sadie got two free tickets to see Rogue Valley..."

I frown. "I thought she said it was next week?"

"She got the date wrong. Anyway, I was wondering..."

I think I know what she's going to ask, and as much as I'd absolutely love to see our favorite band together, I know that isn't a good idea.

"Why don't you go with Sadie?" I cut in.

"She's busy." Violet's gaze drifts across the street, as if she can't bear to look at me when she adds, "And I want to take you."

Oh, God. She's so adorable when she's nervous. Which is exactly why I have to say no.

"Violet," I begin, my tone heavy with warning.

Her gaze snaps back to mine. "Oh, it's not like that. It's... something else."

"What do you mean?"

Her mouth opens and closes a few times, and she sighs. "Okay, fine. I got a call from my old boss this morning, and there's a project manager position opening up at my old company. She thinks I have a good chance of getting it."

I try to keep my expression blank, but there's a pinch in my chest at the thought of Violet leaving. I push it away as she continues.

"I told her I was managing this project, and she asked for a letter of recommendation. It won't count if I get one from Dad, so I was wondering..." she trails off, looking at me hopefully.

"You want me to write you a letter of recommendation?" I scan her face, at the way she looks a little uncertain, as if I might say no. That hurts. "Of course, Vi. I'll write you a great recommendation."

She lets her breath out in a long exhale. "Okay. Cool. Thank you."

"But what does that have to do with the tickets?"

"Oh, well..." She gives a sheepish laugh. "I kind of thought that I might need to, I don't know, sweeten you up a bit."

A laugh rumbles in my chest. "Seriously?" As if I'm not already sweet enough on her as it is.

She shrugs. "I wasn't sure."

God, I'd give anything to step forward and pull her close, to bury my face in her neck and stroke her hair and tell her I'd do pretty much anything for her at this point.

I rake a hand through my hair, thinking. So it's definite, then—she's going back to the West Coast. And I'll be returning to Maine. It's just like she said, this is all temporary, then we go back to our real lives.

And suddenly, I want to make every moment I have left with her count—in all the ways I'm allowed to, at least.

There's no harm in two people enjoying some music together, is there? And Rich will be out of town. He'd want me to make sure she's safe. Besides, what if I don't go with her and she invites Owen instead?

Fuck that.

"Well... if you have the tickets, it seems a shame to waste them," I say, with what I hope is a nonchalant shrug.

Her gaze sparkles as it moves over my face. "It does. You told me I need more time away from work, and I'd really like to see them. Wouldn't you?"

I nod, a grin tugging at my mouth, because I do want to see them—I've never seen them live—and I want to do it with her.

"Cool." Her smile makes my chest ache. "Then I'm looking forward to it."

IT TAKES me forty-five minutes to get ready for the evening. It doesn't help that I sweat through my first shirt, which is absurd because, as I keep telling myself, *this isn't a date.*

For some reason, that makes me even more nervous.

I consider wearing a button-down shirt, then realize that's a bad idea. It's a concert in a converted warehouse, where I'll most likely be surrounded by twenty-year-olds. I don't want anyone to think I'm Violet's dad.

Again.

Eventually I settle on a plain black tee, faded jeans, and boots, styling my hair in the way she seemed to appreciate last time. Then I worry I've put in too much effort, until Violet meets me in the entry hall looking so delicious I want to take a bite out of her. She's wearing a denim mini skirt and some kind of white, ruffled top that cuts across her chest, exposing her shoulders. Her cheeks are flushed with excitement, her blonde hair pulled high into a ponytail. There are a few loose tendrils around her neck, and I want to brush them away and trail my mouth across the soft, exposed skin.

I want to forget the damn concert and take her to bed.

Stop. Now.

"Ready?" I ask brusquely, looking away.

"Yep." She slings a little purse across her body and we head out into the warm evening air, her sweet vanilla scent making me heady as we walk side by side through the Heights.

The venue is only a ten-minute walk, across Old Fulton Street—"Named after the guy who ran the first steam ferry in 1814," Violet says with a grin, and I nearly kiss her right there—then under the Brooklyn Bridge overpass to an old tobacco warehouse on the edge of the water. It's a two-story brick structure with arched windows and doorways. Half of it is a theater used for productions and concerts, and the other half of the building maintains the brick façade with open arched windows and no roof. Instead, the walls contain a paved area and outdoor garden, through which you can see the East River, and Manhattan in the distance.

"This is cool," Violet says as we walk through the garden. The large tree in the middle is strung with bulbs, making it glow as the sun sinks behind the city beyond. The entire garden feels magical and romantic, and if this were a date, I'd be pulling her aside for a kiss.

"Let's go in and get a drink." I head out of the dimly lit garden and into the bright lights of the theater, Violet trailing behind. "The usual?"

She nods, smiling. "Yes, please."

I grab her a Riesling, get a beer for myself, and we mill

about as we wait for the band to start. They don't keep us waiting long, and soon enough the lights dim and the cavernous warehouse fills with music. In spite of myself, I grin over my beer at Violet as they play, glad I decided to come. I love their music, a genre called 'Americana Rock' that encompasses traditional music styles like folk, bluegrass, singer-songwriter and others. I discovered them, purely by accident, when I moved to Maine, and the lyrics of their songs remind me of the natural beauty of places like Kennebec County. Their music will always make me think of the move I made and the peace it brought me.

They play a great set, Violet and I hovering near the back enjoying the beat. I'm relieved to see that it's not all twenty-somethings; there are people of all ages, and I don't feel nearly as old as I'd imagined. I feel right at home, with Violet by my side.

"I love this song!" she squeals, as they begin to play *False Floors*—the song that was on when I scared her shitless in the basement that time. She sets her wineglass down on a table and grabs my hand, pulling me through the crowd, closer to the band. Her hand is warm and soft in mine, her excitement palpable, and I move to the music beside her, feeling more alive than I have in a long time. Her energy is infectious, her smile so wide my heart pounds in response. And the fact that she's still holding my hand in the crowd makes my skin feel electric. It makes me high.

When the song ends, she turns to me, beaming. Her gaze falls to our linked hands and she gives a sheepish laugh, unlacing her fingers. "Sorry."

Don't be sorry, I want to lean in and whisper to her.

Instead I smile, turning back to the stage as they begin a favorite of mine.

Violet leans in to speak to me over the music. "It's so cool to finally see them live." She pauses for a moment, then adds, cheeks pink, "I used to have a little crush on the lead guitarist."

I grin at her teasingly. "Oh yeah?"

"Yeah." An adorably awkward laugh titters out of her. "There's something about a guy with a guitar..."

"I play guitar," I blurt, like a teenager trying to impress his crush.

Jesus fucking Christ.

She twists to meet my gaze, her face lighting with an interested smile. "Really?"

"I'm not very good," I admit. Now I'm the one laughing awkwardly. "But I can play."

She lifts her brows in a way that says she likes that, a lot. And even though I'm not supposed to be encouraging this, I'd be lying if I said I didn't love the feeling I get when she looks at me like that—the way my chest expands, my pulse accelerates.

Then the guilt and disappointment that always follow. The knowledge that I'm falling for a girl I'll never be allowed to touch.

"I need to get some air," I mumble, pulling away from her. I push through the crowd and out into the garden, hoping Violet won't follow me.

Ah, that's a lie.

I expect the garden to be busy with other people getting a breather from the crush of the crowd, but it's not. It's only me and my racing thoughts, along with the sound of music drifting out from the theater into the garden.

I step into the shadow of a birch tree and slump against the bricks, dropping my head into my hands. What the hell am I going to do? Rich is like a brother to me. He's truly the best friend I've ever had—someone I know will always have my back, no matter what.

Well, *not* no matter what; if I made a move on his daughter, it would change our relationship and not for the better.

And yet…

I sigh, grinding the heels of my hands into my eye sockets. I've never met a woman like Violet. Someone who challenges me, who makes me laugh, who constantly surprises me. Someone who looks at me like I'm the best thing she's ever laid eyes on, like I could be her whole world if I let myself. Someone whose smile makes me want to give her everything.

I lower my fist and slam it into the wall behind me. My jaw clenches as the rough brick bites into my skin, but I welcome the pain. Anything to stop myself from storming back into the theater and pulling Violet close.

But it's no use. I spot her wandering through the garden, weaving between the trees until she finds me. The only light comes from the string bulbs on the tree in the garden's center, giving the place an otherworldly feel, but it's enough for me to make out the concern on her face as she steps into the shadow of my birch tree.

"Are you okay?"

"Fine," I mutter, pushing off the wall. I can't be out here with her. I need to be inside, around other people, not alone in the darkness where no one can see us.

"You're obviously not fine," she says as I step past her. "And I know why."

I freeze, then turn back to look at her, breathing hard. We stare at each other in the half light, neither of us daring to move.

Finally, Violet says in a quiet voice, "If you *had* asked me out, what would we have done?"

The question catches me off-guard, and against my better judgment, I answer. "Something like this." I shrug. "Like dinner the other night."

A smile ghosts across her lips. "That was fun."

"It wasn't a date," I snap, and any trace of a smile vanishes from her face.

"I know."

"Neither is this."

"I *know*." She looks hurt by my tone and I hate myself for it.

"Look, Vi, it's not that I don't want..." I screw up my face, rubbing my forehead in agitation, then let the air out of my lungs slowly. "When we started this project, your dad asked me to look out for you."

She cocks her head. "He did?"

"He specifically asked me to make sure you're okay. To take care of you."

"So that's why you've been pushing me away. Making sure I don't work too much, that I eat."

I frown, shaking my head. "That's not—"

"Stop." She lifts a hand, her brows crashing together in frustration. "I'm a big girl. I don't need a babysitter."

Hard to disagree with her there. I'd even said as much to Rich at the time.

But what I can't tell her is that I *want* to look out for her. I *want* to make sure she takes care of herself. Hell, *I* want to take care of her.

So instead I say nothing, and she folds her arms across her chest, staring at me, getting increasingly angry.

"You know what?" she says bitterly. "Maybe I *should* go out with Owen. At least he's man enough to tell me how he feels."

My blood simmers at the mention of him. At the suggestion that he'd be better for her than me. I grind my molars hard, feeling everything boil up inside me until I can't hold it in anymore.

"You want to know how I feel, Violet?"

She gives an impatient, exasperated shrug.

"I feel jealous and possessive." The words spill from me without hesitation. "I feel conflicted. Constantly horny. Ashamed and guilty. I feel... I feel fucking crazy."

"Crazy?" Her brow knits in confusion, and I realize in that moment that she's feeling a lot of the things I am, too.

"Yeah," I murmur. She looks just as lost as I feel, and I begin to soften. "I'm crazy about *you*."

She stills, her eyes wide as they move over my face in the darkness. "You're crazy about me?"

I give a defeated sigh. "What do you think?"

She swallows, her gaze falling to my mouth. "I think you should kiss me."

Oh, God. I'd give anything to do that. Literally anything. Except my friendship with Rich.

"I can't."

My heart jumps when she steps closer. "You mean you *won't*."

I shrug, because really, what's the difference?

She closes the gap between us. "Then I will."

And just like that, her mouth is on mine. Her sweet vanilla smell swamps my senses, the soft brush of her lips enough to make me howl, and when her hand touches my cheek, the world around me disappears. I'm lost to the taste of her, the feel of her. To the way the blood in my body rushes south, stiffening my cock and making my head spin.

The sound of a siren wailing nearby pulls me back to reality, and I stumble away from her, my pulse thundering.

"We can't, Violet." My voice is a desperate rasp I've never

heard before, but I'm barely holding on. I reach for the one thing I know a good guy would say in this position. "You've been drinking."

She huffs in irritation. "I've had half a glass of wine. I'm hardly drunk, Kyle." She stares at my mouth, her chest rising and falling with her quick breaths. "I know what I want, and I'm tired of being treated like a child." She squares her shoulders, lifting her dark gaze to mine. "I'm a grown woman." Her voice becomes breathy, her eyes beg me. "Please treat me like a woman."

I take a step closer, intending to put a stop to this, but I can't. I don't know if it's the romantic feeling of this garden, the secrecy of the darkness, or that I'm a very weak man, but I kiss her again.

Properly this time.

21

VIOLET

I have never been kissed before this moment. I thought I had, but I was so, so wrong.

Kyle's mouth slants over mine, his tongue parting my lips. When it sweeps into my mouth, heat rushes my bloodstream, making my legs shake, my thighs squeeze together with need.

I wind my arms around his neck and pull him into me, stumbling back until I'm pressed against the brick wall. A low groan comes from deep in his throat as my hands thread into his hair. His fist goes to my ponytail, tugging, and my breath stutters against his. No man has ever done that before and I fucking love it.

I feel the heat of him through his shirt—a black tee fitting him perfectly, clinging in all the right places, the very bottom of his tattoo peeking out on his bicep. I'm not the only one who thinks he looks hot as hell tonight. I noticed several women checking him out inside, and hated every second of it. I wanted to stake my territory, pull him away from the crowd and steal all his attention for myself.

Mission accomplished. I can't believe he's kissing me—

he's *letting* himself kiss me—like this. Like a man who thinks this is his last night to live. A man whose time is running out.

I drop my hands to his ass, tugging him against me. A hard ridge in his jeans presses between my legs and I moan, rubbing myself on him shamelessly, desperate for friction. He's so hard for me, I want to weep.

His kiss deepens, long strokes of his tongue over mine, a frantic clash of teeth and breath as he grinds his cock against me, one hand tugging on my hair, the other propping himself against the wall above me. I can't breathe and I'm okay with it. I'd be happy to die like this.

Thankfully Kyle regains some control and lifts his mouth from mine. I gasp in a breath as his lips move along my jaw, down my neck, below my ear. His beard is a rough scrape on my collarbone, sending goosebumps scattering across my skin, making all the nerve endings fire in my body.

"I've wanted this since the day we met," I pant, quivering as his lips make a trail to my shoulder.

He gives a dark chuckle against my skin. "You're not the only one."

I take his face in my hands, forcing his gaze to mine. I hope he can see just how okay I am with this—*more* than okay. My panties are soaked through, I'm so wet and ready for him. It's dark in this garden. We're alone. Would it be insane for him to push my skirt up, unzip his jeans, and fuck me right here? I need it more than I need air right now.

As if reading my thoughts, his mouth curls into a dirty grin. His hand slides down, hooking my thigh over his hip, giving him better access.

"Ohhh," I moan, grinding against the hardness behind his fly, dizzy with need. Each thrust of his hips brings me closer, my mouth finding his neck and sucking on the soft skin below his beard. His woodsy, earthy smell fills my nostrils as I work myself against him, hands gripping his back, so high I never want to come down.

"Fuck yes, sweetheart." Kyle's voice is a rough growl in my ear. "Get off on me."

Something about his command pushes me to the edge. "Oh God, I think I'm going to—"

Light floods the garden and Kyle lurches back. I tug my skirt into place, my cheeks hot as I try to make sense of what's happening. I hadn't realized the music had stopped; people stream out of the theater with drinks in their hands, talking excitedly. The band must have finished their set.

My gaze darts to Kyle, my heart galloping as I try to catch my breath. He discreetly adjusts his crotch, his posture awkward, refusing to meet my gaze. Luckily no one seems to have noticed what we'd been doing, but I don't really care. What I care about is how Kyle won't look at me. The dark flush of red on his cheeks, the way he's hanging his head in shame.

Come back to me, I want to whisper to him. I want to pull him close again and press my face into his chest, rub a hand over his back to tell him we haven't done anything wrong. And I could. We don't know anyone here. But everything in Kyle's body language tells me not to go near him.

I hover by the brick wall, uncertain. I don't want to push him, but I can't leave things there. He finally admitted how much he wants me. He had me on the brink of orgasm, for fuck's sake. I can't just smile and go back in to watch the band like nothing happened.

I force out a heavy breath, pushing away from the wall. The garden feels suffocating and I need space to think.

I step through the arched doorway and out to the path

beyond, not bothering to see if Kyle is behind me. This won't end well, because he won't let it. He won't let *himself*.

Manhattan glitters across the river, a picture-perfect postcard laid out before me. To my left the Brooklyn Bridge looms large, an imposing tower of brick with cables that stretch across the water, sparkling against the black backdrop of night. I turn and wander toward the Bridge, my thoughts spiraling, my body still thrumming. I've never felt so exhilarated, so intoxicated—and it's *not* from the half a glass of wine. It's from Kyle's body, pressed to mine. It's from the way he let himself lose control, just for a moment, to take what he wanted. It's from his words—*Fuck yes, sweetheart, get off on me*—that make me whimper, remembering them. No man has ever said anything so filthy to me; no man has ever instructed me to take my *own* pleasure. It's always been about theirs.

I shiver, even though it's not cold, and wrap my arms around myself as I gaze up at the bridge in all its glory. Despite everything, I can't help but appreciate how beautiful it is. What a feat of engineering it must have been in its day.

I feel a presence beside me, and don't have to look to know it's Kyle.

"It was the longest suspension bridge in the world when it was built," he murmurs after a long, painful pause.

I sigh, my heart heavy. Kyle might be insanely good-looking in that sexy older man who commands a room kind of way, but it's more than that. It's his love of history, his passion for old buildings. It's the way he cares for me when I need it—like the fact that he likely followed me right now so I wouldn't be alone out here in the darkness. So I'd be safe.

Unless...

I turn to him, searching his face. "All those times you

looked out for me; when you built me a desk, when I cut my hand, when you made me take a night off work... did you do all that because Dad asked you to?"

"No." Kyle finally lets his gaze meet mine. "I did them because I wanted to. I care about you."

I nod. I believe him. Because I care about him too.

"I also care about your dad."

My heart sinks. I know what he's going to say, and I don't want to hear it.

"And if he knew..." Kyle shakes his head, casting his gaze out over the water.

"But..." God, this is frustrating. "I get it might be awkward for Dad, but also, you and I are both adults. Why would you even have to tell him?"

Kyle's gaze whips to mine. "Because I would."

"So you're going to tell him we kissed?" I press. "You're going to tell him you had me pinned against a wall, that you almost made me—"

"*No*," Kyle cuts in emphatically. "We stopped before anything happened."

"It doesn't feel like it. It feels like something already happened."

He wipes a hand down his face, looking agonized. "Well, we need to pretend that it didn't."

I huff incredulously. "I don't want to pretend, and I don't think you do, either."

"I'm going to have to." A muscle ticks in his neck as he glares at Manhattan, and I reach tentatively for his arm.

"Kyle—"

"I think you should go out with Owen."

His words stop me in my tracks. An icy coldness trickles down my spine. "Are you fucking kidding me?"

He turns away, but I don't miss the deep scowl on his

face. "No. I think..." I can hear the way he has to force the words out. "I think it's for the best."

I stare at the back of Kyle's head, fury churning through me. It's one thing to say nothing can happen between us, but to tell me to go out with another man—as if I'll simply follow his instructions? As if I don't have a say in my own feelings? My own needs?

I want to scream at how stubborn he's being, but I know that won't help.

I feel jealous and possessive...

His words ring in my ears, and I clench my fists in irritation. I think of the way he practically pushed Owen out the front door, the anger that flashed in his eyes when I told him Owen had asked me out. I think of the way he kissed me back there, how hard he was for me, how he was getting off on me getting off. He's wrong—*we* didn't stop it, we were forced to stop. Who knows how far it would have gone if the lights hadn't come on.

No. He doesn't want me to go out with Owen at all.

I know what I need to do. What might finally force him to act like the powerful, decisive man I know he is.

"Okay," I say at last, trying to keep my voice even. "I was waiting to see if anything would happen with us, but since it won't... I think I will go out with Owen. He was cute." He certainly wasn't bad looking, even if the thought of him does nothing for me. Still, he was nice enough. Spending an evening with him won't exactly be painful.

Not for me, anyway.

Kyle's shoulders stiffen at my words. I wonder if he was expecting more of a fight from me.

Well, he's not going to get it.

"In fact, I'll message him now." I pull my phone out, opening my inbox. Owen's email is still there, unanswered, and I take a deep breath. I send off a reply apologizing for not responding sooner, telling him I'd love to see him and that I'm free tomorrow night. I ask him to text me. "Done."

Kyle still stands with his back to me, hands in the pockets of his jeans as he stares at the river. His posture gives nothing away, but that's okay. I'll need to really call his bluff here, to go out with Owen, and make him see I'm not kidding around. I don't want to play games; I'd much rather that Kyle simply stop fighting this and come home with me now, but this is the way he wants to do things. And I'm not giving up on this, not after getting a taste back in the garden. We practically mauled each other. I've never felt a need for someone so badly, and I'm not going to forget about it now.

22

KYLE

Violet doesn't stay to see the rest of the show. I offer to walk her home, or order her an Uber, but she insists on walking home alone. I want to follow her to make sure she's safe, but I know that's the last thing she wants.

I'm tired of being treated like a child.

Is that what I've been doing? Worrying about her, looking out for her, refusing to lay a finger on her?

Well, that all went to hell tonight, didn't it?

I take a cab to Fruit Street and let myself into the house. Violet isn't back yet and it makes me uneasy, but I force myself up to the top floor all the same.

I know I won't sleep. I can't stop thinking about what happened in the garden; I'm still shaking from it. The way her tongue tangled with mine, the way she pulled me hard against her, the feel of her softness against my stiff cock as she wrapped her leg around me. And, God, the wet patch on the crotch of my jeans that I noticed when we jumped apart. I wasn't sure if it was from me or her. When I think about the fact that she almost came, grinding on me right there in the garden, my dick throbs in my jeans.

But I'm not going to jerk off tonight. Tonight, I'm going to sit with the shame of what I've done, dry humping my best friend's daughter in a public garden, for fuck's sake. I'm lucky the lights came on when they did, bringing me to my senses, or I might have just fucked her right up against the wall. It's like my self control completely evaporated.

But... I couldn't help myself. I've been fighting this so hard, when all I want is to have Violet in my arms, in my bed. I want to make her laugh, hold her close, make her feel good. Hell, I want a future with her.

I sink onto my bed and drop my head into my hands. I can't have any of those things, and I've known it all along. I would never be okay with betraying Rich, and it's probably already too late.

I try to tell myself it's not; after all, we *did* stop, and it won't happen again. It can't, because I did the stupidest thing I could have possibly done—I told her to go out with Owen. Smooth, shiny, age-appropriate Owen. I thought she might protest a little more, maybe say she wasn't interested in him, but she didn't take much convincing at all—even contacting him on the spot.

So that's that. She's going out with him and I have no one to blame but myself. I have to force myself to accept something that makes me want to vomit.

I take out my phone and, with shaking hands, send off the letter of recommendation I drafted for her earlier today. I'd hesitated to send it, for reasons I didn't want to acknowledge, but after letting myself get way too close tonight, I know it's the right thing to do. The sooner we can get back to our normal lives, the better.

At least, I really want to believe that.

The sound of the front door closing downstairs makes my shoulders sag with relief. At least Violet is home safe. Now I can get some sleep.

But I don't sleep a wink. Everything has changed tonight, and I'll never be the same man again.

23

VIOLET

I wake up to a text from Owen—a little too eager, if you ask me—saying he'd like to take me to dinner tonight. We make plans for him to pick me up at eight, which gives me plenty of time to pop out and buy a new dress, then put extra effort into my hair and makeup.

Not that I'm doing any of it for Owen.

Guilt twists through me as I curl my hair in the bathroom mirror. It's probably not fair to drag Owen into this, to use him to get Kyle's attention. I might not be interested in him, but he's not a bad guy. He doesn't deserve to be led on. I make a mental note to ask Sadie if she has any single friends I could introduce Owen to after tonight. Or maybe that barista from Joe's, Daisy. She's about our age, and she might hit it off with Owen.

Today was awkward as fuck. True to his word, Kyle behaved as if nothing happened between us last night. He wouldn't look my way, and he barely said two words to me, but that's not unusual for us. I tried to stay out of his way, and spent the day in the yard, ripping out more weeds, with gloves on this time. I made sure to avoid the ladder, too.

Kyle couldn't have left the house any faster when the workday ended, but I was relieved to have the place to myself. Now I'm putting the finishing touches on my look for the evening, hoping Kyle will be back in time to see me off.

There's a flicker of doubt in my chest and I glance at the stairs. What if he doesn't come home at all tonight? Or worse, what if he lets me go out with Owen without putting up a fight? What if it's all for nothing and this is it—he just lets this go? Just lets *me* go?

I glance in the mirror to apply my lipstick—I'm going for a bold, crimson red to really highlight my pout—fortifying myself. I know Kyle wants this as much as I do. He can only hold out for so long, and once he gives in... Fuck. That will be worth everything. I have to trust that he'll do what needs to be done.

I stand back from the mirror, admiring my reflection. I've styled my hair into loose curls, highlighted my brown eyes with a subtle cat's eye, and I'm wearing a scarlet-red dress with babydoll sleeves, a ruffled hem that skims mid-thigh, and a deep V to show off my cleavage. Strappy black heels complete the look. I wasn't sure about the dress, but since Kyle told me I'm beautiful, I've felt so good. Or maybe it's the way he looks at me—the way he touched me last night. Whatever it is, I've felt a lot more comfortable in my skin lately.

I grab my little black purse and head for the stairs. I haven't heard Kyle come in, but it's almost eight so I might just have to miss him. Maybe he'll be here when I come home. Or maybe I'll take a pic of myself and Owen, and send it to him. Would that be too cruel?

I sigh as I ascend the stairs to the entry hall. My keys are on my desk, so I head into the parlor, only to find Kyle sitting in one of the fold-out chairs with a book open on his lap.

My heart leaps at the sight of him, whether it's because I thought I was home alone, or just because it's him, I don't know. Either way, I purposefully slow my walk across the room, adding a deliberate sway to my hips as I wait for him to notice me.

He doesn't even look up.

Well, whatever. I snatch up my keys in frustration. If he's going to be like that, then so be it. I'm going out with a cute guy tonight, and even if I'm not exactly looking forward to it, who knows? It could be fun.

I'm almost out of the room when the sound of Kyle's voice freezes me in place.

"Are you really going out like that?"

I slowly turn to throw him a look over my shoulder. "Is there a problem?"

Kyle's intense gaze rakes across me, drinking in my shoes, my dress, my hair. I feel a flicker of satisfaction when his eyes finally meet mine again, dark and fiery.

"I haven't seen that dress before," he says, his voice a low rumble.

"Well, you should have asked me on a date."

He ignores me, motioning to my outfit. "I don't think that's appropriate."

I give a snort of irritated laughter. How dare he? "Now you sound like my father."

His jaw tenses, a tendon pulses in his neck. "Don't do this, Violet."

I cock my head, playing dumb. I know I'm being a brat, but honestly? I don't care. It's his fault I'm dressed up to go out with another man right now. I could be in his bed, but he's too damn stubborn to take what he wants.

"Do what?" I ask, the picture of innocence.

Come on, Kyle, I silently beg. *Tell me not to go. Tell me to stay with you instead.*

But he shakes his head, returning his gaze to the book. "Have a nice time."

I'm not prepared for the fury that boils inside me. "I will," I snap, spinning on my heel. "Don't wait up."

I PEER into the windows of Joe's, trying to decide if they're still open. It's almost ten, but the lights are on and Daisy is inside wiping the counter.

The date with Owen didn't last long; my guilt over being out with him under false pretenses won, and I blurted the whole sorry story out before our entrees arrived. He was surprisingly nice about it, but we decided to part ways after quickly finishing our meal. Well, he finished his meal; I sat there feeling awful until it was time to head back to the subway.

The funny thing is, he's exactly the kind of guy I would have liked in the past—clean-shaven and tidy looking, light-hearted and relaxed in nature—but I didn't feel even a hint of excitement when he met me outside the restaurant. Part of me almost wished I did—wished I could be interested in someone I'm actually *allowed* to like, someone who isn't my father's closest friend—but no amount of willing myself to like him made it happen. I was relieved when I could slip away, despite the fact I wasn't eager to get back home to Kyle. I figured I could stop in at Joe's for a while to make him sweat a little more.

Daisy spots me dithering about on the sidewalk and waves me inside.

"Hi," I say, pushing through the door, "I wasn't sure if you were open."

"I'm about to close up, but it's no problem. What can I get you?"

I order a hot chocolate, then lean against the counter with a sigh while I wait.

"I love your dress," Daisy says.

"Thanks. I just came from a date."

Her brow furrows. I know what she's thinking—it can't have been a very good date if I'm here, at ten o'clock, alone, but she keeps this to herself as she focuses intently on steaming the milk.

I laugh. "It wasn't meant to be." I pause, wondering if I should try to set her up with Owen like I'd considered earlier, but she speaks before I can say anything more.

"That's a shame. I think you two would make a good couple."

I falter. "Me and who?"

She looks up from the milk. "The guy who always comes in for a decaf cappuccino. The older one. Kyle, isn't it?"

Despite myself, I smile. "He wasn't my date."

Daisy's delicately-freckled cheeks color. "I just assumed..." she trails off, then continues when she catches my curious expression. "I got a vibe when I saw you two together, and I overheard you talking to your friend the other day. Sorry," she adds, and I shake my head.

"It's okay. You're right: there is something between us. Or at least, there should be."

Her eyebrows rise. "But there isn't?"

"It's... complicated."

"How so?"

I smile wearily. "How much time do you have?"

Her gaze drifts over the empty coffee shop and back to me. "If you don't mind me wiping tables and cleaning while you talk, I've got all the time in the world."

I laugh, sinking into a chair at a nearby table. "Alright then. He's my dad's friend."

Daisy nods, focusing on carefully pouring the hot chocolate. "So he's, what, twenty years older than you?"

"Eighteen," I correct. "I know that's a lot, but... I don't care." The truth is, I've never cared about his age, not from the moment I met him. I care about *who* he is—the man who looks out for me, who teaches me interesting things about the house and the neighborhood, who's reminded me what it means to have a life outside of my job.

"I'm not judging," she says kindly. "I've actually, uh, got a little crush on an older guy who's started coming here every morning."

"There's something about an older man that's so hot, right?" I grin and Daisy nods in agreement.

Fuck yes, sweetheart, get off on me.

Kyle's words from last night replay in my mind, sending a shiver of heat through me, and I add, "I bet they're way better in bed than guys our age, too."

Red streaks across Daisy's cheeks, and she glances away. "Probably," she murmurs.

I cringe inwardly at my big mouth. I hardly know her and here I am talking about sex like we're old friends. Sometimes I forget not everyone is as open about this stuff as Sadie.

"Well," I begin, trying to steer the conversation back to safer ground. "Maybe you should ask him out."

"Oh, no." She glances back at me with a sigh. "I think he's married. I just like to look."

"Bummer."

She sets my hot chocolate in front of me, and I look down to see the most beautiful latte art in the milk—two hearts made of chocolate syrup and foam, linked together.

When I glance up at her, she smiles. "Think of it as a little good luck for you and Kyle."

I can't help but smile back. We're going to need all the luck we can get.

"That's sweet, thank you." I press the lid onto the cup, almost sad to destroy her masterpiece.

Daisy picks up a rag and wipes a nearby table. "So what are you going to do then? About Kyle?"

"I really don't know." I fill her in on all the details—our kiss last night, how he told me to go out with Owen, and how I hope he's back at the house jealously waiting for me to come back from my date. "I like him so much—more than I've ever liked a guy before. I just need him to get over the stuff with my dad." Daisy nods, and I sigh, rising from the table. "Anyway, I guess I should head home."

"No way." She shakes her head. "You need to make Kyle realize what he's missing. Stay out late and make him think you're having a fabulous time. Make him lose it a little." She looks around Joe's, then back at me. "I think this place is clean enough. Are you hungry? I know a great burger place near here."

My stomach rumbles at the mention of food, reminding me I didn't touch my meal earlier this evening. "That sounds really good, actually. I'm starving."

Daisy grins in response, and I wait for her to turn off the lights and lock up, before we head out into the warm night air. As we talk over burgers, my mind strays to Kyle back at the house. Daisy's right—the date with Owen might have been short-lived, but no way will I tell Kyle that. I'll let him believe I had the time of my life, that I might even see Owen again. I'll tell him whatever I need to make him think he could lose me, to make him realize I should never have gone out with Owen tonight.

To make him realize I should be with him.

24

KYLE

Four hours. Violet has been out for *four hours* with Owen. What the hell could they possibly have to talk about for that long?

Unless they're not talking at all.

I think of that sexy red dress she wore when she left tonight, those heels that made her legs look so long and delicious, the way she'd obviously spent a lot of time doing her hair and makeup. She looked like sin, and no man would be able to resist her, least of all some twenty-something guy who wouldn't have a clue how lucky he'd got.

Bile rises in the back of my throat. I lurch from the chair, tossing aside the book I've been attempting to read since she left, and pace the worn floorboards.

They wouldn't be hooking up, would they? Not when less than twenty-four hours ago her mouth was pressed to mine, her hands were on my ass, and she almost came in my arms...

A strange cocktail of arousal and fury swarms my bloodstream and I stop at the window, peeking out onto the dark street. It was light when they left and now it's pitch black. What's taking them so long?

"Fucking hell," I mutter to myself. "Get a grip."

God, I hope she's safe. I figured Owen wasn't really a bad guy. A little shiny and polished, but some women like that. At least he cares about the preservation of historical buildings, I'll give him that much, but is he good enough for Violet? Can he take care of her in the way she needs? With that quick temper and smart mouth, surely she'd bulldoze him before he even knew what was happening.

No, she needs a real man. Someone who's strong enough, both physically, like that time I caught her when she fell off the ladder, and mentally, to match her quick wit, handle her sharp remarks, and bring out her playful side. She needs a man who knows how to worship a woman like her, knows how to touch her perfect body in just the right way and make sure she never feels the need to look for pleasure or comfort anywhere else again.

I turn away from the window and sink back into my chair, scrubbing a hand roughly over my beard. I bet that kid couldn't even grow a beard, he's so damn young.

Like her.

Fuck.

Dropping my head into my hands, I pull in a long, steadying breath. Jesus, what has happened to me? Last night I *told* Vi to go out with Owen. I told her that nothing could happen between us and I practically pushed her into his arms. Now I'm pacing the apartment like a possessive boyfriend, murderous at the thought of him touching her.

But it's more than that. I keep imagining worst-case scenarios in cruel, vivid detail. What if it's not that they're hooking up, but that something terrible has happened? My stomach hollows as I picture her alone somewhere, hurt, or—

The front door opens and I jump from my chair, relief flooding through me in a great wave. Then I realize how fucking pathetic I look, and drop back into the chair, snatching up my book and flicking it open as Violet enters the room.

"Oh." She stops in surprise in the doorway when she sees me. "You're awake."

I grunt, not looking up from the page. It's the same page I've been reading over and over since she left, four hours ago. I couldn't recall a single thing it says.

She sets her keys and bag down on the chair beside me then hovers, letting tension fill the space between us. She's waiting for me to ask how it went, and I'm not going to bite. The less I say to her right now, the better. I've spent the last few hours spinning out over her being on a date with someone her own age, knowing damn well it's exactly what should be happening.

Because I cannot date my best friend's daughter. That would be beyond fucked up.

I let my lungs deflate slowly. Now that she's here in front of me, safe and sound, I feel myself calming down. I was only worried about her being safe, that's all. She was out with a stranger in the city, and anything could have happened to her. It was making me a little unhinged, but now I can see she's fine. It was nothing more than concern for her wellbeing.

She folds her arms and cocks a hip, staring down at me. I diligently study my book, attempting to make sense of the words as her gaze bores into the top of my head. Her foot begins to tap the floor beside me.

Oh, she's good.

With a sigh, I set the book aside. "How was it?"

Satisfaction ghosts across her lips. "It was nice."

Great. Conversation over.

I nod and reach for my book again, as she adds, "He kissed me."

My grip tightens on the cover. Good thing it's a hardback. "He did?"

Of course he did. It was a date. And she's *gorgeous*. He had every right to kiss her.

Unlike me.

I crack the spine of my book and look down, but now I can't even make out the words. They're just a blur of black smudges on the page.

He *kissed* her. She kissed *someone else* tonight. It makes my chest tight and hot with jealousy. In this moment I don't even care that she's the daughter of my friend, I'm so consumed with this sick feeling inside.

I don't *want* her kissing anyone else.

So much for only caring about her safety.

"He did," she replies, not moving from her spot beside me. "He actually invited me back to his place..."

"He what?" I snap the book shut and jerk my head up in shock. "On the first date?" That little shit. I knew he was bad news, I just *knew* it.

Her eyes shimmer with mischief, and I realize exactly what she's doing. She's baiting me. She wants me angry. She wants me to snap and tell her I was wrong, that she shouldn't have gone out with him.

That she belongs with me.

Well, that's not going to happen. As much as it turns me on when she behaves like this—I've had more than one fantasy of bending her over my knee and showing her who's boss—I can't do that.

I just can't.

"I considered it," she says, watching me.

"Don't, Violet."

"You're the one who told me to go out with him."

I grit my teeth, rising from my chair. "You know why I told you to do that."

She looks up at me from under her lashes.

Goddammit. Don't give in to her.

"And why was that, again?"

I shake my head. Fuck, she's infuriating.

"Well." She lifts a shoulder, casually glancing away. "He asked me out again. I think I'll say yes."

My stomach drops. "You can't be serious."

"Why not? I have no reason to say no."

I clench my jaw, glaring at her. The thought of her spending another evening—or, fuck, the *night*—with that greasy little rat makes my skin crawl.

"Unless *you* can give me a reason," she adds, lifting her gaze to challenge me.

God, I love her like this. All bratty and smart-mouthed and needing nothing more than for me to teach her a lesson.

"I can't," I grit out, drawing on my last reserves of self-restraint.

She gives an impatient little huff, staring at me. Her teeth dig into her lower lip and my gaze becomes fixed on it—plump, pink, wet. I remember the way she felt last night in the garden, her teeth grazing my neck, her body soft and pliant against me, her eyes dark and needy, begging me to give her more.

What if I had? What if I'd brought her home and given in to what we both so clearly want? I have the sudden, vivid image of her under me, hair splayed out on the pillow, hands pinned beside her head, her pretty face contorted in ecstasy as I bring her over the edge.

Fuck.

No way is Owen going to be the one who gets to do that to her.

Violet sighs, turning away and heading into the entry hall. "I guess I'll go text Owen about our next date," she calls over her shoulder.

I stalk out of the room after her. "No. You won't."

She stops near the stairs and glances back at me.

Christ. What am I doing?

But I can't stop myself.

"You won't be going out with him again."

Her eyebrows rise expectantly. "And why is that?"

"You know why."

She gives a triumphant little nod, her mouth curving smugly. Fuck, she's so cocky right now and I can't take it for another second.

"Get over here, Violet."

She takes a step in my direction, but I'm too impatient after waiting for her all evening. I cross the entry hall and pull her into my arms, crushing my mouth to hers. She melts against me, moaning as I part her lips and our tongues collide. She tastes like wine, smells like sweet vanilla, and feels like heaven in my arms. My hands tangle in her curls as we kiss hard for a long, desperate moment, then I yank myself away with a low growl.

I should not be doing this. Rich's face flashes into my mind, and I drag an agonized hand through my hair. If he knew, he'd kill me. He'd fucking *kill* me.

I glance at Violet, wavering. It's not too late to put an end to it. I should do it now, before it really begins.

But the truth is, it began the moment I met her in Joe's. It began the moment she smiled at me, the moment I heard her laugh. It's a runaway freight train at this point, and there's nothing I can do to stop it.

I shake off the thought of my best friend, reminding myself how much it hurt to watch her walk out with Owen tonight. How much it killed me when I thought she might be going home with him instead of coming home to me. It instantly brings a scowl to my face, and Violet's brow creases.

"You're angry," she murmurs, and just like that, I feel myself soften. She can be such a ball-buster, it's easy to forget she has a vulnerable side. I think about her telling me she had a panic attack in class that time. I think about the way she cared for me when she hit me with her phone. She definitely has a soft side, and it makes me weak for her.

But I can't let that weakness in now. I can't feel soft and caring for her right now, because if I do, I'll realize what a truly terrible idea this is.

I force myself to harden my features. "I am," I say, stepping close enough that I can feel the heat coming off her. "Telling me you had a great time tonight, that you're going to see Owen again."

Something flickers in her eyes, an understanding of how we're going to play this, and she nods. "You don't like it when I talk about going out with someone else."

"Fuck, no." I lift a hand to stroke her hair, tenderly at first, then I catch myself and pull away. "Don't ever talk to me about another man again."

She gives an indignant huff. "Don't tell me what to do."

I let out a dark chuckle. "Oh, I think you'll like it very much when I tell you what to do, sweetheart."

She blinks, staring at me for a second. I can see her pulse thrumming in her neck, her chest rising and falling. "I think I will too," she breathes, her voice husky as she leans into me. It sends a shot of lust straight to my dick.

"You never wanted to go out with him, anyway," I say, more for myself than anything else.

"And you know what I want, do you?"

"I have an idea." My gaze falls back to her mouth and she shivers. "You want this." I lean down, brushing my lips over the warm skin where her neck meets her shoulder. It feels so good to finally have my mouth back on her that I take my time, tasting the sweet skin below her ear. Her breath falters as my lips move to her earlobe and whisper, "You need to be fucked by a man who knows how to do it right." Her mouth forms a perfect little O, and I chuckle. "You don't have to act so shocked. You just have to tell me I'm right."

She swallows, her pupils wide and dark. "You're right," she whispers.

"Good girl."

Her breath rushes out, a pink blush staining her cheeks. I hadn't meant to say that out loud, but seeing her physical response to those words—I'd bet anything she's already soaked by the way she's squeezing her thighs together—I can't help but give her a devilish smile. I'll call her whatever she wants if it gets her off.

I lean down to take her mouth again, leading her backward until she's against the wall. She hooks a leg over my hip and pulls me into her as her tongue meets mine. I'm tempted to slide that dress up her thighs, push her panties aside, and sink inside her right here, but if there's one thing

I've learned from last night it's that I don't want to fuck her quickly against the wall. I want to take my time.

I drag myself back from her lips, adjusting the throbbing ache in my jeans. Then I slide my hand into hers.

"Upstairs. I want to take you on my bed."

25

KYLE

Violet's eyes are round with anticipation as she follows me up the newly restored staircase. The layout of the top floor has changed since I moved in, now providing two bedrooms with a small bathroom, and my bed is in the farthest one, overlooking the backyard.

Well, I say 'bed,' but really it's a large, double-height inflatable mattress. I'd much prefer to be taking her on a four-poster bed in a stunning hotel room—or, God, in my own bed at home in Maine—but this will have to do. She doesn't seem to mind though, her gaze following me as I lead her across the room and switch on the lamp.

"Is this really happening?" She looks almost nervous, and it makes me pause. No matter how much I want to tear her clothes off and devour her, no matter how much I love playing with her, this will only happen if she truly wants it. I'd never make her do anything she wasn't comfortable with.

"Only if you want it to, sweetheart."

Her pulse beats in her neck as she gazes up at me. "I really do," she whispers.

I pull her close, my heart softening for her again, despite

all my intentions. This won't be a one-night stand, and that will make everything unbelievably complicated, but at this moment I don't care. All I care about is being close to her, to finally exploring this thing between us.

I turn her around in my arms, so her back is to my front, and sweep her hair off to one side as I slowly tug down the zipper on the back of her dress. The scarlet fabric slides over her arms, down her waist, then pools at her feet. I trail my lips along the smooth warm skin of her shoulder, breathing in her familiar scent. My heart is in my throat as she steps out of her dress, still in her heels, and turns back to look up at me.

"Jesus Christ." I slowly, reverently, skim my hands down her waist to rest on her hips. Her hair is a halo of gold around her heart-shaped face, her eyes glassy under dark lashes as she gazes up at me in her underwear and heels. She's a fucking wet dream.

I take her mouth in a torturously slow kiss. My hands slide to her arms, gently lowering her backward. Then I step back to admire her, sitting on the end of my bed.

"This isn't fair," she complains, pointing at me, fully clothed. "You need to take something off."

I grin, reaching behind my neck to pull my T-shirt over my head. It's not like she hasn't seen me shirtless before—I'd thoughtlessly peeled my wet shirt off the day we got caught in the rain—but she stares at me in delight like I'm the Rockefeller tree being unveiled. I can't say I mind the way her eyes gobble me up, the soft hum that escapes her lips as she looks her fill.

But I'm getting impatient.

I kneel at her feet, undoing the straps of her shoes one by one and setting them aside. As sexy as it would be for her to leave them on, I can see them puncturing the air mattress and ruining the moment. Because no way will this be slow and gentle lovemaking. I'm going to ruin her. I'm going to fuck her so good she'll never want another man again.

Christ. I shake my head to myself. *What are you thinking?*

But I know what I'm thinking. It's what I've been thinking since I met her, whether I could admit it or not.

I sigh as I let my gaze sweep across her beautiful body; her soft curves, a freckle on her stomach I didn't know was there, the skin of her thighs creamy and smooth in my hands as I part them and move between her knees. Her underwear is pale pink with tiny bows on it, one between her breasts, the other on the waistline of her panties, like she's a present for me to unwrap. Except, instead of it being my birthday, it feels like I've won the damn lottery.

I slide my finger under the strap of her bra, frowning as I imagine Owen getting to undress her tonight instead of me. The thought makes me want to put my fist through the wall.

"I can't believe you wore this for another man," I growl.

Violet tilts her head, looking at me like I'm an idiot. "I *didn't.*"

I meet her gaze and her meaning becomes clear. She never intended for anything to happen with Owen tonight. It was all a show to get me to give in to her. That's why she dressed up like this, why they stayed out so late. Hell, I bet she didn't even kiss him. She just wanted to make me pay for telling her to go out with him in the first place.

And pay, I did.

I reach around and unhook her bra, watching as she slowly pulls it off and tosses it aside.

Oh, fuck. I have no words for how beautiful she is. There's a slight blush on her cheeks, the pink perfectly matching the rosy buds of her nipples. I stroke a thumb over one and she shivers, arching into my touch. When I take one of them in my mouth, it stiffens as I circle my tongue over the peak. She moans, threading her hands into my hair, parting her legs further. I can feel the heat pouring out of her and it's an invitation I can't refuse.

I lower my hand between her thighs, my cock jumping at how soaked her panties are. She whimpers as I apply a little pressure, and tries to grind against my palm.

"You're so fucking wet, sweetheart."

Her blush deepens. "Now do you finally understand how badly I need you?"

"I'm sorry I made you wait," I whisper into her neck as I gently cup the damp fabric. "I wish I'd had the chance to ask you out the day we met."

She sighs, stroking a hand over my beard, her eyes deep pools of longing as they search my face. "Me too, but you're worth the wait."

Fuck. I close my eyes as her words pierce something in my chest—something I don't even want to think about right now.

I press my mouth to hers, sweeping my tongue over her bottom lip as I slide a finger into the waistband of her panties to tug them down. I have to break the kiss and move back for her to shimmy them off, and impatience has me forcing her legs apart again the moment she's done. Her brows jump at my aggression, but I don't miss the spark of excitement in her eyes, the way her breath hitches in response. Good to know she doesn't mind me getting rough; I can't promise I'll always be gentle with her.

My hands skim down her thighs, spreading her open for me on the edge of my bed. I take in the perfect triangle of blonde hair, her pink, glistening slit. My dick is a heavy ache in my jeans, begging me to get in there, but I need to taste her first. I need to make sure she definitely knows I was worth the wait.

She watches as I slide a finger through her wetness, then bring it to my mouth. Her sweet, musky taste hits my tongue and I groan my appreciation. I lower my mouth between her thighs and lap at her sweet pussy, feeling her spasm against my mouth.

"Oh, fuck," she mutters, trying to clamp her legs closed. It's a reflex, I know, but I'm not having it.

"Keep them open," I growl, pushing her down onto the bed, pressing her thighs back so she's completely exposed for me. And I begin in earnest, covering her with my mouth, drinking her sweet flavor, working my tongue through her slick folds. I pin her legs open, loving how she's completely at my mercy as I suck on her clit, gently dragging my teeth over the sensitive flesh. I know she doesn't mind because she's moaning in response, her hands in my hair again, her hips rocking up to meet the movements of my mouth.

"Oh my God, Kyle, yes."

She tugs on the strands of my hair and my cock flexes in response. I release her legs, pleased when she keeps them spread for me, to relieve myself from the pressure of my fly. If I rub against that any more I'll come in my jeans like a fucking teenager.

I strum her clit with my thumb, then push a finger inside her wet channel, watching as her eyes roll back. It's only one finger, but she's tight as hell, and my cock pulses at the thought of being inside her.

"You have the most perfect pussy," I murmur into her skin. I can feel her tightening around my finger as I alternate sucking her clit and stroking it with my thumb. I press another finger into her and she moans loudly, her body beginning to shake. "You like that, sweetheart?"

"Yes," she rasps as my fingers curl up inside her. "Yes, yes."

"I want you to come for me."

She throws her head back on the bed, her body arching into my touch, the first whispers of her orgasm taking hold.

"Look at me, Violet. I want to see your pretty face when you come."

Her head snaps up, dark eyes meeting mine, lips parting as she pants out her pleasure. "I'm… I'm so close."

"I know," I say gruffly, reaching to pinch her hard nipple, my other fingers drilling her soaked center. I've never felt as intoxicated as I do right now, making this woman feel good. I'd spend forever doing this if she'd let me.

"Yes." Her hips begin to buck and I know she's almost there. "Yes, oh my God, yes."

"That's it." I trail my mouth up her stomach as she quakes against my busy hands. "Be a good girl and come for me."

"Ohhh—"

She tips over the edge and I capture it with my mouth, wanting to feel her orgasm on my tongue, to taste her pleasure. I lap up her wetness eagerly, her taste hastening the urgency I feel to be inside her.

The moment her aftershocks subside, I rise to my feet and shuck my pants, my dick so hard it hurts.

"You're amazing," Violet slurs from the bed, sitting up woozily. "I'm still shaking."

I give her an unabashed grin, feeling unreasonably proud. I don't think anything will top the feeling of making Violet come. It's a high I wasn't expecting.

Her gaze fastens on my stiff cock, her lips curling as she leans forward to take hold of me. Her touch sends sparks shooting down my limbs, heat coiling low in my abdomen. She strokes my length, looking up at me with dark, hungry eyes, and my knees nearly give way. The sight of my cock in her beautiful hands almost makes me come on the spot. I suck in a breath, trying to stay in control.

"I'm not very… experienced," she says, stroking me shyly. We don't often speak of the age difference between us, but I know that's what is running through her mind right now.

"Fuck, Violet, I don't care." I thrust into her hand, then stop abruptly, feeling a flicker of panic. "Wait. You're not a virgin, are you?" Why didn't I consider that before? Why didn't I *ask*?

"No." She smirks up at me. "Sorry to disappoint."

A laugh rumbles in my throat, relieved. "That's not what I meant. I just didn't want to…"

"Steal my innocence?" she says, with a jerk of her wrist that makes me groan.

"You're a lot less innocent than you look."

She gives a throaty giggle, swiping her thumb over the tip of me to collect the bead of precum that's gathered there. I watch as she licks it off her thumb, keeping her gaze riveted to mine.

Jesus Christ. I don't know how much longer I can wait.

She leans forward, looking as though she's about to take me into her mouth, and I force myself to step back, out of her reach.

"Hey," she protests. "I want to—"

"Violet," I warn, my patience waning fast. I'm about to throw her down on the bed and take what I need without waiting another second. Not that I think she'd complain.

"But—"

I shake my head. "I need to be inside you, sweetheart."

Her breath stutters at my words, and she nods. "Okay."

She wriggles up the bed, and I go to climb on beside her, then freeze.

Goddammit.

"I don't think I have a condom." I rub a hand over the back of my neck, feeling unbelievably annoyed at myself. How could I have been so stupid?

But I didn't exactly plan this, did I?

"I do," she says. "But I'm on birth control. And I'm healthy. Are you…?"

Oh, holy Christ. Is she suggesting what I think she is?

I nod, trying not to appear too eager. "I had a full health check a little while ago."

"Then…" She bites her lip adorably, giving a little shrug. "Maybe we don't need anything?"

My head falls forward in disbelief. The thought of being bare inside that sweet pussy is almost too much.

"Unless you want to use one, of course," Violet adds, misinterpreting my response. When I look up she's eying me uncertainly, and my chest tightens.

"I want nothing more than to feel you," I whisper, lowering myself onto the bed. What I don't say is how worried I am that once I do, nothing will ever compare again.

I climb over her, nudging her legs open with my knees. She looks up at me breathlessly as I position myself at her entrance, my heart thundering. She's so beautiful, I almost can't believe she's here, giving herself to me. That I get to be with her.

"I need you so badly," she murmurs, and with that, I thrust into the wet heat of her. She lets out a long, breathless moan, and I swallow it down with my kiss as I attempt to sink deeper.

"Fuck," I grunt between shallow thrusts. "You're so tight,

sweetheart." She spreads her legs wider, trying to invite me deeper, and slowly, I feel her take all of my length. I have to fight the urge to pound her recklessly, pausing to examine her face, to check that I'm not hurting her. She's panting and trying to move on my dick.

"Oh my God." Her fingernails score my back. "You're so much bigger than I realized."

Well, if that doesn't give me an ego the size of Brooklyn, nothing will.

I give a slow roll of my hips, bringing my mouth back to hers. "Does that feel good, baby?"

"Yes," she breathes. "So good."

I slide my hands behind her to grip her ass as I rock into her, and she moans into my shoulder, biting my skin. Everything about her is pushing me further away from my self-control, and I know it won't be long before I snap.

"I've thought about this so many times." Violet's lips move to my ear, her teeth grazing my lobe as I thrust into her. "I made myself come thinking about you."

Jesus Christ. That's it.

I growl as I rise to my knees, forcing her thighs back so I can get deeper. "You thought about me fucking you? Making you come on my cock?"

"Yes." She nods, her breath catching as I increase my pace.

"You touched that sweet little pussy and imagined my tongue?"

"Yes." Her eyes press closed and I growl again.

"Look at me, Violet. Watch me fuck you." When she brings her gaze back to mine, I pump harder. "Good girl."

"I love how bossy you are," she rasps, eyes hazy and unfocused, cheeks flushed with pleasure. "It drives me nuts when we're working together, but right now, I love it. I love how you're taking what you want."

I slow my thrusts, lowering myself to claim her mouth with mine. "What I want is you. You're all I can think about. You're all I want."

"Then take me," she whispers. "However you want me, take me."

I press my forehead to hers, my breathing ragged. I tell myself it's from the sex, but the squeeze in my chest tells me it's more than that. I'm getting in way too deep, way too fast, with the last person I should be looking at, let alone touching, but I don't care anymore. I just don't fucking care.

As I thrust into her, I slide a hand between us to stroke her clit, desperate to make her come again. She wants me to take what I want, but what I want is for her to feel good.

"Yes, yes, yes," she chants, writhing underneath me. She tightens around my cock and I take her hands, pinning them to the pillow above her head. Her body shakes and spasms as I slam into her, trying to hold my own release at bay. It's only when her moans subside, when I'm certain that she's come, that I let my orgasm break.

"Oh fuck, baby." Waves of pleasure crash through me harder than I could have imagined, and a guttural groan tears from my mouth as I bury myself deep, gathering her close. Her lips find mine, our tongues merging as we both slowly come down from the high.

Then we lie there, limbs tangled, chests heaving with shallow breaths. She trails kisses over my shoulder, sighing happily, but my pulse won't slow down. It's not the sex, it's more. It's her. It's the feeling in my gut that I don't want to let her go.

But I have to, because she wriggles away with an embarrassed laugh. "Um, I'm going to go and take care of..." She gestures vaguely to her lower half, and I manage a gravelly laugh.

Shit, it's been so long since I've had sex that I've forgotten my manners.

"No, stay there. I'll get you something."

I pop into the bathroom to find a washcloth, my heart a steady boom in my chest. I expected the sex to be good, but that was something else entirely. That was like finding a lock for some random key that's been on my key chain for years, not realizing how desperately I'd needed to find where it belonged. The way Violet and I fit together… it's like she was made for me. Not only physically, but in every way possible. My heart knew it even before my body felt it, and now I've experienced it in the most carnal, primal way.

Fuck. I don't know how I'll recover from that.

I return to find Violet hovering beside the bed, and hand her the washcloth before turning away as she cleans up my mess. When I glance back, she's looking at me with her bottom lip tucked between her teeth.

"Should I… go downstairs?"

"No." I need her here, with me. I reach for her, tugging her down into my arms. "Stay. Sleep beside me." I nudge my pillow closer and she buries her face in it.

"It smells like you," she murmurs, smiling to herself.

I glance at our surroundings, at the air mattress and single pillow. At least I've got sheets, but still…

"I'm sorry we aren't somewhere more romantic." I press a kiss to her cheek and she turns to face me.

"Um, I was ready to fuck you up against the garden wall at a Rogue Valley concert." She gives me a sly grin that slowly morphs into a soft smile. "It's you I want, Kyle, not some fancy bed. As long as I'm with you, I don't care."

Oh, God. Sweet girl.

I stroke her hair. "Goodnight," I whisper, afraid to say anything more, but she's already dozing off in my arms.

I hold her close, hoping she can't feel the way my heart is jackhammering. Whatever this is between us, I have to find a way to make it last.

26

VIOLET

Golden light streams in and it takes me a moment to remember where I am when I wake the next morning, the heat of the day already beginning, even though it's early. Kyle's arm is slung over me, his head at an awkward angle without a pillow, and I wince at what that will do to his neck. I should have given him his pillow back.

I roll over to face him properly and he stirs at the movement. His eyes flutter open, his unfocused gaze landing on my face, assessing for a moment, then crinkling at the corners into a smile.

"Good morning, sweetheart."

Sweetheart.

My heart melts at his affectionate nickname for me. Every time he called me that last night, I fell a little harder. I knew the sex would be amazing—and I was *not* disappointed—but what I didn't expect was to feel so close to him, to feel... *things*.

"Good morning." I trail a finger down his bicep, studying the details of his tattoo. It's the silhouette of a moose surrounded by tall pines, the peaks of mountain ranges stretching above onto his shoulder. "I love this," I say, touching my fingers to the ink. "Does it mean anything?"

He gives a sleepy nod. "I got it when I moved to Maine. I was hiking one afternoon and came across a huge moose. It was October, which is their mating season, and a bull moose can be quite aggressive during that time. He wasn't pleased to see me."

"Wow." I stare at Kyle, enthralled. "What happened?"

"We had a sort of stare-down, and eventually he turned and left. I was lucky, but felt a weird kinship to this animal, alone in the forest, trying to go about his life without people getting in the way." Kyle shrugs. "The moment felt significant, so I got the ink."

"I love that." I trace a finger over the moose, wondering if I would ever get a tattoo, if anything would ever feel significant enough to permanently etch it on my skin. Nothing in my life has ever felt that meaningful. At least, not in a good way.

Kyle's eyes are a lighter shade of green this morning, hazy from sleep as his gaze moves across my face. I lift my head and shuffle the pillow closer so we can share it. It brings our mouths very close, and I lean forward to brush my lips against his, stroking a hand across the coarse texture of his beard. I know we have work to do, but I don't want this moment to end. I want to stay here and ask him more about his life in Maine, to feel his heart beating against my cheek as I lay it on his chest, to listen to the gravelly way his voice sounds after sleep. All these tiny intimacies I never get with him during the day.

I draw back to study his face, trying to read his thoughts. Part of me worried he'd wake up filled with regret, insistent that we had to pretend this hadn't happened, but the way he snakes his arm around my waist to pull me into him makes me relieved. I hadn't thought much past last night, but now I can't imagine not doing it again. I can't imagine going back to the way we were before.

In an attempt to express this, I open my mouth, but a bang from downstairs makes us both freeze. Kyle's brows slash together and he disentangles himself from me to reach for his phone.

"Shit." He bolts upright. "It's almost eight. The guys will be outside."

There's another noise downstairs, this time louder, and I chuckle. "I think someone is already inside."

Kyle's gaze darts to me. "How would they get in?"

"I gave Dale a key weeks ago," I say, clasping the sheet to my bare chest as I sit up. "I guess he's never had to use it because one of us is usually up."

"Fuck." Kyle scrapes a hand down his face, the color draining from his complexion. "You have to get downstairs without being seen."

"It's only Dale," I mutter, trying not to get irritated at the way he wants to suddenly discard me. "What will he care?"

Kyle shakes his head, swinging his legs over the side of the bed, fumbling for his work shorts. "Your dad hired him, Vi. If he sees us, he might decide to tell Rich."

"Couldn't we just ask him not to?"

Kyle grimaces. "You know how old fashioned he is. I doubt he'd find this"—he motions between us—"okay. He'd probably think I took advantage of you."

"But you didn't," I protest.

"*We* know that, but come on, Violet. I'm nearly twenty years older than you. He wouldn't be out of line to worry and tell your dad."

My blood turns to ice in my veins. "Shit, you're right." I

scramble from the bed, panic rising in my chest. I hadn't planned to fall asleep up here, but I was so tired, so comfortable and relaxed in Kyle's arms after he told me to stay with him. Honestly, it's the best I've slept in years.

But none of that matters now.

I find my bra and panties on the floor, my red dress at the end of the bed. Fuck. I have no choice but to put on my clothes from last night.

I frantically yank on my underwear, then snatch up my dress, all the lovely memories of the night before gone. If I can't find a way to sneak past Dale unnoticed, he'll catch me doing the walk of shame from the foreman's bedroom to mine. And if he tells Dad, then this—whatever this is—will be over. Kyle will probably never speak to me again, let alone touch me.

I wrench my dress into place and grab my heels, turning in bare feet to glance at Kyle. He's pulled on a tee, and his gaze softens as it moves over me, disheveled in my dress.

"Violet—"

A crash from downstairs makes us jump, and I glance at the stairs, my pulse thumping.

"How am I going to get past him?"

"I'll create a diversion," Kyle says, striding across the room. "Just give me a few minutes."

I nod, and he pauses in front of me to drop a kiss on my forehead. It's the lightest touch, but it's enough to reassure me. I watch him descend the stairs, taking a deep breath to calm my nerves. Part of me feels guilty for not being downstairs, ready to face the day, but another part of me—the satisfied, sleepy part of me that woke in Kyle's arms—has hardly thought about work since Kyle kissed me in the garden at the concert. That part reminds me of what Kyle said the night we went out for dinner; that I need to have fun outside of work. I think he might be right.

I tiptoe to the top of the stairs, straining to hear. Kyle greets Dale casually down below, and I inch down a few steps. After a quick peek onto the second floor, I can see no one is there yet, so I continue carefully down the staircase, listening to Kyle chat idly to Dale. When I don't hear anyone else's voices, I relax a little.

"Where's Violet this morning?" Dale asks, and I freeze. "She's usually up when I arrive, working away."

"She must still be asleep," Kyle responds. "I think she, uh, had a late night."

"Good for her." Dale chuckles heartily. "That girl works far too much."

"You're right about that."

I take another tentative step until I'm able to peek over the banister into the parlor room. Dale is standing with his back to me, and Kyle catches my eye as I creep down. If I'm quick, I might be able to dash across the entry hall to the basement stairs and be out of here.

But as I take another step, the ancient staircase creeks. I wince, my heart leaping into my throat as Dale begins to twist around.

"Hey—do you want some coffee?" Kyle calls loudly, catching Dale's arm before he turns. "I'll treat the team this morning. Coffee and bagels."

"Sounds good, boss."

Kyle pulls his wallet from his pocket, fishing out a handful of bills and stuffing them into Dale's hand. "Would you mind running down to Joe's to fetch them? I've got some things to do here." He sends me a quick look over Dale's shoulder and I hastily backtrack up the stairs, out of sight.

"Sure thing."

I wait, listening as Dale's boots move across the parlor floor, and the front door closes behind him. My breath whooshes out when Kyle calls,

"You can come out now, Vi."

"Thank God."

I wander down to find Kyle in the foyer, frowning. "That was close. We almost—"

The front door swings open and Ryan strides in, yawning. "Morning, all. It's going to be a hot one today, I tell ya." He pauses in the doorway as his eyes notice me in my red dress, clutching my heels in my hand.

Shit.

"Well, well, well." His mouth pulls into a smirk. "Someone's doing the walk of shame."

I glance from Ryan to Kyle, trying not to panic. Kyle's face is as white as a sheet, and I realize there's only one thing for it.

"Uh, yeah, I just got home." I give what I hope is a casual shrug. "I went out last night with that realtor, Owen?"

"Oh yeah. I remember him. Good-looking guy. Looks like you two had fun." Ryan winks.

"Mm," I say absently.

Beside me, Kyle grumbles something inaudible to himself. When I slide a look his way, he's scowling at the floor.

"Anyway, I'd better go get ready for work." I back away toward the stairs. "Excuse me."

Ryan chuckles as I head down to the basement, my pulse whipping through me. I quickly shower and change, trying not to think of how unprofessional I must look as I head up to the parlor room. By the time I get there, everyone has arrived for the day, and they're milling about, sipping the coffee Dale got from Joe's.

"Here you go, love." Dale hands me a coffee from the tray with a kind smile.

I take the cup with a nod of thanks and gulp down a few hot sips.

"Heard you had a wild night," Phil says, biting into an onion bagel.

I stuff some bagel into my own mouth so I don't have to answer.

"Owen is a nice enough kid," Dale says, smiling over his coffee. "You could do worse."

I chew my dry bagel, saying nothing.

"What do you think?" Ryan glances at Kyle, who's glowering at the box of bagels on the table. "Would Richard approve?"

Kyle snorts into his coffee, shaking his head.

My face flames red as the guys dissect my love life. Jesus, this is getting out of control.

Dale notices and pats Ryan's arm. "That's enough. You're embarrassing the poor girl."

"Thanks," I mutter, and attempt to steer the conversation back to work. "Okay, so, now the scaffolding is up, we've got the brick guys coming today to work on the façade. We've got tiling to do in the downstairs bathroom, and new hardware arriving for the kitchen installation down there."

I motion to my Gantt chart, feeling a little more in control as I shift back into work mode. We go over what needs to be done for the day, and the guys head off to work. Then I sink down into my desk chair, rubbing my forehead. Not a great start to the morning, but everything seems to be back on track now.

Except for Kyle's change in mood, but I can't worry about that now. There's work to be done.

I spend the next few hours following up on late orders

and finalizing the landscaper for next week. We're going with a local guy who has a company that specializes in small New York spaces. When I saw pictures of the work he's done, in yards similar to ours, I knew we had to have him.

By 11 a.m. I still haven't seen Kyle, and I can't distract myself with work anymore. Everything had seemed so lovely when we woke up beside each other this morning, but ever since I had to sneak downstairs, Kyle hasn't been able to even look at me. What if he's having second thoughts?

I check that Dale and Ryan are working in the downstairs bathroom, while Bob is outside talking to the brick guys, and sneak upstairs, looking for Kyle. Phil is varnishing the banister on the second floor, and I find Kyle in the walk-in closet in the front bedroom, fitting shelves.

I step into the small space, pulling the door closed behind me. Phil has his headphones on and didn't even notice me walk past, so we should be safe talking in here.

"Hey," I murmur, and Kyle glances over his shoulder at me.

"Hey, you."

I chew my lip, watching as he screws the shelf into place. What is it about a guy holding a power tool that is so hot?

"Are you... okay?" I ask, keeping my voice low.

Kyle sets the drill down and turns to face me, but doesn't say anything, just folds his arms and lets his gaze wander over me, releasing a long sigh.

I try again. "Are you having regrets about last night?"

He gives a slow shake of his head, fire igniting in his eyes. "Fuck, no."

I shiver at the low, rough edge to his voice. He glances over my shoulder at the closed door and steps closer, lowering his mouth to my ear.

"I haven't been able to stop thinking about how pretty you look when you come."

Jesus fucking Christ.

I huff out a breath, feeling hot and restless all over. God, I want him to kiss me. Immediately.

But Phil starts whistling out on the landing and Kyle growls under his breath, yanking himself away from me.

"You need to go."

I can't help but frown at his change in tone, and he shakes his head.

"You need to go, so I don't fuck you right here in the walk-in closet." He swallows, raking his eyes up and down my body. "Stay away from me for the rest of the day, okay?"

My frown deepens and he looks pained.

"Stay away and I'll reward you later, sweetheart."

Oh, God.

Anticipation tingles in my stomach at the thought of seeing him again tonight. I've never wanted the workday to be over more.

27

KYLE

I should regret it. I should have rolled over this morning, taken one look at the daughter of my closest friend lying naked in bed beside me, and been riddled with guilt.

But the only thing I felt when I saw Violet's sleepy face smiling at me from my stolen pillow—besides the stiffness in my neck—was happiness. A blazing, full-body joy I haven't felt in years, if ever. It's a sensation I never felt in the courtroom, or on completing a cabin renovation in Maine; a sensation I never felt with Lisa, even on our best days. It's a feeling of completeness I can't describe, something too intangible to put into words.

And just being able to reach out and pull her close, to feel her warmth and softness nestled in against me… it was impossible to dredge up any feelings of regret in that moment, despite what I knew I should feel.

It seems that what I *should* feel and what I *do* feel are two very different things lately.

The afternoon drags on forever. Dale and Bob talk about going out for a beer after work but I make my excuses. I asked Violet to give me space for the rest of the day because it's impossible to focus when she's in the room. Every time I catch sight of her, I think of her beautiful, naked body spread out on my bed. I think of how it felt to be inside her. How it felt to pleasure her.

But the day is long and empty without her, and after lunch, when Dale and I are discussing the kitchen installation for the basement and he mentions how happy Violet looks today, I have to hide my smile. By the time the crew finally leaves for the day, I'm torn between asking Violet out to dinner and just taking her on the floor of the parlor room. I should be exhausted after we were up so late together, but being around her fills me with energy and makes me buzz in a way I haven't for years.

I wave Dale and Bob off, impatient to talk to Violet. She's not in the parlor room, and a quick visit to the top floors tell me she's not there, either. I plod down to the basement, where Dale and Ryan were working today, but there's no sign of her. Unease snakes through me as I consider that maybe she was all too happy to give me space today. Maybe *she's* the one having regrets. She did spend the evening with a much younger man, after all. Maybe she's decided I'm too damn old for a woman her age—and I couldn't blame her one bit.

I notice the door to the yard is open, and tentatively poke my head out. Violet is by the back wall of the garden, a pile of weeds at her side. She's made good progress out here, even though it's not part of her job. I think she enjoys it.

She doesn't notice me, but seeing her makes me feel a hundred times better. I think of how she came to find me in the walk-in closet today, the spark in her eye when I told her I'd reward her later, and any doubts I have vanish. It might be unconventional for a young woman like her to be attracted to a guy my age, but she's made it very clear that she is. I can't explain it. I only know I'm a lucky bastard, and I won't waste any chance of being with her. Not anymore.

"Hey," I say, approaching her through the tangle of weeds that's swallowed up the old patio furniture back here. I rake a hand self-consciously through my hair, wondering if I should have showered or at least looked in a mirror before finding her. Probably, but I just couldn't wait.

She spins around, wiping the back of her arm across her forehead in the warm evening air. At least she's got gloves on this time. Her face lights with a smile when she sees me.

"Hey. Is everyone gone for the day?"

I nod, running my eyes over her. She's in a purple cotton dress with thin straps, her shoulders taking on an olive glow from spending more time out in the sun. It suits her. Her hair is pulled back in a ponytail again, like when we went to the concert, and I imagine pushing her up against the brick wall here to finish what we started that night.

But there's something I need to tell her first.

"Last night wasn't just a one-time thing for me," I say firmly. I've thought about this a lot today. I might not know what the future holds—and I can't even begin to think about Rich—but I can't pretend last night didn't change things for us.

She pulls her gloves off and tosses them aside, letting her breath out slowly. "Good. It wasn't for me, either."

A grin threatens my mouth, but I don't give in to it yet. "We've already crossed the line..." I pause, the words I'm not saying hanging in the air between us. "I don't want to go back. I don't think I could, anyway, after last night."

Her eyes shimmer as they move over my face. "Me neither." She pulls her bottom lip between her teeth. "But what about..." She gestures vaguely. It seems she can't bring herself to say it either, but we both know she's referring to her father. I ignore the spike of guilt I feel and step closer.

"Well, since your folks are out of town, maybe we could spend the next two weeks..." I roll my hand, searching for the right words. "Exploring whatever this is. We could take that time together, until..." I trail off, not sure what I'd planned to say. Until what—they come home and we stop? Could I even do that after two weeks with her?

But it's the best plan I have right now. The only plan.

She looks up at me as I close the distance between us. Her hairline is damp with sweat from working out in the heat, and there's dirt on her forehead, but I've never wanted her more.

"I like that idea," she whispers.

This time I let the grin win. "In that case, I want to take you on a date. A proper date. The one I should have taken you on all along."

Her smile is pure delight and excitement, and my chest tightens. I brush the dirt from her forehead with my thumb before lowering my mouth to hers. When I tilt my head to deepen the kiss, she pulls back, wrinkling her nose.

"I'm disgusting right now."

"I like you like this." My voice is husky as I bury my face in her neck to breathe in her scent and taste the salt on her skin. I drag myself away and motion to my dirty work shirt. "But I'm gross. I should—"

"You're delicious." Her hand fists in my shirt, tugging me back to her. "I like you all sweaty after a hard day's work. All *dirty*." She gazes up at me from under hooded lids, her lips curling into a naughty smile that suggests her words have more than one meaning.

"You like me dirty, huh?" I trail a fingertip along her collarbone and heat flares in her eyes.

"Fuck yes."

I let out a low growl and claim her mouth again, nudging her back against the brick and caging her inside my arms. Her fingers thread into my hair as she tilts her head, parting her lips. My tongue sweeps into her mouth and she welcomes it with a moan, stroking it with her own.

"Fuck, Violet," I rasp, already hard for her. "I've waited all day to have my hands on you."

"Then put them on me." She takes my hands from the wall, placing one on her breast, the other on her thigh. "Touch me." Her skin is silky soft under my palm, her breast firm and her nipple hard.

I groan into her mouth, stroking my thumb over the stiff peak through her dress, sliding my other hand up her thigh to the edge of her panties. "You want me to touch you here, sweetheart?"

"Yes," she breathes. She parts her legs for me and I can't help myself. I grind my stiff cock at the apex of her thighs, aching to be inside her. I should probably take her inside, but down by the back wall we're hidden from neighboring houses by the vibrant green foliage of the magnolia tree. I can't wait anymore.

"You want me to fuck you here?" I rumble into her neck. "Make that pretty little pussy of yours come in the back garden?"

She moans, lowering her hands to tug at my zipper. "Yes," she pants as my fingers hook into her panties and slide through her slickness. "Fuck me right here." Her hands slip into my boxer-briefs and grab hold of me.

Christ, she's amazing. She's a fucking fantasy come true.

"I love having your hands on my cock." My voice is raw as she strokes me, sending pleasure coursing through my bloodstream. I try to return the pleasure, but it's hard to focus with her perfect hands jerking me.

"And I love touching you." She quivers against my hand before tightening her grip on me. "I love how big you are, how hard you get for me. I've been wet all day thinking about you."

"Fucking hell, Violet. The mouth on you." I push two fingers into her moist tightness and she expels a heavy breath into my ear, letting go of me as she rides my hand.

"I need you right now." She pushes my underwear over my hips. "I need you inside me."

She doesn't have to tell me twice. I shove her panties out of the way and sink inside her with a low moan. She's tight and warm and perfect, and I let out a ragged breath as she hooks her legs around my waist, letting me hold her against the wall.

"This is what I wanted you to do in the garden at the concert," she says as I rock into her.

"You would have let me fuck you against the wall?" I change the angle and thrust into her hard, watching her bounce on my dick. Her eyes roll back and she can't answer with anything other than a nod. "I wanted to, sweetheart. Fuck, I wanted to so bad."

Her mouth finds mine, her hands digging into my hair as I pin her against the bricks, driving myself deep inside her. She sucks on my tongue, letting me pound her hard.

"You're such a good girl," I grunt between thrusts. "Taking my cock like this."

"I love it." Her nails rake over my scalp. "And I love when you call me that."

I draw back enough to see her face. "You love being my good girl?"

"Yes." Her voice is a breathy tremble, her cheeks flushed. She holds my gaze as she begs, "Say it again."

"My. Good. Girl." I punctuate each word with a deep thrust that makes her mouth open around a silent moan. Then I drop my mouth to her neck and suck on her soft, hot skin, my hand finding her ponytail and tugging. "Are you going to be a good girl and come for me, sweetheart?"

"Yes, I'm—" That's all she can get out before I feel her clamp down on my cock, shaking and shuddering in my arms. Watching the pleasure wash over her face sends me over the edge too. I plant myself deep inside her, crushing her to the wall as my orgasm rips through me and I fill her.

"Ouch." Violet's laugh brings me to my senses and I reluctantly withdraw from her, setting her down onto shaky legs.

"Are you okay?"

She rubs her shoulder and guilt lashes through me when I see the red mark left from where I had her pinned against the brick.

"Shit. Look what I did to you." I brush a thumb over the skin, then press my mouth to it in a soft kiss. "Fuck, I'm sorry, baby."

"I don't care." Her eyes are glassy, her mouth curved into a dazed smile. "That was..." She shakes her head as she gazes up at me. "I've never had sex like that."

I chuckle as I stroke a hand across her flushed cheek. "I swear, I didn't come out here to do that."

"I'm not complaining. We should end every workday this way."

My face drops to her shoulder as I gather her into me, imagining a life where I get to do exactly that. Would it ever be possible? Is there a world in which I get to be with her and keep Rich as my friend?

"I need a shower," Violet says, laughing as she squeezes her legs together to hold my seed inside her.

I like that thought, a lot.

I take her hand and turn to head back inside. "Let's clean ourselves up and get some dinner." I'm tempted to join her in the shower, but then I know I'll never leave the damn house, and I want to take her out.

She lets out a happy sigh as she follows me. "Sounds perfect."

I press a kiss to the back of her hand, then head up the stairs, leaving her to get ready. As I shower, I force dangerous thoughts about the future from my head. Now is all we have, and that's enough.

It will have to be.

28

VIOLET

"Tell me again why we're here?" I glance at Sadie, shielding my eyes from the midday sun. I'd planned to spend Saturday in bed with Kyle, but when Sadie told me she'd be in Brooklyn Heights, I knew I couldn't blow her off. I'm not sure if I should tell her about Kyle or just let it run its course during the next two weeks while Mom and Dad are out of town. Nothing can come of it, as much as I might want it to, so it seems pointless to even mention it to her.

Sadie motions to the store in front of us: a white-painted brick building with the words 'Books Are Magic' in bold script above the window. A line of people snakes out the door onto Montague Street, with us bringing up the rear.

"We're here so I can get these signed." She holds up a stack of romance novels, explaining that local author, Tessa Bailey, is here doing a book signing. "She writes the *best* sex scenes."

"Nice," I murmur. Sadie keeps talking, but I'm not listening—my mind has strayed to my own sexy scene in the garden with Kyle yesterday. We had a lovely dinner last night, and even more delicious sex, but there's something about the way he fucked me against the garden wall that afternoon, all sweaty and dirty and desperate to have me, that makes me shiver. And God, the way he spoke to me, the things he said...

"Um, hello?"

I blink, focusing my attention back on Sadie. More people have joined the line and Sadie has moved up a few steps, her head cocked in amusement as I hastily shuffle forward.

"What's going on with you? Thinking about work again?"

"Not work, no." I cringe, staring down at the sidewalk as my cheeks heat. I've hardly thought about work at all since the Rogue Valley concert, and I'd be lying if I said I didn't feel guilty. This project is supposed to be my top priority, but to say I'm distracted is an understatement, and since Kyle finally gave in and let me into his bed... the house could have burned down around us and I probably wouldn't have noticed. This isn't like me at all.

"What..." Sadie leans in closer, her eyes narrowing. "Is that a *hickey* on your neck?"

Oh, Christ.

I slap a hand to my hot skin, turning away from Sadie. *Did* Kyle give me a hickey? I didn't notice, but I do remember his mouth all over me last night. I stifle a giggle at how we've been acting like high schoolers since the crew left yesterday, unable to keep our hands off each other.

Sadie's wild red curls bounce as she laughs, attempting to get another look at my neck. "It is! Oh my God, Vi, what the hell?"

"It's... Um..." Ugh, she's not fooled for a second. "Okay,

yes," I say, lowering my voice and glancing at the line of people around us. "It might be a hickey."

Sadie's grin is as wide as her eyes. "Please tell me your dad's hot friend gave that to you?"

"Shhh!" I smack her on the arm. "*Don't* call him that. His name is Kyle."

"But it was him?"

"It... might have been." I'm trying for nonchalance but my mouth betrays me by hooking into a giddy grin.

She lets out a little squeal of delight. "I can't believe this! Oh my God. Tell me everything."

I give her a shortened version of what happened in the garden at the concert, the date with Owen, and everything that followed after that. Sadie is positively vibrating with excitement as we follow the line into the bookstore—a long space lined with bookshelves under a ceiling of solid oak beams.

"Wow. That is so hot." Sadie shakes her head in disbelief. "What about your dad?"

"My folks are out of town for a couple weeks. The plan is to just... I don't know, be together for that time, and then..." I trail off, gnawing on my lip as I contemplate what will happen, two weeks from now. Will we go back to working as we were before? I think of Kyle's words from yesterday—*I don't want to go back. I don't think I could*—and wonder what his plan is for when my parents return to the city. And we're both going back to our real lives in a month or so anyway, and...

I shake the thought from my head. I'm getting way too ahead of myself here. And more importantly, I've taken my eye off the goal: doing an awesome job with this project so I can secure a proper project management job afterward, and prove to my dad that his belief in me all these years hasn't been for nothing. Unease billows through me as I consider how distracted I've been.

"And then?" Sadie prompts, but we're at the front of the line now and she's distracted by handing her books over to be signed, and gushing all over the author.

I step back with a smile, watching my friend chat with Tessa as she signs Sadie's books. Sadie is one of those people who's always upbeat, always sunny and positive. She knows who she is and what she loves, and never feels guilty for having fun. Sometimes I wish I was more like her.

I wander through the bookstore, perusing the tables laid out along the center. A small book about Brooklyn Heights catches my eye. It's full of beautiful pictures of the neighborhood, with quotes from well-known writers who lived there, like Walt Whitman, Truman Capote, and Henry Miller. I flip to the inside cover, surprised to find it signed by the author, who is also local, and know instantly I have to get it for Kyle. A smile plays on my lips as I glance up to find Sadie turning away from Tessa. She's glowing as she weaves her way across the store, arms laden with even more books.

"That was so cool," she says when she reaches my side. "She was just as nice as I thought she'd be."

"I'm glad. There's nothing worse than meeting your hero and finding out they're an asshole."

Sadie gives a solemn nod. "Exactly. But she was awesome! They call her the Queen of Dirty Talk."

Dirty talk.

You're such a good girl, taking my cock like this... You want me to fuck you here? Make that pretty little pussy of yours come in the back garden?

Kyle's dirty words from yesterday flash through my head and I huff out a breath, feeling heat curl through me at the memory. No man has ever talked so filthy to me and it's the hottest fucking thing. Everything about him is hot, from the way he takes control in bed, to the way he holds me close and kisses me, feather-soft, afterward.

Sadie's eyes are glittering with mirth when I finally glance back at her. "You're thinking about Kyle again, aren't you?"

I chuff a laugh. "Is it that obvious?"

"It is," she says affectionately. "I said *dirty talk*, and you were away with the fairies. Does Kyle talk dirty?"

I nod, my cheeks warm.

"Ugh, I'm so jealous. I bet he likes to be in charge, too. He's a real stern brunch daddy."

I laugh again at that term. "Tim isn't like that?"

She lifts a shoulder, her gaze sliding away. "He's sweet, but sometimes I wonder if he's… I don't know, *enough* for me."

I frown. There's something in her tone that sounds off, and I open my mouth to ask more, but she pushes her mouth into a smile.

"Anyway, I want to hear more about Kyle. I bet you're hardly getting any work done at all now." She gives me a grin that's meant to be cheeky and playful, but her words bring the guilt back again.

"Actually, I have been distracted," I mutter, clutching the Brooklyn Heights book to my chest.

"Of course you have." Sadie leans against a table of books, eying me. "That's normal. I'd be distracted with that hottie walking around all day."

I give her a faint smile, and she sighs.

"Vi, you know you have… *issues* with work, right?"

"Issues?"

"Yeah. You always have. It's why we didn't really keep in touch when you moved away, and why I'm always on you to take a break. You let your career rule your life, and that's admirable, but it comes at a cost."

Huh. Kyle said basically the same thing to me that first night we went to dinner.

"I think it's great you're having a little fun with Kyle. Why not?"

I twist my lips to one side. "Because I—*we*—have a job to do."

"Sure. That will get done. I know you won't let everything fall apart. That's not who you are. You need to trust yourself a little more. Trust that you can do a good job on the project while also having a life outside of work. Work-life balance and all that."

You deserve a life outside of work too. Who are you when you're not working?

I think of Kyle's words at dinner, and realize Sadie is right. I've done nothing but work for years, to the exclusion of everything else in my life. I'm allowed to have fun, and it doesn't have to mean everything at work falls apart. I can do both.

Sadie's gaze drops to the book in my hands. "What's that?"

"Oh." I glance down. "Just something I thought Kyle would like."

Her mouth tugs into a knowing smile. "There's no way you're only in this for two weeks, babe."

29

KYLE

"I like this orange color," Dale says as he passes Violet in the basement. "I wasn't sure about it at first, but it's growing on me."

"Thanks, Dale. It's called Autumn Apricot." Violet grins, brush in hand. She chose a rich apricot for a feature wall in the basement, and it works well with the cream kitchen countertop and navy-blue hexagonal tiled backsplash. She had to remove her 'bedroom' from the basement when we started working on this floor, but it hasn't mattered—she spends every night in my bed.

Violet glances at me over her shoulder as Dale leaves the room. Admittedly, I wasn't sold on the color choice at first either, thinking it might be too much, but I'm glad she chose something bold. It works.

I told her she didn't have to paint it herself, but she's been very firm on using her work time pro-actively and being involved in a hands-on way. Even though we've never taken time out of the workday to spend together, I know she feels guilty about spending her evenings with me instead of working. It's like she's trying to cram twice as much work into her days to make up for it.

"I told you the apricot would work," she says with a satisfied smile.

I chuckle, wandering closer to the stepladder she's standing on. She's wearing her denim mini skirt and a black tank top, and with no one around I'm tempted to drag my lips over the exposed skin of her shoulder, to shove her skirt up and bury myself inside her.

"It works," I murmur, watching her paint. She's very careful, paying attention to every stroke of the brush, wanting it to be perfect. That's Violet.

I press my face to her shoulder, inhaling the sweet vanilla scent of her skin before pulling myself away and upstairs, where I won't get myself into trouble.

The past two weeks have gone way too quickly. It's like I blinked and they were over. One minute I'm kissing Violet in the backyard, telling her we have two whole guilt-free weeks together, the next Rich is texting me to say he's looking forward to getting back to the city and checking in on the progress at the house. I want to wind the clock back and start over.

I sigh as I head upstairs to find the guys taking their afternoon coffee break in the parlor. We've had the specialist come in to redo the plaster in here, and soon this area will be painted too. I stand in the doorway, proud of how far we've come.

"Looking good, huh, boss?" Phil grins from where he's lounging in a folding chair.

I nod. "Yeah. I'm really happy with the way we've struck a balance between the historical and the modern."

"You ever think about doing this full time?" Bob asks. He

holds out the box of leftover donuts from this morning and I take the last cruller.

"I *do* do this full time."

"Not in the city," Ryan points out. "This must be quite different from what you do back home."

Back home.

I think of my cabin by the lake, the place I yearned for when I first got to New York, but have thought about a lot less since I've had Violet in my bed. Kennebec County felt like home from the moment I moved there, but lately I've felt right at home here, with Vi. It's almost as though we've lived an entire lifetime in the last couple weeks, and I'm not sure I can go back to Maine, to the life I had before. To my life without Violet.

But what choice do I have? Rich and Diana return to the city today, and this has to end. I could ignore the guilt while her parents were out of town, but I don't think I could look Rich in the eye knowing I'm secretly sleeping with his daughter. I couldn't live with myself.

Besides, even if we didn't have the issue of Rich, things still couldn't be any more than they are. My life is in Maine, and Violet's life is on the West Coast. We said we'd spend two weeks exploring this, and now our time is up.

"Yeah, it's different." I tear off a piece of cruller with a frown.

"You have to admit it's nice to work on these grand old buildings," Dale says with a wistful smile. "So much history. I like to see them restored like this."

Ryan nods in agreement. "I'd be interested in working on more places like this. If you decide to stay in the city, I think we make a pretty good team."

I cast my gaze across the crew, all looking at me expectantly. "What are you saying?"

Bob chuckles. "We're talking about doing this on other houses. Starting a business that specializes in historical restorations in these old New York neighborhoods."

"Well, *you'd* run the business," Phil says. "We'd be the crew."

My eyebrows spring up in surprise. "You've discussed this?"

"Sure." Dale sets his empty coffee cup down. "We were all at a loose end before Richard hired us for this project. As good as it will be to see it finished, I'll be sad when it's over."

I scratch absently at my beard, contemplating the idea. They're a good group of guys, hardworking yet easygoing, and we do make a good team. But the thing that's made this entire project tick over so smoothly isn't us. It's Violet. It's her meticulous planning, her staying on top of every aspect of the project, her energy and enthusiasm. As much as I love these historical buildings, as much as I've enjoyed this project, I don't think it would be the same without her.

I finish my cruller, saying nothing. The guys disperse to continue working for the afternoon, and I trudge upstairs to sand the floorboards. Most of the work is done up here, so we're moving on to finishing the floors. I spend almost two hours sanding, lost in thought, before heading into the bathroom to wash the dust from my hands.

I stare at my reflection in the mirror above the sink, thinking about Violet. I've felt like a different man these past two weeks. There's a light in my eyes I haven't seen in a very long time, a smile that won't leave my mouth. Only now it's fading, knowing what's coming.

"There you are." Violet appears in the mirror behind me, smiling. "I've finished the last coat on the basement wall. It's going to look good."

I exhale, turning to lean back against the sink and

study her. She looks different lately, too—her skin is a darker shade of olive from working in the garden, her complexion pinker and healthier thanks to less time in front of her laptop, her eyes bright. All the sex is probably helping, but it's more than that. She's happy in a way she wasn't when she arrived here, and so am I. If only we could freeze time and live inside the past two weeks forever.

She glances over her shoulder to check we're alone, then steps closer, between my outstretched legs, sliding her arms around my waist. Her face tilts up to mine and I brush my lips over hers with a deep sigh, my heart aching in a way I'm not used to. A way I'll never get used to. I want to tell her that I don't want it to be over, not yet, but I know it will only hurt us both if I drag it out.

A buzz in my pocket jolts me from my thoughts, and Violet steps back, pulling her own phone out. We stare down at our screens in tandem.

Rich: We're coming out to the Heights this evening. Let's meet for dinner, the four of us, so you can update us on the house.

My shoulders sag with disappointment, which is quickly chased by guilt. I should be happy at catching up with my friend and his wife for dinner, but all I can think about is how this is it. I have to face Rich and I can't keep lying to him. I need to end things with Violet. It's the right thing to do.

I send a reply telling him we'll be there, then stuff my phone back in my pocket with a weighted sigh. I glance up to find Violet gazing at me, her eyebrows knitted, her bottom lip tucked between her teeth as she slides her phone away. She knows what's coming and she doesn't want it any more than I do.

"I'm sorry, sweetheart," I murmur, stepping forward to press a chaste kiss to her hair.

"Me too."

"It's just what needs to be done."

She swallows. "I know."

Her gaze finds mine and I weaken, lowering my lips to hers for one last kiss. But knowing it's supposed to be our last sends urgency flooding through my veins, and I haul her hard against me, devouring her mouth with mine. She whimpers, tightening her hold on me, and I reach past her to slam the bathroom door closed.

If this is the end, I need to make it count.

30

VIOLET

Our kiss is frenzied in a way it's never been before, tinged with desperation and haste. Our time is up and we both know it.

When Kyle shuts the bathroom door, I know his intentions. The crew is still downstairs, chatting in the parlor room before they pack up for the day, but he doesn't seem to care. Neither do I.

He plunders my mouth with his tongue, hands roaming my back, moving down to my ass, holding me against him. Somehow, in the space of a few weeks, he's become both my safe place and the person who makes me feel the most daring. I think of all the things we haven't had the chance to do yet, and my heart squeezes.

He moans softly into my mouth as my hands stray down his front to find he's already hard for me. I know what I want to do—what I need to do. I need to give this to him, to make him feel good, to leave him happy and satisfied once this is over, instead of riddled with the guilt I know he's carried for the past two weeks.

I drop to my knees on the tiled floor in front of Kyle and undo his zipper, letting his erection spring free from his boxer-briefs. Without wasting any time, I take hold of him and lick his salty tip, savoring his taste. His breath hisses out as I draw him into my mouth and swirl my tongue around the head of his cock.

"Oh, fuck." His hips rock, and he takes a handful of my hair, holding it back from my face. He doesn't force himself into my mouth, but I want him to. I want him to take everything from me.

I hold the base of him, taking as much of his length as I can to the back of my throat, gagging on his size. I know it's twisted but I want to suffer for him, want this to hurt, to know I've given him my all.

"Jesus." He gives a low growl as his cock hits the back of my mouth and I gag again. His hips thrust a little harder, driving him down my throat, and I moan, my eyes watering as he grips my hair tighter.

Good. I want him to use me. I want him to feel as good as he's made me feel these past two weeks.

His other hand comes to tenderly stroke my cheek as he thrusts into my mouth. "You are *such* a good girl," he rasps. Heat rushes to my center and I press my legs together, squirming with need at his words. Nothing will ever match the feeling I get from Kyle calling me his good girl. Is that fucked up? Probably. But I'll replay those words in my head every time I come for the rest of my life.

I look up at him, meeting his gaze as he fucks my mouth. His eyes are dark and wild, the rhythm of his hips becoming more frantic, and I expect he's going to come at any moment, but he pulls himself away.

"Holy shit, that was incredible. Almost made me come in

that sweet little mouth, but that's not what I need right now."

His hands cradle my face to tug me to my feet, and he takes my mouth in a bruising kiss. As his tongue scours mine, he yanks my panties down my legs with rough hands, tossing them behind him. Then he spins me around until my hands grip the sink, facing the mirror. He pushes my skirt up over my hips, his eyes finding mine in the reflection. Without a single word, he thrusts hard inside me, and ecstasy rockets through my body from head to toe. We stare at each other in the mirror, our faces slack with pleasure as he grips my hips and pumps into me.

"Fuck, Violet." Kyle's voice is a rough, breathless scrape in my ear. "You feel like heaven. Like you were made for me."

"I think I was." The words tumble from my mouth without a thought, but I realize once I've said them, that's how it feels—like I was made for him. Like he was made for me. Like we're made for each other.

Yet we can't be together.

My heart twists as his gaze sears into mine in the mirror, the same realization written all over his face. I drop my head and press my eyes closed to contain the emotion rushing up inside me, but Kyle takes my chin in his hand and gently tilts it up, bringing my gaze back to us.

He buries his nose in my hair, his front pressed to my back, his arms wrapped around me tight. His eyes are still on mine in the mirror, one hand fumbling to release my breasts from the front of my tank top. He rolls my nipple between his fingers and thumb, his mouth on the shell of my ear. The feeling of his hot breath sends shivers through me, and when he pinches my nipple and thrusts deep, my legs shake.

"That's it, sweetheart," he says gruffly. He knows my body like a book he's read a hundred times. His hand drops between my legs to stroke my clit, and I shudder as the pleasure builds in my core. "I need you to come for me. I need to feel you come one last time."

"Yes," I whimper, quivering against his touch. The intensity in Kyle's gaze spears me right through the heart, and I dissolve in his arms as my orgasm hits.

"There we go. That's it, baby girl." He gives another hard thrust, driving the pleasure into every cell of my being as he joins me in his release. Letting out a bestial growl he fills me with his liquid warmth, clutching me to him as we ride our orgasm together.

I lean on the sink, Kyle's heart hammering against my back as we catch our breath. He's still holding me, still inside me, his chin resting on my shoulder. I twist my head to brush my lips over his. I wish we could stay in this bathroom forever, but I know the real world is waiting for us out there. We're meeting my parents for dinner and there's no hiding from the reality of our situation any longer.

Kyle draws breath to say something, but a knock on the door has us springing apart. We glance at each other, eyes wide with alarm as we silently fumble to straighten our clothes.

"Be right out," Kyle calls, his voice shaky. I have no idea who's out there, or why they've come all the way to the top floor to bang on the bathroom door, but this is not good.

I glance frantically around the room, but my panties are nowhere to be found. Where the hell did Kyle put them? I have no choice but to pull my skirt lower and squeeze my legs together awkwardly to contain the sticky mess, wishing I had time to clean myself up.

Kyle takes a deep breath then cracks the door open.

After a quick peek outside, he pulls it fully open and we both take a tentative step out. It appears we're in the clear until we reach the landing at the top of the stairs, where Ryan is waiting for us with a shit-eating grin. My pulse scrambles at the sight of him.

"What have you two been up to?"

I swallow, glancing at Kyle, who wipes a hand across his face with a sigh of weary resignation.

"Whatever it was," Ryan continues, his expression growing serious, "you should probably know that Richard and his wife are downstairs."

My heart stops. "My parents are here?"

Ryan nods, eyes swinging between me and Kyle.

"Fuck," Kyle mutters to himself, the color draining from his face.

I gulp in a breath. I should be embarrassed about Ryan catching us, but that's the least of my concerns right now. "Do they know..."

Ryan shakes his head. "I told them you were sanding the floors, which is what I *thought* you were doing, or I wouldn't have come up."

Kyle looks at Ryan desperately. "Please promise you won't—"

"I won't mention it," Ryan says dryly, with a wrinkle of his nose that says he'd rather he didn't know himself. "It's your business, but you should probably come downstairs."

Kyle quickly smooths a hand over his hair and beard, looking at me. His eyes are ringed with worry, his lips pressed into a flat line.

So this is it. This is how it ends. We have sex in the bathroom like the world is ending and boom, it does.

Okay, I know that's dramatic, but that's what it feels like. For the first time in my life I have something outside of my job that excites me, that makes me feel alive, and I don't even get to keep it. I don't get to keep *him*.

My throat feels tight as I say, "I guess we should..." and gesture to the stairs vaguely. Kyle gives a grim nod, and I woodenly follow him and Ryan down the stairs, trying to ignore the way my heart cries out in protest.

31

KYLE

My stomach is in knots as I descend the stairs, knowing Rich and Diana are down there. Thank God it was only Ryan who found us, but even that's bad enough. I can't believe I was stupid enough to have sex with Violet upstairs while the crew was still here.

And yet... I wouldn't change a thing. I can still feel her in my arms, still see her face in the mirror when she said she was made for me.

Because she was made for me, I'm sure of it. She challenges me in a way that no woman ever has. She cares about the things I care about. And God, the way her body fits with mine... Yeah, she was made for me, alright. I just don't know how I can make it a reality with Rich.

We arrive in the entry hall just as Bob and Dale are leaving. I wave them off, noting Phil has already gone. Ryan mouths "good luck" as he grabs his bag and ducks out the front door.

"Kyle!" Rich appears in the entry hall, beaming. "There you are."

"Sorry. We were finishing the sanding upstairs." I'm disgusted by how easily the lie rolls off my tongue, then equal parts relieved and guilty that Rich accepts this without a second thought. Because he trusts me unequivocally.

"Di and I were just having a look around," he says as Diana joins us in the hall. She pulls me in for a hug then smiles as Violet descends the stairs behind me.

"Hi, honey."

"Hey, guys." Violet's cheeks are flushed a deep pink and she clears her throat, stuffing her hands into the pockets of her skirt as she comes to stand beside me. "How was the trip?"

"Wonderful." Diana clasps Rich's hand. "We had the best time. I'll have to share the photos with you."

"Sounds good." Violet smiles in a way that doesn't touch her eyes, her gaze downcast.

"What are you doing here?" I ask, trying to be casual.

"It's my fault." Diana laughs. "I couldn't resist popping in before dinner to sneak a peek at the place."

"It's looking fantastic," Rich chimes in. "You should both be so proud."

Violet's gaze clashes with mine, then slides away. "We are," she mumbles.

Rich smiles at us. "You two make a good team. We're lucky to have you."

I pull my lips into some semblance of a smile for my friend. My stomach is a tornado of guilt and shame as I think about the fact that we were just upstairs, having sex. My seed is probably still inside her at this very moment.

I sneak a glance at Violet. She shifts her weight, clamping her thighs awkwardly as we stand in the foyer.

Oh my God, I'm right. I should feel even worse about

this, but some sort of primal, animal part of me loves knowing my seed is running down the inside of her thigh. It's as if I've claimed her, made her mine, like I so desperately want to do.

Fuck.

I grind my jaw, hating myself. How can I want her *this* much and still be Rich's friend? He's like a brother to me and I can't imagine my life without him.

Only now, I can't imagine my life without Violet. And that makes everything a thousand times more complicated.

I SET my beer down with a sigh. Rich chose a Mexican restaurant on Montague Street, and even though the food is amazing, I can't appreciate it. Violet is quiet beside me, barely touching her food or meeting my gaze.

Meanwhile, I'm struggling to keep my eyes and hands off her. We showered and changed before heading out, and she's wearing the same white, off-the-shoulder top she wore to the Rogue Valley concert, her blonde hair falling in gentle waves onto her shoulders. Even with her somber mood, she looks radiant and beautiful, and all I want is to pull her close.

"What do you have planned for the long weekend?" Diana asks me as she swipes a tortilla chip through the guac.

I sip my beer, trying to get my thoughts in a row. "The what?"

"It's Fourth of July weekend in three days," Rich reminds me. "We were going to invite you both over for dinner on our terrace."

"Oh. Right." I forgot it was nearly the holiday weekend. I

glance at Violet, trying to appear as if I couldn't care less what she's doing. "Will you go?"

She lifts a shoulder, twirling her margarita glass. "I don't have anything else planned."

I should be glad that she'll at least be there, but being around her and not being able to touch her, to kiss her, is torture. Everything is torture now.

Violet excuses herself for the restroom and I watch her go, wishing I could follow her to steal a moment alone. But what's the point? I can't keep lying to Rich. It was one thing while they were out of town, but to sneak around when he could catch us? To have to face him, knowing what we're doing? I can't do that, and this afternoon was the wakeup call I needed.

"Unless you're planning to spend the weekend at the lake," Diana adds, bringing my thoughts back to the conversation.

The lake.

An idea germinates in my head, bringing with it a tiny bud of hope.

Shit, yes—the lake! That's what I'll do. I'll take Violet up to the lake with me. We can spend a few days away from the city, alone. We can swim, and I'll cook for her, and there will be no one to make us feel like we're doing something wrong. It might not solve all our problems, but if it buys me a few more days with her, I'll do it. I'll do anything for that.

"Uh, actually, I was." I reach for a tortilla chip and casually lift it to my mouth.

"That's a great idea!" Rich grins over his beer. "We should all come up for the weekend."

My eyebrows jump. "Who are you and what have you done with my friend?" My mouth hooks into a mocking smile. "You've literally just got back from vacation."

He chuckles. "And it was a hell of a lot more fun than the office, I can tell you that."

I shake my head, laughing quietly. This is not the Rich I know, and that's a good thing.

But they can't come up to the lake. That would defeat the entire purpose.

"I'd love to have you guys stay, but..." I rack my brain for what I can say to put them off, and know there's only one thing for it. "I've actually, uh, met someone," I begin, treading carefully. I don't want to lie, and this gives me the chance to be somewhat honest. "I was hoping I could spend the weekend with her up there."

Diana's face breaks into a grin. "That's great, Kyle! Tell us about her."

The corkscrew of guilt turns in my gut. I should have seen that coming.

"Uh, well... it's new, and I'm not really ready to talk about it yet." At least that much is true. "But..." I shake my head, looking down into my beer bottle in an attempt to hide my smile. "She's amazing." Then I fold my lips closed to stop myself from blurting out words I can't take back. Words like, "She's your daughter, and I think I'm falling in love with her."

Diana reaches for my hand and squeezes. "I could tell something was different about you. It's wonderful to see you happy."

"Thanks," I murmur, unable to meet her eye. I don't know if she'd feel the same if she knew who it was we were discussing, but one problem at a time.

"Alright." Rich sends me a sly smile. "We can do the holiday weekend without you if it means you're finally getting back out there." He loads a tortilla chip with black bean dip, changing the subject. Or at least, he thinks he is.

"How's it been working with Vi? She giving you any trouble?"

She's giving me many things, but trouble isn't one of them.

I can feel the heat on my neck as I shake my head. "She's been great," I say, trying my best to keep my tone even. I remember how worried she is about impressing Rich, and add, "Very good at what she does. She's the reason the entire project is running so smoothly." It's easy to say because it's the absolute truth.

Rich beams at me. "I knew she'd be great." He reaches for Di's hand with a proud sigh. "Our little girl is all grown up."

There's a punch of nausea in my stomach. God, I hate it when he calls her that.

Rich's gaze swings back to me with a genuine smile. "Thanks for looking out for her on this project."

I drop my gaze to my drink, giving a stiff nod, overcome by so much guilt I can't look at him. Instead, I set my beer down and rise from the table, needing a second to stew in my self-loathing alone.

"Could you excuse me for a moment? I have to... make a quick call." I make a show of pulling my phone out as I step away from the table and head to the back of the restaurant, looking for the restroom. It's around a corner and along a corridor, and I find it just as Violet steps out.

My heart lifts at the sight of her. She's so lost in thought, her head bowed, she almost walks right past me.

"Hey." I put a hand out to softly touch her arm and she stops, looking up at me with sad eyes that make my chest tight, that make any guilt I'm feeling evaporate. What matters is *her*. Us.

She attempts a faint smile in response, then looks past

me as if to keep walking. I grab her hand and tug her back into the restroom, locking the door behind us.

"What are you doing?"

"Come up to Maine with me for the long weekend," I say in a rush.

She blinks. "What?"

I take her hands in mine. "I want you to spend the holiday weekend at my cabin with me."

Her eyes widen in surprise, a hint of a smile touching her lips. "Are you serious?"

"I'm so fucking serious. I know we said two weeks, but..." I shake my head. "I'm not ready for this to be over, Vi."

She stares at me for a long moment, and I wonder if she's having second thoughts of her own, but then she pushes up onto her toes to kiss me. I wrap her in my arms and hold her close, relief making my heart beat hard in my chest.

It's not over yet. It doesn't have to end yet.

"That sounds amazing," she whispers, burying her face in my neck. She draws away with a huge grin. "I can't wait to see your cabin. But..." Her grin wobbles. "What will we tell Mom and Dad?"

I swallow. "I told them I met someone and will be spending the weekend with her in Maine." Violet's mouth pops open in surprise. "I was very vague," I add quickly. "Said it was new and I didn't want to talk about it."

She nods, running her gaze across my face for a beat. "Are you sure... Look, I know this is a big deal, but are you sure we couldn't just tell them the truth? It might be awkward at first, but..."

I think of Richard calling Violet his 'little girl,' of the way he thanked me for looking out for her, how much he trusts me.

"I can't—" The words lodge in my throat. "Your dad would kill me." I sigh as I stroke her hair. "You're not the only one who's worried about letting him down, sweetheart."

Her face falls, and she nods. "Yeah, I get it."

I take a deep breath. "If that means you don't want to come to Maine, I understand."

"I do want to," she assures me, taking my hand. "I really do."

I exhale slowly, lifting her hand to press a kiss to the back of it. *Thank God.*

"But what will I tell them? I already said I don't have plans..." She gnaws on her bottom lip in that sweet way of hers, and I tug it free with my thumb.

"Tell them Sadie invited you away for the weekend. She'll cover for you, won't she?"

"Yeah. Okay." She nods, a wide smile spreading across her face. I dip my head to capture it with my mouth, loving the way she melts against me with a happy sigh. Then I force myself away from her before I lose all control and fuck her in a bathroom for the second time today.

32

VIOLET

I turn Kyle's pickup truck onto the gravel driveway, an excited smile twitching on my lips as I pull up in front of a stunning lakeside cabin. Apart from a quick stop for groceries, we've been on the road for six straight hours, but I don't mind. If there's one thing I've missed since being back in the city, it's driving, and Kyle was all too happy to sit back and relax for the drive.

Well, he didn't relax, so much, as slide his hand up my thigh while kissing my neck and telling me how sexy I looked driving his truck, until I told him to stop so we could arrive in one piece. After that we put Rogue Valley on and enjoyed the drive, chatting about music and work and Maine.

Now we're here, and I'm glad. We've spent the past two and a half days since dinner working hard on the house, mainly to assuage my guilt about leaving town for a few days and lying to my parents, and while part of me still feels bad, another part of me is giddy at the thought of three whole days alone with Kyle in this beautiful setting. I'm doing my best to let that part of me win.

"Home sweet home," Kyle says as I shut off the engine. We step from the truck, stretching after the long drive, the evening air a warm embrace after the cool air conditioning of the pickup. We left work in the early afternoon to get a head start on any weekend traffic, arriving in time to catch the last rays of sun as it inches toward the horizon, casting a golden trail across the lake and bathing the cabin in a warm glow.

My breath catches as I take in the view before me. The cabin is clad in natural cedar shakes, with a red metal roof and a screened-in porch to one side. It sits at the edge of the lake, perfectly placed to capture the vista of the water, shrouded in pine trees. I know there are other cabins nearby, but as I follow Kyle to the porch, I can't see anyone else. It feels like we're alone in the wilderness, in the best possible way.

Kyle sets our bags down to open the door, then leads me inside. He flicks on the light as the sun sinks further behind the forest across the lake, and I step into a large, high-ceilinged room. I twirl on the spot, marveling at the space as I take it in. The living room and kitchen are open-concept, with wooden beams spanning the cathedral ceiling above, and a front wall that's almost entirely glass, designed to maximize the view over the water. There's a wood stove in the corner, and I sigh dreamily as I imagine sitting by that stove in the winter, looking across the frozen lake. Behind the kitchen is a hallway, and off to one side is a set of stairs leading to a lofted bedroom, overlooking the space below.

"Wow," I breathe, running a hand across the white-washed pine walls. "This place is beautiful." The whole cabin feels cozy and welcoming, and this is only emphasized by the craftsmanship of the place: the detail in the wooden banister on the stairs, the cabinetry in the kitchen, the rough oak dining table. I can see Kyle's touch everywhere I look, and my heart feels like it could burst at what this man can do. With blinding clarity, I understand why keeping the historical details in the house at Fruit Street matters so much to him. It's the history, yes, but it's more than that—it's staying true to the building as it should be. It's respecting the soul of the house. I can feel that in this cabin in a way I never have, and it makes me glad I got to work with him on the house in Brooklyn.

Kyle steps behind me, sliding his arms around my waist and nuzzling his face into my hair. "I'm so glad you're here, sweetheart."

I sigh, sinking back against his solid warmth. Honestly, I can't imagine being anywhere else in the world at this moment. I can't explain it, but I feel like… I don't know. Like I'm finally *home*.

"Me too," I whisper, turning in his arms to press my mouth to his. He returns the kiss then draws away from me with a chuckle.

"If I start kissing you, I won't stop." He tucks my hair behind my ear, smiling down at me tenderly. "Why don't you settle in while I cook us dinner?"

I lift my brows. "You're going to cook?"

"Why do you think I stopped at the market?"

I laugh. "Fair point. Okay, well, I could help?" I'm not great in the kitchen, given almost everything I eat comes out of a packet, but thankfully Kyle doesn't put this to the test.

"No." He drops a kiss on my forehead. "You've been driving for hours. Go relax, I want to cook for you." He grabs the grocery bags and saunters into the kitchen. "I bought some fresh fish, but if you're not into that I could make—"

"I love fish," I say, and he grins. I watch him unload the groceries and pull out pots and bowls, setting out ingredients. He grabs a large knife and begins dicing red onion with the confidence of a man who's done this hundreds of times before.

Oh, God. If he's a good cook too, I'm in huge trouble.

I tear my gaze away and grab our bags, heading toward the stairs. The banister is smooth under my palm as I climb into the loft, inhaling the faint smell of pine. The loft is a mezzanine floor under sloping rafters, with a front railing open to the main living space below. A queen-sized bed sits on a large rug under a window, beside a nightstand with a small lamp and a stack of books. I set my bag down and lower myself onto the bed, lying back to stare up at the ceiling.

This is where Kyle sleeps, I think, rolling over to smell his pillow and examine the books on the nightstand. There's one I recognize, a paperback called *Old Brooklyn Heights*, which contains a very detailed history of the houses in the neighborhood. It's the same book I purchased from Barnes & Noble on my trip with Sadie. There's also a book about the philosophy of stoicism, some kind of historical novel, and a book about anxiety, which surprises me. I pick that one up and flick through it, noticing several dog-eared pages with highlighting and notes inside. I think about how Kyle knew I'd had a panic attack, and feel a pinch in my heart. It seems there's more to him than he's let on, and I want to know it all. I want to know *him*.

I hold the book to my chest, looking around the bedroom, listening to Kyle humming to himself as he works away in the kitchen. Just being here, getting a glimpse into his world, fills me with warmth from head to toe. I stretch out on the bed with a sigh, feeling more at peace than I have in ages. I'm not thinking about work, about Dad, about anything other than the man who brought me here.

The man who brought me home.

I WAKE to a hand stroking my cheek. "Dinner's ready."

I suck in a breath, bolting up, wondering where I am. Through bleary eyes I see Kyle, perched beside me with an amused smile.

Right. I'm on his bed, in his cabin.

"Sorry." I rub my eyes. "I must have dozed off."

"I'm not surprised," he says affectionately. "It was a long drive, and you've worked your ass off the past couple days. And let's face it, this bed is a lot more comfortable than the air mattress."

I stretch and yawn, my nose picking up the scent of food. My stomach rumbles and I'm suddenly famished. "You mentioned something about dinner?"

Kyle rises to his feet with a chuckle. "Yep. It's downstairs." I stand too, and he pulls me close, brushing his mouth over mine. "Having you here, in my bedroom..." He shakes his head. "It feels too good to be true."

I grin, leaning into him. "I can assure you, it's not. And as soon as you've fed me, I'll make that very clear."

Heat simmers in his gaze, but he steps back and motions to the stairs, clearly fighting the urge to skip dinner and go straight to bed. I follow him across the loft, watching him duck in what I can only assume is a habit. With his height and the slope of the roof rafters, it wouldn't take much for him to smack his head.

Downstairs, he leads me out onto the screened-in porch where he's set up dinner, laid out with candles that flicker in the warm evening breeze. He's crammed the table with dishes, and I cast my eyes over the spread in wonder.

"What is all this?"

"Ceviche, cilantro-lime rice, tostadas, salsa, and guac," he says, boyishly proud of his efforts.

My heart does a back flip as I glance from him to the food. No man has ever cooked for me like this before. If it tastes half as good as it looks, I might have to keep him.

He hands me a glass with a grin. "And a mojito," he adds, clinking his glass against mine. I take a sip, the minty-lime flavor waking my taste buds.

"Wow, that's good." I take another long pull, and Kyle's grin tugs wider.

"Thanks. I have mint growing here, so I like to use it."

He can build houses, cook, and use fresh, home-grown produce to create mouth-watering cocktails. And that's before we even get to the part about him being a stern brunch daddy (thanks, Sadie).

I'm well and truly fucking screwed.

He motions for me to sit at the table and I do, watching as he serves up the meal.

"Ideally the ceviche would be made with fish I'd caught myself," Kyle says, setting a plate in front of me. "But the market catch is fresh today, so it's the next best thing."

I remember him saying he likes to fish. And he plays guitar. And then there was that whole law career he used to have. I marvel at this man before me, seeing him in a new light. Is there anything he can't do?

We tuck into our meal and I groan my appreciation as the fresh, zesty flavors explode on my tongue. The food is so good that I can't even pause to tell him, I just shovel it into my mouth before reaching for seconds. He watches me devour his efforts with a satisfied smile, his eyes sparkling as he sips his mojito.

Once I'm full, I push my plate away with a contented sigh. "Oh my God, that was so good."

"I'm glad you liked it." He shakes his head, his mouth curved in amusement. "I've never seen you eat like that."

An embarrassed laugh slips from me as I wipe my mouth with my napkin. "Maybe I would if you cooked for me every night."

"I wish I could." The humor fades from his expression, his eyes piercing mine in the flickering light of the candles. My pulse skitters at the suggestion in his words, because how amazing would that be, spending every night with him? The food, sure, but *him*—being with him, for real.

Could that ever be a reality for us?

I swallow, leaning over to kiss his cheek, but a buzz in my pocket stops me short. I don't want anything to interrupt the perfection of this moment, but habit has me pulling my phone out to check anyway. My eyebrows jump when I see who the text is from.

Deb: Hey, Vi! Hope you're well. Just want you to know the letter of recommendation helped a lot. We should hear in the next week or two. I've got a good feeling about this!

I slide my phone away with a frown. Instead of the shot of elation I expect to feel, my stomach gives a nervous, uneasy ripple. For the first time I can honestly say that the thought of going back to my old life doesn't make me excited in the slightest. Sitting out on Kyle's screened-in porch, drinking mojitos and watching the sky fade from a cloud-studded purple canopy to a jet-black abyss shot through with stars, I feel a million miles away from that life. From the person I was in that life. When this project wraps up, I'm supposed to go back to it. I have my car and my apartment and now I might even have my dream job waiting for me.

But what if I don't want that anymore? What if what I want is everything I've had over the last month? Work, sure, but finding satisfaction in doing less of it, and balancing it out with more of everything else, including this man beside me. Would that ever be possible? Does he want that too, and more to the point, could we find a way to make it work with Dad?

If there's one thing I know after this evening, it's that I'm not ready for this to be over, either. Not now, not in a week from now, maybe not ever.

I'm falling in love with Kyle, and I'm not ready to let him go.

33

KYLE

"This place is paradise." Violet drops into the Adirondack chair beside me with a happy sigh, kicking her feet up onto one of the rocks surrounding the unlit fire pit in front of her.

"Mm," I agree, my face tilted to the mid-afternoon sun. We're a few feet from the lake on the lawn below the cabin, drinking mint juleps.

I roll my head to the side, lazily gazing at Violet as she reclines in the sun. She's wearing that same purple cotton sundress she had on in the backyard when I had my way with her at Fruit Street, only this time it's over the top of a bikini. We've spent the past two days swimming in the lake, eating fresh food, listening to music, and having so much sex I'm surprised my dick hasn't fallen off. Tonight is our final night before we head back to New York tomorrow, and like the last time, I wish it wasn't about to end. In fact, it seems to hurt even more now.

When I decided on the spur of the moment to bring Vi up here, I'd been thinking about getting out of the city somewhere we could be alone. What I hadn't considered was that I wasn't taking her just anywhere, I was bringing her *home*, into my oasis by the lake, my fortress of solitude. In the four years I've lived in this cabin, I've never brought a woman home, and now I know why.

I was waiting for the right one.

"I bet you don't want to return to the city tomorrow," Violet murmurs, sipping her drink. "If I lived here, I'd never want to leave."

I turn her words over in my mind. As much as I've enjoyed being home—even more so with Violet here—the quiet surroundings aren't soothing me like they used to. I can't quite believe it, but I think I miss the buzz of the city. I'd assumed that going back there would be triggering after everything I experienced, and while it took me a while to settle in at first, lately it's been totally different. I'm not at the firm, and being in Violet's company has changed everything. Then there's the work itself, the challenge of tackling a major project and working with a team. Violet was right, I have missed the challenge of harder work, I just hadn't realized it. In fact, I hadn't realized a lot of things until I met her, like the fact that during the past four years I've become a bit of a recluse, hiding away in my cabin and only choosing projects I knew I could handle on my own. Working with Violet, with her relentless drive and ambition, has reminded me of how good it can feel to immerse myself in a project I'm passionate about. She's reminded me it's okay for work to be a source of satisfaction and enjoyment, too.

Violet, on the other hand, seems to have gone in the opposite direction. Since we left New York, she's barely mentioned work; instead, she's easily unwound into the long hours of swimming, eating, reading, and generally relaxing. I didn't expect her to fit into this place so well, but she does. She fits here, with me.

As I gaze at the beautiful woman beside me, I realize that's why we work so well together: we balance each other in all the right ways. Without Violet, I'm a recluse who hides from anything that might push me too hard, and without me, she's a workaholic who never lets herself rest. Together, there's harmony.

"Would you ever consider staying in the city?" I hear myself ask.

Violet mulls this over as she sets her drink down. "It has been on my mind," she admits. "I'm not sure I really want to go back to the West Coast. But... my life is there. And if I get this job—"

"What if you got a job in New York?"

She pushes her sunglasses up onto her head to look at me properly. "That would be great, but I don't have contacts there."

"You have me."

Her mouth quirks into a smile. "I mean for work."

I set my own drink down, trying to ignore the anxious twinge in my stomach. "I do, too. The crew spoke to me about starting a company doing historical restorations full time. Well, it would be my company, and they'd work for me," I add, thinking of how they phrased it. "Or... it could be *our* company."

Violet's lips part in surprise. "What are you saying?"

"I'm saying that you are the reason this project ran so smoothly. That you could, maybe... stay in the city and work with me on more projects." There's another uneasy ripple in my gut, and this one is harder to ignore. Am I really considering leaving the carefully-constructed comfort of my life here to start over in New York? The city I intentionally left behind?

She stares at me. "As a business partner? Or..."

I nod, my heart drumming as I say the next words. "Yes, as my business partner, but also..." I swallow. "As more."

It's not until the words are out of my mouth that I realize how badly I want this. I don't want to live like a recluse in my cabin anymore, afraid of my life getting messy again. After these past few weeks with Violet, there's no way that could ever be enough for me now. Even if the thought of upending my whole life makes my pulse surge.

Her face lights with an incandescent smile. "Are you serious?"

It's the smile that calms my nerves, that reminds me why I'm even considering something that, two months ago, would have had me running back to Maine with my tail between my legs.

"I don't want this to end, Vi. Not after this weekend, not... I just don't want it to end." I take her hand in mine. "Do you?"

"No," she whispers, eyes moving over my face. "But there's more to this than just us, right? What about Dad?"

I grimace, feeling that familiar gut punch of guilt. "God, I can't even think about that."

She gives a deep sigh. "You're going to have to think about it. Yes, we could both move back to New York, and yes, we could work together, but... we can't actually *be* together if we don't tell Dad about us."

And there it is—the thing I let myself forget, up here at our little oasis by the lake. The thing that's *really* standing between us and happiness.

Violet twists in her seat to face me squarely. "Why are you so reluctant to tell him? I understood when we didn't know what this was, but we're talking about building a future together. We can't have that without him knowing."

I look down at my hands, my stomach sinking. She's right. We can't have that life without him being on board. And I can't imagine any scenario in which I tell him, and he's okay with it. Anxiety rises within me.

"Your dad was there for me during a really tough time in my life. He had my back when no one else did, and I took on this project as a way to repay him for everything. Then he asked me to look out for you..." I shake my head. "Getting together with his daughter feels to me like the ultimate betrayal. It goes against everything in the friendship code, especially after all we've been through."

Violet nods, nibbling on her bottom lip. "Can I ask what happened when he was there for you?" When I don't answer, she adds, "I saw that book about anxiety on your nightstand, and you knew I'd had a panic attack that time in class. Is that... related?"

I sigh. I've been waiting all weekend for this question. I knew she'd seen the book because it was lying beside her the night I found her asleep on my bed, open to a heavily-annotated page. That book became my bible as I navigated my way through the transition into my new life here. I don't rely on it as much as I once did, but it comes from a defining period in my life.

"Yes," I say at last, realizing that I actually want to share this with her. I want to tell her about what drove me out of the city, because I want her to know the real me. And because I know she won't judge me for what I've been through.

"The reason I knew you'd had a panic attack is because I used to have them. I had a lot of them."

"Oh, Kyle." Her face lines with compassion and she

takes my hand, lifting it to her lips. "I only had the one and it sucked. I can't imagine having more."

A grim laugh chuffs out of me. "Yes, well, I didn't have much choice. They started at work, mainly because of the stress of the job. I thought it was a heart attack at first, but then I learned the truth. I figured I had a handle on them, using a combination of meds to help, but ultimately, because I never removed the stress, I didn't remove the symptom."

"And Dad helped with that?"

"He took on some of my cases to help lighten my workload, talked me into going to therapy. And then..." I take a deep breath. This is the part that makes me look the worst, and I hate it. "My girlfriend, Lisa, couldn't deal with it, couldn't deal with me. She ended things and kicked me out of our apartment."

Anger ignites in Violet's eyes, and I love her for it. "She kicked you out? When you were at your lowest point?"

"Yes, but things were on the rocks with us for years, I just didn't want to see it. Or rather, I was too busy and preoccupied to see it. Your mom and dad took me in without a word. They were there for me when my whole life fell apart."

"Wait," she murmurs, her eyes round. "I remember that. Not the details, but I remember someone from Dad's work staying with them for a while when I started at DigiSwap. That was you?"

"That was me, sweetheart. I was a wreck, and your dad is the one who helped me get my life back together. He helped me find my place here, made sure I got a huge severance when I left the firm, and he's called me every week since to make sure I'm all good. He's truly the best friend I've ever had."

"Right." She gives a slow nod. "That's why you don't

want to tell him about us. I understand so much more now." Her breath comes out in a long, slow stream, and she reaches for her drink again. "Honestly, I'm not that thrilled about telling him either. He hired me to manage this project, and instead I ended up getting together with the foreman. Hardly a model of professionalism."

"Not *instead*," I correct. "You've done an amazing job with the house. Your work hasn't suffered at all."

"Well." She lifts a shoulder. "There's also the other thing I've kept from him about my job for the last four years." She cringes. "So really, I have two reasons to disappoint him." She stares down into her drink, looking morose, and I watch her with a heavy heart. As worried as she might be, I don't think Rich will be half as disappointed in her as he will be with me. She's young, she's allowed to make mistakes. I'm old enough to know better.

"Anyway." She drains her drink and turns to me, doing her best to paint on a smile. It's a single word, but it's enough to tell me we're shelving this conversation for the time being, and part of me is relieved. I want everything we've talked about, but I don't have the answers we need right now.

Violet's gaze flits to the lake, shimmering bright in the sun. "Have you ever gone skinny-dipping?"

A quiet laugh escapes me. "No. I have neighbors."

She gives a cursory glance over each shoulder. "They can't see."

"Not from here, but they have a perfect view of the water. You can see their houses from the lake."

A mischievous smile slides along her mouth. "So?"

I lift my brows. She can't be serious. Old Mrs. McGrady next door would probably have a stroke if she were to glance out her front window. And then there's Tom Marley, the guy who lives on the other side of me. He's nice enough, but I've seen him leer at the young checkout girls at the local market. The thought of him getting an eyeful of Violet's perfect body makes my skin crawl.

But she's already rising from her chair and pulling her sundress over her head to reveal the black bikini underneath. Her complexion is a shade darker after more time in the sun, her shoulders now dusted with tiny freckles. I think again about how much this place suits her, and how I wish we didn't have to leave.

My train of thought completely derails as she unties the strings of her bikini top, letting it fall to the ground. The bottoms follow. My eyes trail her skin, wanting to touch her for the millionth time this weekend, but then I catch myself. When I meet her gaze with a stern look, she giggles.

"Let's go."

I blink. It's hard to focus with her naked. "What?"

"I'm going in," she says with a grin. "Come on."

"No way." I snatch up her dress, holding it out with a frown. I love every inch of her curves, but they're for my eyes only. "You can't go out there like that."

Her brow arches in challenge. "Why not?"

"Violet—"

Pivoting on her heel, she strides toward the dock.

"Don't you dare—"

But she's in the water, laughing her head off, before I can finish. "Come and get me," she calls, standing in the shallows so the water only reaches her belly button, her beautiful breasts on full display.

Jesus.

I rise from my seat with a shake of my head. It's hard to be mad at her when she's so damn sexy, then I picture Tom on his front porch, eyes feasting on her.

No fucking way.

"Get back here," I growl.

"You're not going to join me?"

"No, and you're getting out. Now."

She pouts. I'm reminded of the woman I first met, the one who could be so smart-mouthed and bratty, who needed me to teach her a lesson. Maybe it's time I did.

"Get out right now, Violet, or there will be trouble."

Her eyes flash. Why do I get the sense that's exactly what she wanted to hear?

She slinks from the water, a naughty smile playing on her mouth. I throw her dress to her and she pulls it onto her damp skin with fire in her gaze.

"Come here." I reach for her but she sidesteps me, heading defiantly into the house. "Violet," I warn, starting after her, and she shrieks playfully as she tears up the steps. I follow her inside, grabbing her wrist as she heads for the stairs to the loft. I don't want her there. I want her here, on the sofa.

She gives a gasp of mock surprise as my hand closes around her wrist. "What are you doing?"

"I told you not to go out there naked. What the hell?"

She glares at me brazenly. "And *I* told you not to tell me what to do."

I shake my head in disbelief. She's doing this on purpose, surely. She's trying to push my buttons, like the old days. And God, I want to play along.

"Sweetheart," I say, a wicked laugh rumbling from my chest, "you know that's not how this works."

A whimper comes from her mouth as I push her down onto the sofa, but it's not a sound of shock, or pain. It's a sound of arousal. Her hands move to her thighs, inching her dress up slowly, teasingly, and my cock flexes at the searing heat in her gaze.

"You're right," she purrs. "I was bad. I guess the question is, what are you going to do about it?"

I lower my mouth to hers, close enough to kiss, but refusing to touch. "I have an idea."

34

VIOLET

Kyle yanks me up, spins me around, and pushes me forward until I'm on my knees, arms along the back of the sofa. He's always been a take-charge kind of guy when it comes to sex, but there's something about the rough way he handles me now that makes heat rush to my core. His hands push my dress up, exposing my bare ass, and excitement sparks in my abdomen when I glance back to see his dark gaze riveted to my backside. What's he going to do?

It doesn't matter. What matters is that I've distracted us both after that conversation by the lake. I still can't believe he asked me to stay in the city with him. That would be amazing, but unless he's prepared to tell Dad the truth, it can't be a reality. Talking about his panic attacks, about how much Dad supported him, made it pretty clear why he's so reluctant to tell him. That's not going to change. As hard as it is to swallow, maybe Kyle and I were only ever meant to have a few weeks of fun. The thought makes my heart wilt, but I push that feeling aside. This is exactly why I wanted a distraction. I don't want to think about the difficult things to come. I want to have fun with him now, while we still can. And it was all too easy to push Kyle's buttons, like I used to. I've almost missed his grumpy side.

"I told you not to go in the water," Kyle growls behind me. His hand strokes my butt cheek, feather soft, and goosebumps rise on my skin.

"I know." I wiggle my butt, realizing that what I want is for him to spank me. It makes me feel like some sort of deviant, craving that, but I don't care. I want him to hurt me, just a little, then make it feel better.

His hand lifts from my ass cheek and my heartbeat quickens in response. When it lands again with a loud crack, I jump in surprise. It takes a second for the sting to come, but when it does, I suck in a sharp breath. The pain gives way to a rush of pleasure almost instantly, and wet heat pools between my legs.

Again, I want to beg. *Again*.

I glance at him over my shoulder, trying to let him know how much I like it. There must be something on my face that makes it clear, because his eyes glint as he lifts his hand again.

"You didn't listen, Violet."

This time the pain is more of a hot burn, spreading through my lower half like melted honey. I let out a low groan and lift my butt higher. No man has ever treated me like this, and I can't believe how much I love it. Now I know what's been missing from my sex life this entire time.

"Only bad girls don't listen."

Kyle's hand meets my ass again and I whimper, squeezing my thighs together. I can feel how wet I'm getting and I need him to touch me there. He notices and forces my legs apart, sliding his hand between them.

"Fuck," he murmurs to himself. "You're soaked. You fucking love this, don't you?" He drops to his knees behind me and spreads the back of my thighs, dragging his tongue through my slick folds. "This is exactly what you wanted, isn't it? For me to spank your ass and tell you that you really shouldn't be such a brat if you don't like the consequences."

He's right—it *is* what I wanted, even if I didn't realize until his hand struck my backside. But he's wrong about the rest, because I *do* like the consequences. I fucking love them. I'll be his brat anytime if this is how he responds.

I want to tell him this, but I'm dizzy from the way his tongue is stroking my clit and dipping inside me. His hands are on my ass cheeks, massaging the pain away as his tongue slides across me. I'm not prepared for the way he licks higher, to a place I've never been touched before. I inhale a short breath of surprise, and he hesitates before touching his tongue to the tight ring of muscle again, his fingers circling my clit as he does. I can't help the moan that escapes me. My head spins from the pleasure, from the way it feels so naughty but so damn good.

He kisses his way up my back, peeling my dress over my head as he rises to his feet again behind me. "You like that, sweetheart? You like me touching you there?"

I give a tiny nod, unable to meet his gaze because of the heat coloring my cheeks. Yes, I like him touching me in the most intimate of places, but part of me is too shy to admit it.

"I thought you did." He lets out a low, rough chuckle. "You can tell me. Tell me you like the way my tongue feels on your perfect ass."

Jesus fucking Christ.

My breath stutters at his filthy words. I press my legs together, desperately needing friction, and I can feel the slickness running down the inside of my thighs. I've never been so turned on in my life.

"Say it, Violet."

"I... I can't," I whisper, my face burning. As much as I love every dirty word from his mouth, I can't seem to make myself repeat them back to him.

He tuts behind me, and a second later his hand comes down on my backside again, bringing with it a hot sting of pleasure. The moan I release is embarrassingly loud.

"Still refusing to do what I tell you," he mutters, his voice laced with disapproval. I know we're only playing, but it tugs at something inside me, and I search his face to make sure he's not serious. The sinful smile hinting at his lips reassures me.

"I'm sorry." I stick my bottom lip out in a show of exaggerated remorse. "How can I make it up to you? I want to be your good girl again."

He grunts, letting his eyes fall closed for a moment before they lock on mine. His jaw is hard as he peels his tee over his head and kicks his swimming trunks off, the dangerous gleam in his eye making my heart bounce against my ribs in excitement.

"You can take my cock," he growls, lining myself up behind me. "And you can come for me." He grips my hips and plunges into my wetness without hesitation, and for a few seconds I see nothing but stars as the pleasure of being filled melts through me.

"Yes." I rock back against him, already breathless from the feel of him. "I need it." The sensations building in my core tell me I'm not far off, and when I feel Kyle's hand slide between my butt cheeks and touch that taboo spot again, my legs shake. He presses gently, sending a new surge of rapture through me as he enters a place I never knew I wanted him. No. *Need* him.

"Fuck yes," Kyle grits out when I moan. "Now come on my dick like the good girl you are."

That's all I need to hear. The wave crashes over me and I lose myself in sensation as Kyle buries himself to the hilt, scooping an arm under my stomach to hold me up as I become boneless with pleasure.

He's chuckling when I finally come to. "I lost you there for a moment."

I shake my head, vision blurred. "I've never come so hard in my life."

He lets out a groan, stepping away and withdrawing from me. I'm instantly hollow at the loss of him, but he lowers himself onto the sofa beside me, gathering me onto his lap, and I swing a leg over to straddle him, guiding him back inside me.

"I want you to come again," he says, his hot breath tickling my lips. "Ride me, sweetheart."

Honestly, at this point I'd do anything he asks.

I lower myself fully onto his length, sighing at how hard he is, at how well he fills me. He dips his head to take my nipple in his mouth, sending a zing to my core when he pulls it roughly between his teeth. He feels so good at this angle that I can't help but take my time, slowly moving myself up and down his shaft, reveling in the sensation of him filling me so completely. We fit together in a way I've never fit with anyone, and before I can stop myself, I say,

"I *was* made for you."

Kyle's gaze meets mine from under hooded lids, his cheeks flushed as I work myself on him. He opens his mouth to say something, then closes it, swallowing the words. My heart flutters at the way his eyes become intense as they search mine, at what he might have been going to say. I hold my breath, waiting for him to find the words, but instead he captures my mouth with his, pouring everything he feels into a scorching kiss. His hands cradle my head as he thrusts up into me, our breaths mingling with a sudden desperation that wasn't there a moment ago.

God, everything about this man makes me weak. I'm in over my head and I don't know how to get out. I don't *want* to get out. I want to drown in him. I try to focus on the physical sensations as our bodies move together in a frantic rhythm, but my chest aches too much. I wasn't supposed to fall this hard and now it's too late. It's way too late.

"I love watching you ride my cock," Kyle rasps, eyes hazy as he rocks up into me. "I love it. I love... *Fuck*," he curses quietly to himself, the movement of his hips stilling, the haziness in his eyes clearing as he swallows hard, focusing on me properly. "I love *you*, Violet. I love you so damn much it hurts."

My heart stops. For a split second, I think I've imagined him saying those words, but the vulnerability in his expression tells me I heard right.

He loves me.

"I..." The words catch in my throat.

He loves me.

His hand smooths my hair tenderly. "You don't have to say anything back," he murmurs, but I shake my head, needing him to know.

"I love you too." I stroke a hand softly over his bearded cheek, huffing a tiny laugh. "It wasn't part of my plan, but I fell in love with you anyway."

The relief in his eyes tells me everything I need to know. He bared his heart to me, not knowing whether I'd say it back, but hearing those words from him makes my heart fill my chest. How could I not love him?

Then his mouth is on mine again, our kiss imbued with a new depth as we hold each other close and move together. This time when I come he follows, clutching me to him like he never wants to let me go.

35

KYLE

The pounding of my heart wakes me. I'd dreamed I was back in court, but instead of being the attorney I once was, I was the one on the stand, being cross-examined by Rich, no less. I couldn't speak. Literally, my mouth didn't work, in that strange way that happens in dreams. The funny thing is, Rich was trying to prove my innocence, but I knew I was guilty and when they told me I was free to go, my legs wouldn't move. Rich was leaving without me, and I was stuck. Panic clutched at my chest, waking me in a cold sweat.

I lurch up in bed, groping the covers around me for... I don't know what. It's only when I see the plaster details on the ceiling above me, the soft orange glow of a nearby street lamp falling through the open window, that I remember where I am.

Not in court. Not with Rich. I'm on an air mattress in his house in Brooklyn Heights, with his daughter sound asleep beside me.

I take a moment to calm down, doing the deep breathing exercises I've perfected over the years. In: one, two, three, four. Hold: one, two, three, four. Out: one, two, three, four. Hold: one, two, three, four. Repeat. Box breathing, it's called.

Once my hands have stopped trembling and my heart has ceased hurling itself against my ribcage, I reach for my phone to check the time. Five in the morning. Too early for Violet to be up, but I know I won't get back to sleep. Not after being woken by what I'm certain was the start of a panic attack. The first in years.

I climb gingerly from the mattress, trying not to wake her. She rolls over, snuggling into her pillow with a soft sigh. My heart sighs in response. God, I love this woman.

I pace the floor, feeling that anxious energy inside me, like a coiled snake ready to pounce. My ears are ringing again like they do when I'm stressed. If I've learned anything, it's that ignoring this feeling will lead to more trouble.

There's only one thing for it.

I pull on my running shorts and tank, stuff my earbuds in, and lace my shoes. The morning air is balmy when I step outside, typical of this time of year. It might be pre-dawn, but the heat clings to the city streets, making it feel suffocating no matter the time of day. It occurs to me that as much as I might want to stay in the city with Violet, I'd still rather spend my summers at the lake. Maybe we could find a way to have both.

This idea percolates in my mind as I turn onto Cranberry Street, heading for Columbia Heights. Already I'm feeling better, just from moving my body. In fact, I can almost forget what woke me. The dream that made it abundantly clear what a terrible friend I am. The familiar feeling of panic as my body tried to warn me that something was wrong.

I cross Columbia Heights, coming to the Fruit Street

Sitting Area, adjacent to the Promenade. The first fingers of dawn reach across the sky, and on the other side of the East River Manhattan is stirring. I sink onto one of the park benches, taking in the view as my breathing settles.

I can't forget the dream. I can't ignore the message from my body. As much as I'd like to, I know I can't keep living like this.

Violet and I arrived back from the cabin a week and half ago, and nothing changed. After we both confessed we'd fallen in love, there was no going back to how things were. There was no ending it, despite both of us being uncomfortable lying to Rich. Instead, we've avoided every request from him to meet up, throwing ourselves into work on the house.

And now, it's complete. The crew finished up with us yesterday, and today Rich and Diana will stop by to see the final product. After that... honestly, I don't know what's going to happen. Violet and I haven't talked any further about the idea of staying in the city and working together, being together. I know we both want it, and I know there's only one way we can make it happen. I either need to man up and tell Rich, or let her go, but telling him will mean losing him. I have to choose between my best friend and the woman I've fallen in love with.

Then there's the impact it could have on Vi's relationship with Rich, too. I can't stand the thought of being the reason they might fall out. I'd never forgive myself.

The images from my dream flash back to me and I grimace, rubbing the back of my neck. I've had feelings for Violet since we met, and I don't have any more answers now than I did then. If anything, it feels a million times worse.

I cast my gaze across the river, my heart heavy as the sun slowly turns the sky a gentle gold. I never thought I'd fall in love with Violet, and I certainly never thought I'd fall back in love with this city. Yet, here I am. Turns out coming back to New York for this project was exactly what I needed after all.

I check the time with a sigh. It's after six; time to head back to the house. Violet and I need to have a serious chat before Rich arrives, and dread weighs heavy on me as I plod half-heartedly through the Heights. I don't know what the outcome of that conversation will be, but either way it will mean losing someone I love.

Warm light spills from the windows of Joe's Coffee as I pass, and I'm about to step inside when I see the 'closed' sign is still up in the door. With a frown I turn to go, then notice the brunette barista—Daisy—waving to me through the window. She approaches the door and unlocks it.

"I'm not technically open for another fifteen minutes, but you can come in."

"Thanks." I follow her inside and she locks the door behind me.

"Let me guess—decaf cappuccino and triple shot Americano?"

"Yeah, thanks." I pay for the coffee, then find myself drifting over to the spot where I first met Violet, by the framed history of the area on the wall. I sink down into a chair as I wait for Daisy to make our drinks, so lost in thought I don't even notice they're ready until she sets the to-go cups on the table in front of me.

"Everything okay?" she asks. "You seem a bit glum."

I can't summon the energy to lie, so I simply give a solemn shake of my head.

She gazes at me for a moment, then tentatively says, "I hope this isn't out of line for me to ask, but... does it have something to do with Violet?"

My brows spring up in surprise. "How do you...?"

Her mouth curves into a little smile. "You know when she went out on a date about a month ago? She actually spent most of that night with me." Daisy gives an awkward laugh. "The date was a bust, then she and I went for burgers. I made her stay out late so you'd get jealous and make a move."

I stare at her in disbelief. "You're kidding."

"Nope." She grins. "Did it work?"

"Did what work?"

"Did you ask her out?"

I cringe as I recall how I devoured her before asking her out, but it definitely worked. "Yes."

Daisy eyes me for a moment, then lowers herself into the seat opposite. "I know things are a little complicated, with her dad and all."

"She told you about him?"

"She did. We had a lot of time to kill."

I chuff a morose laugh. "Right." There's an awkward silence during which neither of us seems to know what to say, so I reach for the coffees and rise to go, when Daisy speaks again.

"Violet's really cool. I hope things work out with you guys."

And my whole body slumps back down into the chair in defeat. I haven't had anyone to talk to about this, and unburdening myself on our local barista hardly seems appropriate, yet the words rise to my tongue anyway.

"I'm not sure they will. Things with her dad make it almost impossible."

Daisy gives a quiet nod. "I understand. But it's not every day you find someone you really care about, right? I guess you need to decide if she's worth fighting for."

"Her father is my best friend. He's like a brother. He'd never forgive me if he found out."

"Well, I don't know him," Daisy concedes. "But I do know you can't predict the future. You can't know for sure how someone will react to something. If you tell him, there's the possibility he might understand. But if you let her go, it's definitely over."

I stare at Daisy in astonishment. Why didn't I think of it like that? She's right—I can't predict with absolute certainty what Rich will say or do, but if I let her go, I lose her.

And suddenly, the answer is simple.

I thank Daisy for the coffee and chat, then I head out into the morning air, knowing exactly what I need to do.

36

VIOLET

For a brief moment, when I wake to an empty bed, I wonder if Kyle has jumped in his truck and left town. Part of me would understand. He's been adamant that we can't tell Dad anything from day one, and even after our time at the lake he's made no mention of doing so. That means we're no closer to figuring our shit out.

My heart gives a thump of relief when I hear the front door close, and ten seconds later Kyle appears in the room with two cups of coffee.

"Morning, sweetheart," he says, handing me one with a smile. He's in his running gear, which I haven't seen for a while. We've spent most mornings doing a different kind of workout, but I sense today isn't one of those days.

"Thanks." I take a sip of the strong coffee, wondering how today will unfold. Mom and Dad are coming this afternoon to view the house, and I'm not sure what will happen after that. As someone who likes to plan everything meticulously, this is new territory. I feel untethered, but in a different way to how I felt after losing my job. Then, I could always plan next steps, send out resumes to at least feel like I had some control, but with Kyle… I can't control what he'll decide. I can't control what my heart will do.

He kicks off his running shoes and sinks onto the mattress beside me, pressing a kiss to my forehead. "I've made a decision," he announces firmly. "I want to tell Rich."

I almost drop my coffee. "You do?"

"Yes. And I want to do it today."

Jesus Christ. Did he have a lobotomy while he was out?

"Why are you so sure all of a sudden?"

He rubs a hand absently over his beard. "I almost had a panic attack early this morning."

"Oh, shit." I twist to face him properly. "Why didn't you wake me?"

He cringes, letting his gaze fall from mine. "I managed to stop it, and I didn't want to bother you."

I think back to what he said at the lake, about Lisa getting annoyed with him and eventually ending things. No wonder he wanted to keep it from me.

But I'm not her. I'm someone who knows what a panic attack feels like, and I'd never wish that upon anyone.

"Hey." I touch his arm gently. "You never have to hide that from me. I want to be there if they happen, okay? I want to help."

"I haven't had one in years," he murmurs. "But all this sneaking around, worrying about what Rich will say…"

I squeeze his arm. "I understand."

"Then I went for a run, and I popped into Joe's. While I was there, I chatted with Daisy…"

This makes me smile. I've been into Joe's for coffee but haven't had a chance to really talk to Daisy since we went for burgers on that fateful night. Still, I remember how sweet she was, how much she was rooting for me and Kyle.

"And what did she say?"

"First of all," Kyle says, casting me an amused smile, "she told me that your date with Owen wasn't quite what you made it out to be, and that you actually spent most of the night with her."

A laugh escapes me. "Alright, fine. You got me. It was a ploy to get you into bed."

He dips his head to press a kiss to my mouth. "I'm glad it worked," he murmurs, breath warm against my lips, eyes forest-green and dancing with love.

I touch his cheek. "What else did Daisy say?"

He sits back with a sigh. "She said we can't know for sure how Rich will react, and she's right. We should at least try." Kyle's eyes meet mine again and little lines of worry form between his brows. "I can't keep lying to him, Vi. So, I think we should show your folks the house and then"—he steels himself with a deep breath—"tell them about us. Okay?"

A knot forms in my stomach. I've been waiting to hear these words from Kyle for weeks, but now that he's finally saying them, I feel uneasy. I've poured everything I have into this project, wanting Dad to feel like I've done a good job, and today is the day I discover what he thinks and whether he's impressed, and proud of what we've achieved here. If he's proud of *me*. The thought of telling him that I'm sleeping with his best friend makes my gut churn, and that's before I even think about coming clean on the whole misunderstanding regarding my career.

But when I look at Kyle's handsome face, gazing at me affectionately in the golden morning light, my chest fills with warmth. I want a future with this man, and there's no getting there without explaining to Dad. Besides, Kyle's right—it's time to be honest. I can't keep lying to my parents, about any of it.

"Okay." I snuggle into Kyle's side, pushing away that niggling sense of unease and filling up on hot coffee instead.

We spend most of the day cleaning and tidying the house. I usually loathe cleaning, but it's good to be moving. My body twitches with nerves and I can't sit still. There's nothing like sweeping and scrubbing and polishing to take the edge off my anxiety.

I've never considered myself an anxious person, but learning more about it from Kyle has me thinking. I've always felt restless when I'm not working, like I have energy I need to channel into a project, and when I stop, there's nowhere for it to go. It's only lately that I'm wondering if that's unhealthy, if it's driven by more than ambition. Then there's the whole panic attack in class thing.

But I can't worry about that now, not with everything happening today.

I set the broom aside and smile as I appreciate the back garden. This might be my favorite part of the property. I love being out here, under the beauty of the magnolia tree. Now that it's finally tidy, it's a lovely space. The landscaper turned out to be a guy who lives two houses away at number 18 Fruit Street, and he was excited to work on another yard in our block of buildings. He removed the remaining weeds and old patio furniture, cleared a large paved space for new furniture, and added a border of small shrubs along with a grassy area under the magnolia tree. I can see myself setting up Adirondack chairs, like the ones Kyle has at the lake, and sitting in the shade, reading. I never thought I'd be that person, but being away with him in Maine changed me. Being around him changed me. I've learned to slow down in ways I didn't know I needed, and I feel so much better for it.

I glance around the yard one last time with a sigh. I'm going to miss this place. I've enjoyed being out here, and it makes my heart sad to think that someone else will get to enjoy our work. That it was never for us.

I reluctantly head up to find Kyle in the entry hall. "Everything tidy upstairs?" I ask. We packed away our stuff so it would be clear for Mom and Dad's visit. I know we've agreed to tell Dad, but I'm not sure where we'll stay tonight, or what the next step will be. Packing up our things felt very final, in a way I didn't like.

"Yep." Kyle pulls me close and lowers his mouth to mine in a soft kiss. "So we'll show them around the house first, then we'll tell them."

I nod, swallowing against the nerves that rise rapidly in my chest. Kyle seems oddly composed, like he's accepted his fate now that he's made the decision.

"Do you want to tell them, or should I?"

I consider this for a moment. "I think I will, if that's okay?"

"Of course." Kyle squeezes me tight, then steps away when there's a noise at the door. It's Dad, letting himself into the house.

"Hello, hello," he says jovially. My heart vaults into my throat at the sight of him. This is going to be harder than I'd thought.

"Hey, guys." I glance past Dad as Mom enters behind.

"Hi, honey." She pulls me into a tight hug. "I feel like I haven't seen you in forever."

Kyle and I have been avoiding Mom and Dad since we got back from the lake, knowing it would be too hard to lie to them face to face, and guilt tugs at me as I squeeze Mom back. When she pecks Kyle on the cheek and his eyes meet mine, shadowed with guilt of his own, I know I have to go through with this. Even if the thought of it makes me feel sick.

Dad smooths a hand down his tie, glancing at Kyle. "Time for the big reveal?"

A grim smile twists Kyle's lips. "Something like that."

I take a deep breath, plastering on a confident expression. "Where do you want to start?"

"What do you think, Di?" Dad glances between us. "Should we start in the bedrooms?"

My pulse surges, as if he's hinting that he already knows about us. Which is utterly ridiculous.

Get a grip.

"Sounds good," Mom says.

We follow Kyle as he leads us to the top floor. He explains to Mom and Dad about the restoration of the staircase, pointing out the features on the original banister as we climb. Then he walks us through two small bedrooms, one of which has been ours for the past month, and into the bathroom. We kept the color scheme neutral for the bedrooms, only bringing color into the bathroom. The emerald tiles might be my favorite. The color is bold, but the subway tile is a classic shape. It's the best of both worlds.

Dad's eyebrows rise when he sees the bathroom, and I can't tell if he's impressed or not. He can be so hard to read sometimes, and my stomach clenches as I watch his impassive face.

We head down a level to the second floor, which has two large bedrooms and another bathroom, this one slightly bigger. Kyle explains how the rooms would have been laid out originally, before the indoor plumbing, and I can't help the joy I feel as he talks about the work, his gaze occasionally coming to mine, warm and proud.

After that, Kyle leads us back to the first floor, through the front and back parlor, and the balcony—or the 'tea room'—that overlooks the yard.

"This is beautiful," Mom gushes as we head into the front parlor, but Dad rubs his jaw in silent contemplation.

I glance around, realizing it doesn't look like much without furniture, and feel a brief flicker of panic that we didn't think to stage the house to really showcase it. What if Dad can't picture it the way we can? He remains quiet as Kyle notes the ornamental plaster work that's been restored, including the rosette around the pendant light fixture in the center of the ceiling, and the way he's painstakingly stripped back the paint on the original walnut mantel.

"This is probably my favorite room," Kyle says, looking around the parlor we've spent so much time in.

"Mine too," I murmur. His eyes meet mine for a moment and he sends me a tiny smile. It's enough to make my pulse relax a little.

Everything will be okay.

Kyle leads us downstairs to the basement, which is a large, open-concept space. The kitchen runs along one wall and the dining area opens out through bi-fold doors into the yard. I chose an apricot and navy-blue color palette for the kitchen, keeping the rest of the room a warm off-white. I love the simplicity of the color scheme, how it feels fresh while still respecting the historical touches of the space.

Mom runs a hand across the kitchen counter. "I love these colors."

I smile, looking to Dad for his approval as we lead him through to the yard. He's still deep in thought, and my stomach nosedives as I wonder if he hates everything. He asked us for modern and this isn't exactly that. I might feel inordinately proud of the work we've done, but it's not really what he requested. At least, not originally.

We stand in the yard, Dad taking it all in, and I wring my hands miserably. Why didn't I fight Kyle harder on the whole historical thing? How could I let Dad down like this?

"I'm sorry," I blurt, and Kyle's gaze zips to mine. I plow on. "I know you asked for modern, and this isn't—"

"Violet." Dad puts his hand on my arm to stop my nervous rambling. "This is... I have no words. This is so much more than I could have imagined. I'm astonished."

I turn to Kyle, uncertain. Am I hearing right?

"I'm so glad you talked me out of gutting this place and turning it into apartments," Dad continues. "So much would have been lost."

Mom nods vigorously. "I agree."

Beside me, Kyle beams. His pride is contagious, and warmth tentatively spreads through me. Dad isn't disappointed—he loves it!

Thank God.

Dad grins back at Kyle, taking his hand in a hearty handshake. "I knew you were the right man for the job."

Kyle chuckles, but I hear the nervous thread running through it. The house is only half of the issue here.

Dad turns to me. "I'm so proud of you, Sweetpea. I knew you could do it."

I want to bask in his praise but I can't let myself fully appreciate it. Not when I know what's coming.

"Thanks, Dad, but—"

My phone buzzes in my pocket, interrupting my words, and I swear I've never been more relieved in my life. I check the screen and when I see it's Deb calling, I hold up a finger and mouth an apology as I answer the call. Anything to postpone this.

"Hello?"

"Vi!" Deb's voice is high and excited. "I'm just calling to tell you"—she pauses briefly for dramatic effect—"the job is yours!"

Surprise socks me in the gut. After everything going on with Kyle and the house, after the weekend at the lake, I'd all but forgotten about the job at DigiSwap.

"It's... what?" I ask, Mom, Dad, and Kyle watching with interest.

"It's yours. Scott was going to call you, but I asked if I could do it. After everything we've been through, I wanted to give you the good news myself. You can start right away."

I open and close my mouth, unsure how to respond. My dream job is being handed to me on a platter right when I'm about to tell Dad I want to stay in the city with Kyle, and I don't know what to say. This wasn't part of the plan.

"Wow, that's... Thank you." I pause, glancing at the others. My head is spinning. "Can I call you back? I'm kind of... in the middle of something."

"Of course," Deb says kindly. "It will be so good to have you back here, Vi."

I end the call without responding and slide my phone away, my heart rattling in my chest.

"Who was that?" Kyle asks lightly.

"My old boss." I shake my head, still trying to process it. "She offered me a project manager job back at DigiSwap."

"That's wonderful!" Mom squeezes my shoulder, but I don't miss the tiny lines of worry forming on Kyle's brow.

"I guess," I mumble, rubbing my face.

Dad looks puzzled. "Why aren't you more excited? You're going to take it, aren't you?"

I glance between my parents and Kyle, thinking about the untruths hanging between us, and suddenly feel suffocated. Dad is so happy and proud of me, and for what? I've been living a lie for too long and it's time to let him and Mom know the truth.

I release my breath slowly. Here goes nothing. "There's something I have to tell you guys." I pause, realizing that's not all of it. "Actually, there are two things I have to tell you. But... one at a time."

Mom glances at Dad, his brows tugging together in concern. My stomach pitches dangerously.

"I... I've never been a project manager before this house project. I was an assistant to one, but that was all." I keep my gaze fastened to the floor, shame washing over me as my confession spills out. "I'm sorry I let you believe something that wasn't true, and I shouldn't have accepted this job."

My parents are quiet for the longest time, and when I can't stand it anymore I force my gaze to meet Dad's. He's regarding me with nothing but love, and confusion swirls through me. Did he not understand what I just told him?

But before I can ask, he simply nods, and says, "We know."

"You... what?"

He sighs. "We know about your old job, Sweetpea. When I called your office asking for you on the day you were let go, your boss mentioned you were her assistant."

"She did?"

"Yes. She told me how sad she was to lose you as her assistant. I was surprised, and I asked her to clarify, but yes, she said you'd been her assistant since you started at the company. I guess since I always rang you directly it had never come up, but the way she spoke about what an asset you'd been, and how she wanted to promote you rather than let you go…" Dad lifts a shoulder. "I knew it didn't matter. You should have been a project manager, and that's what counts."

Mom gazes at me with compassion, and I glance from her to Dad in disbelief.

"So you gave me the job on this house knowing I had no experience?"

"I gave you the job on this house knowing you'd do an excellent job, Vi."

I blink, absorbing this. *He knows.* He's known, maybe not the entire time, but he knew when he hired me. Beside Dad, Kyle gives me a gentle smile, and relief flickers faintly in my ribcage. Dad knows, and he's not mad, even though he probably should be.

"And look, it all worked out," he adds, smiling. "You've secured the perfect job."

There's a lurch in my chest. "You think I should take it?"

"Of course." Dad's brow knits with confusion. "Isn't that what you've been working toward this entire time? It's the job you should have had all along."

Guilt tunnels through me. "I'm so sorry I wasn't honest. I'm sorry I disappointed you."

He pulls me into a tight hug. "Nonsense. I've never been prouder of you than I am right now, Vi." When he draws away to gaze down at me, his eyes are warm with love. "You could never disappoint me."

I'm seventeen again, under the hot lights of that stage for the debate tournament, only this time Dad *did* show up, and he's cheering for me in the audience like no one and nothing could ever mean more to him than me. Hot tears sting my eyes and I look down at my hands while I blink them away.

Kyle shifts his weight, reminding me he's there, and my

stomach crumbles. I've told Dad the truth about my inexperience and he's not angry or disappointed. I think of all the times I've worried about letting Dad down, all those times I've felt like nothing but a big disappointment to him, but I was wrong. He's never been disappointed—he's proud. Prouder in this moment than ever. I can't ruin that now.

I think about Kyle nearly having a panic attack this morning, about how appalled my parents will be when I tell them I've spent half my time working on this house not actually working, but in bed with Dad's friend. Dad will take back all the lovely things he said—things I've needed to hear for years—and who knows what he'll say to Kyle. What if it leads to more panic attacks? What if life gets bad for him again?

My heart slams loudly in my ears and suddenly, I realize, it's too high a price to pay. For both of us.

"What was the other thing you wanted to tell us?" Dad asks.

I open and close my mouth, the words trapped in my throat as I look at Kyle. There must be something on my face that tells him what I'm thinking, because his expression shifts from one of anxious expectation to grim resignation. His shoulders sag and he sighs deeply, turning away.

"Nothing." I wrench my gaze from him. "It was... it was just that."

"Well, I think we need to celebrate," Mom says, and Dad nods in agreement.

"Absolutely. A fantastic restoration of the house and a new job!" He grins at Kyle, who can barely muster a smile, and I press my eyes shut against a rush of unexpected tears.

"Dinner and drinks on us. What do you say?" Dad looks at me excitedly and I try to swallow down the lump in my throat.

"Sure," I murmur hoarsely. I flick a gaze to Kyle, and he shakes his head.

"I'm not feeling well." He rubs his forehead, not meeting my gaze. "I think I'll take a raincheck."

Dad's face falls. "Are you sure? We'd love for you—"

"I'm sure. Sorry, guys. Go celebrate as a family. I need to pack the truck and get ready to leave in the morning anyway."

My heart twists at his words, but I force myself not to react. What did I expect? I'm not telling Mom and Dad about us, so that means it's over. It has to be. Kyle doesn't want to keep lying and neither do I. And then there's the project manager job that Dad thinks I should take...

This is the right thing to do, I tell myself. It's what the plan was all along: finish this project then get back to my real life. Dad's right, I can't turn down that job offer. And I can't hide things from him anymore. I don't have a choice.

I tell my parents I need some time to shower and get ready, then I'll meet them at a restaurant on the Upper West Side in a few hours. They agree, reluctantly leaving after Kyle insists he can't come.

Then the door shuts and only me and Kyle remain in the house, and I burst into tears.

37

KYLE

"Hey," I say softly as Violet crumples before me.

"I'm sorry." She wipes her eyes with trembling hands. "I couldn't do it. You heard what Dad said about being proud of me, even after I lied about my job. I just couldn't do it."

I nod, hesitating before pulling her into my arms. I'm not sure if I should, but I can't stand to see her upset.

"I know." I stroke her hair gently. "I understand, Vi."

And the thing is, I *do* understand. She feels like she has to choose between the love of her father and me, and I don't blame her one bit for choosing Rich. I had my own reservations about telling him—it wasn't until a few hours ago I decided I was prepared to go through with it—so if she feels like she can't do it, I get that. A small part of me is almost relieved I don't have to hurt my friend.

It doesn't mean my heart isn't broken, though.

She looks up at me, eyes glistening with tears. "I'm so sorry," she says again.

"It's okay." I have to force the words out, because even though it doesn't feel okay, I know it's what she needs to hear. "The time we've spent together has been amazing. But... maybe that's all it was supposed to be. Maybe anything more is too hard."

"We could try again to tell him—"

"Shh." I press a finger to her lips, shaking my head. I'd never be okay with making her do something she doesn't want to do, just like she never pressured me to tell Rich when I didn't feel like I could. "I don't want to come between you and your dad."

"I don't have to take the job," she says feebly.

"You should." I wipe her moist cheek. "I'd never forgive myself if I let you throw away this opportunity for me."

"But that means..." Her eyes search mine, filling with tears again. "It's over."

I swallow, my throat rough with emotion. "Yeah."

"I don't want it to be over," she says through her tears. I wipe another one away, a sharp ache piercing my chest.

"I don't want that either. But... I think it has to be."

More tears spill from her eyes and I gather her close again, blinking as my own eyes moisten. She shakes with sobs in my arms and I want nothing more than to kiss her pain away, but I know I can't do that anymore. Instead, I let her cry as much as she needs, knowing I won't get to hold her again. Knowing that whenever she cries in the future, someone else will be the one to hold her, to comfort her.

Eventually, she pulls away, wiping her face. "I guess I should go to Sadie's tonight. Hopefully I can get a flight out tomorrow."

The thought of Violet going back to the West Coast and out of my life makes me want to pull her close again, to tell her she can't go. I ignore the pain lacerating my heart and nod.

"Unless I stay, for one last night?" she ventures, almost shyly.

God, I want that. I want every last second I can have with her, but now that we've decided not to tell Rich, it feels more wrong than ever. And if I kiss her again, if I touch her again, I won't be able to let her go.

"I think..." I try to clear the thickness from my throat. "I think it would be too hard."

"You're probably right." She takes a deep breath, finally regaining some composure. I, on the other hand, feel as though I'm on the brink of falling apart. "What will you do?"

I lift a shoulder. "I'll pack up the truck and head back first thing tomorrow." I want to leave as soon as possible, but I feel too raw, too shaky and emotionally wrung out to trust my driving tonight.

She nods, gazing up at me from red, puffy eyes. We stand in the entry hall looking at each other, both of us fighting the urge to take it back. It takes all my strength not to reach for her again.

Just when I think I can't take it for a moment longer, she sighs deeply and drags herself upstairs. I busy myself going down to lock up the bi-fold doors to the backyard, my heart clenching as I remember catching her when she fell from the ladder, remember the way we couldn't keep our hands off each other by the back wall. What will I do without her in Maine? How will I go back to my life as it was? Will everything in my cabin remind me of her now?

I get lost in thought in the basement, and by the time I finally haul myself back to the entry hall, Violet is standing there with her belongings.

"I'll call you a cab," I offer, but she shakes her head.

"I've ordered an Uber. Thanks, though."

I step forward, hesitate, then lift my hand to touch her

cheek one last time. "For what it's worth, the past two months have been the best of my life."

"Mine too," she whispers. Her eyes shimmer with unshed tears again.

God, what am I doing? Letting her go like this? Saying goodbye to the woman whom I'm pretty sure is the love of my life?

But what else can I do? I can't force her to tell Rich. I can't ask her to sacrifice her relationship with him, and I can't ask her to give up this job for me. It's me who has to make the sacrifice. She never promised me more. I shouldn't have had anything at all, truth be told, and I'm lucky I got what little time with her I did. It's time to let Violet go. It's the right thing to do.

"I hope the job goes well. Just... promise me you won't go back to working insane hours and not looking after yourself."

She lets out a small, watery laugh. "I promise. Thank you. For everything." She hovers for a moment, then steps up onto her toes to give me one last, soft kiss. I have to clench my hands into fists to stop myself from touching her, holding her close and not letting her leave.

When she steps away, my heart howls in protest. My voice cracks as I say, "Goodbye, Violet."

"Bye, Kyle." She grabs her bags and heads out without looking back.

The door clicks shut, and I slump back against it, letting the tears fall.

IT'S NOT an exaggeration to say that last night was one of the worst of my life. I barely slept. I probably should have driven back last night because I feel even worse now, but I can't stay in this house for a minute longer. Everything reminds me of Violet, of our time together, and I need a clean break. I need to return to Maine and get my life back on track. Somehow.

I get everything packed up and ready by six in the morning. It takes several trips to lug everything down to the entry hall, and on the final trip I stop short with surprise when I see Rich letting himself in through the front door.

"Oh. Hey." I set the last of my stuff down on the pile. "What are you doing here?"

"You didn't think I'd let you leave town without saying goodbye, did you?"

"How did you—"

"Violet told me you were leaving first thing."

I ignore the pain I feel at hearing her name as Rich holds up two cups.

"Got you a coffee."

"Is it—"

"Decaf, yep. I remember."

My chest almost caves in with guilt and sorrow. He's the kind of friend who remembers things like that, who comes to see me off first thing in the morning. I don't deserve him.

Rich studies me, head tilted. "Are you still feeling unwell?" He hands me my coffee with a concerned smile. I barely have the energy to take it from his hand, let alone smile in return.

"No, I... didn't sleep well," I mumble, sipping the hot liquid. Today, of all days, I could use the caffeine, but I know it would only make me feel worse.

"You look like you've been hit by a bus."

I feel it.

Normally I'd laugh at this, say something smart-ass in

return, but I don't have it in me right now. I shift my weight, wanting to change the subject. "How was dinner?"

"Would've been good to have you there. Violet wasn't quite herself." His brows draw together as he seems to recall the evening. "In fact, she looked downright miserable."

"She did?" I ask cautiously. The thought of her suffering makes something twist sharply in my ribcage, and I wince. Did she sleep any better than I did? Has she left for the airport yet? Does she feel as empty as I do right now?

"She did, although she wouldn't say why." He's quiet, sipping his coffee as he studies me. "You look pretty miserable yourself, buddy."

It's impossible to hide how I feel, so I give a small nod, pretending to check my bags.

"I don't get it." Rich gives a puzzled shake of his head. "You were both so happy when we had dinner at the Mexican place. Vi was excited to go away with Sadie for the long weekend, and you'd met some mystery woman you couldn't wait to escape to Maine with."

I grimace, rifling through my duffel bag as if I'm looking for something—anything—so I don't have to meet Rich's gaze.

"Then you finish up here, and it couldn't look better. You've blown me away with this place." He chuckles quietly to himself. "But will either of you let yourself enjoy it? No. You're both leaving as if you can't get out of town fast enough. Honestly, the way you two are acting, it's as if..." he trails off slowly and I focus intently on zipping my bag back up, then rummaging through my toolbox. But there's not much I can pretend to look for in there, and when I hazard a glance at Rich, he's staring at me, the cogs in his head almost visibly turning. My blood turns to ice in my veins.

Oh shit. Oh fuck. Please, God, don't let him figure it out.

I straighten up and square my shoulders, as if I have nothing to hide. "Well, I should be heading..." But I can't finish the sentence with the way Rich's expression has hardened into stone.

"Is there something I should know?" he asks, his voice cool and steady in a way that sends a shiver of fear through me.

"What are you talking about?" I attempt a light laugh, but it sounds hollow and he just shakes his head, gaze narrowing.

"I'm an idiot." His mouth hangs open in shock as he pieces everything together, and I seriously contemplate dashing out the door to my truck. "How the hell did I not figure this out before?" His eyes flare with anger. "You didn't go to Maine with some mystery woman, did you?" Thankfully, this question is rhetorical, because he continues. "And that day, when you both came downstairs, all flushed..."

I press my eyes shut in shame. He's putting the puzzle together too quickly for me to keep up.

But what did I expect? He's a fucking excellent attorney. He's right, he probably should have figured it out sooner. I was just too wrapped up in Violet to think about it.

"She said she had two things to tell me yesterday, but she only told me one." Rich sets his coffee down, making a visible effort to stay calm as his steely gaze meets mine. "So maybe you can tell me. I'm only going to ask once, and I expect you will be honest with me."

I swallow, my pulse skyrocketing as I give a shaky nod.

"Was there something going on with you and Violet?"

I can hardly breathe. I don't want to tell him because this is the whole reason we broke up, but I suspect it's far too late for that now.

And honestly, I'm so tired of lying to him. I can't do it anymore.

"Yes," I say hoarsely.

His eyes darken with fury as he stares at me, speechless.

"It's over," I add, but that doesn't make it any better. We both know I've done the worst possible thing and betrayed him.

He's quiet for a long time, letting me stew in my guilt. Finally, he says, "She's only twenty-five."

"I know how old she is."

"How *young*, you mean."

This grates a little. Yes, she's young, but it's not like she's eighteen. She's a strong woman who knows her own mind, and I don't think he always gives her enough credit. "She's a grown woman," I remind Rich.

"She's my *daughter*, Kyle. She was vulnerable after losing her job, and you thought you'd make a move? How could you—"

"Hey, wait a minute." I raise my hands. "That's not what happened."

Rich folds his arms, gaze challenging me. "Then what happened?"

I hesitate. What am I going to say, that I fought it as much as I could, but she pushed me to the point of no return? I could never throw her under the bus like that. If I'm going to lose Rich over this, I can at least make sure she doesn't lose him too.

"Okay," I mumble, forcing yet another lie out of my mouth. But this one is for Violet. "It was... it was my idea." I glance up quickly. "I never pressured her, or anything. She was interested, but... yeah, I instigated it."

Rich's face reddens with rage, a vein throbbing in his temple. I've never seen him so angry, and it makes my pulse whip through me. There'll be no coming back for us now. There will be no saving our friendship, and it's my own fault.

"I trusted you," he spits. "I asked for your help. I asked you to look *out* for her, for God's sake, and instead you took advantage of her."

"I didn't... I mean, she's not a *child*. She's—"

"She is to me. You knew that. She's my little girl, Kyle. My only child." His lips snarl in disgust, but he still hasn't raised his voice. I expected him to yell, maybe hit me, but he only stares at me silently, eyes wild with fury.

This is worse. Much, much worse.

I want to tell him I'm in love with her, that it wasn't only physical. That she's made me feel more alive in the past two months than I have for the past two years, and that I think she feels the same, even though she's left. That we didn't tell him because we didn't want to hurt him, that we feel awful for betraying him, and we've sacrificed each other for him.

But then I think of Violet standing in the entry hall with shaking hands yesterday, how relieved she was that Rich didn't know the truth, how afraid she's been of letting him down. It's not my place to tell him these things, to risk him blaming her. She's made her choice, and now I want to do everything I can to protect her from the fallout of this.

"Is this why you wouldn't take my money?" Rich asks, face twisted in outrage. "Because you thought you'd take my daughter instead?"

"Jesus," I mutter, grinding the heels of my hands into my eye sockets. "You've got to be kidding. Come on. You *know* me, Rich."

"I thought I did." He steps away with a shake of his head, his eyes cold as they move over me. "But the man I knew would never do this. After everything I've done for you..."

His words are like a punch to the gut, but it's what I deserve. I make one last attempt to protect the woman I love, hoping my plea will register through his anger. "Promise me you won't hold it against Violet. It's not her fault."

For the first time, I think he might actually hit me. His eyes widen with disbelief and he steps forward, fists shaking at his side. "Of course it's not her fault," he grits out. "You're the one in the position of power here. You should have known better. I thought you *were* better." There's a moment where he seems to contemplate striking me, before turning swiftly on his heel, suit jacket flying out behind him as he strides across the foyer to the front door. Then he pauses, turning back to say, "Don't ever speak to anyone in my family again."

"Rich—" I begin, but it's no use, he's already yanking the door open and thundering down the front steps, and there's nothing I can say that will make a blind bit of difference. He's hurt, and after everything I said, I don't blame him. I'd feel exactly the same in his shoes.

My old therapist once told me that one way to deal with anxiety is to follow any worries through to their worst possible outcome. He said that if you did that, you'd find you could always cope with the worst case scenario if you absolutely had to.

Well, the worst has happened. I've lost the woman I love and my best friend, within the space of twenty-four hours. It's going to take me a long time to piece my heart and my life back together, but I'm still here. I will survive this, like I've survived everything else.

I take a few faltering breaths to calm myself, then I numbly load up my truck and begin the long drive home.

38

VIOLET

I manage to get an early flight out of New York the next day, arriving home in time to change before heading to the office.

My apartment looks exactly the same when I finally let myself inside. I don't know what I was expecting. Just because I've lived an entire lifetime and become a different person in my time away doesn't mean that anything here has changed. My apartment is as charmless and impersonal as it always was, and for a second I stand in the doorway wondering if I dreamed the entire thing; being let go, flying to New York, managing the restoration of the house on Fruit Street, and falling in love.

If it wasn't for the hollow pain in my chest, I might even believe I did.

I drag my bone-tired body into the shower with a deep sigh. I didn't sleep at all last night and not because Sadie and Tim were having sex. They were surprisingly restrained, instead sitting on the sofa and listening to me pour my heart out. Tim even gave me a hug before heading off to bed, but Sadie hauled her comforter out into the living room and curled up on pillows on the floor beside the sofa, refusing to leave me alone.

For a long time, I cried in the darkness, thinking not just of Kyle, but of my friend and her kindness, of the city I knew I would miss, of that beautiful cabin in Maine that I'd never see again. Then I cried for what Dad told me, that I hadn't disappointed him, that he was so proud. I'd never realized, but seventeen-year-old me had waited to hear that for a long time. Now, she didn't know what to do with it.

Long after I thought she was asleep, Sadie whispered to me in the darkness, "Are you okay, Vi?"

I sniffled into my pillow. "I will be."

There was a long pause, during which it felt like Sadie and I were back at high school, lying on the floor in her mom's basement, refusing to sleep because we wanted to talk about boys all night instead. I knew in that moment I was really going to miss her when I went home, and my eyes pricked with tears again.

"Are you sure..." She hesitated for a beat, as if considering whether to actually ask the question. "Are you sure this is the right thing to do?"

"No. I'm not sure at all." My words had surprised me. I'd spent all evening convincing myself that I was doing the right thing, that it was best for everyone. It wasn't until my friend asked me, alone in the darkness, that I let myself face the truth.

"Maybe you could try talking to your mom about it?" she suggested. I had considered that, more than once, but I could never ask Mom to lie to Dad for me. And I'm not entirely sure she'd be all that impressed with me getting together with Kyle, either.

"I can't."

"It's such a shame," Sadie said. "You've been like a

different person since you came back, in a good way. I've never seen you so happy."

And I'd never felt so happy, but was that worth hurting Dad for? Losing his respect and everything I'd finally got from him? Was it worth passing up this huge opportunity for my career?

I had no answers, so I stayed quiet. Besides, I'd already made my decision. Kyle was leaving town and I had a plane ticket for early in the morning. I couldn't change my mind now.

"I'm going to miss you," she whispered into the quiet, and that's the last thing she said before finally falling asleep.

I switch the shower off and step from the steam, looking at myself in the fogged-up mirror. This is the first summer in years where I've gotten a tan, and if it wasn't for the dark circles under my eyes and permanent downturn to my mouth, I'd say I look better for it.

Thankfully, my concealer works wonders. The smile is harder to fake, but I tell myself it will get easier with time.

It has to.

DEB GREETS me with coffee at the office—something I'm not used to, given it's always been my job. She throws her arms around me in the foyer, giving me a face full of ebony curls as she squeezes tightly.

"I'm so glad you're back, Vi!"

Her enthusiasm coaxes a small smile from me, and I step away, adjusting my blazer as she grins. "Thanks, Deb. For all this."

She hands me a cup. "Of course. I meant everything I said. You deserve it. In all the time you've been my assistant, you've been like an assistant project manager anyway."

In the glass and mirror-lined elevator, I realize for the first time how shiny this place is, how polished and reflective and modern. I miss the textured plaster walls of the townhouse on Fruit Street, the creak of the oak stairs, the worn wooden floorboards under my feet. My first instinct at this thought is to text Kyle, to tell him how much I miss the house—how much I miss *him*—but as soon as I notice my hand snaking toward my purse for my phone, I let it fall back to my side. I can't text him and tell him those things. That wouldn't be fair.

Besides, I tell myself, this is what a workplace should look like. Modern and professional. Not some hundred-and-fifty-year-old house where you sneak off to fuck the foreman in the bathroom. It's as if I've forgotten what it means to be professional, and I grimace, reminding myself what an incredible opportunity this is for me, what a massive step forward it is in my career.

The elevator lets us out on the third floor and I follow the click of Deb's heels across the open-plan office to the doors along the far wall. A few people call out in greeting and say how good it is to see me, and I muster a wave and nod in response.

For some bizarre reason I feel like I might cry, so I focus on taking deep breaths as we head for Scott's office. This is what happens when you don't sleep all night, then jump to a different time zone and immediately start a new job. It messes with your system.

Deb raps on Scott's door, then steps inside with me in tow. Scott leans back in his desk chair, clasping his hands behind his head when he sees me. He's the picture of relaxation, and I think of my promise to Kyle. Maybe working with Scott will be easier than I'd thought. Maybe life could be different this time.

"Glad to have you back, Violet." He rises from his chair to shake my hand. We know each other well, but I appreciate the way he's trying to make me feel welcome again.

"Thanks, Scott." For the first time, I feel a tiny zip of anticipation. Maybe this will be okay. Maybe this will even be good. "I'm glad to be here."

He motions for me to sit in the chair opposite his desk and Deb leaves, closing the door behind her with a grin. I sink onto the stiff vinyl chair, sipping my coffee while Scott taps away on his keyboard, saying nothing. He's exactly as I remember him—salt and pepper hair that's thinning on top, slight paunch threatening his waistband, deep-set grooves on his forehead from hours of frowning at his computer. He can't be much older than Kyle, but he couldn't be more different. I try to picture him with a hammer in his hand, or swimming in the lake, and shudder. I don't see myself falling in love with this guy, and that can only be a good thing.

"Right, we've got a lot to do," Scott says, interrupting my thoughts without looking up from his computer. "We're already way behind, so the next month will be all hands on deck, yours especially."

I frown. Exactly how many hands does he think I have?

His gaze shifts to me. "Are you up for the challenge?"

I suppress the sigh that wants to rush from my mouth. I know what this means; late nights, early starts, back to the grind. Back to life the way it was before, whether I want that or not.

Stop it, I scold myself. *This is what you've worked for. You need to stop thinking about Kyle, about New York, and focus.*

I take a deep breath, paint on a bright smile, and nod. "Absolutely. Let's get to work."

39

KYLE

The nail gun shoots straight through the pine, securing the board to the wall. I step back and survey my work, waiting to feel a sense of pride or achievement, but I'm still as numb as the day I arrived back in Maine, a month ago.

The first thing I did was call Muriel Murdoch to ask if she still needed the work done on her cabin. I'd recommended Dixie, another contractor I know, but he was busy all summer and Muriel was still waiting, so I jumped at the chance to work on her place, despite my earlier reservations. I knew I needed a really good project to sink my teeth into, so I wouldn't have time to think about Violet or Rich.

I've made good progress on the house, but not such great progress on the other things. Not a day goes by that I don't think about my friend, about how hurt and betrayed he must feel by my actions. The absence of his regular check-in phone calls asking me to come back to the city only amplifies my guilt. Yet I can't bring myself to feel regret about any of it. If anything, I regret not fighting harder for Violet.

She's in my thoughts day and night. I can't stop replaying

the time we spent together. As I'd suspected, everything in my cabin reminds me of her. Part of me wants to burn the place to the ground, much like it seems I did to my life back in New York.

I lower the nail gun and pull my tape measure from my tool belt to measure the length for the next board. It's after seven and I should pack up and head home for the day, but I can't stand the thought of going back to my empty cabin. I know I'll only stare at the ceiling and think of Vi, of the life we almost had together.

I wonder how things are going for her at the new job. If it's what she wanted, if she's happy. I hope so, and I sure as shit hope she isn't doing what I'm doing, working increasingly long hours so she doesn't have to face how miserable she is. I hope she's not miserable at all.

I get one more board up, my back protesting at the effort. With a sigh, I realize I need to call it a day or I'll end up paying for it later. Part of me is ashamed at how easily I've slid back into my old habits of over-working to avoid my life, and another part of me just doesn't fucking care.

After Violet, after the project in New York, after Rich's parting words... nothing matters. I've never felt so broken. Not after doctors told me I was having panic attacks, not after I had to leave my law career and my relationship fell apart, not after running away up here to lick my wounds. Maybe because the life I'd had back then hadn't made me very happy, on reflection. Not like I felt with Violet, working on the Fruit Street house, waking up beside her every day, walking with her through Brooklyn Heights...

I haul my toolbox into the back of my truck and drop into the driver's seat. The sky is darker than usual. Summer is almost over and fall is creeping in, but tonight it's made worse by a cluster of heavy rain clouds blotting out any remaining light.

I force myself to start the truck and put it in gear before slowly, numbly, peeling out and heading to the cabin. The entire drive I'm on autopilot and it's not until I'm climbing the stairs to the screened-in porch that I realize I've driven home.

That can't be good.

Inside, I kick off my work boots and reach for my phone, absently ordering a pizza. Then I clutch my phone tightly, staring at the screen.

I want to call her. I want to hear her voice, to tell her how much I miss her, that I think we made a mistake, but I haven't heard a word from her since it ended, and it doesn't seem fair to reach out to her now. Not when she's on the other side of the country, in a new job, getting on with her life.

Not when Rich told me never to speak to her again.

I'm trying to respect them both, respect what they've asked for, but it's not easy. I wonder if Rich has shared it with Di, if he's confronted Violet about it, if she's told him what happened between us—the truth of how it went down—or if he's kept our argument to himself.

I shake my head at myself, dropping my phone and reaching for a bottle of water from the fridge.

Every day. Same damn thought loop, every day. I know it's not helping, ruminating like this. I've tried to use some of the skills I learned in therapy to help with compulsive thoughts, but they're not working. It's not just in my head. It's the gut-deep, heart-wrenching feeling of losing the woman I love. The best friend I've ever had.

My phone buzzes on the counter and my pulse leaps as I

reach for it. I never get texts, but that doesn't stop me from checking my phone around the clock.

Just in case. In case she's reached out.

The text is an automated reply from the pizza place telling me my order is on the way, and as I set down my phone, sadness threatens to engulf me. My throat grows tight and I take a long chug of my water, wishing it were something stronger.

How can it still be *this* hard, even after a month? I know how heartbreak works—this isn't my first rodeo. Admittedly, I've never fallen as hard for anyone as I have for Violet, but it's always followed a predictable pattern. By this stage, things are supposed to be getting easier. You're supposed to realize it was for the best, and life is supposed to start feeling good again.

Why isn't that happening? Why does it feel like with each passing day I'm falling apart even more? I've been in this dark place before, but this time it's worse. The person who helped me through it last time is gone from my life, and I have no one to blame but myself.

The pizza guy arrives with my food, and I take the box and set it on the coffee table without opening it. I don't know why I bothered. I'm not hungry.

Outside, the sky cracks open and rain falls in thick, heavy sheets.

Fucking perfect.

I sink onto the sofa, head in my hands, and something digs into my lower back. Twisting to look, I fumble between the couch cushions and pull out a small book. It's the one about Brooklyn Heights that Violet bought for me, because she saw it and thought I'd like it. The last time I read it was when we were here for the holiday weekend together. It must have got shoved between the cushions while we were having sex.

No, that wasn't just sex. That was when I couldn't hold my feelings in any longer, when I finally confessed I'd fallen in love with her, and she admitted she felt the same.

Fuck.

Misery grips my heart as I run my hands across the smooth cover, imagining her in the bookstore, thinking of me. I flick absently through the book, wishing I hadn't found it. It's yet another reminder of everything I've lost.

I'm about to set the book down when something catches my eye—an inscription on the inside cover that I hadn't noticed before. It's in Violet's loopy scrawl, and it says:

You were right. Some things are worth fighting for. Vi xx

My breath catches in my throat as I reread her words. I know she's referring to the house and the fact that I fought for a historical restoration instead of modernizing the building, but in this moment my heart reads more than that. It reads it like a sign from Vi, asking me to fight for her. For us.

I stare at Violet's words, clarity striking me like the lightning flashing across the lake outside. I fought with everything I had for the house, but didn't fight for her at all. I simply let her go. She was afraid to tell Rich, but I didn't even try to talk to her about it, and after all that, he knows anyway. I didn't fight for her; I didn't fight for my friendship with Rich. I let myself give up and walk away. Hell, part of me was even relieved when Violet said she couldn't go through with it. Because here's what I couldn't admit to myself; that sense of panic I'd felt when I woke that morning wasn't only about keeping our relationship from Rich, it was about the idea of turning my entire life upside down, moving to New York, starting a new business... The thought of such a huge step felt overwhelming. When Violet let me off the hook, it was all too easy to accept, to choose not to fight for something that scared me so much.

Well, I'm tired of taking the easy road, of backing down from things that feel hard. It's time to go after what matters to me, and that's Violet.

I spring from the couch with renewed energy, snatching my keys off the counter and striding out to my truck without a second thought. I need to talk to Rich face to face. I need to apologize for how it went down, to tell him I'm in love with his daughter and that I think we're meant to be together. That I'll do whatever it takes to be with her, even if that means losing him, even if that means moving my life to the West Coast.

It's a risk, but if the past month has taught me anything, it's that I can't live without Violet.

40

VIOLET

I close the door to my office with a soft thud, glancing at the time as I settle in at my desk. It's been a long day, and I'm not nearly done yet. I should order some dinner, but I'm not hungry. Over the past month my appetite has vanished. The only good thing is I've lost the few extra pounds I was carrying around, plus a couple more. My coworkers think I'm on some kind of health kick, but the truth is a lot less glamorous.

I'm sad.

I don't *want* to feel this way. It makes no sense. I've got the job I've wanted for years. I'm making a lot more money. Scott and the rest of the team are great. Sure, I'm working longer hours than I'd like, but a few months ago I was used to that. In fact, I reveled in it.

All in all, I should be thrilled. It's like my life has finally come together but I can't enjoy it.

I've never missed someone as much as I miss Kyle. Every day, I pick up my phone to text him and stop myself. It's hard to believe that in two short months my entire life was upended so much that it now seems wrong when he's *not* there. My bed has never felt so empty. My nights have never felt so lonely. And my heart...

My heart has never felt so tender and bruised.

And the worst part is that I did this to myself. He was ready to tell Dad, and I'm the one who chose not to. I'm the one who chose to move here and take this job, to give up on Kyle.

I lean back in my chair with a deep sigh. Work keeps me busy, and that's good, but my heart isn't in it. I've even developed this unpleasant little habit of crying in the bathroom in the afternoons. Sometimes it's the only way I can get through the day. I didn't get the chance today because we were super busy, and now the sadness has built up inside me to the point that it feels like I'm about to burst.

Just a few more hours, I tell myself.

My phone buzzes with a text from Mom, checking in. Dad called not long after I arrived back in Silicon Valley, but I was swamped at work, and, admittedly, wanting to avoid him. I sent him and Mom a text saying I loved them very much, but I needed some space to focus on settling back into work, and promised to call them soon. They respected my request, but I guess a month without a call from me is pushing it.

Then there's Sadie, who calls most days to check on me. I take her calls, and try to be as perky as possible, but I don't know how much she believes me. If only she was here so we could sit on her sofa and talk about life. I wish she was dragging me out to a bookstore with her, making me take time away from work to go for coffee. I miss her so much.

I stare at my phone, then reluctantly press call on FaceTime. Maybe seeing Mom and Dad will cheer me up. In fact, I realize as I push my mouth into a smile to greet them, avoiding them for the past month has probably contributed to my shitty mood. This will make me feel better.

"Hi, honey!" Mom grins at me through the screen and my eyes instantly prick with tears.

Shit.

I clear my throat roughly. "Hi, Mom. Where's Dad?"

She gives an affectionate chuckle. "He's in his study, as usual. How are things with you? Have you settled in okay?"

I let my gaze drift around my office. I've settled in more than okay. I'm back to where I was before visiting New York, working all hours of the day and neglecting every other aspect of my life, only now with my own office and a bigger salary.

And a broken heart.

A sob escapes me before I can stop it, and Mom's face softens.

"Oh, Violet, what's wrong?"

I glance at the door to my office to make sure it's closed, trying to compose myself. Where would I even begin? With the job I never should have taken, or the man I never should have fallen in love with?

As if reading my mind, Mom says, "It's Kyle, isn't it?"

Surprise makes me jolt in my seat. "How do you know?"

"Your father told me."

My stomach plummets. "Told you... told you what?"

"That you and Kyle were together while working on the house."

I open and close my mouth, my pulse whipping through me. "He *knows*?"

She nods, gazing at me as I process this.

Dad knows? Did Kyle tell him? Why didn't Dad call me? Well, he did try to call me, didn't he? It was me who asked him not to.

My head spins with so many thoughts I don't even know where to start.

"So it's true, then?" Mom asks gently. "You and Kyle?"

I blink as more tears spring to my eyes. I have no reason to hide, no reason to lie if they already know. Besides, I might have moved across the country, but that doesn't mean things with Kyle are over, because they aren't, not in my heart. I'm more in love with him than ever.

"Yes," I whisper. "I fell in love with him."

Mom gives me a small, knowing smile. "I can see why. He's a lovely man."

I stare at her in shock. I don't know what I was expecting her to say, but it wasn't that.

"He is." I swallow, my belly knotting as I wonder what Dad must think. "Did Dad—"

"I'll deal with your father, don't worry." Mom sighs. "But you should probably talk to him."

That is the absolute last thing I want to do, but Mom's right. I need to talk to him. I've hidden away, using my new job as an excuse, for long enough.

"Okay," I say shakily.

Mom leans away from the screen. "Rich! Violet's on the phone, come say hello."

I listen as he shouts a response in the background, a rock sitting heavy in my gut. God knows what he's going to say to me.

But when he appears on the screen, he's smiling. "Hi, Sweetpea. How are you?"

Just seeing him makes my eyes well with tears again. I try to hold them back but it's no good. The floodgates have opened and I can't stop them now. Tears spill over my cheeks and drop onto my keyboard, and I reach for a tissue before I'm forced to call IT.

“Violet, what’s wrong?” Dad asks. “Is it something with work? Is the job not going well?” He looks at Mom who is off-screen and obviously nearby, but I can sense she wants me to say this to him myself.

“It’s not that.” I wipe my face, trying to pull myself together. “It’s... Mom told me...” My heart is a jackhammer as I try to find the words. “Mom told me you know about me and Kyle.”

Dad nods, his gaze dropping to something on his desk. “Yes.”

I take a fortifying breath. “How did you find out? Did he tell you?”

Dad grimaces, still not meeting my eyes. “He didn’t have to. After the project wrapped up, you both seemed off and I knew something wasn’t right. I put two and two together, and when I confronted him, he admitted it.”

I rub my forehead, feeling awful. “I’m so sorry,” I mumble. “Can you forgive me?”

Dad’s head snaps up. “I’m not angry with *you*. It’s him I’m mad at. He’s the adult in this situation.”

A weary sigh gusts out of me. Why am I not surprised he views it in that way?

“No, Dad,” I say firmly. “We’re *both* adults.”

His brows crash together. “He shouldn’t have pursued you, Violet, especially not after what you’d been through with losing your job. I asked him to look out for you—”

“I don’t need looking out for. I’m not a child.” I sigh impatiently, and somewhere in the background I hear Mom chime in.

“No, you’re not, and your father needs to get used to it.”

Having Mom’s support makes me feel bolder, so I add, “He didn’t pursue me. I pursued him.”

"It's okay," Dad says, ignoring Mom. "You don't have to defend him. He told me it was his idea, that he instigated it."

I shake my head in disbelief. Why would he do that? Why would he tell Dad that he pushed me, rather than the truth?

My eyes prick with tears as I realize why. He tried to protect me, to make sure Dad blamed him and not me.

"He lied," I whisper. "He would have said that to make sure you didn't think badly of me, but the truth is..." I sniff, dashing a hand across my cheek. "I pursued him. He was a complete gentleman, and fought it every step of the way. But we..." My words die off as another sob slips from me.

Dad's frown deepens. "Stop trying to protect him."

"Richard," Mom scolds in the background, but Dad waves her away.

"I'm not trying to protect him," I insist. "He was worried about betraying you. He agonized over it constantly."

"Then why did he do it?" Dad snaps angrily.

"It wasn't only him. It was both of us. It was me, pushing him, because there was something..." I swallow. "We fell in love. I loved him. I *still* love him."

Dad's eyes widen with shock. "You can't be serious."

"*Richard*," Mom says, more forcefully this time, and Dad glances away from the screen. "You're not in the courtroom now. This is your daughter, for Christ's sake. Listen to her."

Dad turns back to me with a wary look.

"I *am* in love with him," I murmur. "He's your closest friend. Surely you can see how lovable he is."

Dad shifts his weight uncomfortably. "But he's nearly twenty years older than you!"

"So? Mom is four years younger than you."

"That's not the same thing, Violet."

I lift a shoulder. "It doesn't matter. That's not how love works."

"Look," Dad says, his tone one of exaggerated patience, "just because you've developed a little crush on—"

"That's not what it is!" I cut in fiercely.

"Oh for God's sake," Mom interjects, shoving Dad aside until she appears on the screen beside him. "You're being ridiculous, Richard. I was younger than Violet is now when I married you, when I gave birth to her. She's old enough to know how she feels."

"Mom's right." I give her a shaky, grateful smile. "We fell in love. We were planning a future together. He had this idea to start a business restoring old buildings, and we were going to work together, like we had at the house. Honestly, Dad..." I shake my head in frustration. "I know I'm *your* child, but I'm not *a* child anymore. I know my own mind, my own heart."

Dad rubs his chin in thought, his hand scratching the five o'clock shadow. He glances from Mom to me, and eventually lets out a long sigh. "I guess you're right. I'll always see you as my little girl, but it's true, you're not little anymore. Even Kyle said that."

Just hearing his name from Dad's mouth is enough for my eyes to well again. "I've never been happier than I was with him."

"Not even at the new job?" Mom asks.

"No. I should be, because it's perfect, but I'm not. I miss Kyle. I miss Sadie. I miss you. I miss New York." The words come tumbling out in a rush and I don't even try to stop them. "I wish I'd never come back here. I wish I'd told you about me and Kyle, that I'd stayed and we'd made things work." Then I flop back in my chair, limp with relief. For the first time in a month, I feel lighter, unburdened, because I've admitted the truth. Not only to Dad, but to myself.

"You know, I've never seen Kyle as happy as he was working on the house," Dad admits quietly. He chuckles to himself. "I didn't think much of it until he told me he'd met someone, but I certainly didn't think it was you. Now I understand."

My heart squeezes. Would Kyle forgive me if I went to him and apologized for running away to the West Coast, instead of telling Dad and fighting for us? He was so calm and accepting when I told him I couldn't go through with it. He almost seemed relieved. Maybe he was glad that it hadn't gone any further. Maybe he's moved on with his life and is happier without the drama.

A notification pops up on my computer screen, bringing my mind back to work. I have so much to do, and I probably shouldn't be wasting time on this call, but I can't bring myself to care.

"Did you mean what you said?" Dad asks gently. "About wishing you'd never left the city?"

I nod.

"Then will you come back?"

I chew on my lip, unsure how to respond. "I want to, Dad. But without Kyle..." I sigh. "And what would I do for work? How would I—"

"One thing at a time," Mom assures me. "You can figure the rest out when you get here."

"Maybe. I don't know if it's the right thing to do."

"You said you know your own heart," Dad reminds me. "What is it telling you?"

That's easy. It's the thing I've been ignoring all month now, since I got back to Silicon Valley.

"To go home."

"Then come home," Dad says softly.

"Do you want us to come get you?" Mom offers, and I shake my head.

"No. I'll work my two weeks notice and pack up my apartment."

"Are you sure?" Dad's brow crinkles with concern. "We could easily get a flight—"

"Thanks, Dad, but I need to do this on my own."

My heart beats harder at the thought of moving back to the city, and that's how I know it's the right move. Maybe I won't get to be with Kyle, maybe it's all too hard after everything we've been through, maybe I hurt him too much and he won't want to try again, and I'd understand.

With or without him, I realize, I don't belong here. I belong in New York. I belong near my family, near Sadie, in the city that makes me feel alive. No job is worth giving up all the best things in life. Not even this one.

I let out a long breath, feeling the first tentative shoots of hope unfurl. I don't have any plans, any idea of what I'll do once I get there, but I have to try. I want a life that's more than work, and I have Kyle to thank for realizing that.

Who are you when you're not working? he once asked me.

I really, really want to find out.

41

KYLE

The sound of tapping on my truck window wakes me.

I drove for five and a half straight hours through the night, fueled by adrenaline and determination. It wasn't until I pulled up outside Rich and Diana's building at three in the morning that I realized how poorly I'd timed it, and there was nothing to do but pull over and try to snooze in my truck until morning. I didn't think I'd fall asleep, but when I crack my eyes open in the pre-dawn light I realize I must have dozed off.

The tapping on my window comes again, and I rub my eyes, turning to find Rich's unimpressed face staring through the glass. He's in his suit, briefcase in hand, up at his usual ungodly hour to head into the office. Meanwhile, I'm in yesterday's work clothes, my eyes gritty from lack of sleep, my pulse lurching at the sight of my friend.

I straighten up in my seat and roll the window down.

"You're parked illegally," Rich says dryly.

Not an excellent start, but at least he's talking to me.

He leans forward to peer into the truck, sliding his gaze across my face. "And you look like shit."

"I feel it." I scrub my hands over my face. My beard is back to being the shaggy mess it was months ago, my hair so unkempt I need my cap to hide it from the world. I'm the man I was before Violet and I met, only this time I know what's missing from my life.

Rich lets out a long sigh. After studying me for what feels like an eternity, he walks around the truck and opens the passenger door, easing himself onto the seat. Then he sets his briefcase down at his feet and pulls the door closed behind him, turning to face me. This emboldens me to talk, to tell him why I'm here and to try to make amends.

I take a deep breath, tense with anticipation for what's to come, but before I can get the words out, Rich says, "I owe you an apology."

I'm so stupefied by his words that I check over my shoulder to make sure there isn't someone else he's talking to instead. "I don't..." I scratch my cheek. "What?"

His chuckle makes my shoulders relax down from my ears. "I was going to drive up to Maine to speak to you this afternoon."

I twist to face him properly. "You were?"

He nods, his face growing serious. "I don't like that you kept it from me, but I shouldn't have been so hard on you. Violet told me what really happened."

I let my gaze fall to my lap, my heart jumping at the mention of her name. "When?"

"Yesterday. She asked for some time to settle into work, so I didn't push it. Then she finally called last night. She's..." I glance up to see Rich shake his head, frowning. "She's not happy."

There's a twinge in my chest. "Is it the job?"

"The job's fine," Rich says, shrugging. "She said it's exactly what she wants, but that didn't stop her from crying throughout our entire call."

The twinge turns into a dull ache. *No, not my vibrant, strong, determined Violet.*

"She was crying?"

Rich tilts his head, expression softening. "She misses you, said she wishes you'd both told me what was going on and that she'd never left New York."

Oh, wow.

I pull in a long, steadying breath. Maybe there is hope for us after all.

"And you?" I ask tentatively. "If I were to go out there and see her, what would you think of that?"

Rich's brow wrinkles. "Look, I don't love the thought of you with my little girl—" he cuts himself off with a shake of his head. "My daughter. But... I also don't enjoy seeing her so miserable. If being with you is what makes her happy"—he gives a resigned sigh, eying me warily—"I wouldn't stand in the way."

For the first time in a month I feel like smiling.

"But you shouldn't go out to the West Coast."

I furrow my brow. "But I—"

"She won't be there. She's packing up and moving back to New York."

My heart nearly stops. "She's coming back? For good?"

Rich nods.

"But what about the job? Everything she's worked for? Is she sure she wants to leave it all behind?"

"She is." He leans his head back on the seat, his eyes carefully surveying my face. "You really care for her, don't you?"

I swallow. It's such an odd combination, that he's both

my best friend and the father of the woman I love. You'd think that would make things easier, but it doesn't.

Either way, I won't lie anymore.

"I'm in love with her, Rich. I'm sorry, there was nothing I could do to stop it. I didn't want to feel this way, trust me. But..." I stare at my hands. "She's smart, and beautiful, and she challenges me. We balance each other out in the best way. And the chemistry between us..."

Rich holds up a hand, his nose scrunched with an uncomfortable smile. "I don't need to hear any more."

I chuff an awkward laugh, relieved when he joins in. "I'm sorry," I say again. "This is weird. I'm probably not what you imagined for her."

"No, but it's not up to me, it's up to her. And if you're the guy she's chosen, then I'll have to make my peace with it."

Emotion clogs my throat. Rich has forgiven me, and it's all thanks to Violet, to her telling him the truth, despite her fears.

"I need to see her..." I clear my throat, pulling my cap off to shove my hand through my hair before tugging it back on. "Do you think she'll want to see me when she's back?"

Rich's smile is wry. "I suspect you're the main reason she's returning. She said she missed us and the city, but it's obvious she misses you more. I didn't want to get her hopes up so I didn't say anything, but I planned to drive up this afternoon so we could talk. I want her to be happy, Kyle, and I think that involves you being here with her. She also mentioned something about a business you wanted to start together?"

I finally let myself smile. "We did talk about that, yeah." This time I feel no anxiety at the thought of moving here for her, leaving my life behind to start a new one with her in the city. I feel nothing but hope and excitement. I just had to go back to my old life in Maine to realize it.

"As far as I'm aware she doesn't have any other work lined up," Rich says. "So she might still be interested."

God, I want to grin like a fucking idiot. How is it possible I could still get everything I want?

I tamp my enthusiasm down with the reminder that nothing is final until I talk to Violet, until I'm holding her in my arms again and can see she still wants that too.

"When will she be back?"

"Two weeks." Rich's gaze catches on a taxi driving past. "She has to give her notice and pack up her apartment, but then she'll be here."

"Has she found a place yet?"

"Actually..." He glances back at me and smiles. "I was thinking of offering her the Fruit Street house. I haven't listed it yet, and I know she loves it there."

My mind works overtime as I contemplate being with Violet again. "I want to live there with her, Rich." I'm rushing ahead of myself, but I can't help it. Ever since it's started to feel like a reality again, all I can think about is my future with her, and us being in that beautiful house, the house she and I worked on together.

I want to buy it from him, actually. I could offer him a decent deposit now, but I won't have the kind of money to pay for it in full for some time. Maybe after we've built the business and—

I force myself to breathe, reminding myself nothing is certain yet.

Rich nods, lost in thought. He might take a little time to come around to the idea of me living with Violet, so I'm not going to push it now.

"Can you not tell her we spoke?" I ask. "I'd like to do it myself."

He nods, retrieving his briefcase from the floor of the truck. "I don't want to be the messenger between you two. Besides, she has a lot going on with leaving her job and moving."

I scrub a hand across my beard, thinking. Two weeks. I won't interfere while she's wrapping up work and packing, that wouldn't be fair. No, I'll wait until she's back in the city, until we can talk properly, face to face. In the meantime, I can do some more work for Muriel then pass the rest onto Dixie. I might not be moving back to the city immediately, but I don't want anything tying me to Maine. I want the freedom to be with Violet, if she'll still have me.

Now I just need to get through the next two weeks.

42

VIOLET

"This place is amazing," Sadie says, closing the door as we step inside. "You guys did an awesome job."

I turn to take in the familiar entry hall at Fruit Street. It's exactly as I remember it, and despite everything that's happened over the past few months, I feel proud as I look around.

Sadie sets a box down and lunges at me with a grin, wrapping me in a hug. "I'm so happy you're back for good!"

I laugh, my bags slipping from my arms as my friend squeezes me tight for the hundredth time since she picked me up from the airport. "Me too." And I truly mean it. I might not know where things stand with Kyle, but the minute I touched down at JFK, I knew I'd made the right decision.

It's been a difficult couple weeks, especially because I felt awful letting Deb down after she'd gone to so much trouble to get me the job. She was surprisingly understanding, and said she'd let me know if she heard of any positions opening up with her New York contacts. But the truth is, I'm not sure if I want to work in an office anymore, not after working in this beautiful house.

I haul my bags up the stairs with Sadie in tow. I've brought a stuffed suitcase and two duffel bags, and the rest of my belongings will arrive sometime this week. It's not a lot, just a few boxes of books, clothes, and other bits and pieces. All the furniture in my apartment came with the place, and I sold my car because having a car in the city is a pain. Besides, the money will come in handy to tide me over while I figure things out here. It was nice of Dad to offer me this place, but I don't know what he'll be expecting for rent, and I'm not sure I want to live in this huge house alone. If things don't work out with Kyle, I'll be reminded of him at every turn.

"In here," I tell Sadie as we head to the far bedroom on the second floor. I've chosen this floor because it's the one with the fewest memories. But as I tug open the doors to the walk-in closet, I'm hit with the image of Kyle holding an electric drill, installing the shelves the morning after we first had sex. I remember how I'd found him in here, how all I wanted was to be close to him again.

Like now.

I sigh as Sadie pulls my old air mattress out from the box I'd left at her place, then flips the switch to inflate it.

"You're going to need a better bed than this," she says as we stand and watch the mattress slowly inflate. "I don't know how you slept on this for so long."

A sad smile touches my lips as I think of the nights Kyle and I spent sleeping, among other things, on his air mattress. It was surprisingly sturdy.

Sadie can read my mind. "Have you called him?" she asks gently.

I shake my head. "I've tried to focus on the move, and

honestly, I wouldn't know where to start. What would I even say?"

"That you miss him?"

I pull my old lamp from the box and place it on the floor beside the bed. That doesn't feel like enough, somehow, just telling him I miss him. I need to apologize, to ask how he's been, to see if he's happy, to ask if he ever thinks about me. I need to tell him I made a mistake and that I'd give anything to go back and change the decision I made that day. I need to tell him that I've never been in love like I am with him, and that I want more than anything to have the future we talked about.

But that all feels like too much right now.

"Maybe," I murmur, turning my back to her as I pull a fold-out chair from the box. I focus on finding a spot for it, hoping that signals the end of the conversation.

Sadie spends the next twenty minutes helping me unpack my clothes and set up my makeshift bedroom, while I fight off her insistence that we go furniture shopping immediately. I don't want to buy anything until I know what my living situation will be, and I'm too drained to even think about it at the moment. Eventually she senses that I just want to be alone, and I walk her down to the front door to see her off.

"Thanks for picking me up from the airport," I say. "That's a true mark of friendship."

She laughs, pulling me in for another hug. "Of course. You won't get rid of me now that you're back."

"I know." I squeeze her. "And I'm glad."

She draws away with misty eyes. "I'll pop back later tonight to check in, okay? We could get dinner?"

Gratitude warms my chest at how caring she is. "Thanks,

but I'm supposed to be going to Mom and Dad's for dinner tonight. Let's catch up tomorrow."

"Okay. I'm only a phone call away if you need me."

"Thanks, Sade." I close the door behind her, my heart hollow as I climb the stairs back to my floor. I'm happy to be back in the city, happy to see my friend and be back in this wonderful house.

But without Kyle, it's bittersweet.

I flop onto my bed with a weary sigh. I'm exhausted after the past two weeks and it doesn't take me long to drift into a deep sleep.

A CREAK on the other side of the room wakes me. I'd forgotten how different this old house is to my apartment back in Silicon Valley. It's alive in its own way, creaking and shifting, depending on the weather or the time of day. It's got a personality that new houses don't have, and that's one reason I love it so much.

My eyelids flutter open to see the afternoon sun dipping behind the neighboring buildings through the back windows. It's early fall and the city feels different—cooler, but also cozier, even more welcoming. I'd forgotten how much I love autumn in New York, and I wish Kyle was here with me. We'd walk the streets of Brooklyn Heights as the gold and orange leaves fall around us, the air crisp with the promise of winter. We'd sit in Joe's and sip hot coffee, watching the world turn white with snow outside. We'd pick out a Christmas tree together and decorate it, then we might go up to Maine to sit by the wood stove and look out over the frozen lake.

God, I want that so badly it hurts.

I need to call him, now I'm back in the city. I can't simply sit here and miss him. I need to hear his voice, to know I at least tried.

I roll over on the bed, looking for my phone, and the skin nearly jumps from my bones. There, in the fold-out chair by the door, sits Kyle.

My brain short-circuits as I try to make sense of what I'm seeing. I must still be asleep. I must be dreaming. Either that, or I miss him so much I've started hallucinating.

But he looks up from the book sitting in his lap, his eyes lighting when he sees me. He sets the book aside and rubs a hand nervously across his face. "I'm sorry. I came to see you, but you were asleep. I didn't want to wake you."

I sit up on the mattress, my heart somersaulting. He came to see me. He's really here. I'm not imagining it.

"Of course, it now occurs to me that sitting here while you were asleep is probably a bit creepy," he adds, his brow dipping with worry. "If you want me to leave, I'll go."

I shake my head, at a loss for words. It's like I wanted him so badly that I somehow made him appear.

"Rich told me you were back today." The anxious creases in his forehead ease when I smile tentatively. "I probably should have given you some time to settle in, but I couldn't wait. I've waited for two weeks and it nearly killed me."

He's known I was coming back all this time?

"I'm sorry things didn't work out with the job," he says, rising from the chair and coming to perch on the end of the bed. He's wearing his faded jeans and a dark green Henley that brings out the color of his eyes, sleeves pushed up to his elbows.

I run my gaze across his handsome face. He looks tired, but he's clearly had a haircut and beard trim recently. It reminds me of the first time he did, and how it forced me to acknowledge my attraction to him.

I clear my throat, trying to focus on what he said about my job. Now that I'm here, now that he's in front of me, that's the last thing on my mind. "Yeah, well," I mumble. "It wasn't the same once I was back there."

He gives me a compassionate smile, studying me. God, I must look like shit. I'm not wearing a lick of makeup and I've probably got a hybrid bed-hair, plane-hair look going on. I lift a hand in a futile attempt to smooth it, then give up.

"So you're back for good," he murmurs, and I nod. "And Rich knows about everything that happened between us." I nod again, uncertain about where this is going. He's only a few feet away from me, and I want nothing more than to throw myself into his arms. After a pause, he adds, "Your dad invited me to dinner at his place tonight."

"Me too." My pulse ramps up as Kyle shuffles closer, and it occurs to me that if he isn't here for the reasons I hope he is, dinner will be pretty awkward.

"He gave me his blessing to be with you, Vi." Kyle swallows, a tiny vulnerable line forming between his brows that makes my heart press against my ribcage. "Is that something you might still—"

He doesn't get the rest of the words out because I lunge at him, covering his mouth with mine. It's not a very good kiss. It's sloppy, and we're both laughing, but his arms are around me again and that's all I care about.

When I run out of breath, I draw away to meet his gaze. "You were going to ask if we could be together, right? I didn't let you finish, but I assumed—"

"Yes, sweetheart." He drops a kiss on my forehead, chuckling. There's a light in his green eyes as they gaze at me affectionately. "I've missed you like crazy. I'm sorry I didn't fight harder for us."

"No." I stroke a hand over his cheek, loving the way he lets out a tiny sigh at my touch. "I shouldn't have walked away. We should have told Dad like we'd planned, and I'm so sorry I didn't go through with it."

"I understand why you couldn't. I couldn't either, really, but..." He shrugs. "Rich figured it out anyway."

"Was he really awful?"

Kyle chuffs a humorless laugh. "It wasn't great, but I don't blame him. I would have felt the same way in his position." He looks down at me, one hand rubbing gentle circles on my back. "So... you're back in New York and Rich is okay with us. I don't know what to do with myself."

A smile curls along my lips. "Yes, you do. Move in here with me, and we can start the restoration business."

He shakes his head, and for a brief second I think he's saying no, then I realize it's an expression of disbelief. "You really want me to live here with you? To work together?"

"More than I've wanted anything."

"Fuck," he murmurs quietly. "How did I get so lucky?"

I gaze at him, my body humming with joy. Even after I walked away from him and let him down, he still wants everything we talked about. We still have a chance to be happy. My heart is so full it's overflowing.

"I'm the lucky one, Kyle."

He lets out a rough exhale, taking my mouth in a slow, passionate kiss. Then I'm tugging him on top of me, his woodsy, earthy smell making me dizzy as his weight pins me to the bed.

"I missed you so much," I say between wet, urgent kisses. My hands are already on his shirt, pulling it over his head so I can trail my mouth across the ink on his shoulder.

"I missed you too, baby." His lips are on my neck, one hand reaching down to hook my leg around him. I feel his hardness dig into my belly and heat rushes through my bloodstream.

"Clothes." I can barely get the words out as I kiss him deeper, tugging at his belt buckle. "Off."

He laughs and lifts himself off me to strip, and I take the chance to wriggle out of my jeans and sweater, kicking my underwear aside. Then it's just me and him, skin to skin, mouths and hands everywhere.

"I thought about this every single day," Kyle rasps as my hands close around his cock. "Being with you, touching you. How soft and warm your skin is." He dips his head to take my nipple into his mouth, fingers sliding between my legs to where I need him so badly. "Fuck, sweetheart. You're already wet for me."

"You're not the only one who thought about this every day." I arch into his touch, the swirl of his finger sending a jolt of pleasure down to my toes. But I don't want to wait anymore—I want him as close as he can be. "I need you," I whisper, guiding his rigid length to my entrance.

Without missing a beat, he thrusts inside me, where he belongs. His mouth finds mine and we hold each other close, rocking together, making up for all the time we've spent apart.

"I love you so much, Violet." He lifts himself up enough to gaze at me, each roll of his hips bringing me closer to the edge.

"I love you too," I reply, loving the way his eyes darken at my words. "I can't wait to live with you. To work with you. To be with you every day."

"Fuck. Yes. Baby." He underscores each word with a thrust of his hips that makes me moan loudly. "I can't fucking wait." He captures my moans with his mouth, driving himself deeper until my hips are bucking underneath him, until we're lost in sensation, in each other.

After, when my head is resting on his chest, listening to the gentle thrum of his heart, I realize I've never been happier than in this moment. This time, I'm not worried about my career, about what I'll do next with my life. This time, there's no hiding things from Dad. There are no secrets, no guilt, no fear.

There's only me and Kyle, and the house we made beautiful together.

43

KYLE

I'm grinning like mad when Rich opens the door. Violet is beside me, her soft hand in mine, and my friend welcomes us with a smile.

Well, he looks at our joined hands, coughs, then fixes on a smile as he lets us in. I'm sure this will take some getting used to for him, but I don't mind. I won't hide my love for his daughter any longer.

"Hi, Dad." Violet throws her arms around Rich. "I missed you."

"I missed you too, Sweetpea." He releases her, watching with a fond smile as she goes to find Diana. His gaze swings to me, and he extends a hand stiffly, saying nothing but "Kyle." I hesitate at the formal greeting, but he laughs, pulling me into a hug. "I'm kidding. But"—and here his tone grows serious as he lowers his voice in my ear—"if you ever hurt her, I will kill you."

I pull away with a grim laugh. "I believe you, but don't worry, Rich. All I want is for Violet to be happy."

He studies me for a moment, then nods. "I believe *you*." And with that, he turns for the kitchen. "Beer?"

"Sure, thanks." I follow him to find Diana chatting excitedly to Violet. I haven't had a chance to speak to Di since everything happened, and I'm not entirely sure how she feels about us.

"Kyle, honey. It's so good to see you." She throws her arms around me, planting a kiss on my cheek.

When we pull apart, I gaze at her uncertainly. Maybe she doesn't know? Would Rich really not have told her?

She pats me on the arm. "Don't look so worried. I think you two make a good couple." Her mouth curves into a knowing smile. "Even before Rich told me, I had a feeling there was something going on."

When I glance at Violet in surprise, she laughs, leaning her head against my arm. "Thanks, Mom. We're very happy."

Rich hands me a beer and I take a long pull, relieved there doesn't seem to be any tension between us. Yes, it's an unusual situation, but only until we all get used to it.

I watch as Violet sips her wine, talking to her parents about her flight to the city. We spent the afternoon in bed, talking and laughing and making love. She's lost weight since I saw her last, and even though I'll always find her beautiful, I do miss her extra curves. More than that, I'm worried she lost weight because she wasn't taking care of herself properly. It makes me eager to cook for her every night, to look after her in all the ways she needs.

She laughs at something Diana says, and I smile at the sound. Her cheeks have taken on a pink glow that wasn't there earlier today, partly from the sex, but she also seems to be glowing with happiness.

I know how she feels. I wasn't sure how she'd react when I showed up at the house, but once I saw her beautiful face so peacefully asleep, I couldn't leave. It took all my strength not to climb onto the bed with her, but I managed to restrain myself, and I'm glad I did. She was surprised to see me, shocked, even, but it didn't take me long to realize how happy she was to see me, too.

And now I get to live with her, to work with her, to build a life with her. I don't have to hide what I want and how I feel, and I've never felt more grateful, more excited about my future.

We follow Rich and Diana through to the living room to sit with our drinks. Violet sinks easily onto the sofa, motioning for me to join her. I hesitate, wondering if I should snuggle beside her like I so desperately want to, but she tugs me down by the hand before I can second guess myself. Then I tuck an arm around her and she cuddles into my side with a soft sigh. When I finally force myself to glance at Rich, he's smiling.

"So what's the plan for you two?" Diana asks over her glass of wine.

"Well, assuming Rich is okay with it, I'd like to move into the house on Fruit Street with Vi."

I'm relieved when Rich nods. "You'll sell your place in Maine?"

I glance at Violet and worry flickers in her gaze. "No." I press a kiss to her forehead, careful to avoid clocking Rich's reaction. "I was thinking I'd keep that, and we could find a way to split our time between the two places."

Violet's face lights with an radiant smile. "Really?"

"Yeah. What do you think?"

"I love that idea! The cabin is so lovely. Maybe we could spend summers there."

Summers at the lake with this beauty? I can't imagine what I've done to deserve it.

"Sounds perfect." I turn back to find Rich holding out an envelope. "What's this?"

He glances between Violet and me, sighing. "Consider this my formal apology."

I laugh as I reach for the envelope, expecting tickets to a show or something. My heart stops altogether when I find what appears to be the deed to the house on Fruit Street.

"Rich..." I look up, confused. "What...?"

He sits back to casually sip his beer. "Well, neither of you let me pay you for the work you did."

I stare at my friend, dumbfounded. "You can't possibly be serious."

Violet leans forward to examine the document in my hand, and her eyes widen.

"But we *wanted* to do that work for you, Dad. We don't need—"

"Then think of it as a very early wedding present," Rich says with a shrug.

My heart beats double time at his words and I cut an awkward look to Violet. "Uh, we're not—"

"No, not yet." Rich's gaze moves between the two of us. "But you will."

I stare at my best friend, at the warmth in his eyes, and my chest feels like it's about to burst. He's right. I haven't let myself think about it for even a second, but I know without a doubt that I will ask Violet to marry me at some point. There's nothing I want more than to make her properly mine, especially now that I have Rich's blessing.

When I look back at Violet, her cheeks are pink as she studies her wineglass. Leaning into her ear, I whisper, "Do you think you might like to?"

Her wide eyes flick to mine. "Like to what?"

I lift a shoulder, trying to appear nonchalant as my pulse ticks nervously in my wrist. "Get married someday."

"Is that a proposal?" she whispers back.

I mean, yes, I could ask her right now. My feelings won't change, not after everything we've been through to get to this point, but we've only just gotten back together. I don't want to scare her. There's no need to rush—we've got our whole lives together.

I swallow. "It's a... pre-proposal. For someday."

Her eyes shimmer with an excitement that sends my pulse skyrocketing. She leans in to brush her lips against my earlobe, whispering, "Then I pre-accept."

My self-restraint weakens and I turn my head to take her mouth in a soft kiss, sliding my hands into her hair.

She wants to marry me. Not now, at least that's not what I asked, but she sure seems happy about doing it one day.

Fuck.

The sound of Rich clearing his throat makes me reluctantly pull away from Violet's lips. I look back at him, grimacing at the uncomfortable chuckle he emits.

"Sorry, Rich. I shouldn't—"

He holds up a hand. "You should. I don't know how I missed it before, but you're obviously very much in love. I'm happy for you. We both are." He pauses to glance at Diana, who vigorously nods her agreement. "It's going to take me some time to get used to seeing... this." He motions to us vaguely, his nose wrinkled in an awkward smile. "But that's my issue."

"We'll try to go easy on you," Violet teases, squeezing my hand.

"But we can't accept the house," I add. "It's too much."

Rich shakes his head, guilt shadowing his eyes. "It's the

least I can do after the way I spoke to you, Kyle. After I came between the two of you."

I open and close my mouth, unsure of what to say. He didn't come between us, not really, but I know my friend, and I know he won't let this go. So instead, I say, "I have another idea. I want to buy the house from you."

Violet grabs my arm, mouth open in shock. "Do you have that kind of money?"

"Not yet." I turn back to Rich. "I'll need some time. A few years, at least." Laughing, I look back at Vi. "This business is going to do well, especially with you running things. I can feel it."

She laughs too, her face lit with love. "I think so too."

"Okay," Rich says, bringing my attention back to him. "But I'll cover what would have been the down payment. We can work out the details later."

Violet shakes her head in disbelief. "Are you sure, Dad?"

He reaches across the coffee table to squeeze her hand. "I'm sure, Vi. I'm thrilled to see you two in that house. Seems like the right thing after the hard work you put into it."

She looks at me, speechless, and I grin back. "You want to live there, sweetheart?"

"Yes," she breathes. "I want to live there with you." The love in her voice makes my heart glow hot in my chest, and her eyes grow darker as she holds my gaze. I force myself to look away, mentally counting the minutes until we're alone again.

"Tell me more about this business idea," Diana says. "You're going to restore old buildings in the city, is that right?"

Violet nods. "We want to keep the history of the buildings but make them work for the modern homeowner, like we did on Fruit Street."

"I'll get started tomorrow," I say decisively. "I need to contact the crew and see if they're still interested. We can draw up a business plan, and—"

Violet puts a finger to my lips. "That sounds good. Great, even. But first, can we take a few days off? You and me?"

My eyebrows spring up. "Seriously?"

"I want us to spend a little time together before we jump into all that."

"*You* want to take time off work?" My mouth pulls into a teasing smile and she pinches me on the arm.

"Is that so hard to believe?"

I lean closer. "What do you want to do?"

She arches a brow that suggests she can't say in front of present company, then adds, "We might want to purchase some items for the house, pick up some of your stuff from the cabin. We can walk through the Heights and enjoy the weather. We can meet Sadie and Tim for dinner. Go to a museum, or something. We can just... spend time hanging out."

I release my breath in a long, steady sigh. I've never felt prouder of her than I do in this moment, actively taking time off work to live her life, to relax, to do what makes her feel good. And I know there will be many more moments in our future where I'll feel proud of her, that I'll never stop feeling proud of her.

"That sounds perfect, Vi." My voice is scratchy with emotion, and I take a long sip of beer to pull myself together. How did I end up here? I have my best friend across from me, the woman I love beside me, and a future I've never been more excited for stretching out in front of me. I'm not worried about the challenges that will come my way, because with her by my side I can handle them. With Violet in my life, anything feels possible.

I pull her close and kiss her temple. *She's* the reason life feels good, and that's how I know.

How I know she was made for me.

EPILOGUE

Head to:
www.jenmorrisauthor.com/swmfm-epilogue
to read an exclusive *She Was Made for Me* epilogue!

Did you enjoy *She Was Made for Me*? Reviews help indie authors get our books noticed!

If you liked this book, please leave a review on Amazon. Or you can leave a review on Goodreads. It doesn't have to be much—even a single sentence helps! Thank you.

ACKNOWLEDGMENTS

I'd like to thank the following people:

Carl and Baxter, first and foremost, always. You're my reason for everything.

Samara Reyne, Sarah Side, Amanda Wood and Katie Wyrill. Thank you for always encouraging and believing in me.

Rachel Collins, thanks for not only your awesome editing skills, but the informal role you've taken on as my author coach (whether you realise this or not, haha). You always remind me I'm not terrible at this, and you help me to keep pushing forward when I feel like my work is garbage and I want to give up.

Julie Olivia and Alicia Crofton, for critiques and proofreading. Enni Amanda for always helping me with my blurbs.

Kira Slaughter, Emma Grocott, Tammy Eyre, Andi Cowan, and Michele Voss, for beta reading and being my tireless cheerleaders.

Elle Maxwell for her fabulous cover design and illustration, as always.

Tessa Bailey for kindly agreeing to let me include her in the book-signing scene.

All my ARC readers and reviewers. There are way too many to name, but you all help me so much. Thank you for your time, energy, and enthusiasm.

And to all readers who've taken a chance on this story. Thank you.

A few other notes:

Rogue Valley is a real band, and their music is fab. You can find them on Spotify. I'd recommend their songs *False Floors*, *Orion*, *Shoulder to Shoulder*, *The Wolves & The Ravens*, *Icebox*, *Bay of Pigs*, and many others.

If you like the sound of Kyle's cabin, you might like the show *Maine Cabin Masters*. His character, cabin, and work in Maine was inspired by this awesome show. You can find out more about the show and the people who run the Kennebec Cabin Company at mainecabinmasters.com.

ABOUT THE AUTHOR

Jen Morris writes sexy escapist romance set in New York. She believes that almost anything can be fixed with a good laugh, a good book, or a plane ticket to NYC.

Her books follow people with big dreams as they navigate life and love in the city. Her characters don't just find love—they find themselves, too.

Jen lives with her partner and son, in a tiny house on wheels in New Zealand. She spends her days writing, dreaming about New York, and finding space for her ever-growing book collection.

She Was Made for Me is her fifth novel, and the first book in the *Forbidden on Fruit Street* series.

ALSO BY JEN MORRIS

If you enjoyed *She Was Made for Me,* you might also like the *Love in the City* series—especially books three and four, *Outrageously in Love* and *The Love You Deserve*. Both are forbidden romances, with The Love You Deserve also being age gap (my fave trope!).

Stay in touch so you don't miss anything:

Find me on Instagram and Facebook: @jenmorrisauthor

Subscribe to my newsletter for updates, release info, and cover reveals: www.jenmorrisauthor.com

See all the book inspiration on Pinterest: www.pinterest.-com/jenmorrisauthor/

Made in the USA
Las Vegas, NV
05 October 2023

78584497R00215